*It was time.*

Time to get rid of the baggage and explain. As far as forgiveness was concerned, Mark didn't hold out much hope.

"The hardest thing I've ever done—" He forced his gaze to remain locked with Mara's. "I did... that night...to you."

There, it was out. He wasn't surprised by her instant recoil. Instinctively he reached out and captured her wrist.

"You asked, damn it. Now hear me out. It's not exactly easy for me, either, you know."

"Then don't do it. Don't say anything," she whispered. "Just let it go. Please, Mark...I've got enough to handle."

"Then tell me what it is and we'll share it. There is something, isn't there?"

Mara gazed at him, stricken.

Dear Reader,

Welcome to Silhouette Special Edition...welcome to romance.

The hot month of July starts off with a sizzling event! Debbie Macomber's fiftieth book, *Baby Blessed*, is our THAT SPECIAL WOMAN! for July. This emotional, heartwarming book in which the promise of a new life reunites a husband and wife is not to be missed!

Christine Rimmer's series THE JONES GANG continues in *Sweetbriar Summit* with sexy Patrick Jones, the second of the rapscallion Jones brothers you'll meet. You'll want to be around when the Jones boys bring their own special brand of trouble to town!

Also this month, look for books by some of your favorite authors: Celeste Hamilton presents us with an emotional tale in *Which Way Is Home?* and Susan Mallery has a *Cowboy Daddy* waiting to find a family. July also offers *Unpredictable* by Patt Bucheister, and *Homeward Bound* by Sierra Rydell, her follow-up to *On Middle Ground*. A veritable light show of July fireworks!

I hope you enjoy this book, and all of the stories to come!

Sincerely,

Tara Gavin
Senior Editor

Please address questions and book requests to:
Silhouette Reader Service
U.S.: 3010 Walden Ave., P.O. Box 1325, Buffalo, NY 14269
Canadian: P.O. Box 609, Fort Erie, Ont. L2A 5X3

# SIERRA RYDELL

# HOMEWARD BOUND

Published by Silhouette Books
America's Publisher of Contemporary Romance

For Renee—
champion, futurist, twin soul

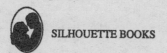

SILHOUETTE BOOKS

ISBN 0-373-09900-2

HOMEWARD BOUND

**Books by Sierra Rydell**

Silhouette Special Edition

*On Middle Ground* #772
*Homeward Bound* #900

---

## SIERRA RYDELL's

first novel for Silhouette Books—*On Middle Ground*—
was a finalist in the 1991 Romance Writers of America
Golden Heart contest.

She has traveled extensively, even managing to see
such exotic locales as Crete and Egypt with her twin
sister during their college years. Her hobbies include
everything from singing to ballroom dancing—she
taught classes at Stanford University—to Kenpo
Karate—"I'm thinking of writing a romance called
*Ninja's Passion.* Just kidding!"

She lives in Anchorage, Alaska, with her husband and
her recently born baby, Forrest. And although she's
been writing full-time since 1986, she's also an actress
and model, and runs a talent agency.

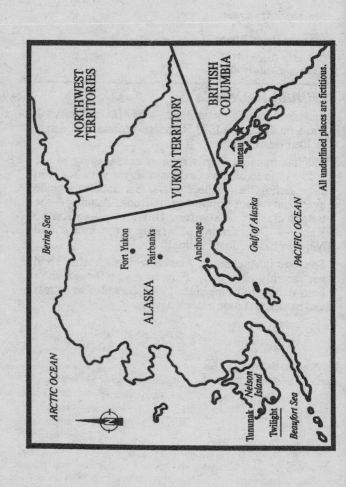

NORTHWEST TERRITORIES

BRITISH COLUMBIA

YUKON TERRITORY

Bering Sea

Fort Yukon

Fairbanks

Anchorage

Juneau

Gulf of Alaska

PACIFIC OCEAN

ARCTIC OCEAN

ALASKA

N

Tununak

Nelson Island

Twilight

Beaufort Sea

All underlined places are fictitious.

## Prologue

*H*e was crying.

Devastated, Mara listened, her ear pressed tightly against the plywood door, her entire being oblivious to the subzero Alaskan temperature that turned her tortured exhalations into white puffs of mist. She knew it was nearing dawn, knew that soon the villagers would awaken to face another midnight-black day, the sun a distant springtime dream.

He was really crying.

Oh, God. The deep, muffled sounds tore at her heart, yet still she hesitated to enter the one-room cabin. She remained, ear pressed against the thin wood barrier, straining to hear something, anything, that would help decide her next move. But there were no such signs in the clear, silent air, and she was left surrounded by cold, her heart pounding, her indecision trembling as much as her body.

He wouldn't welcome her intrusion. For nearly all of her eighteen years, *he'd* been the strong one, her best friend and protector. And now it was her turn. Lia, his sister-in-law, was dead, lost to the Bering Sea. Only the doctors in Fairbanks knew whether Mark's older brother, Jacob, would even survive this February night. And was it only a few weeks ago that Mark had survived his own plane's crash?

How much pain could one man endure? And how would she live with herself if she walked away? Eyes squeezed tightly shut, she concentrated a few moments longer on quelling her pounding heart and the trembling in her hands. She didn't know how to comfort him, but she knew she had to try. Next to Milak, her grandmother, he was her best friend. He was also the man she'd loved, it seemed, forever. She twisted the knob and entered.

The room was pitch-black except for a ray of blue-gray moonlight that streamed in from the single frost-encrusted window. It spilled across the bottom half of the double bed in an off-center triangular swatch. Mara's breath caught.

He was naked. Mesmerized, her gaze traveled with equal parts awe and embarrassment over the smooth, curved buttocks, and the sculptured muscles of his thighs and well-rounded calves. His upper body lay shadowed, but it, too, sent her heartbeat skyrocketing. She'd never seen a naked man before. Quickly, before she lost the little bit of nerve she had left, she stripped off her traditional sealskin parka and gloves and stepped out of her handcrafted mukluks. As she straightened, she automatically flicked her waistlong hair behind her back. Then she slowly, carefully, tiptoed to his side.

"Mark?" she whispered, her eyes riveted to his body.

He turned over restlessly, one powerful forearm moving up to cover his eyes. Her face flamed, and she took an instinctive step backward. His maleness was too potent, displayed too frankly, for her untried innocence. Helplessly she glanced at his long-limbed nakedness, transfixed by the triangular patch of black curls, so like her own, yet so very, very different. She stared until she realized what she was doing. Then her horrified gaze flew once again to his shadowed face.

He lay still, but she knew he wasn't asleep. The tortured rasp of his breath gave mute evidence to the battle he was fighting to control his emotions. She was certain now that he hadn't heard her enter, hadn't sensed her presence or even her questioning whisper of his name.

As her eyes adjusted to the semidarkness, they widened to huge pools as she saw the wetness streaking his cheeks. Her own tears spilled unrestrained, practically blinding her, so deeply did she feel his pain. With a helpless moan, and with his need for comfort so obvious, she discarded her virgin inhibitions and slid gently onto the bed. Yet before Mara even had the opportunity to absorb the first-ever sensation of his body alongside hers, the mattress creaked and the totally unexpected weight of him pressed down upon her.

Panic swelled, but she controlled it, sensing his sudden tension—he was aware of her presence. Afraid he'd pull away, she reached out, her hands touching bare, muscled shoulders, then sliding around his neck to pull him even closer, so that his head nestled in the curve between her neck and shoulder. He shuddered. Beneath her ear she could hear his heart begin to pound in heavy, thudding strokes. The sound was labored, but not painfilled. It was different. It made her aware of her body, and of his. Especially of his. Uncertain, Mara drew back. Instantly she felt his arms close tightly around her.

"Don't let go," he said hoarsely.

Mara swallowed, totally unable to speak. Yet to deny him anything was beyond her, so she heeded his request and gave in to her own temptation, following her instincts to kiss the chest she'd dreamed so long of kissing, tasting him for the first time, and refusing to think of anything beyond easing his pain, beyond her love for him....

Mara heard the ragged intake of his breath. Within her, new feelings stirred, feelings of warmth and need and desire. She loved him so much. As she felt him pressing against her, Mara quivered, all at once aware of the rising tide of heat. His heat. He was burning up. His heart was pounding deeply now, and his skin was hot. The blaze burned through her shirtlike hip-length cotton *kuspuk*, making her breasts flush, her nipples harden. She gasped, somewhat frightened by her body's reactions, but her hands never ceased to soothe and stroke and caress.

As her fingers smoothed down his spine to stop just before the gentle upward curve of his buttocks, he moaned, then moaned again, his lower body surging suddenly against hers with a force that momentarily robbed her of breath. Then he drew back, his movement forcing her to release him, his breath coming in fast, hard pants. When his mouth suddenly fastened on hers with a needful abandon that seemed to want to devour her, Mara froze. She'd never been kissed before. At least not like this, not as she'd imagined a woman would be kissed by the man she loves.

"Mark..." she croaked when he released her lips.

But he didn't stop. He hadn't even heard her, it seemed. His hands were unsteady as they swept the *kuspuk* up and over her head. Her stammered protest seemed futile in light of the fact that, deep inside her, she wanted what he was doing. But it was happening too fast!

Mara moaned as his hand found her breasts, squeezing together the cotton-covered mounds in a grip too experienced for her first time. Then he was opening the front clasp of her bra, his hand rough as it pushed aside the flimsy fabric, his mouth hot as it swept down and captured a small, tender nipple. Mara cried out at the bittersweet tugging, her back arching upward, the involuntary response a loud proclamation of her own helpless desire. His low growl of pleasure filled her mind and heated her body with soft, dewy moisture. She loved him so much. Mara breathed the words as she threw back her head, her usually gentle hands agitated, as if the pleasure were too beautiful to be borne.

Mara could think of nothing but the awesome wonder of their passion. Eyes squeezed shut, she touched him, learning the hard-muscled contours of his steely arms, the rounded curve of buttocks she'd spent years fantasizing about. Her hands slid up to his neck, digging into the short black strands of hair at his nape before sliding down again to rest along the flat, tight abdomen. There she hesitated, wanting to, but unable to bring herself to, reach under and explore the nest of curls and touch the pulsing shaft that jutted needfully between their heated bodies.

When his mouth left her breasts to fasten again on her lips, Mara sighed, opening up to his deeply masculine appetite. Her breasts burned from the heat of his chest as it pressed against her. His kisses demanded, and she gave him everything, wanting his heat, his possession, more than she had ever wanted anything in her life. She didn't think about the consequences, for there could truly be none now that she knew he loved her as much as she loved him. When he tugged impatiently at the waistband of her jeans, she trembled, but managed to control her shaking fingers enough to help him with the snap and the buttons, as anxious as he was to touch and explore and discover.

She felt his hands skim along her bare thigh, sliding the offending denim and the small cotton panties down and away. When she was naked except for the leather-and-feather wristband she never took off, she shivered, the heady glow of discovery and need giving way to an inkling of fear. She sighed nervously as she realized what they were about to do. Then he was pushing her back, spreading her out beneath him. Her legs were stiff now and reluctant to part, and her once-curious hands were uncertain as they strained against the tensed contours of his bare waist. Mara gasped helplessly when he reached beneath her thighs to cup her buttocks and lift them as his knee parted her legs for his possession. Her frightened eyes focused on his straining and engorged manhood. Tears filled her eyes, and she started to cry.

He froze at the sound of her sobs. Mara's emotions, which seemed always to be tuned in to his, sensed the exact moment when he realized, *really* realized, what was happening between them. He swore, and she cringed. Through her tears she watched him rear up off the bed and stalk to the switch beside the front door.

Immediately the room was flooded with bright, glaring, revealing light. Then he whirled, smoldering rage filling eyes gone cold and devoid of passion.

*"What the hell was that all about?"*

He said it so softly. For some inexplicable reason, that just made her cry harder. What did he think it was all about? She looked up from her splayed position and blushed a hot red at his blatant nakedness.

He was an intimidating sight. Mara's eyes skirted the strength of his arousal and fastened hastily on the thick veins that stood out on his muscled biceps then moved up to his taut neck, square chin and piercing black eyes.

All her life she'd looked into those eyes. Countless times she'd seen them bright with laughter. But not recently. And not now. Never had she seen his eyes convey such unparalleled disbelief and contempt, such uncompromising disgust and hardened resolve.

"You want to tell me what you're doing here?"

Afraid, Mara scrunched instinctively into the pillows bunched up at the headboard, her tears abruptly curtailed in the face of his totally unexpected anger.

"I—I came to be with you."

His eyes flicked over her. *"Be* with me?"

Abruptly Mara's shocked brain regained its ability to function. She cried out and lunged for the nearest thing at hand—her discarded jeans and panties. Her face flamed as she made a second grab for the crumpled sheet at the foot of the bed. She could feel the cold chill of the air on her bare thighs. Her breasts swayed forward, in full view of Mark's stunned eyes. She felt like dying, her mind clamping down on all but the most basic of needs. Somehow she managed to jerk the cover over her lower body and flick the long, thick curtain of her hair over her bared breasts.

*"Be* with me?" he repeated.

"Not like this . . . I didn't plan it."

She was humiliatingly aware of her nakedness and the stunned disbelief it was causing in the man studying her. As Mark's gaze roamed over the wild tangle of her hair, which couldn't quite conceal the fullness of her breasts, Mara felt deep shame enter her soul. She bowed her head.

"I came because I thought you might need me," she managed to say, holding on to her composure with great difficulty. She didn't see the sudden sympathetic comprehension that widened his eyes, nor the cold resolve that just as quickly clouded his features. Mara shuddered as embarrassment burned through her body.

"Stand up."

She had thought things couldn't get worse than they already were. She had been wrong. "What?" she choked.

"You heard me."

"Mark! Please—"

He cut her off. "Get up."

Her glance flicked wildly to the thin sheets covering her nakedness, then over to the door, so far out of reach.

"You've got to get up to get out." His facial expression was blank. His chest, however, was heaving in and out with some strong emotion. Rage? Disgust?

"Please . . . why are you being like this? I thought we were friends."

"Friends? You do this with all your . . . friends?"

The way he said it . . . Mara shivered, clutching the sheet with nerveless fingers. Her glance never left his face. Cold and unfeeling, he glared back at her stricken stare, and she admitted to herself that she was completely out of her depth.

"My *friends* know what to expect when they get here."

Mara couldn't quite stifle the pain his words wrought on her fragile composure. She jerked her eyes away from his. Her face flushed. "I told you! I didn't plan—"

"*Stand up.*"

The command sliced, knife-blade sharp. Startled, Mara jumped, and the springs on the mattress squeaked. Her gaze snapped to his. Nothing, in all the years she'd fantasized about intimacy with Mark, had prepared her for their brief passionate exchange, or for this awful aftermath.

"I—I can't. Please, don't make—"

"You can and you will," Mark snapped, interrupting her. "Because you damn well don't want my help."

He was right. She didn't want him touching her. The moisture between her legs now felt like a betrayal, because she knew that, deep in the cradle of her womanhood, desire still stirred. Mara felt the rhythm of her heartbeat increase as she faced that bald fact. In order to leave this nightmare scene she'd have to get dressed, and in order to get dressed she'd have to drop the sheet.

Mara blanched.

How could she have been so stupid, so awfully innocent, as to think he'd welcome her with open arms? Beneath the sheet, her shivering legs began inching to the edge of the bed farthest from him.

"Wrong side, Mara."

She cast one last, pleading glance toward him. He stood tall and straight, determination etched into his frozen features, his eyes unyielding as they coldly pierced the distance between them. She couldn't allow herself to feel, for to do so would shatter what little remained of her composure.

She swung her legs off the edge of the mattress. Her dainty, sock-clad toes hovered, then eased to the bare floor with hardly a sound.

"Hurry up."

She flinched, shoulders hunched, eyes fearful and teary. Though he stood across the room, she felt threatened by the menacing touch of his eyes. He remained unmoved by her tears. She pulled the covering with her as she slowly stood, letting it drape around her waist, obscuring her nakedness.

"I want you to look at me." He crossed to stand a few feet from her. "A good long look. What do you see?"

Mara could hardly see anything for the tears that blinded her sight. She sniffed and wiped at her eyes, fear and humiliation and a lingering desire burning confusingly through her body, short-circuiting her ability to talk, much less reason coherently. "I don't understand."

He sighed, clearly impatient. "What do you *see*, Mara?"

"A—a man?"

"Yes! And you want to know what I see? I see a girl. Not a woman, Mara. A *girl*." He suddenly reached out and pulled the sheet from her hands. Mara cried out at the unexpected exposure. Her eyes squeezed tightly shut. It seemed her only defense. She didn't even hear the soft moaning sound of pain that came from her throat, or see the agonized self-disgust briefly flare across his face as his eyes swept over her peaked nipples and lingered on the triangle of curls no other man had ever seen.

"Open your eyes, Mara."

Jerking spasmodically, she shook her head violently. Tears rolled unheeded down her cheeks. Why was he behaving like this? She didn't understand what was driving him. "Please . . . Mark . . ."

"Open your eyes and tell me what you see!"

Mara's eyes snapped open. Her gaze just happened to land on his softened manhood. "Oh, please! Let me go!"

"Fine. Go," he said, then stepped away from her and bent down to the foot of the bed, where her panties, bra, *kuspuk* and jeans were piled in a hastily discarded heap. He picked them up with a casual disregard that emphasized his sophistication and her naïveté. "Just so you know— I'm not turned on by naive little girls with teenage crushes."

The raging self-disgust in Mark's voice went unnoticed by Mara, for she felt as if she'd just received a crippling blow. *Crushes?* What was he talking about? She *loved* him! Wanted to marry him!

For endless seconds she stood frozen, eyes pinned on the clothes in his hand, praying, hoping, she wouldn't be sick as the rest of his words played through her mind. *I'm not turned on by naive little girls with teenage crushes.* But the softly spoken words crescendoed in her mind as their awful meaning sank in.

He'd never love her.

Suddenly she felt violated, and all she wanted was to leave, to get out from under his falsely adult patronization. He had responded to her— She wasn't so young that she hadn't felt the need in his kisses. But once he'd realized just what was happening between them, he'd pulled back, leaving her to deal with the continued presence of needs she'd only just begun to investigate. She'd sacrificed her fears to ease his pain, and he'd returned the favor by ripping a gaping hole in her future! And all because, to him, she was just a little girl.

Blinking rapidly, she pulled on her jeans, then ran to the door, jerking on her parka, boots and gloves, stuffing her bra and panties and the *kuspuk* in a side pocket. She knew she'd never be able to wear them again without remembering. As her hand wrenched open the door, Mark's voice cut through her retreat.

"I don't need anyone, Mara. Never forget it."

The pain-filled statement made her pause. She turned, her eyes drinking in the picture he made, standing so casually, unconcerned about his own nudity. His lack of arousal was as obvious as his arousal had been earlier. The truth ripped her soul, and with a cry she turned and fled into the night.

## Chapter One

The dining/living area of his brother's newly remodeled three-bedroom home smelled appetizingly of a blend of Yup'ik Eskimo and *kass'aq*—white man—dishes: his sister-in-law Ann's mouth-watering biscuits, his mother Oopic's broiled seal and the dried low-bush cranberry pie that his sister, Siksik, had insisted on baking to celebrate *kaugun*, the arrival of June and of fishing season.

They'd just finished dinner. Mark Toovak lay sprawled across an oval braided rug, his hands making a pillow for his head as he gazed up at the wood-frame ceiling. Twenty-four-hour daylight marked this time of year, and Mark knew that everyone in the village—including ninety-two-year-old Milak, whose speculative gaze he sensed as she settled herself slowly into Jacob's brown lounger—felt the electric excitement that came with the annual resurgence of life-giving food. Yet this year Mark wasn't excited. In fact, he was finding it damn hard to maintain the lighthearted attitude he'd so carefully cultivated these past four years.

"What's the matter, Uncle Mark? You sick? You didn't eat much."

Mark grimaced. How was it, he wondered idly as his gaze left the ceiling to connect with Patrick's, that eleven-year-old boys invariably asked the one question you didn't want asked? Sitting up, he playfully cuffed the boy on the chin. May as well tell them now, he decided.

"I guess I just wasn't all that hungry tonight, Patrick. I found out Friday that Crosswinds Siberia won't operate this summer. I'm going to have to cancel the tours I booked."

Mark's fingers dug into the beige rug and clenched. He waited for an explosion that never came. At least not from Patrick.

"Bummer."

A corner of Mark's mouth twitched. Leave it to Patrick to make a molehill out of a mountain.

"Yeah, major bummer," Mark repeated, watching the boy plop down, then reach for the tangled pile of sealskin rawhide that Mark knew his brother, Jacob, was using to teach his adopted son how to knit a fishing net. Mark kept his gaze fixed, waiting for the rest of his family's reactions. This time, he wasn't disappointed.

"Cancel your tours?" In the middle of scooping the remaining seal meat into a small plastic container, his mother stopped her task and followed swiftly behind her husband. They settled on the couch in front of him.

"What about the money you've already paid?"

Good ol' Jacob. He wasn't Twilight's business manager for nothing. Mark smiled, though it didn't reach his eyes.

"Spent. No way to get it back. I prepaid for the planes, the helicopters, the equipment, everything. Russian rules, not mine. I guess they want to make sure that when things like this happen, they don't get stuck without those American tourist dollars coming in."

"Things like what?" asked Ann's sixteen-year-old daughter, Sharon, from her position in front of the television.

"But that's not fair!"

Mark gazed at his sister's outraged expression. She was sixteen, too. And with her boyfriend, Billy, away at college, lots of things in life seemed unfair. Again he shrugged, knowing that at twenty-nine things weren't a hell of a lot fairer.

"Back up, son," ordered his father, Ben Toovak.

The deep concern in the elder Toovak's voice brought a frustrated slant to Mark's lips. His father took all his responsibilities quite seriously. Most especially his role as mayor of their small village of Twilight. Crosswinds Siberia's closing meant lost wages and work for the entire village.

"Now, what do you mean you won't operate this summer. Why not?"

"No interpreter. Randall broke his leg. He's a rock climber, though not a very good one, apparently. Anyhow, bottom line is that he can't come. And I've just told you what that means."

"You need a new interpreter?" Patrick asked.

Mark frowned. "It's not that easy, sport. Randall and I traded expertise, not money. He got to hunt and fish for free and, in return, I got his services for my clients."

Mark grimaced, not really expecting his joke to lighten the mood. Sometimes he felt like cursing their familial right to question him like this. He didn't like people digging into his business. He didn't like the dependency and obligation that came from loving and being loved—from close ties of any kind, if the truth be known. Four years ago he'd decided he wouldn't knowingly accept responsibility for anyone except his family ever again. That was why he'd begun Crosswinds Siberia in the first place. The business was seasonal, the clients ever-changing, the obligations—both business and personal—minimal. For him, it was the perfect job.

So how had he let himself become dependent upon an interpreter? Now his entire business was in jeopardy. And judging from the anxious expressions on their faces, his family knew it. He shook his head, disgusted with himself.

"We'll work something out," murmured Ann after a few silent moments had passed. She sat balanced on the wide, padded armrest of the second brown lounger in the room, her arm curved possessively along her husband's broad shoulders.

Ann was a kind woman, Mark knew. He looked from his brother's wife to the month-old baby boy sleeping peacefully in the curve of Jacob's arm. Had only eighteen months passed since the math and science teacher had moved her two children from Anchorage to live in their village? Single-handedly she'd changed Jacob's entire outlook on life. And everyone, including him, had been grateful. So when she'd begun her personal crusade to ensure that Twilight's Yup'ik students could compete scholastically against their *kass'aq* counterparts, he'd promptly donated the start-up funds for her computer-literacy program. And he'd kept on donating. He believed in education. He believed in progress. They gave people choices, made them less dependent on aid. He was big on independence. Real big.

"I've already planned to join you at fish camp this year, Jacob. We'll be able to catch more with me there to help."

"You can offer no payment for an interpreter?"

Milak's question was in Yup'ik. Though she understood much, she spoke little English. Mark held the old healer's gaze, disturbed by the narrowed intensity in eyes that commonly saw more deeply than most. Uncomfortable, he shook his head, then looked away. But he could still feel Milak's studied concentration.

"I used what was left of last summer's earnings to prepay this summer's tours. And even if I did have some extra cash, it wouldn't be nearly enough. Russian interpreters, so I've found since last Friday, are expensive."

"What about the other outfitters? Maybe they could give you some leads, or, better yet, let you contract one of their interpreters."

"Don't you think I tried that, Jacob? But most headquarter out of Magadan, and that's too far from where I am in Provideniya, even if I could afford to pay their rates, which I can't. I refuse to rely on the Russian airline, Aeroflot, to fly anyone anywhere in Russia on time. I'm on a strict time schedule, and so are—" he sighed heavily "—so *were* my clients. A late interpreter is as bad as no interpreter."

"There's no one?" asked Mark's mother.

"The only company I thought might work was Asia Tours, but it turned out they're strictly Kamchatka Peninsula. They don't offer the Chukotka District in their program and their interpreter wasn't eager to go anyway. It's not exactly a pleasure cruise. Mention taking a hike into remote Siberia and most people look at you weird."

"I wouldn't, Uncle Mark," Patrick chimed in, his hands busy with the rawhide. "Sounds rad to me. Dad and I can go with you sometime if you want."

"And what about me, young man?"

"Aw, Mom. Hunting's the man's job. Dad said so." He looked up, his innocent face confused by the subdued amusement of his family. "What'd I say?"

"Nothing." Jacob looked momentarily abashed by Ann's teasingly raised eyebrow. "But since you listen so well, remind me to teach you about tact, son." He smiled as he said it, his expression warm with love. "And the sooner the better."

Mark stood, aware of a dozen-plus eyes following his purposeful stride toward the door. He was beginning to feel trapped by their concern and frustrated by his inability to ease it. He needed space. And distance. Bending, he laced up his high-tech court shoes, then pulled his denim jacket off the peg by the door.

"You're leaving?" his mother asked softly. "But we're not finished...."

Mark paused. He couldn't explain what he was feeling, so he didn't try. "There's nothing you can do, Mother. I've looked into everything, and it's either too expensive or...too expensive." He forced a smile. "Thanks for the dinner, Mom, Ann. You, too, little raven. Great pie." He pulled open the door.

"Mara speaks Russian," Milak offered softly, almost absently.

"Mark, wait!" Siksik turned to Milak, her black eyes suddenly bright, her voice hushed with suppressed excitement. "Do you think...do you think Mara would do it?"

Abruptly the heavy atmosphere evaporated and the room filled with excited voices.

"Milak, what a wonderful idea!" exclaimed Oopic, switching to Yup'ik in her excitement. "As one of us, she would not need payment."

"Who's Mara?" asked Patrick, his head bobbing from one person to another.

"You'll need to call her first thing in the morning," ordered Ben, a big smile on his broad, weathered face.

Again Patrick asked, "Who's Mara?"

"Work out the details tonight. That way, when you call her, you'll be able to give her an idea when you'll need her," his mother suggested.

Mark wasn't listening. The mention of Mara's name sent a shaft of pain into his gut. He couldn't remember a time in his life when he'd felt so completely lost. And he also couldn't remember ever being crueler or making a bigger fool of himself than that night with Mara. He'd tried to forget, but who was he kidding? Four years hadn't dimmed the image of midnight-long hair shielding full breasts. Embarrassed, Mark felt hot blood creeping over his cheeks.

"Come, sit down, son," Oopic urged him in gentle Yup'ik. "There is much to discuss. Much you will need to plan. We will help."

Mark hesitated. As far as he was concerned, his family had "helped" him enough for one night.

"Mara...she's at the university in Fairbanks, right? Just graduated?" asked Ann, aware of Mark's reluctance, but not of its cause. Siksik nodded.

"They used to be best friends before she moved away to college," Ben said.

Again Mark flinched. They *had* been good friends. But that had been before the crash, before Lia died, before Mara witnessed his tears. The last made him distinctly uncomfortable. He'd lowered his guard that night. His bitterness and his pain had overwhelmed his judgment.

Shame—emotional, physical—wrapped around his chest. He doubted she would call him a friend. Not after what he'd said, what he'd done. He'd been a heartless bastard four years ago. To think, to remember, that Mara had only wanted to help! And he had deliberately betrayed her fragile trust.

But there had been reasons. Reasons that still existed today, reasons that would never go away. He hadn't wanted to do it, but the attraction for him in her eyes, his temptation by the sight of her body, and his own shocking vulnerability to both, had forced him. Inwardly, he cringed, realizing he hadn't seen her in four years, hadn't even known she'd graduated, much less that she could speak Russian.

"Mom, who's Mara?"

"Zip it, Patrick," Sharon ordered. "You're getting on people's nerves."

"Just a moment, sweetheart," answered Ann before turning once again to Siksik. "But I thought her major was in Native anthropology?"

"It is, but her minor is Russian."

"Oh, okay, now I see." Ann turned to her son, who was just opening his mouth. "Mara is Milak's granddaughter."

Patrick looked at the old healer for a long, wondering moment, his expression showing clearly that he was having trouble picturing her as anything other than the ancient woman she was now.

"Mark."

Milak had to repeat his name before he heard it. He blinked and focused, aware now of her studied observation.

"You will take me home?"

He stiffened, surprised by the commandlike request. Usually Milak enjoyed lounging after one of his family's Sunday dinners. Dread filled him. Either he could stay and stomach their enthusiasm or he could accompany Milak. Damn. He didn't need this!

Recrossing the room, he politely offered his arm. As she stood, their eyes met. Did Milak know?

They left his curious family behind them and moved silently to the narrow plank pathway connecting most of the village's homes.

Mark adjusted his long stride to match the slow, deliberate tread of the woman beside him. Though her advanced age made speed an impossibility, it had not dulled her mind or her eyes. She missed little, and had a sharp, decisive tongue. As a healer, she was her own walking advertisement. Her fingers were mobile, her back was straight and her teeth, miraculously, were her own. She was old, but not worn, and she continued to shoulder the concerns of three generations of Twilight's children with a calm reverence that never failed to remind Mark just how much he had yet to learn of life.

As they passed the two-story high school building, Milak paused and turned toward the great gray-blue expanse of the Bering Sea. In summer it was alive with sound as waves formed, rolled and crashed into the pebbled shoreline. Her black eyes roamed the source of their yearly sustenance, her waist-length white braid swinging rhythmically behind her back. She inhaled deeply.

"*Kaugun* marks a time of great joy," the old healer said in Yup'ik, her voice like the sound of the sea inside a seashell. She dropped her arms, her face tilted to the hazy sun.

"Yes," he murmured, for in the past June *had* been a good month. But not this year.

"Fish are plentiful, children run freely and with much laughter. The days are long and warm," the old healer said.

"Yeah," Mark agreed aloud. In summer, fishing was a twenty-four-hour occupation for Twilight's subsistence-dependent community. Fall was a time for hunting and for gathering grasses, seeds, flowers and berries. And winter brought dances and celebrations and family gatherings, traditional pastimes used to celebrate culture and community. He didn't like winter much. Too many bad memories.

"Our world is full in June."

Yeah, full of trouble, Mark thought bitterly.

"But Mark Toovak, man of sky machines, is not so full. Mark Toovak is empty, sad," the old healer said, continuing down the wooden pathway. She walked steadily, eyes forward, expecting his presence at her side, her brown, sun-wrinkled arm curled into the crook of his elbow.

"Learning Randall broke his leg has made me sad, yes," Mark said evasively. His stomach tightened. *Man of sky machines*. Hell! She didn't pull her punches, did she?

Her knowing eyes turned abruptly and peered into his soul. Then she once again faced forward. She waved her free arm. "You never speak of the crash, do you?" the wise old woman asked.

For crissakes! Did she think it was a topic for Sunday-dinner conversation? In midstride he bent down, momentarily dropping her arm to reach for a child's carved-driftwood storyknife half buried in mud. Little girls used the *yaaruin* mostly when they played in the sand by the shore, illustrating the hunting stories of their ancestors. He wiped the six-inch-long blade against his jeans, then proceeded to toss it in the air, end over end. "No," he said finally, to make sure she did know. "I don't."

"Take care not to cut yourself. My supply of dried angelica root is low."

Mark looked uncomprehendingly at the old woman for a second, then at the *yaaruin* in his hand. Shrugging, he stuck it in his back pocket.

"You are indeed like your *inua*. You wander, yet you always travel the same road."

Mark grunted at the not-so-subtle dig at his spirit guide, the caribou. "Being *stubborn* has nothing to do with it. It's over, done. Why talk about it?"

"Do you want to fly again?"

Mark turned on the narrow pathway and faced her. "I don't even think about it," he said, aware it was only a half-truth. Though he longed to pilot another aircraft, he didn't want the headache, the responsibility and the dependence of other people that flying the medevac plane had wrought on his system. So he didn't dwell much on his lost career. The pain went too deep.

But he did think about flying. He missed the sensation of freedom, the oneness that came with solo communion with the heavens. He missed that indefinable something that came over him in the sky. He didn't know why he hadn't again piloted. Was that part of him forever buried? Was the pilot in him too frightened? Was he dead?

"How do you do it?" Mark asked, aware he was thinking about it, even though he'd just said he didn't.

The old healer chuckled, and they resumed walking. "You sound like Mara when she tried hiding something from me. As a child, I told her the eyes are a window into the soul. Read the eyes and you see the pain. See the pain and you can heal. She didn't like that any more than you." She looked up at him.

Mark endured her stare and kept walking, stiff at the seemingly nonchalant mention of her granddaughter's name. He knew better. Here it comes, he thought. His heart began pounding, and he felt it necessary all of a sudden to remind himself that he was a grown man who didn't need a lecture on proper conduct. Then he remembered just who he was with. He was young compared to her. Being ninety-two gave one a unique outlook on lots of things.

"You are alike, you and she," the old healer continued. "You both live with pain. You both walk alone." She shook her head, her long white braid undulating with her movement. "You both bury your feelings, denying they exist. You have both found new paths, and care not that the road is unhappy. You are both confused."

"No, we're not." Mark knew he sounded childish. "At least I'm not. I know exactly what I'm doing and why."

"Do you?"

Again he stopped, his black eyes taking in the frail woman. "Yes, I do." His voice rang with sincerity. For the first time in minutes, he felt on solid ground. The depth of his belief made him feel slightly embarrassed, the way he often felt when Milak dispensed her herbal medicine. He just didn't believe in all that ancient mystical herbal stuff.

For long minutes, the Bering Sea breeze flowed around them. Milak said nothing, her eyes seeing more than Mark wanted her to see. "Four winters have passed since you last soared the sky. And four winters have passed since Mara left her home. I see there is much left to say. I see—"

"Too much?" Mark said, interrupting her. Abruptly he started walking again. He didn't offer his arm.

"Talking eases much pain," the old healer said as she followed behind him.

Mark said nothing. But he did slow down, cursing his own sense of propriety. He spotted Milak's two-bedroom house with relief.

"Darkness feeds pain." The old woman waved her hand across the sky. "Use the light and its warmth. June is the time of plenty."

He didn't have anything to add, so he didn't. They traversed the remaining distance in silence. At the front door, Milak entered, then turned.

"I have a task for you."

Mark swallowed a groan. Damn. Now what?

Taking off his shoes, he entered her home and stopped just across the threshold, gazing in renewed disbelief at the room before him. It was a museum. Except for the modern window and the tattered recliner, and an even older cookstove, Mark would have sworn he'd entered a time warp. The floors were draped with skins: wolf, bear, seal and walrus. There were inflated walrus-stomach containers, dried and filled with strange, scent-heavy liquids. Two long-handled spears with carved stone blades stood upright in a corner. And there were filled grass baskets of every size and design, even plates and spoons carved out of driftwood. Along one wall hung an old but magnificent beaded headdress, along another an equally impressive collection of driftwood, ivory and feather spirit masks carved to depict the union between man and animals and earth. The woman's one-piece reindeer suit was truly magnificent. A masterpiece of functionality that by virtue of its advanced age was now art. It came to him suddenly that Mara had grown up amid these ancient symbols, smelling the dried herbs, seal oil and dried mosses burning in the several large, shallow clay lamps, called *naniqs* that were strategically placed about the main room to provide light. As he watched, Milak lit several, illuminating the room and throwing two magnified silhouettes up against a wall hung with another beautiful collection of ceremonial dance fans. Then she moved into the small connected kitchen and set about making tea. Great, Mark thought. Obviously this was going to take a while.

"Mara crafted some of those," Milak said, noting his interest in the multicolored circular dried-grass fans, some ringed with polar bear hair, others with owl feathers and still others with reindeer hair. Mark was impressed. And disturbed. How had Mara survived in this place? No wonder she'd gone away to college.

"You spoke of a task," Mark murmured. For some reason, Milak's home made him feel like whispering.

Instead of choosing to sit on the lounger, Milak settled down on a silver-haired wolf pelt, legs loosely crossed in front of her, each hand holding a cup. The physical feat would have taxed a much younger person, but Milak handled it with ease. Bewildered by the apparent paradox of her behavior, Mark settled down beside her and accepted a carved-driftwood cup. No telling how old it was. He preferred coffee, not tea, and in a mug, also preferably manufactured in this century.

He sipped the chamomile tea, catching the spicy scent of labrador leaf. It was hot. It burned his insides. It cleared his mind.

"I had a dream last night. It spoke of times gone by, of family far away, and of the future."

Dreams? He didn't want to hear about dreams. Too many of his own were nightmares. "The task, Milak. You wanted me to do something for you?"

"Ah, you are yet a young caribou. The old ones have more patience."

"The old ones are dead," Mark replied, smiling into his cup.

Milak chuckled. "There is much to be learned in death. I do not fear the final lesson, I only delay it. All things become known in time."

"Delay your death? What are you talking about?" Though the tea burned hotly down his throat, he shivered. He didn't like talking about death. Death filled him with fear and with memories.

"Did Mara ever tell you of my family?"

Mark frowned and looked up from the tea to the white-haired healer. "Do you always answer one question with another?"

"One man's question is another's answer."

Mark's mouth opened, but when he couldn't think of a single reply he shut it again.

Milak nodded. "You learn quickly. Perhaps you will succeed."

Mark sighed, tired of playing word puzzles. "Okay, Milak—we'll do it your way. No, Mara never told me about your family. She didn't much discuss her parents."

"Not her parents, mine."

"Yours?"

She nodded. "As I said, I had a dream. My *inua* led me on a long sea journey."

Through their years of growing up as playmates, he'd learned much from Mara about the healer. And one of the things he'd learned and remembered was that her spirit guide was the Bearded Seal. "Where did Tungunqut take you?"

"We journeyed across the Bering Sea, back in time fifty years," the healer said, curling her hands around her cup. She fell silent, lost in thought.

After several moments had passed, Mark asked, "Across the Bering Sea . . . to Russia?"

"Then, as now, our *umiaks* carried my family from old Sireniki across the Sea to Saint Lawrence Island. But one day, almost fifty years ago, I alone made the journey. And that same day Stalin made the Sea change. The Iron Curtain divided the Sea. The Iron Curtain divided me from my family." The old woman paused, nodding at Mark.

Mark nodded back, enthralled. He'd heard about hundreds of Yup'ik Eskimo who'd been cruelly cut off from their relatives by the strong arm of Stalin's 1948 edict. He just hadn't realized any of Twilight's people had been among that sad group. He sighed, grateful for the shifting in Russian/American relations. At least now the Yup'ik could again freely sail the two hundred and fifty short miles separating Siberia from Alaska's coast.

"Bearded Seal took me home. Though their spirits still live in grandchildren as namesake, the bodies of my parents and my brothers are now gone."

Mark remained silent.

"Except for one—an older sister. She, too, is healer."

"An *older* sister? Older than you?" Mark asked, astounded.

"Didn't I just say so? For a young man, you're hard of hearing, aren't you?"

Mark grinned, aware once again that Milak could talk just like everyone else when she chose to. She just didn't choose to very often. An image thing, Mark decided. Who ever heard of a healer who didn't frustrate the hell out of a person by speaking in riddles?

"What about this sister?" Mark asked, suddenly aware of the keen intelligence shining out of her piercing black eyes. Milak was not only a powerful healer, but she was also an excellent negotiator with a clever knack of making her plans seem like someone else's. That way, she never forced anyone to do anything he didn't want to. Smart. Real smart. Now all he had to do was figure out what she wanted.

"Change is coming. Coming to Twilight. Coming to my sister...coming to me." The old woman set down her cup and stared across the room to the windowsill, at a wood-framed photo of Mara.

Mark frowned. "What change? When?"

Milak shrugged, her gaze never wavering from the photo. "I want you to bring Mara home."

For perhaps the space of two seconds, silence encompassed the room as Mark tried to stem a sudden and overwhelming feeling of walls closing tightly around him.

"You're kidding, right?" He jerked to his feet. The hot tea sloshed over his hand, and he swore. "Why should I fly to Fairbanks when you can just pick up the phone over at John's store and call?"

The old healer abruptly turned away from the photo of Mara, her entire body radiating an aura of great emotion. A knot formed in his stomach, and he was suddenly overcome by the sense that she was desperate.

*Milak desperate? Why?* He could find no answers in the eyes that gazed at him.

"You know why. She won't come unless you bring her."

That made even less sense. Mara loved her grandmother. Mark was certain that she'd *walk* home if she had the slightest knowledge that Milak needed her. He stared. Was the old woman crazy? He hunkered down again, squatting on the balls of his feet. They were face-to-face.

"Milak, what's going on?" he asked softly, his confusion plain. Twilight's healer was old. Frail. Talking of death and of unusual dreams. And she was strangely tense. He'd never seen her like this. Not even Mara's mother's death—her own daughter's death—had created such an outpouring of uncontrolled emotion. "Tell me," he urged. "Whatever it is, I'll help."

"You will do this?" the old woman asked, suddenly clenching his arm with surprising power.

It wasn't really a question. It was an order. She stood, and so did he.

"Milak, Mara loves you. Dream or no dream, she'll come if you call. You don't need me."

"Then why has she not visited? Four years I have waited. It is time. The dream has set the stage."

Again the dream. Even though Mark didn't believe in all that mumbo-jumbo stuff, he felt a shiver shimmy up his spine. He also felt trapped between his desire to remain aloof and his desire to help the old woman. Her granddaughter had obviously made her own life plans. She'd left Twilight. How did Milak expect him to alter them? What did she expect he could say that would bring her home?

Mark glanced into Milak's face. She believed in the dream, even if he didn't. And she needed her granddaughter, even if he had to suffer through the hell of the damned to bring her back home.

"What about if I called her? Would that do?" he asked, almost desperately, picking his words with care.

The old woman looked at him for a long, searching moment. "You tell me," she said, slowly, wearily. Then, from the pouch in her *kuspuk* she withdrew something.

Mark looked down. The wrinkled hand held a garment. Mark recognized it instantly, and his head shot up.

It was Mara's *kuspuk*, the one he'd pulled off her four years ago.

## Chapter Two

*Granddaughter?*

Maacungaq. *Grandmother... is that you?*

*Come home... time... runs out...*

Mara opened her eyes. The air in her bedroom was hot. From the center crack in the double-lined curtains, fierce sun rays lit the room's darkness. Mara stared up at the ceiling, her body drenched with sweat, muscles trembling from prolonged tension. How long had she lain clenched like this? Minutes? Hours?

She trembled beneath the sealskin comforter, her mind racing. The dream had been so vivid, and her grandmother's voice so frail and so weak. Did the healer really want her to come home? Or was the dream a manifestation of her own secret longing?

She missed her grandmother. She missed her home and her people. And, though her life was full, it wasn't fulfilling. Part of her would always be in Twilight.

Tungunqut had visited her often since her move to the university. She'd never questioned the dreams. She'd never wanted to. Always Tungunqut brought comfort and a cultural connectivity Mara craved in her *kass'aq* surroundings. She'd needed those dreams. She still needed them now.

But this dream was different. It didn't reassure, it frightened.

*Come home.*

She shuddered at the whispered command. What to do? Her grandmother was ninety-two. Spiritually powerful, but physically frail. Could she afford to gamble that the dream was just that—a dream?

No. Dream or not, real or not, she had to find out. Had to see for herself. And telephoning was out. The village only had one phone. Privacy was, therefore, rare. Besides, Milak had insisted that she *come* home, not that she *phone* home. She sat up abruptly, her gaze fixing on the radio clock on the nightstand beside her bed.

Six o'clock Tuesday morning. How soon would the first flight for Bethel leave? Throwing back damp sheets, she scrambled from the bed and hurried toward the bathroom. Opening the shower stall, she turned on the spigot, then pulled her oversize University of Alaska at Fairbanks Nanooks T-shirt over her head. When she caught her own glance in the mirror, tears filled her eyes. Her grandmother was her only family. If anything happened to her . . . Eyes closed, she bent over the sink.

*Granddaughter. Time runs out. . . .*

Mara's head snapped up. Her black eyes were enormous as she gazed unseeing at her reflection. This was no dream. This was real. All her energies were centered inward as she let her thoughts wing with Tungunqut back through the sea of dreams, back to the frail woman lying among familiar furs, waiting for her.

Mara didn't question what she was doing, didn't pause to analyze the images gathering in her mind.

*Maacungaq. Grandmother . . . I'm coming home.*

Then she stepped under the spray—and thought of Mark.


Mark was coldly furious with himself. Grabbing his knapsack, he slid from the cab, slammed the rear door, then walked around to the driver's side, waiting impatiently as the cabby fumbled around for change in an all-too-obvious attempt to get a larger tip.

Yeah, sure, buddy. Mark pocketed the bills and the change, then strode purposefully toward the brown three-level apartment complex. Of all the stupid, foolish things . . . He'd told himself, over and over and over: Do not get involved in other people's problems. He knew better! Right then he should have been helping Jacob assemble the necessary gear for the move to fish camp, not playing messenger boy for a very odd and possibly senile old lady. Climbing every other step to the third floor, he wondered just how to handle the next few minutes.

They'd be long ones, that was for sure. Maintaining his usual detachment wouldn't be easy, and it might even be impossible. He wished he could shove a note under Mara's door, return to the cab and leave. Better yet, he wished he'd called her late last night, when he arrived. But he hadn't, and damn himself for an honest man, he'd known full well he wouldn't. He'd promised Milak. Something he didn't do lightly or often. Two days ago, Milak hadn't had to say a word. The garment in her hands, Mara's discarded *kuspuk*, had said it all. And his red face had screamed his guilt. This was likely to blow up in his face, just like the explosive situation he'd found himself in four years ago.

Damn it! What was he supposed to say to the girl? *Hi, I happened to be in the area and thought I'd drop by? By the way, Milak's gone crazy.* His lips twisted into a cynical smile. The latter might be true, he acknowledged irritably as he arrived at Mara's door, but there wasn't a chance in hell she'd think his unscheduled appearance was a friendship call.

He shifted from one foot to the other, uncharacteristically indecisive. Several witty openers sprang to mind and were immediately rejected.

So then, what?

He could apologize. Explain why he'd said what he had, why he'd done what he'd—

Forget it, Mark decided as a chill enveloped him. To apologize meant he'd have to reopen a part of his past he'd closed forever, and he couldn't do that, wouldn't do that—ever. His frown deepened. All he wanted was to deliver Milak's message and drag Mara's absent little butt home for a visit. He wouldn't even be here if she hadn't stayed away so long. Taking a deep breath, he decided to wing it. Grim-faced, he raised his hand and knocked.

Mara was sitting on her bed, her hair wet, her body shivering in its warm terry-cloth robe, her dry-eyed gaze unfocused as she stared down at her trembling hands.

Every molecule of her awareness was fixed on controlling the huge and painful waves of denial that had been trying to seize control over her rational thoughts since she realized that going home meant seeing Mark.

Four years. Four years, and still the mere thought of him made her want to curl up into a tight ball of painful humiliation and die.

Mara's chest heaved as the images played out in her mind. Four years, and she could still hear his condemning words and see the disgust in his eyes as they roved over her nakedness. A sob welled up within her, but she stopped it.

Bastard.

Her lips flattened as she faced the mocking black eyes projected with stunning clarity in her mind's eye. She stared at the man she'd once loved.

Mark Toovak.

Thinking his name rattled her soul and roused the embers of her anger into full-blown rage.

She no longer loved him. He'd killed that four years ago. He'd almost killed her, too, but she'd survived, though at great expense. Mara shifted her gaze from her hands to a small, intricately designed grass basket no bigger than a half-dollar. Her grandmother had crafted it. The grandmother she hadn't seen in four years.

Her throat constricted. *Oh, Maacungaq,* she screamed in silent anguish. *Do I have to go home?*

Four years. Four lonely years.

And all because of that bastard.

A low moan escaped her throat.

She had given him her friendship, and he had thrown it away like trash. Even worse, she had given him her love, and Mark had not only dismissed it as an inconsequential crush, but had denied her an adult's respect by calling her a little girl. But the most unforgivable of all—the move that had forever killed her love for him—was his insulting tug on the sheet. Even now, four years later, she could barely bring herself to even think about that awful instant when he'd stripped her naked.

Damn Mark Toovak.

Anger ripped through Mara. And shame. Images flickered through her mind, clear and sharp, of old but wise black eyes that had not once questioned a granddaughter's sudden leave-taking or pleaded for a granddaughter's presence.

Until now.

Mara wasn't aware of slowly moving her head back and forth in silent denial. Her throat and lips were dry. A chill silence enveloped the room as she sat, huddled, concentrated on that one moment of the past. But gradually, as her muscles relaxed and her thoughts moved beyond the initial shock of realization, she calmed enough to allow other thoughts to filter in, thoughts that further steadied her.

Four years she'd lived with this pain. And in those years, though she hadn't succeeded in burying the humiliation, she had eventually managed to understand that whatever had prompted Mark's behavior, it wasn't anything she'd said. She'd been naive, certainly. But that innocence couldn't have prompted Mark's cruelty. And, understanding that, Mara further concluded that it wasn't Mark's behavior that had kept her from going home all these years.

It was her *reaction* to it. The experience had controlled her, prompted her to leave her home and everyone she loved.

Well, no longer, Mara resolved as a determined glint sparked her usually soft eyes. It was time she called a halt to his psychological control over her mind and actions. She had a life of her own now, a career that didn't include him, a future she was excited about. Mark was a part of her past. She would not give him the satisfaction of messing up her future, too. Her grandmother needed her. Mark Toovak or no Mark Toovak, she would go.

Mara bounded off the bed and into some clothes. She was fixing her bed when she heard a knock on the door.

"Just a minute!"

Giving her sealskin comforter one last swipe, she made for the door. There was only one person she knew who would drop by at six-thirty in the morning, and that was Wally. Like her, he was an Alaskan Native, only his family lived in interior Alaska and was Athabascan Indian. They'd met as freshmen, both nervous and uncomfortable in a *kass'aq* environment so far removed from their respective cultures. Often they studied late into the night together, sharing their fascination with Alaskan Native anthropology.

Impatient, she bypassed checking the peephole, unlocked the chain and the dead bolt, then jerked open the door. "Wally, I can't talk right now, I'm getting ready...." she began, and heard the frustration in her voice fade to stunned silence.

"Hello, Mar—*Mara?*"

"*Mark?*"

Mark Toovak was on her doorstep!

Shock forced her eyes wide open and froze her muscles. Her mind scrambled, unable to process the evidence of her own eyes, leaving her unprepared, helpless, unable to cope. But, though rational thought had deserted her, her senses nevertheless continued to smell, to see, to reject!

"Go away! I don't want you here!" She started to slam the door.

Guessing her intent, Mark swung his knapsack into the rapidly diminishing space, then shouldered his way inside.

Mara immediately retreated. He was too big, and too powerfully male. "Get out of my apartment."

Mark shook his head, staring at her as if he'd never seen her before. Dressed in tangerine leggings and a cropped white T-shirt, she looked modern and attractive. *And about ready to throttle you with her bare hands,* Mark concluded from the agitated flexing and clenching Mara was doing. The phrase *dead meat* skirted his thoughts, and he silently thanked Tuntu, his spirit guide, the caribou, that she hadn't come to the door wielding a knife. Yup'ik women were known for their expertise with the U-shaped blade called the *ulu.* He frowned, uncomfortably aware that she had every right to want to cut him up.

"Look, we need to talk."

"No." Mara swallowed against the urge to run from the apartment and leave him there. "No. Forget it. Whatever you feel you need to say, I'm not interested."

Mark's grim expression became grimmer. "Interested or not, you'll hear me out," he said abruptly, fighting to control his own trapped feelings. Damn Milak and her meddling! Why couldn't she just have picked up the phone?

"You might as well get used to me, because I'm not leaving until you hear me out."

He couldn't have chosen a worse set of words. Mara gasped, her already pallid features going white with remembered pain and humiliation. "I want you to leave."

"Fine," Mark said tightly. "As soon as you're packed." Mark's glance took in her too-bright eyes and trembling lips. His gut clenched. Viciously he pushed the weakening feeling aside. He didn't want to hurt. He didn't want to feel. He didn't want to be involved, damn it! His expression hardened. "Milak needs you."

Mara's breath caught. "What's wrong with Grandmother?"

"Nothing. At least, nothing I know of. But she has been acting weird. Talking about dreams and . . . stuff."

Mara gaped, thinking of the dream she'd had. "Dreams? What kind of dreams? And what do you mean, she's been acting weird? Weird how?"

She was worried. Mark's hands clenched. He didn't care, he told himself. In fact, he hoped it would keep her thoughts away from him. Apart from that, he had no feelings for her at all.

"Our flight for Bethel leaves at 8:30," Mark continued, making up his mind, then striding impatiently into the living room past a stunned Mara. It was obvious she wasn't about to invite him in. "It's 7:15 now. Get a move on. Time's running out."

Mara experienced the horrifying sensation of her well-ordered world once again being torn from under her. *Come home. Time... runs out....*

His stance aggressive, Mark scanned the living/dining area for closets. How, he wondered when he spotted one and started toward it, how was he going to make it through the next few hours? To look into her eyes was to see her condemnation of him. To look at her body was to be reminded of its sensual allure. His mind reeled as he pulled open the door to face neat rows of canned goods. Not there. He headed toward another closet, his movements tightly focused as he blocked out the pain.

Mara watched Mark's studied concentration as he invaded her domain, unable—for the moment, at least—to confront him. The short black hair she remembered was long now, wild and wavy and distinctly uncivilized as it brushed his shoulders. Overall, he looked older, harder, more cynical. That didn't surprise her. The youthful fullness of his face was gone. Angles defined him now. His shoulders were still straight and broad, like those of all the Toovaks, and his chest had filled out, barrel-thick and strong. Blue jeans stretched tightly over muscled thighs, the coarse material accentuating his male potency in a way that made Mara acutely uncomfortable. Everything about him was leaner and even more unconventional than ever before, from the gold-studded caribou emblazoned on the back of his denim jacket to the court shoes on his feet. Hearing another muffled oath, she snapped out of her reverie.

"Tell me about the dreams," Mara ordered, following him. There was now no doubt left in her mind. She was going home.

Slowly Mark's head emerged from yet another closet. His expression was distant, withdrawn, and something twisted in Mara at the thought that he could behave so callously, as if he'd completely dismissed that night from his mind. On impulse, she decided to try to follow his example. She didn't want him knowing how much anguish he'd caused her or how drastically he'd altered her life. She didn't want his pity, either. In fact, she didn't want anything from him. Not even an apology.

Staring into Mara's unfocused eyes, Mark fought a silent battle against an almost overwhelming urge to leave. He'd promised himself never to be the cause of anyone's pain, and he could see pain so plainly in her eyes. But he'd also promised Milak, so he was stuck. "Your suitcase. Where is it?"

"Hall closet. Now tell me about the dreams," she repeated.

"Ask Milak. I'm just her messenger boy." Mark knew he was being a jerk, but he had a right to protect himself, didn't he? Let Milak explain it to Mara. It wasn't really his business.

He strode down the short hallway and seconds later emerged from the closet holding a worn brown vinyl suitcase in one hand. Unceremoniously he shoved it into her arms. "Ten minutes, tops. And lose the outfit while you're at it. Unless you want to give your grandmother a heart attack."

Mara flushed; she could feel it. She was struggling for a reply when a knock sounded on the door. Mark got there first.

"What?"

"Do you mind?" Mara snapped, grabbing the door and swinging it wide open. She turned an apologetic smile on her visitor. "Hi, Wally."

"Hey, babe! I brought breakfast. Didn't know you had company."

Mark eyed the young man and his bag of donuts.

"Do you like donuts, sir?"

*Sir?* Who did the kid think he was talking to—his grandfather? Mark reached for the bag, inwardly satisfied with Wally's immediate frown, and peeked inside. Jelly-filled. He hated jelly-filled donuts. Reaching in, he pulled out two and bit into one. "Thanks."

Wally's expression was speculative, and he commented dryly, "Mara loves jelly-filled donuts. Of course, at our age, we can eat pretty much anything."

Mark almost choked. Quite deliberately, he bit into the second donut. "Hmm . . . Me, too."

"Wally, I'm so glad you came." Mara's smile didn't quite reach her eyes. Ignoring the tension between the two men, she introduced her visitor. "Wally, this is my . . . this is Mark. Mark Toovak."

The look that passed between the young Athabascan and Mara was intimate, friendly, and filled with unvoiced questions. Their closeness irritated Mark, though he couldn't come up with any reason why. He turned toward the living room, expecting Wally to follow. But he didn't.

"Glad to see me, huh? I tell ya, babe, everyone loves the donut man."

Yeah, right, Mark thought sourly as he settled uncomfortably on the sofa with his donuts. Some jelly oozed onto his jeans. He grimaced.

Mara nodded as she bit into a donut. She liked Wally. He was the only male she'd met during her years at the university with whom she could relax and be herself. So when she headed to her bedroom with Wally in tow, she didn't think about how it would look to Mark.

"I need you to do me a favor."

"Sure, whatever you want, babe. What gives?"

Their voices faded down the short hallway. Mark remained seated for all of one minute. Then he stood, stalked over to the trash can standing beside the refrigerator and tossed away the revolting donut, pleased with the squish it made on contact with the bottom of the bag. Then he turned away, disgusted with himself. The guy was just a kid. Too young to be a threat.

A threat? Now where had *that* come from?

He scowled. What were they doing in there? He washed the jelly off his hands. He wiped his jeans. He looked at his watch. Then he smoothed a hand over his hair. Then he decided enough was enough. He marched down the hallway.

And entered another world.

As when he'd set foot in Milak's home, Mark gazed around him in disbelief. Except for the double bed, the single desk, the closet and the carpeting, he would have sworn he was in Milak's home. Grass baskets occupied one corner of the room, their contents filling the room with familiar herbal smells. One of the spirit masks Jacob had carved adorned the wall above Mara's bed. And on yet another wall, dance fans of every size were artfully arranged. Mark stared, recalling Milak saying Mara crafted dance fans. Then his eyes fell to the bed and the huge sealskin comforter. And to Wally, who was shrewdly observing him from his sprawled position on top of it.

With obvious concern, Mara was finishing a sentence from her location in what Mark assumed was the bathroom.

"Go by my office. Their names and numbers are on my computer. Tell them it's a family emergency and that I'll be back as soon as I can, but that if they need their translations immediately to contact Peg at home. Her number's on the computer, too. And oh, yeah, I almost forgot. You'll tell Dr. Gordon? I don't want him to think I'm not dedicated to the project."

In anthropology, a doctorate was almost a requisite to being taken seriously in both corporate and academic societies. Dr. Gordon was her newly appointed adviser and he'd encouraged her interest in studying Yup'ik languages and their Russian ties. He'd even secured her a research grant.

"He knows you're interested, babe," Wally replied, looking Mark right in the eye.

Mark arched one brow. The kid could use some lessons in subtlety.

Wally made a pillow out of his hands and settled back on the bed. Mara's bed. He was jerking Mark's strings, and Mark knew it. But as much as he'd enjoy teaching Wally a lesson in manners, he refrained. If Mara liked the oversize runt, that was her prerogative. All he had to do was get Mara home to Milak. After that, his life was his own again.

So he smiled at Wally. A superior smile that said, *Try anything and you'll be sorry.*

Wally looked at him with dislike.

Mark was satisfied. "Get a move on, *babe*," he called out.

At the sound of Mark's voice, Mara dropped the brush in her hands. It crashed down on the vanity tile with a loud noise. She blushed, cursing the nervousness that blitzed her usual dexterity. Of all people, why had her grandmother sent Mark? Why had she sent anyone, for that matter? The dream had done its work; she'd understood the psychic summons. Even Wally was acting strange, and he was usually relaxed and easygoing.

She changed into a pair of jeans and a white polo shirt, still considerably irked by Mark's remark. Just because she'd moved away, that didn't mean she'd forgotten what it was like at home. Fashion was considerably more conservative.

She gathered up the remaining toiletries, and was just moving toward her bedroom when an intense wave of heat seared her from inside out and dizziness caused her to make a wild grab for the countertop. The bright room dimmed as her sight blurred, then narrowed. Her fingers grasped the countertop as she blindly willed her body not to give in, not to faint. Only the bald fact of Mark's and Wally's presence kept her on her feet.

She could see her reflection in the mirror on the vanity, see the pain in her eyes, but she couldn't move, couldn't have called out even if she'd wanted to. The heat blurred her vision as beads of perspiration ran from her forehead into her eyes. The dizziness in her head was overwhelming. It fluctuated, like a stormy ocean wave, pounding, receding, then pounding again.

Trembling fingers reached for her toiletry case. The room was still spinning, but she finally managed to pull out a small vial, unscrew the lid and pop a pill into her mouth. Then she collapsed on the toilet seat, her head hanging between her legs, and waited.

Hopefully, it wouldn't take long.

If only she knew what *it* was.

For six months the doctors—specialists in endocrinology and urology—had tested, prodded and pricked her body for clues, to no avail. The best they could say was that she was suffering from a hormonal deficiency, possibly thyroidal, possibly even adrenal. Mara was getting sick of possibles.

She wanted certainty, needed to know what was wrong with her, why her body was fine one minute and not the next. They weren't even sure it was a disease, because they couldn't find any similar cases in their medical texts. They'd offered pills, but no cure.

And lately, even the pills were losing their effectiveness.

Mara prayed that this time they would work, and work quickly. A few minutes later, she was rewarded with a clearing of her head and an ebbing of the heat flushing her from inside out. As soon as she could, she stood and ran a cool cloth over her face, studying her reflection for any telltale signs.

She didn't want anyone to know. Not Wally, not Milak, and especially not Mark. Gathering the vial, she snapped it shut and threw it into her toiletry bag. Then she took a deep breath and reentered the bedroom.

She squirmed under Mark's rigid stare. He looked down at his watch. "Ready?"

Instead of replying, she tossed the toiletry bag into her suitcase, then snapped it shut. Both Mark and Wally moved to heft it.

"I can do it myself, thanks." Sensitive to the strange tension between the two men, she handed Wally her apartment key. "Stay awhile if you want," she offered, then gave him a hug. Wally wanted to prolong it, but she pulled back, her black eyes telegraphing her surprise. He looked serious for a moment, then grinned sheepishly and released her. She hefted her knapsack and suitcase. "Water the plants, please. And take out the trash, okay? I'll call when I get some idea when I'll be back. Thanks for taking care of business for me."

"Yeah, sure, babe. You've got your tape recorder? Dr. Gordon won't be so uptight if you get a jump start on your research."

"I got it," she remarked on her way to the front door. Mark and Wally were right behind her.

"We need to call for a cab," Mark commented, heading for the phone he'd seen mounted on the wall beside the refrigerator.

"No need. We'll take my car."

Mark turned. "You can drive?"

The real surprise in his tone annoyed Mara considerably. Though *he* still considered her a little girl, she most definitely was not. And the sooner Mark Toovak realized that irrefutable fact, the better.

Mara turned and smiled at Wally. A genuine smile that had Wally blushing and Mark frowning. She was proud of her accomplishment. There weren't any cars in Twilight, or anywhere else on Nelson Island, so she'd never needed to learn until her arrival in Fairbanks.

"Wally taught me. And he also helped me pick out my Subaru. I don't know what I would have done without him."

Wally preened.

Mark merely gritted his teeth and hefted his knapsack, his restless stance a clear indication that time was ticking away. That Mara sensed his impatience was as obvious as her unhurried but efficient departure. She'd changed, he acknowledged, as he followed her out of the apartment and into the hallway. He could tell the suitcase she carried was heavy. Instinctively he reached out.

Mara hesitated, uncomfortably aware of that long-fingered hand. She shuddered, oblivious to Mark's suddenly closed expression, aware only of her aversion to his presence in her life, even if it was only temporary. She wished he weren't here, that Milak ,hadn't sent him, that he hadn't come.

But fighting over a suitcase was stupid, she reasoned, and she let it slide from her fingers in such a way that she didn't have to touch him. If Mark noticed, he didn't comment, and Mara picked up her pace, grudgingly acknowledging that its weight had slowed her down. Her black high-top tennis shoes squeaked on contact with the dew-wet pavement. Her old dark green Subaru beckoned her. Pulling out her keys, she opened the hatchback. Mark laid the suitcase and their knapsacks inside and slammed the door. Mara ignored him as best she could, but it wasn't easy. He more than filled the passenger seat, threatening her hard-won composure. She didn't like feeling threatened. Determinedly she concentrated on maneuvering the car into morning-rush-hour traffic.

"Tell me about Grandmother. You said she's been acting weird. Is she sick?"

Her question fell into the silence between them. Wasn't he going to answer?

She shot him a quick glance, then almost wished she hadn't. He was staring out the side window. Waves of thick black hair framed a profile that was harshly defined in the bright morning sunlight. Mara could see that his mouth was a thin line of simmering impatience.

He was deliberately ignoring her.

Mara's fear for her grandmother turned to anger, and all the anguish and shock and denial she'd been suppressing for the past few hours, ever since the onset of the nightmare and Mark's appearance, surged forward.

"I asked you a question."

Her voice echoed loudly in the empty silence. Mara didn't care. Again she flicked him a glance. His left hand lay relaxed and still along his thigh. Not even a flicker of an eyelid proclaimed he'd even heard her at all.

But she knew he had. Though it wasn't visible, Mara could feel the tension in his body, like a swiftly running current beneath an ice floe. At this moment, he was completely focused on the busy morning traffic, as focused as he'd been when his sole intent was to get rid of her. With a shiver of foreboding, Mara recognized the mood, but this time she refused to be intimidated.

"Answer me, Mark," she ordered. "Is Grandmother all right?"

Mara didn't delude herself into believing her niggling had caused him to turn slowly and face her. But whatever the motivation, she suddenly wished he hadn't, because the eyes he turned on her were coldly furious, giving Mara the impression he was at the end of his patience, that he'd rather be anywhere but here, with her, in the small confines of the car. A chill feathered her skin.

"A stupid question, Mara," Mark finally replied with cruel bluntness. "Otherwise, why would I even *be* here?"

Mara flinched. He was right, of course. "But—"

"But nothing." Mark fought the irrational urge to jump out of the car, to get some air. What he needed was to get home. People knew to leave him alone in Twilight. He muttered an oath. "You need something to think about? Concentrate on the traffic. You miss that plane and it'll just be that much longer before I get home and you get some answers."

"But Grandmother's—"

"For crissakes! You haven't even talked to your grandmother in years," he said coldly, accusingly. "As far as I'm concerned, you can wait a few more hours."

At that, Mara gasped. "Why, you—" Several colorful names came to mind, and she said them all.

"Impressive," Mark taunted with a soft chuckle that abraded Mara's nerves. "Be sure to show off your new vocabulary when we get home. Milak may not like it, but maybe a few more kids will decide college is worth something after all."

"You bastard," Mara blurted out. "Why can't you answer a simple question?"

Mark's mouth curved into a chilling smile. Good. He wanted her mad. Mad would keep her at a distance. Mad might even shut her up, though he seriously doubted it. The old Mara was very definitely gone, and the new Mara... Well, he didn't want to deal with the new Mara at all.

He surveyed the picture she made, her hands clenching the steering wheel, her shoulder-length black hair seemingly electrified with anger and her black eyes flashing defiance. His eyes darkened as they took in the silky texture of her skin, tanned golden from the hot June sun. They'd shared so many good times growing up together. He remembered feeling a real pride knowing he was her hero. Back then, in her eyes, at least, he couldn't do anything wrong. That close, remembered warmth and companionship, despite its uncomplicated simplicity, stirred within him an unexpected longing. A longing he no longer deserved to feel. Abruptly his smile faded.

"Just get us to the airport," he ordered, then deliberately turned away, shutting her out. "And when you talk to Milak, tell her to stay the hell out of my life."

Milak slipped the fifty-year-old reindeer-skin suit from its display on the wall and carried it to her recliner. Her old but nimble fingers stroked the one-piece garment, sliding up and against the grain of the reindeer fur, up and around the wolverine-fur cuff that bordered the deep hood. Her sister had spent much time tanning the furs, then sewing the pieces together. The winters were long in Siberia.

Our ways will survive, she thought.

She settled the heavy garment more firmly in her lap. Forty-plus years ago, when she'd been torn from her family, from all that was familiar and secure, this suit had represented her connection with her past. Now it would be her key to the future. She stroked the fur softly.

Our ways will survive, she thought, her hands trembling. She would not let them die. Not while her sister still lived. Not while continuity was within her power.

Sixteen-year-old Siksik Toovak knocked on her door and entered, a gentle smile of welcome on her youthful face. "Mother baked some pan bread. I thought you'd like some," she murmured shyly, her voice soothing with its promise of youth.

"*Assirtuq,* thank you. Your mother is kind to this old woman. I'll have it for lunch."

Siksik nodded and crossed the room softly, her tread light, unobtrusive. Her *inua* was the Raven. She, too, was a healer. But she wasn't the One. There was only one who could be. And she wasn't here yet. Milak's hands stroked the reindeer fur.

"Do you need anything?" Siksik asked.

Milak shrugged. "I am old, there is much that I need. But of those things, time is the most precious."

Siksik nodded. "I could use three years in a day," she said wistfully.

"He is Tuntu, the caribou. He wanders, much like your brother, Mark," Milak replied, aware of the girl's longtime love for the absent eighteen-year-old Billy Muktoyuk.

Again she nodded. "If I truly had wings, I would fly."

"Child, it will take more than Raven's wings to bind the caribou. You will have to go hunting for your mate. The Raven flies high, yet Tuntu wanders far. You may not find it so easy to live such a life."

Siksik looked startled, then strangely thoughtful. The door closed quietly behind her.

Milak rose from the recliner and laid the precious fur on the seat. Then she crossed to the table, unwrapped the pan bread and tore off a small wedge, savoring the taste as it settled in her mouth.

As she ate, she watched the village outside her small window with shrewd, alert eyes. The warm June air had everyone outside. The village was busy, for *kaugun* was the season of renewal. Children, brown and happy, chased each other between the houses while their parents looked on with indulgent but work-weary smiles. Milak felt a deep serenity at the thought of the role she'd played in their lives. Many had problems; she knew them all, had helped cure some, had soothed others when cures were not possible. It was a good legacy, one that provided long years of satisfaction to offset occasional pain. It could be a lonely legacy, she knew, having had her own family lost to her. But family was never truly lost. Not for the healer.

"Our ways will survive," she repeated, taking one last bite. Then she reached into the pocket of her *kuspuk* and withdrew an old envelope and a blank piece of writing paper. It had been forty years since she had last used the written word, last needed it to communicate. Milak sighed, thinking of secrets kept and secrets yet to be revealed. Sitting down on her furs, she began to write.

# Chapter Three

Mark deplaned, his eyes on the group of villagers smiling and milling around waiting for the unloading of supplies, his mind on Mara. He pulled her suitcase from the cargo bay of the Twin Otter and backtracked in time to see her greeted by several surprised and delighted friends.

She was laughing and talking excitedly in Yup'ik, her smile wide, infectious, her eyes teary. Watching her bend slightly to hug an elderly man, he got the distinct feeling that she'd missed Twilight a lot and was deeply happy to be home.

The likelihood disturbed him. He didn't want Mara too happy about this homecoming. He didn't want Mara at home at all. Her eyes condemned him, forcing him to relive that night. He didn't—wouldn't—do that. Even now, years later, the pain was too great, and the memories were too vivid. Especially those of Mara's sweet passion, a passion he'd cruelly and deliberately killed. Mark's fingers clenched on the handle of the suitcase, but except for that, he showed no indication of his thoughts. As far as he was concerned, the sooner she left, the better.

*And the sooner you get her to Milak, the sooner you'll be off the hook,* he reminded himself as he moved silently through the small crowd of excited villagers. Mark ignored the noticeable ebb in their conversations as he passed, ignored, too, their concerned and caring gazes. Nodding a curt greeting to no one in particular, he paused just to Mara's left. Already he could feel the stress leaving his body. He was home. People knew to leave him alone here. In another few minutes, what Mara Anvik did or didn't do would no longer concern or involve him.

Mara turned, sensing Mark's presence. Self-conscious, she wiped at the tears on her wet cheeks. For a moment, she'd enjoyed the luxury of forgetting all about him. "I imagine you're eager to get back to—" she floundered, aware suddenly how little she knew about Mark's life now "—whatever. Anyway, you don't have to wait." She reached for her suitcase.

Mark hung on, and their fingers brushed. He ignored Mara's immediate and reflexive withdrawal. "I promised Milak I'd bring you home," Mark responded brusquely. "I like to finish the things I start."

He waited, impatient, as Mara said goodbye to her friends, watching her blush as several of the younger men tried to pin down a time for their next meeting. When Mara finally started out, he trudged behind her in brooding silence, immediately realizing that the calculated move had been a mistake.

Four years had changed Mara Anvik. The pigtailed child who had run after him like a faithful puppy was gone. From his vantage point, Mark could see that she was very definitely a woman now.

She had always been a cute little girl. Now, at what—twenty-one—Mark gave a brief shake of his head. She was twenty-two... and dangerous.

Her legs, encased in designer blue jeans that fit as tightly as her orange leggings, were long and slender. The soft curves of her hips swayed gently as she walked, calling his attention to the snug fit of the denim as it molded her bottom. And even from his distance Mark could see the sunlight reflecting brightly off the rich, deep blackness of her model's haircut. Although he couldn't see her breasts, he had a perfect memory of them, their fullness, their weight, their taste....

*Damn.*

A painful tightness seized his chest, and he paused in shock, staring at the woman walking ahead of him with fast, sure steps.

Damn her.

Four years. In four long years he'd never once felt so much as a flicker of need, of desire. His resolve was inviolate. Or so he'd thought, until a few hours ago, when his past had finally caught up with him.

Mark's lips thinned into a forbidding line as he finally, slowly, resumed walking, purposefully directing his gaze and his thoughts away from Mara and out toward his surroundings.

Looking at his village in the bright sunlight of an early evening, Mark realized it looked worse than poor: crumbling and unpainted homes, backyards littered with rusting snowmobiles and four-wheelers, torn fishing nets piled high against gnarled driftwood. Everything was worn, old. Unwillingly he wondered about Mara's thoughts. The years had changed the village. He followed Mara's own slowing steps past John Muktoyuk's general store, with its rotted wooden beams and sagging porch, past the tiny village church, where the council of elders held their monthly meetings, and past the new high school, deserted now, but alive with community activity during the cold winter months. Finally, thankfully, they arrived at her grandmother's two-bedroom home.

Mara paused. Her eyes closed. When she opened them, Mark tensed. There were tears in her eyes.

"It's dying, isn't it?" she murmured softly, her rigid composure threatened by the sadness and poverty all around her. She looked back at the dilapidated village, the children's tattered clothes, then up at him. Unthinking, the old Mara who had always looked to Mark for advice asked plaintively, "What are we going to do?"

Mark froze at the sweet, implied intimacy in that "we." His eyes narrowed. "Why do you care?" he questioned, his tone full of detached indifference. "You've got a college degree, a business of your own, from what I heard back in your apartment, a future that doesn't have anything to do with *this.*" His arm whipped out suddenly and slashed at the air, an angry counterpoint to his relaxed, uncaring stance. "You've escaped. Why not enjoy it and stop pretending you give a damn what happens—"

"But I do!" Mara protested angrily.

"Sure," he drawled, seemingly unperturbed by her vehemence. "You and Mr. Donut have life all mapped out, I'd bet. And you know what? I'd also bet none of the roads lead back here."

He dropped her suitcase then and turned away, tossing a last, ironic remark over his shoulder. "Enjoy your *visit.*"

"Mark." Mark half turned, not looking, but listening. "The last thing I need right now is everyone in town whispering about us, or asking questions. They have enough worries, they don't need this. Just stay out of my way, okay?''

He laughed, then stopped instantly. "I intend to."

"Good. And for the record, you've got a diploma, too, *and* a career as a pilot. They don't have anything to do with this, either.'' Mara's arm repeated the slashing movement, though she knew he couldn't see it. "If those are your criteria, why do *you* care?''

Mark whipped around, his eyes icy and uninviting, a stranger's eyes.

"Who said I did?" Mark lied coldly, menacingly. "I'm sick of the old ways. The old ways are what's killing us." He turned and faced the village. "Look around, Mara. You said it yourself. Twilight is dying. And if people like Jacob—like Milak—don't wake up and look, *really* look..." Abruptly he turned again and saw that Mara's anger had been replaced by a look of frightened confusion. "You better make these few days last," he warned. "Once Milak's gone, there won't be anyone here capable of holding the village together. Not Jacob, not my father, nobody.''

Mara stared at him in shocked silence, the frightened confusion transforming slowly into sick disbelief. Her heart pounded.

"Wh-what are you talking about?''

"We're starving," he said bluntly. "And not just for food. What we need is technology. We need to modernize. That's the key. That's where our future lies. The council... I could talk myself hoarse and it wouldn't change their minds. They just don't see....''

Mark's voice faded as he realized how much of his feelings he'd revealed. Mara was staring at him. Then her anxious gaze flicked toward her grandmother's house. "Don't worry," he said. "Siksik's been taking care of her for you.''

As far back as Mara could remember, Mark's sister had wanted to be a nurse. They'd been corresponding for years, mostly about Grandmother's activities.

Except those updates had never included news about Mark. Though she and Siksik were six years apart in age, Siksik's longtime love for Billy Muktoyuk, who was at UCLA on a basketball scholarship, had somehow tuned her in to Mara's teenage crush on Mark. The young girl's sensitivity had alternately frustrated and relieved Mara over the years.

She cringed. *I shouldn't have stayed away so long,* she acknowledged guiltily as she started apprehensively up the first step. Mark stopped her with a quick gesture toward her suitcase.

Just then the door opened and Milak stepped carefully out onto the small sagging porch.

Mark saw Milak through Mara's eyes. The healer's usual braids were undone, her long white hair hung nearly to her waist, a wispy white curtain smoothed flat by a beaded headdress he'd never seen. The *kuspuk* she wore was also of an unfamiliar design and marking. On her feet were summer mukluks of reindeer. In her right hand was a long, narrow driftwood cane.

A cane? Mark's glance focused on the stick held upright in an obviously trembling hand. She looked about ready to fall down. What was going on here? He looked at Mara. Her face was white with shock.

"Grandmother?" Mara whispered, her stunned voice barely audible.

Either something major had happened during his absence, or something didn't add up, Mark reasoned. He felt as if he were seeing a Milak he didn't know—a dying woman.

"As always, Tuntu returns." The old woman spoke to Mark, yet her glance remained fixed on Mara. "You have done well. Come inside."

"Look, I'm sure you two have a lot to talk about, so I'll just—"

"We will have tea to celebrate the homecoming."

Milak extended her free hand to her granddaughter. With a heartfelt cry, Mara ran up the remaining two shallow steps and into the old woman's embrace.

Mark tensed, uncomfortable watching the emotional reunion. He didn't want any tea. And he couldn't remember the last time he'd celebrated anything. He'd done as she'd asked, and he should be free to go on his way.

Then he made the mistake of looking at Mara. Her eyes telegraphed confusion, worry, and a silent plea that he not upset the old healer with a refusal. Convincing himself it was a scene he was trying to avoid, he hefted the suitcase and, swearing under his breath, followed the murmuring pair into the house.

It was humid and overly warm inside. Mark's comfort level dropped even further. Milak was acting strange, Mara was in shock, and all he wanted to do was get out.

Some celebration.

He gazed at the two women. The strong family resemblance between them was startling. Mara's round face and prominent cheeks mirrored Milak's features. Their eyes were a similar shape, and both seemed to see into a person, commanding attention without words.

Mark set down the suitcase and waited by the door, aware that rushing Milak was impossible. She'd make the tea when she was ready, and not a minute before. In the meantime, he'd endure this farce as long as he could. But he wasn't giving himself, or Mara, any guarantees.

Milak drew back and gently fingered her granddaughter's shoulder-length hair. "Indeed, times have changed. Seventy years ago, I, too, wished to cut my hair."

"Then you like it, Grandmother?"

Mark heard the plea in Mara's voice, watching as she moved gracefully out of the embrace with her grandmother and toward the small kitchen area. Her thick jet-black hair swung about her shoulders, and Mark drew in a suddenly shaky breath. He knew what that hair felt like. He remembered tugging on the pigtails, remembered its silky texture, remembered, most of all, how it spilled midnight-black over the fullness of her breasts. Suddenly he had a feeling that he knew why she'd cut her hair. Then, almost as if she were conscious of his thoughts, she swung around to face him, her expression wary.

"So, why didn't you cut it?" Mark asked Milak, more for an excuse to break his odd mental connection with Mara than because he had any real interest in Milak's seventy-year-old hair problem. He settled himself on a wolf-fur rug, accepting the ancient wooden cup Mara handed him.

"Custom," Milak answered, picking up her sister's one-piece reindeer-skin suit before settling herself in her recliner. "During my youth, all women wore braids."

Mark observed the motion, saw the reverence with which Mara's grandmother smoothed her wrinkled hand along the tanned reindeer hide. He'd noted Mara's startled reaction to the one-piece suit almost immediately upon entering the house. He recalled her once telling him that Milak had never allowed her to play with it, even touch it. Yet today it lay draped across Milak's lap much as one would drape an old afghan. He watched as Mara handed Milak a cup of tea.

"It's a good thing I'm not a healer, then, isn't it, Grandmother?"

Mark caught a glimpse of a strange expression crossing Milak's face. Fear? Worry? Desperation? Mark shrugged, reminding himself that, cane or no cane, whatever was bothering the old woman was Mara's concern now, not his. He looked down at the healer's hands. They trembled as they clutched the driftwood cup and lifted it to her lips.

Milak paused just before drinking. Sensing that this was to be a toast, Mark reluctantly lifted his cup.

"It is *kaugun,* the time of renewal," she said, then looked over at him, waiting for his toast.

"Enjoy your visit," Mark said to Mara, raising his cup, stressing the last word.

"It's good to be back," Mara offered as her toast, and smiled at her grandmother. She ignored Mark.

"*Assirtuq.* Good." Milak said. She took another sip of tea, one hand softly stroking the reindeer fur. Tension seemed to pour from her; her body was stiff with it and some unknown agitation.

"*Assirtuq,*" Milak repeated.

Abruptly Mark decided he'd had enough. Standing, he settled the driftwood cup on top of Mara's suitcase. "I imagine you two have lots to catch up on," Mark repeated, feeling nervous in the face of Milak's unusual behavior. "Thanks for the tea. I'll see myself out."

"Has my granddaughter agreed to help her old friend?"

Almost through the door, Mark swallowed an oath. He should have known something would prevent his clean escape. Turning, he eyed Milak with real irritation. "Help isn't necessary. I can take care of my own problems."

"What problems?" Mara asked, her gaze flickering uncertainly back and forth between the two.

"Never mind, Mara. Your grandmother's just butting in to something that's not her concern."

"Then she knows not of your need for her?"

Mark's stomach clenched at Milak's odd terminology. *I don't need anyone,* he'd shouted at Mara that night. For an instant, their gazes locked, the condemning words floating heavily between them. Mark swallowed another oath. He'd meant what he said. Might as well deal with it.

"Your grandmother seems to think you'd be only too happy to spend five weeks in Siberia with me."

Five weeks in Siberia? Mara's eyes widened in horror.

Mark's lip curled at the expected rejection. It was past time for his exit. A curt goodbye, and he was gone.

Mara remained silent, listening to Mark's footsteps fading away, sighing deeply as the tight knot of tension in her shoulder blades eased. Her reactions to Mark were proving difficult for her to handle. This morning, she thought, she'd done just fine, but since then, things had been going steadily downhill.

The flight had lasted seemingly forever. He'd slept, or pretended to sleep, and rather than suffer more of his insults, she'd thankfully joined his charade and closed her eyes. But even that hadn't helped dispel her distress. His proximity unnerved her completely and made her uncomfortably aware of her shortcomings. Would she ever be able to move past it? Would he? She looked up and met her grandmother's glance. Flustered, she asked the first thing that came to mind.

"What was that all about?"

"He needs someone to go to Siberia with him." Milak restated the obvious, her expression intent and watchful.

Mara squirmed. "Why? And why me?" she asked in Yup'ik.

"Does it matter, child? You have said nothing, yet your face has refused him. He will not ask again."

Mara was confused by the slight reprimand she sensed in her grandmother's voice. "I'm only here for a short while, and—" she paused, seeking the right words "—I want to spend the time with you . . . not him."

"I know this, daughter of my daughter, but he was once your friend."

"Yes. My best friend." Even had she been able, she wouldn't have denied Milak's assumption that their close friendship was a thing of the past. Given their strained behavior toward one another, Milak couldn't help but notice.

"Then why do you refuse his request?"

"I told you. I want to be here with you. And besides, I didn't actually say no, Grandmother."

"And he didn't actually ask, Granddaughter."

Mara fidgeted, unprepared to discuss Mark when there was the more important subject of her grandmother's summons to talk about. "Tungunqut has told me that time runs out."

Milak nodded her understanding, but said nothing for a long while. Mara worried about her grandmother's silence. The sounds of the village were amplified in Mara's brain as she eventually stood and retrieved Mark's cup and carried his and her own to the kitchen area of the room. Washing them out, she missed Milak extracting a letter from the pocket of the reindeer-skin suit.

"Come here, Granddaughter."

Upon hearing her grandmother's voice, Mara immediately set down the cup, wiped her hands on a dishrag and settled on the floor at the woman's feet. But instead of initiating the discussion she'd anticipated, Milak surprised her by handing her an envelope.

"It's from Russia!" Mara noted immediately. Intrigued, she peered closely at the small rectangular envelope and the old, unfamiliar stamp. She looked up with a question in her eyes and met Milak's narrowed glance. "Who would write to you from..." She raised the letter close to her face, trying to read the postmark in the dim light. But it was faded.

"The envelope comes from Sireniki," Milak replied slowly. Mara was too busy examining the envelope to take note of the careful editing of Milak's words. "My older sister lives there. She, too, is healer. She has sensed the end of her days."

*Shock* couldn't begin to describe the effect of this news on Mara. She looked up, the letter in her hands forgotten. "Your *sister?* Grandmother, I didn't even know you *had* a sister. And she's a healer, too?"

Milak looked momentarily startled. "Mark did not tell you."

"Mark said he'd come for me, and that you were acting weird." Mara repeated his exact words, riveted by the strain in her grandmother's aged face. "Was he supposed to have told me about your sister?"

"That one hears much and believes little." Milak looked pointedly at her granddaughter. "You would tie yourself to such a man?"

Mara's face flamed, then paled as the significance of the words sank in. "I have tied myself to no man," she murmured, aware it was the literal truth. Her shameful behavior had not been repeated. Even Wally, with all his caring and concern for her, had failed in his attempt to break through the barrier of fear and anguish and embarrassment that overcame her at the mere thought of intimacy with a man. Desire frightened her now.

"I—" Mara swallowed and had to start again. "I can't believe I have a grandaunt and you never told me. And you say she is dying? How do you know this?" Then Mara answered her own question. "The dream, yes?"

Milak's wrinkled hand lifted, almost touched hers, then dropped back to the reindeer-skin suit on her lap. "She made this, my sister. And the *kuspuk* I wear, and the headdress of beads. It is all I have of her and of my life before the Bering Sea changed, before Stalin separated me from my family."

Mara gasped, all the distressing thoughts about intimacy and desire swept aside as her knowledge of Russian language and history forced the ramifications of Milak's calm statement to the forefront of her mind.

"I see you understand," Milak said slowly. "The pain was great, my granddaughter. You know this pain of lost family. I loved my daughter, your mother, and the husband she chose and I accepted as son. You understand that to endure you push away the past and seek what comfort you can in a new future. For fifty years I have done this. For fifty years I have lived each minute of each day of each season of each year aware of my family but lost to them. When Tungunqut traveled back across the Bering Sea, he took me home. Yet only one remained. And soon she, too, will be gone." Her fingers trembled as they stroked the fur, and then one hand stretched forward and softly, apologetically, patted Mara's hand.

Mara's eyes welled with tears that dripped on to the letter. She wiped at the drops, and blinked rapidly. "Why did she write to you now? Our people have crossed the Sea in freedom for three years."

Milak paused, her gaze sliding away. "Maybe she was ill, or busy. Life in my home village was hard, there were few luxuries. Maybe there was no paper. Maybe she didn't know where I was. Maybe she thought me dead after so many years. These things are unknown to me."

Mara nodded, her heart grieving for her grandmother. Perhaps it was true that every instant of life affected every other— If her grandmother hadn't been separated from her family, she herself wouldn't have been born. If she hadn't been so besotted, she and Mark would still be friends. The cycle was endless and interconnected.

"Why didn't you visit her?"

Milak raised her eyes, her expression sorrowful. "And leave our people here without a healer?"

"But I could have..." Mara began, only to realize she couldn't have. She'd been in Fairbanks, nursing a falsely broken heart, while her grandmother suffered in silence. "I wasnt here, so you couldn't go," she murmured, guilt-stricken. "And now she's dying."

Milak's expression didn't condemn. She was a healer, Mara knew. She wouldn't knowingly inflict hurt or pain or guilt. Mara sighed and handled the letter. "You want me to read it?"

Milak nodded.

Curious, Mara opened the envelope, taking no note of its yellowed condition or of the white freshness of the letter inside. She scanned the shaky, unfamiliar script and quickly realized it wasn't in Russian. She looked up, confused. "What language is this? I can only make out every fifth or so word. And I'm not even sure about that."

"It is the language of my people. Few of us survive, so, as with all things unused, the language dies."

Puzzled, Mara again scanned the words. "It's definitely a Yup'ik script, but it's not Central Yup'ik."

Mara knew from her studies in Native anthropology that Central Yup'ik was the most widely known Eskimo language.

"It is Sireniski. Read it to me, Granddaughter."

"But I just told you—"

"Read whatever you can. I will understand."

And so, for a half hour, Mara struggled with the letter, deciphering a word here, a phrase there. Yet Milak seemed to understand. Eventually they reached the end, and Mara looked up, already dreading hearing her grandmother's words.

"Her time is near. I must travel home," the old woman said, her eyes glowing bright and fierce with determination. Her frail body fairly trembled with it, Mara thought as she laid down the letter.

She didn't know how many more shocks she could stand. She felt the sudden tension in her grandmother's body, a living presence, as if she were drawing in energy. Concerned, she leaned forward and laid her hand over her grandmother's trembling one. "Grandmother, you must know you can't travel to Russia."

"I must record the sacred teachings."

Mara scrambled for anything that would deter her grandmother from this path. "You're ninety-two," she began, head pounding. "Such a trip would not be easy. So many things—unexpected things—could happen. And our people need you here." She stared directly into her grandmother's eyes, and sensed she wasn't being heard. "Listen, this isn't a good idea. I know you want to see your sister, but it's too dangerous for you." She reached out and lifted one wrinkled and trembling hand. "These teachings aren't as important as your *life.*" She kept her voice quietly under control, challenging her grandmother's authority no more than necessary. "I don't want you to go."

The old healer sighed with deep understanding and then lapsed into silence for a long time. Again the sounds of village life became a backdrop to the heavy, waiting silence in the house. Mara's blood pounded in her temples while she waited for her grandmother's decision.

"Our ways must survive," Milak finally said. "If I do not go, what will become of our people?"

"They'll die if you leave," Mara blurted out, remembering Mark's warning. "Don't you realize how important you are to the community? How your connection to our ancestors in Russia makes you unique? You're a living link to our past, Grandmother. In you, we have a representative of our cultural and spiritual past and present. How could you even think of jeopardizing that connection by making this trip?"

Silence fell after her impassioned speech. Mara waited, her gaze fixed on the letter, wishing she could read it herself. Maybe a different interpretation ... something that wouldn't sound so dire to her grandmother's ears. *"Maacungaq."* She paused, still hoping for a reply. But none was forthcoming. Then she had an idea. A dangerous one, possibly—given her own unpredictable medical condition—but it would spare her grandmother. "Grandmother, what if I went in your place? Would that be possible? Would you allow this?"

Milak's refusal was immediate. "Only I can record the sacred teachings. You must remain here in my place. This you can do. The other ... is too much to ask."

"But I haven't asked! I'm volunteering, Grandmother, I'm—"

"Enough! I have decided."

## Chapter Four

Walking quickly, Mark headed for the shoreline. He was furious, ready to tear something apart. It had been a long time since he'd felt so powerful an emotion, but the burst of wild frustration and anger he'd felt at Milak's purposeful intrusion into his affairs had come on him in a flash, all but shattering his control. The old woman had guts, just like her granddaughter, Mark acknowledged as he trudged onward. A few children were still playing outside. They paused, silent, as they always were in his presence, and watched him pass. A breeze brushed across his face, lifting the hair off his neck, cooling him and billowing out his denim jacket. When he reached the shoreline, he stopped and took a deep breath, looking out to sea, avoiding the sky completely.

He rarely searched the sky anymore. The open expanse, the seemingly endless freedom, filled him with a bitter longing. And flying as a passenger—as he did for his summer tours—only increased that longing.

Mark took another deep breath. This was good. He needed this. A cool breeze for a hot summer's evening. Shoving his hands deep in his back pockets, Mark listened to the soothing lapping of the water as it rushed in to shore, the complaints of occasional gulls as children chased them away and the sharp, excited barks of the village's few huskies.

A few hundred feet down the pebble-strewn shoreline, men worked at repairing their walrus-skin *umiaks*. A few had more modern aluminum skiffs with old outboard motors, but all had piles upon piles of fishing nets. For a while he watched, drinking in the familiar noises, letting the scene distract him. But then the frustration and the uneasiness returned. He kicked at the wet sand.

Couldn't Milak have left well enough alone? He'd done as she'd asked, he'd brought her precious granddaughter home for a visit. Why had Milak mentioned his trip to Siberia? He hadn't planned on asking Mara for help, despite everyone's insistence that she'd do it, no questions asked. Crosswinds Siberia would just have to fold. He'd suffered worse. He'd survived. He'd just have to hope he and Jacob hit a good run and caught a lot of fish. Then, if fish prices didn't plummet and the season wasn't called off early . . .

Damn! Again he kicked at the sand, his violent movement unearthing a child's forgotten *yaaruin*. Memory engulfed him as he nudged the storyknife with his foot. He'd carved Mara's first *yaaruin*. He'd been thirteen; she'd been six. Her eyes had been round as saucers, and her genuine delight had swelled his chest with pride.

He wished, for just an instant, that she would look at him that way again.

Disgusted with his emotionalism, he turned away, leaving the shore and the *yaaruin* behind. Patrick called him three times before the young boy's voice penetrated his troubled thoughts.

"Hi, Uncle Mark." Patrick stopped playing with a group of friends and automatically tagged along beside him. "I've been thinking about your predicament."

An involuntary smile tugged at Mark's mouth. Patrick was a good kid—precocious for an eleven-year-old, a little too sensitive at times, yet all in all, a real trooper. Mark slung one arm around the boy's slim shoulders.

"Predicament, eh, sport? Good word." Mark grinned at Patrick's sour expression. Ann had told him one Sunday evening that she was insisting both Patrick and Sharon learn a new vocabulary word a day during their summer break.

"Yeah, I suppose so. But I sure wish Mom would pick some easier ones. It's hard to make up ten good sentences. My brain's about to explode."

Mark chuckled, Mara and Crosswinds forgotten for the moment. "Guess it comes from her being a teacher. You'll just have to take it like a man and live with it."

"Yeah, I guess so, but it's not at all conducive to having a good time."

"It usually isn't." Mark laughed. "But it sounds like her exercise is working."

Patrick picked up a rock and tossed it in his hand. "Pretty gross, huh?"

Wisely Mark remained silent.

"So, do you wanna hear it?"

"Hear what?"

"The idea. You know, to help you out of your predicament."

No, he didn't want to hear Patrick's idea. "Sure."

Patrick looked at him strangely. "You okay, Uncle Mark? You still don't look too good."

"I've been away for a couple of days," Mark offered as an excuse. "I'm tired."

"I wish *I* could fly somewhere. If I knew Russian, you could take me, Uncle Mark. I'd love to go."

"Your mom and dad would probably have something to say about that."

"Not Dad, he's cool. But Mom can be—" Patrick paused, as if he were searching for something "—overprotective."

Mark nodded, trying not to laugh again. "Moms are."

"So, what's Milak's granddaughter like? Is she—" his young voice dropped to a whisper "—weird, or anything like that?"

Intrigued, Mark whispered back. "Weird?"

"Yeah, you know, spooky...like Milak."

Oddly enough, Mark found himself wanting to defend the old healer. "You shouldn't disrespect your elders."

"But I'm not! It's just that... Doesn't she make you feel—" again his voice dropped "—kinda strange, as if she can see right through you?"

Having felt that himself too often in the past three days, Mark couldn't help agreeing. "Milak's like that. I suppose being so old, she doesn't see things the way we do."

"But she's not really blind."

Mark bit back a laugh. "No, Patrick, she sees as well as I do." Better, probably, he thought, knowing her. "She's just so old her perspective is different. She was born before the invention of the television, you know."

"Really? Wow!" Patrick's eyes widened. "So, what's her granddaughter like?"

*Stubborn, distracting, a pain in the butt.* "A lot like her grandmother," Mark replied, aware the sarcasm was lost on Patrick.

"Then I guess if she's gonna be your interpreter, you don't need to hear our idea."

"She's not gonna be my interpreter," Mark revealed without thinking.

"She's not? Why?"

*Because I couldn't handle it,* Mark realized suddenly, reminded of those taunting, swaying hips. "It's been four years since she's visited her grandmother. She wants to spend some time with her."

"Oh. Bummer." Then Patrick's face lit up. "Wanna hear our solution?"

"Who's we?" Mark asked first, eyeing his nephew with growing concern. Just how many people had he been talking to?

"Everybody—all the kids, mainly—but mostly me," Patrick answered proudly, unaware of Mark's growing horror. "I thought that maybe someone's dad or mom might have a relative that spoke Russian that wouldn't mind going with you, so all the kids went home and asked, and guess what?"

"What?" He really didn't want to hear this.

"Billy's grandfather's sister has a brother-in-law who lives on Saint Lawrence Island, and he speaks Russian."

While Mark was busy working through the confusing family tree, Patrick continued. "Anyway, Billy's grandfather's sister said she'd ask her brother-in-law if he'd go, and he said sure."

Mark stopped walking, astounded. "What's the man's name?"

"Charlie Naneng. But there's only one problem."

There was always a problem. "And what's that?"

"He can't walk too good."

"Why not?"

Patrick shrugged. "He's kinda old. Ancient. Like Milak, you know?"

Unfortunately, he did know. "So if he's that old, how is he supposed to help me?"

"Well, we were thinking about that...."

Spotting Jacob's house, Mark abruptly decided to drop in on his sister-in-law. Hopefully, Jacob would be at work. "Look, sport, I gotta talk to your mom, okay? Thanks for the help—you really did a good job—but I'll handle it from here."

Patrick smiled proudly and ran off, yelling at the top of his lungs at some friends he'd left behind.

Feeling lucky to have escaped, he entered the house through the arctic entryway and knocked on the inner door. No answer. Again he knocked, louder this time, thinking that Ann was probably dealing with baby Josh and hadn't heard him. When there was still no answer, he decided to let himself in.

He saw them immediately. Ann was on tiptoe, arms wound around his brother's neck, her body tight against his. Jacob's big hands were positioned just below her breasts, around her rib cage.

Deep in a kiss, they were too involved to notice him.

Mark went still. Heat climbed from deep inside him, and he wanted to leave, to turn away, but his body wouldn't move. The burning was intense, painful, acutely uncomfortable.

"You two better stop that unless you're looking to increase the pack again." His voice was a rough croak in the small silent room. Startled, Ann jumped.

"Ever heard of knocking?" Jacob asked, one bushy brow raised, a half amused, half serious expression on his face. Unembarrassed, he released Ann and eased down on the couch.

"You ever heard of listening?" Mark shot back, feeling an unexpected jab of some undefined emotion—envy? longing?—at their comfortable and obvious intimacy. Then he shrugged it off, along with his shoes. His life was perfect. Just the way he wanted it. How many people could say that?

He took his time settling into the recliner, politely avoiding Ann's reddened cheeks, giving her a few minutes to calm herself. "I know Patrick's outside, but where are the other two? Don't they know it's dangerous to leave you alone with this animal?"

Jacob laughed, a satisfied masculine sound that started Ann blushing and pulling away again. He was trying to make her sit beside him. Her jostling drew Mark's attention to her milk-full breasts, reminding him yet again of Mara. He scowled, watching as Ann teasingly slapped away Jacob's questing hand.

"Sharon's over at your mother's house with Siksik," Ann responded, her gray eyes sparkling as she played the lover's tug-of-war with Jacob. "Patrick's outside with Paul, doing who knows what, and baby Josh—bless his napping little soul—is out for the count."

Aware suddenly that he'd likely interrupted what little private time they had these days, Mark stood again, intending on peeking in on his nephew and then leaving. But Ann, with her mother's senses on full alert, was way ahead of him. She shook her head vehemently. "Forget it, Mark."

Already halfway across the living room, he paused. "Not even a peek? With all that curly brown hair, he's so cute. Doesn't look at all like Jacob."

"Watch it, little brother."

Ann laughed, her face still becomingly flushed. Jacob tugged one last time, and she gave in to his insistence and sat down. "You wake him, you get him back to sleep. That's the deal."

Mark hesitated, scowling at his brother's amusement.

"She means it, too," Jacob added as he picked up a copy of the *Tundra Times* and began leafing through it. "When he's upset, Josh can make twenty minutes seem like an hour."

"Two hours," Ann piped in. "So, unless you're prepared for that, I'd suggest you come sit down again and tell us where you've been and what Milak said to you last Sunday after dinner. We've all been dying to know."

"Not all of us." Jacob muttered from behind the newspaper. Absently he tugged on a strand of her curly brown hair.

"Well, maybe not you so much." Ann smiled and deliberately pulled the paper aside, letting her hand curve tenderly along his brother's cheek. "But that's because you're the strong, silent type." She gave his cheek a kiss.

Jacob's glance snagged his. Mark raised an eyebrow. Jacob just smiled and, when Ann pulled away, resumed reading.

"Anyway, Mark," Ann continued, unaware of their silent communication. "Us weaker, talkative folk need gossip to stay alive. So sit."

Resigned, Mark sat. Though her gentle meddling regularly grated on his nerves, he figured it was either her or Jacob—Kegluneq, the wolf—or his mate. Easy choice.

"Milak can be so mysterious, can't she?"

"It's an image thing," he responded, beginning to count the minutes to his escape. "Milak wanted me to bring Mara home."

The newspaper ruffled, but apart from that, Jacob gave no indication he cared about his wife's conversation with his brother.

"She did?" Ann's expression was confused. "Why not just call?"

"Hell if I know," Mark muttered.

"Milak's got phone-o-phobia."

"There's no such word, sweetheart," Ann informed Jacob absently, her attention fixed on Mark. "All right, so she hates phones. Someone else could have done it. I would gladly have helped her out. Why, after all the things she's taught Sharon and Patrick about Yup'ik history . . ." Her voice faded, then strengthened as, apparently, another question occurred to her. "Why you, Mark? Why not Jacob or Ben?"

Hell if I know, he wanted to repeat, but couldn't, because it would be a lie. He did know why. "Maybe because of our friendship." Mark had to swallow hard on that one.

"That's right, Siksik told me you two grew up together."

"Mara had a crush on him. Real cute." Jacob chuckled, his eyes meeting Mark's. "Don't you think?"

Mark refused to say just what he thought with Ann present. Jacob grinned, aware of Mark's irritation and enjoying it.

Ann sighed. "Well, phooey, that wasn't so mysterious. The way she said it—'You will take me home'—everyone got the impression a bomb was about to drop."

Mark shrugged, his expression carefully neutral, but Jacob's glance captured his just long enough to make Mark uneasy. Then his brother shrugged and pulled Ann into the curve of his body. The newspaper lay discarded.

"What's she look like?" Ann repeated, unaware that her son had asked him that same question only minutes earlier.

Mark scowled. For crissakes! Why was everyone so interested in Mara's looks?

"Mark?"

"Milak," he replied curtly. "She looks like Milak, with short hair and no wrinkles." Jacob's rumbling laugh grated on his nerves. And on Ann's, too, apparently.

"Jacob, hush!" Ann said threateningly, though her eyes sparkled with humor. "I'm working here, can't you see that? It's not every day that Mark's so conversational."

Jacob laughed.

Mark grimaced and abruptly decided it was past time he left. "Look—" he began.

"You're not going yet, are you?" asked Ann, overriding his words. "You haven't even told us anything about her yet."

Mark swallowed an oath. He didn't want to hurt Ann's feelings, but she was definitely crowding him. "She's not staying," Mark revealed. Everyone would find that out soon enough anyway, he figured.

"Not staying?" Ann blinked. "But, why? We all thought that she'd be only too happy to help you."

"We didn't all think that," muttered Jacob.

Ann's swift glance effectively shut him up this time.

"She's here to visit Milak." He stood. "I gotta go."

"But we haven't even talked about fish camp!" Ann said, her voice distressed. "Surely there are plans—"

Abruptly the baby started crying. Ann jumped up off the couch and started across the living room. "Now, sit down, and don't leave, Mark Toovak," she ordered, waiting until he'd complied, albeit reluctantly. "I'll go see what's up and then bring him out for a visit with his uncle Mark. He's probably just hungry...."

Her voice faded as she left the living area. For a long, long moment, there was no sound but that of Ann's cooing assurances. Mark wavered, clearly undecided whether to stay. The uneasiness that had been with him since his arrival condensed into an icy certainty. He should leave. He should leave *now*.

He and Jacob rarely agreed on much, even though they were family and only two years separated their ages. Jacob was a traditionalist. Mark thought of himself as a progressive. Last year had been a milestone. They'd managed to compromise on the subsistence issue, because a united front had been necessary to combat the state government's threat to their ancestral hunting and fishing rights. Ann had been the bridge. Without her, his liberal and Jacob's conservative viewpoints might never have merged.

But there were other problems. For instance, Jacob had never respected Mark's need for distance. Mark didn't expect him to respect it now.

"You didn't ask her, did you?" Jacob questioned, as if he'd heard every word of Mark's thoughts.

"Ask who what?"

"Don't be dense, little brother. You know who. Mara. You didn't ask her, did you?"

"No, I didn't. But don't worry, *older* brother. Her grandma took care of it. Like you, she seems to enjoy sticking her nose into other people's business."

There was a long, taut silence. Then Jacob shifted his position on the couch. Mark's tension increased.

"Crosswinds *is* my business," he eventually replied. "And not only because I'm the village financial manager, either. It's because Crosswinds is Native-owned."

Mark flicked a quick glance at the darkened hallway. Where was Ann?

"Come on, Mark," Jacob urged, a faint edge of irritation entering his usually calm voice. "You know the drill. When something good happens, we all benefit, when something bad happens, we all suffer."

When something bad happens...

"You don't think I know that?" Mark's voice was raw with suppressed emotion, for he was fighting against a sea of memories. He remembered the crash of his medevac plane like it was yesterday. He'd forced himself to confront the husband and daughter of the patient he'd been transporting.

"Mommy's not coming home? Make her come back, Daddy," the little girl had pleaded.

Her father had looked at him with tears in his eyes for his wife and his child and their ruined lives. The sight had crushed him, effectively chaining his will. Right then he'd become numb. And later, when Jacob narrowly survived a trip on the Bering Sea that claimed the life of his first wife and best friend, Mark had become despondent. And resolved.

No more responsibility. No more anguish. No more involvement.

Abruptly Mark stood and looked down on Jacob. The last thing he needed was a lecture. He already knew that the failure of Crosswinds Siberia would hurt innocent people. Pain twisted in his gut.

"Tell Ann—" His voice frayed into silence. "Tell her I'll visit Josh another time."

"Stay," Jacob ordered, concern for Mark in his voice and his eyes. "You shouldn't be alone right now. If you'd just relax that wall around you, you'd realize you're in no shape to cheer yourself up."

"I'm fine."

"No, you're not."

"Look, if you and everybody else would just back off and give me some space—"

"You've had space," Jacob said, interrupting him. "Space doesn't work. I've been there, remember? Lia was my wife, Jonathan my best friend. I know what you're going through."

"The hell you do."

"That's right. It's hell. And I do," Jacob finished. With a powerful movement, he surged up and closed in on Mark. They stood less than a body's width apart. "What's happened to you, Mark? People tiptoe around you whenever you come out of that house of yours. The kids think you're a walking spirit! Nobody knows what to say, much less what to do for you.''

"Try leaving me alone," Mark replied coolly, under control again. "That's all I need, Jacob. All I want."

Jacob continued as if Mark hadn't spoken. "Don't be stupid. I just told you space doesn't work. So you crashed the pla—''

"Forget this," Mark broke in, and with a sharp twist of his torso he turned and headed for the door.

Jacob followed, watching as Mark angrily shoved his feet into his shoes, then hunkered down to lace them. "You can't even talk about it, can you? For Pete's sake, Mark! It wasn't your fault."

"Wasn't it?"

"No! Or have you conveniently forgotten the storm?"

Mark finished tying one shoe, then switched to the other. "I haven't forgotten anything." Not the terrified screams, not the pain-filled moans, not the final, awful silence. Nothing. He stood.

"You can't go through the rest of your life feeling guilty over something no one even blames you for," Jacob persisted, his usually calm voice strained.

"*I* blame me."

"I blamed myself, too, but that's no reason to destroy one of the few good things in your life."

"Mara's fine," Mark answered without thinking.

Jacob looked at him oddly, the silence between them stretching tight. Finally, Jacob spoke. "I was talking about Crosswinds."

Mark ran a hand through his hair in a gesture of barely restrained frustration. "I've had enough, okay, Jacob? Just move out of the way."

Jacob stayed put. "What's the matter with you? Do you *want* to fail? Is that it? Because if you do, you're right on target. Mara's your only hope of saving Crosswinds, and you know it."

Anger, and something else, swept through Mark. "I make my own way, brother. In my own time."

Jacob just stared at him. Mark could see the muscles clench in Jacob's jaw. As a rule, Mark knew, Jacob didn't get angry. He just got quiet. After a moment, Jacob said tightly, "Four years is a long time to travel alone. What are you afraid of? That I'm right? Or that I'm wrong?"

Mark took a sharp breath. It had been a mistake to come here. If he hadn't let Patrick rattle him, he'd be at home now, packing for fish camp and away from Jacob's smart mouth and uncomfortable questions.

"I'm not afraid of anything," Mark snarled, and at that moment, at least, it was true.

"You're not afraid of anything and you don't need anybody," Jacob said, taking a single step forward. Involuntarily Mark thought of his brother's *inua*, Kegluneq, the wolf. Kegluneq was, above all, a hunter, but he was a protector, too. And suddenly he knew what Jacob was doing.

"Whether you believe it or not, I'm on your side," Jacob said carefully, unknowingly confirming Mark's suspicions. "I know you're hurting, even if you won't own up to it. It's just— Damn it, Mark! Why did you mess up your only chance? Because you did mess it up, didn't you?"

Mark didn't answer. He couldn't. His throat was closed.

There was another long silence. When Jacob spoke again, his voice was resigned, sad, full of remorse.

"I'll say it once more. *Mara is your only hope.*"

"And I'll say it once more, brother— I make my own way. In my own time. Now get the hell away from the door." Jacob's parting plea followed him down the muddy path.

"Go see Mara. And whatever you did, *undo it.*"


Mara exited her grandmother's house, her neck muscles stiff with tension, no clear destination in mind. She hadn't felt such a whirl of confusion and fear since the night she'd stood outside Mark's house, listening to him crying. Then she'd made the wrong decision, and the shame of it had changed her life. She didn't want to make another mistake, one that might result in her forever losing her grandmother's trust.

Just the thought made her sick. She had to do something, had to find an acceptable solution. Her grandmother clearly thought herself capable of making the trip. Was the old healer right and her young granddaughter wrong? Was she being overprotective of a ninety-two-year-old who leaned heavily on a cane? Even Mark's controlled demeanor had been ruffled by the sight of that crooked driftwood stick.

Her feet carried her away from the houses, toward the Bering Sea. It was early evening, and most of the village women were inside their homes, busy preparing dinner for their families. As she walked, the familiar sound of the waves rang in her ears. Even the air was different, she thought contentedly as she brushed a hand through her windblown hair. She took a deep, calming breath. She was fiercely glad to be home, glad to be among her people again.

For an instant, the memory of Mark peering at her intently, his gaze hooded with masculine assessment, flashed into Mara's mind, shaking her newfound calm. She shoved the thought aside, certain the fleeting expression couldn't have been attraction. Though she knew firsthand that he was a sensual man, knew, too, that his long-limbed attractiveness had only increased with the passage of time, she also knew that he'd never considered her more than a tagalong nuisance. Even now, four years later, nothing had changed. He was still leading, she was still following. Well, from now on, she was through being dependent upon him. He'd suffered through his good deed and could now go on about his business—whatever that was.

She was so far into her thoughts that she was almost upon Siksik and her friend by the time she looked up and focused. Donning a smile, she ran over and hugged the smiling young woman.

"My goodness, Siksik! When did you grow up? You're as tall as I am!"

Siksik sighed, then laughed and hugged her back. "You look very nice yourself, Mara," she responded shyly, and turned to introduce her friend.

But Mara forestalled her. Extending her hand, she said brightly, "You're Sharon, right? Not a lot of spiral perms around here. Hi, Siksik's told me so much about you in her letters. It's great to finally meet you."

"Same here." Sharon grinned self-consciously and nudged her head in Mara's direction. "Rad hairstyle. I remember seeing it on the cover of a fashion magazine last fall."

Mara's amazed glance took in the sixteen-year-old's carefully arranged hairstyle. The light breeze from the Sea only enhanced its windblown attractiveness. "I'm impressed. You want to be a cosmetologist?"

"I think she could be a model," answered Siksik loyally.

Sharon blushed. "I just watch hair, that's all. The model who had that style was pretty famous, too, so it was easy to remember."

"You have some time to visit? We could go to my house," Siksik suggested, her expression hopeful.

Since Mara had questions of her own to ask Siksik, she acquiesced, aware she owed Siksik a great debt for her care of her grandmother. "Sure, I've got some time," Mara responded, and followed the pair to Siksik's parents' home.

Once inside, Mara looked around her and smiled, surprised to be reminded of the happy times she'd spent here, many of them with Mark. Siksik's parents' home was a comfortable mixture of traditional and *kass'aq* items. Mara seated herself on one of two recliners and gazed at her longtime friend as Siksik busied herself preparing tea. Siksik's waist-length black hair was simply styled in a one-inch-thick braid that dangled down her back. She wore the traditional white cotton *kuspuk* and a pair of cutoff jeans that showed off a pair of long, suntanned legs. Except for having exchanged the *kuspuk* for a large, neon-colored T-shirt, her friend Sharon was dressed identically. As Mara watched Siksik perform the traditional tasks, she was suddenly aware of how untraditional she must appear, with her modern haircut, designer-label jeans and crisp white polo shirt. She frowned, uneasy with that image, and with the vague feelings of displacement it generated. It had taken her a long time to become comfortable in the *kass'aq* world. Had she done so at the expense of her ease in her own?

The disquieting question joined the other worries queuing for time in her mind. Deliberately she buried it, too, and smiled at Siksik.

"Where are your parents? I would have thought they'd be home by now."

"Dad's making some phone calls over at John's store, and Mom's buying something for dinner." Siksik handed her a cup, then handed Sharon one, as well, before seating herself on the large oval rug on the wood-plank floor between the two recliners. For an hour the three talked as old friends, sipping tea and exchanging stories. Both Siksik and Sharon were eager to hear about college life, and Mara obliged with a few of the more humorous tales of her early years.

"I can't wait," Siksik said after one story. She smiled, her beautiful eyes sparkling. "You know I'm studying for the GED, don't you?"

Mara nodded, her feelings still ambivalent about her friend's plans. While she would likely pass the high school equivalency test, the diploma would in no way ensure her acceptance into UCLA, Siksik's goal. And it certainly didn't guarantee success with Billy. Mara sighed, aware her young friend could be deeply hurt sometime in the near future.

"When are you planning on taking the test?" Mara asked.

"Probably this winter, if I can keep up my study schedule. That way, if everything works out, Billy and I could be together as soon as January of next year."

"Have you written and told him your plans? Does he know how you feel?" Mara swallowed and asked the most important question. "Does he feel the same way?"

Siksik's face lit up with a bright, rosy blush. "After I performed the solo in the Woman of the Sea dance at last year's Christmas potlatch, we were together all the time. It was great!"

"But has he told you how he feels?" Mara persisted, aware she was pushing, but concerned for her friend.

"Billy doesn't even know she's coming," Sharon muttered, clearly disgusted. "She wants it to be a surprise."

And it would be, Mara was certain as she watched Sharon roll her eyes. "You don't like Siksik's plan?"

Sharon shot Siksik a guilty glance.

"It's all right, Sharon," Siksik murmured, her expression sad but resigned. She addressed Mara. "Sharon thinks I'm being silly. She thinks that Billy's gone, and that he's probably forgotten all about me."

"Siksik, I didn't say it like that!"

"But that's what you meant," Siksik continued, her gaze unconsciously pleading as it settled on Mara. "I've got to try, don't I? I mean, I love him. Isn't love worth the risk?"

Mara was definitely the wrong person to ask. What should she say to the girl? Siksik was sixteen and ready to take on the world for Billy Muktoyuk's love. Mara had been eighteen when she'd risked it all for Mark. What could she say that wouldn't sound jaded or negative? Love was supposed to be worth any risk, Mara knew, but was it truly love Siksik felt, or was it just a crush, as hers had been?

"What if you go down there and everything turns your way— you get accepted into UCLA, Billy falls for you big-time and he makes it as a professional basketball player. What about your dream to become a nurse for our people?" Mara sighed, her expression earnest as she focused on Siksik. Out of the corner of her eye, she noticed Sharon nodding her agreement. "Billy may or may not need you," she continued. "He may or may not love you. But we do need you, and we love you, too. Giving up a dream hurts. I know, believe me, I know. All I can say is, don't do it lightly."

Suddenly Mara's eyes stung. Poor Siksik. She was trying to be brave, but her confusion shone in her eyes.

She was such a nice girl. Too bad she had such an awful brother. Mark. Her heart thudded once, hard, causing her hands to clench tight around her tea mug. What was she feeling? Rage at his lack of remorse? Fear that those midnight-dark eyes would pierce her false calm to wreak havoc on her emotions again?

He was a coldhearted tyrant, an overbearingly stubborn man. Mara could hardly believe she had ever called this dark, disturbing stranger her best friend.

He made her palms sweat, her knees tremble. And his *voice*. It was cool and disdainful. The essence of all her nightmares—and once, a lifetime ago, her dreams.

"Mara?"

Mara jumped, her reverie shattered.

"You okay?" asked Sharon.

"Yes, yes . . . of course," Mara answered, aware that both girls were looking at her oddly.

"Milak said much the same thing yesterday, when I took her some pan bread for lunch," Siksik was saying.

Mara nodded, embarrassed by her lapse yet pleased that her advice had matched her grandmother's.

"So, how long will you be here?" Sharon asked.

"I was planning on a week, but now..." Mara filled them in on her problem with her grandmother. Since Siksik had spent so much time with the healer, her advice might help Mara make a decision about what to do regarding Milak. "So what do you think? She's absolutely determined to visit her sister, and I don't think she should."

"I don't think so, either," Siksik replied. "Last winter was difficult for us all. Many villagers were sick, and though I helped as much as I could, there were many things I didn't know or understand. She was very busy. Since then, she's weakened. She used to visit her patients. Now they come to her. And mostly she sits in her chair on the porch every day, except on Sundays when she has dinner with us at Jacob and Sharon's mom's house, or when the council of elders meet. Then she goes to the church."

The picture Siksik was painting filled Mara with uneasiness. "Was all this stuff in your letters? Somehow, I never got the impression Grandmother's health was failing."

"That's because it isn't. She's just getting old."

"When did she start using a cane?"

"A cane?"

Mara nodded. "When I came home today, she was leaning pretty heavily on it."

Siksik's eyes widened in alarm. "I don't know, Mara. I brought her some lunch yesterday, and she didn't have it then."

"And she hasn't mentioned falling down or anything like that?" Mara asked, her disquiet growing.

Siksik shook her head. "Even if she did fall down, Milak probably wouldn't say anything. She thinks she's invincible."

"That doesn't sound like Grandmother."

"I don't understand why she would...why she would think herself able to make such a big trip," Siksik said quickly. "Just last week, Billy's grandfather came to see her for something, and she told him to slow down and let his son handle the move to fish camp. And he's in his seventies."

The trio was silent until Sharon ventured, "Well, something's surely weird. I had a friend back when we were living in Anchorage whose dad was a doctor, and he didn't even know he had cancer until my girlfriend's mother forced him to go see a doctor about his sore throat. Maybe the same thing's happening to your grandmother. Maybe she doesn't know she shouldn't be running around anymore."

Mara nodded, her thoughts focused on her grandmother.

"These scroll things—" Sharon began.

"Sacred teachings," Siksik amended.

"Yeah, sacred teachings. They must be pretty important."

"Not as important as her life," Mara answered, looking up. "Our people depend on her. She's much more than our healer. She's a symbol." Frustrated, Mara stood and paced the living room. "What am I going to do? How do I persuade her not to go?"

"What do you know about this place?" Sharon was idly twirling a strand of her long brown hair around her finger. "What did you call it?"

"Sireniki."

"Okay. Sireniki. Is this village like ours? I mean, does it have telephone service? Electricity? A post office?"

"The letter was postmarked from there," Mara offered, uncertain about the rest of the answers. It was obvious she'd need more information.

"Then why can't her sister just box 'em up and send them here? One of those overnight jobbies, you know. It'll probably be expensive, coming all the way from Russia, but if you fork out the moolah, and if her sister makes a copy and insures the package, then there's no real risk, is there? And your grandma can stay put. She could have the stuff in her hands day after tomorrow."

Mara brightened, then, almost immediately, frowned again. "It's a good idea, Sharon, but that still leaves me with one problem. My grandaunt's dying, and Grandmother wants to see her one more time."

"Oh, yeah, I forgot that part. Bummer," Sharon murmured, terminology borrowing from her brother. "But you did ask if you could go in her place?"

Dejected, Mara sat down again. "Same problem. She wouldn't even consider it. My grandaunt is the last living member of Grandmother's family. Is it any wonder she won't let me go in her place? I'd want to go, too, if it were my sister."

Siksik had been suspiciously silent for several minutes, her thoughts seemingly far away. "I know what you could do," she said hesitantly.

Mara looked into those black eyes that were so like Mark's and prepared herself for something she might not like. "What, Siksik?"

"Has my brother talked to you about Crosswinds?"

"I haven't even seen Jacob yet," Mara offered. "What's Crosswinds?"

"Crosswinds Siberia, Incorporated," supplied Sharon. "And it's not Jacob's, it's Mark's hunting and fishing business. He does it during the summer. But not this summer, I guess. He told us last Sunday night that he's got major problems."

Mara was having difficulty keeping tabs on the conversation. "Mark's got problems with his business? What does that have to do with me?"

"The Russian interpreter he normally works with broke his leg," Sharon answered. "Siksik mentioned that since you and he had grown up together, and were best friends and all . . ."

Mara gasped, her shocked gaze pinned on Siksik's flushed expression of dismay. The sudden and ringing silence in the room was deafening.

"Hey!" cried Sharon. "Am I missing something here, or what?"

Siksik's head bowed for a moment, and then she looked up, her big eyes full of remorse. "I'm sorry, Mara. I know how you feel about him—at least, I think I know—but I couldn't just watch him lose everything again."

*"Your grandmother seems to think you'd be only too happy to spend five weeks in Siberia with me."*

"Does someone want to explain what's going on here?" Sharon repeated.

"Old history," Siksik replied.

Sharon's mouth formed a silent *Oh.*

"I turned him down," Mara revealed a moment later, grimacing as she recalled her silent rejection. "Can your idea still work?"

"I imagine, but if your grandaunt's so sick, time's critical, isn't it?"

"What are you suggesting?"

"Mark has a camcorder. And he knows Siberia. Ask him to guide you there. You can pick up the sacred teachings and put your grandaunt on video for Milak to see when you get back. She can write her sister a letter, and you can bring it to your grandaunt."

Mara nodded, aware Siksik's plan made sense. Her grandmother could stay home *and* see her sister one last time.

"Looks like Mark's your only hope," Sharon muttered.

Mara looked up from the carpet she'd been studying. "But in return I have to be his interpreter, right?"

Siksik nodded.

Sharon shook her head. "Bummer."

## Chapter Five

Out of the corner of her eye, Mara caught the sharp edge of daylight as it pierced the lamplit interior of the *qasgiq*, a square building that, in generations past, had housed the single males of the village. Time and *kass'aq* influence had changed that custom. Today it was Twilight's spiritual center, predating even the church. And tonight the villagers celebrated the launching of an *umiak*. Tradition demanded it be done properly. Unfortunately, Mara thought as she busied herself, the crumbling *qasgiq* was the proper place.

Apparently even *he* knew it. Uneasy relief flooded her veins, and she looked quickly away from the door, concentrating on the food she was packing in preparation for the evening's entertainment. She didn't need to see the latecomer's face to know who had entered.

Mark. A distinct tremor of nervousness now replaced the relief. She took a calming breath, telling herself that at least she wouldn't have to go to his place. Now that he'd arrived, she could ask him after the ceremony.

Would he go for it? Would he agree to an exchange of her services as an interpreter for his as a guide?

Mara cringed as she sealed a plastic container. Logically she would say he had about as little choice in the matter as she did.

Sharon had said he was in financial trouble, and Siksik had said
Crosswinds Siberia was important to him. Well, it had better be,
Mara knew, because if it wasn't, she'd have no choice but to go
alone. She'd made at least one firm decision during the early hours
of this morning: She was going to Sireniki, and her grandmother
was not.

If only there was someone besides Mark who knew the area. Just
the thought of having to spend the initial days getting to her
grandaunt and then, later, five one-week tours in the wilderness of
Siberia with him made her ill. Involuntarily, her glance collided
with Mark's narrowed assessment from across the *qasgiq*. There
was anger in his eyes. Anger, and something else she didn't want
to analyze.

Looking away, Mara waded through rows of villagers seated in
a large semicircle many deep, to her grandmother's side where the
old healer sat talking with other village elders. Mara rested her
hand for an instant on the shining white hair, gently fingering a red
bead on the priceless Siberian headdress that she now knew was her
grandaunt's, silently asking if there was anything her grandmother needed. When Milak's warning gaze swung toward the
back, where Mark stood, then to her again, Mara swallowed,
maintaining her smile with great difficulty, aware that hiding anything from her grandmother was virtually impossible.

That was why she'd decided before coming here this evening to
tell her grandmother about the plan. But the healer's position
hadn't budged. It was too much to ask, she'd continued to insist,
despite Mara's vehement denial that it was not so. With a final
gentle stroke along her grandmother's hair, meant to soothe her
more than to give comfort to Milak, Mara edged along the walls
toward Siksik, who was excitedly waving her over to where the
performers had gathered. The dances were about to begin.

Siksik stood next to Sharon. Both girls were dressed in embroidered white cotton *kuspuks* and sealskin mukluks, and in their
hands they carried the traditional circular dried-grass dance fans
edged in polar-bear hair. The men in the group whispered their
greetings, and Mara nodded, glancing at their short jacket-type
parkas and plainer, less ornamental dance fans. Ever conscious of
Mark's lurking form in the doorway, Mara smiled at their nervousness and then waited with breath held as the drummers,
Mark's father among them, began an insistent, pulsing beat. The
dance would tell a simple story of the difficulties of the hunt, the
man's work, and then the difficulty of the preparation of the meat,

the woman's work. Mara had never questioned the gender-specific division in the work effort, for each was necessary and vital to the survival of a family unit. If the male was a bad hunter, the family would starve; if the woman failed to preserve the meat and prepare the skins properly, the family would starve. The responsibilities were different, but they were equal and shared.

The drummers were seated on the floor opposite the villagers, chanting accompaniment as their bodies swayed forward, to the right, to the left, and then back to their original position. Mark's father began telling the story, the drummers' bodies keeping rhythm with the beating of the drums.

Two men came forward, and the dance/hunt began. The driving, inescapable rhythms of the drums were slow at first, but then they sped up as the hunt gained momentum. There were muffled sounds of delight from the audience as children and elders alike followed the well-known movements.

Mara smiled, herself absorbed by the sensual, fluid storytelling motions of the young men's hands and strong bodies as they mimicked the undulating sweep in walrus-skin *umiaks* across open seas and past treacherous ice floes. Watching their bodies, she was reminded of Mark's, and she paled at the explicit images.

Sensing she was being watched, she looked away from the male dancers to catch Mark's thoughtful gaze. He stood leaning against the door, his posture relaxed, yet Mara felt his unease across the room. She also felt his quick, dismissing once-over. A blush overrode her pallor, and his eyes narrowed speculatively before he raised a sardonic eyebrow, then returned his focus to the performance. Mara exhaled rapidly, her heart tripping, her mind wondering whether he'd somehow discerned her thoughts in the dim light of the seal-oil lamps. She sincerely hoped not.

When the drummers stopped, the dancers received enthusiastic applause from fathers, mothers, uncles, aunts, cousins and neighbors. Smiling and taking one last, insecure little swipe at her two long braids, Siksik looked at Mara.

"Have you asked him yet?"

Mara shook her head, her expression anxious. "But I will before we're finished here. I really can't put it off anymore."

Sharon tugged on Siksik's arm. "Let's go. It's our turn to wow 'em dead."

Mara smiled, hearing a plaintive, "Too bad Billy's not here" filter back through the crowd as the two young women joined another group of teenagers to perform the woman's part of the ritual dance.

The dancing continued long after Sharon and Siksik finished their performance. Mara watched, her senses alert to Mark's movement as he settled down beside Jacob, Ann and Patrick, who welcomed him with smiles and hugs. Ann passed him baby Josh, and to Mara's surprise he cradled the infant with confident ease. Bemused, Mara missed Ben asking her grandmother whether she wished to sing a song for the children. He held out his drum.

An expectant silence fell among the gathered. Then, stretching out her arm, Milak accepted the large, flat, oval-shaped drum.

Alerted by the unusual absence of sound, Mara looked away from Mark and the baby, her gaze colliding with her grandmother's intent observation. When the old healer beckoned her, Mara stiffened, then acquiesced.

"Granddaughter, you remember the Dance of the Healer?"

It was practically the first adult dance she'd ever learned. Milak's question reverberated around the room. Even the babies were quiet. Mara swallowed against a suddenly dry throat, aware she was the center of attention. Her stomach clenched. What was her grandmother up to?

"I—I don't know," Mara stammered in her bewilderment. "You must know I haven't danced it, or anything, for that matter, in a long time."

For some reason known only to her grandmother, Mara realized, her reply satisfied the healer.

"Then you will dance now, and I will sing. This is acceptable," Milak concluded in Yup'ik.

This is *acceptable?* Not to her it wasn't!

Anger and denial reigned uppermost in the youthful eyes that gazed pleadingly back at the seated woman. But except for a slight softening, and the barest impression of something deeper—something almost desperate, that threw Mara into deeper confusion—Milak's composure remained fixed.

Mara felt a terrible tautness enter her body. She would have to dance. Whether she wanted to or not, whether she understood her grandmother's motives or not, both were irrelevant, for she could never disrespect her grandmother, either publicly or privately. The fact that she was soon to go against her grandmother's express wishes already weighed guilt-heavy on Mara's mind.

Her face clouded with uneasiness, Mara made her way hesitantly to the center of the performance area, terribly embarrassed and overly conscious of her too-modern clothes, searching frantically in her mind for the steps learned so long ago, steps she hadn't thought of in years.

But Milak still had other ideas. "Wait. You will wear this headdress."

Numb, Mara retraced her steps and accepted the fragile beaded artifact. It settled like a crown on her head. The three horizontal rows of tiny blue beads sewn on a red felt background edged in ermine lay against her forehead like a sweatband, and another double row of beads, these alternating white and black, hung down around her chin, like the elastic of a regular hat, but very loose. Softly she moved her head, enjoying the gentle sounds as the beads tinkled with her tentative movements. Murmurs of wonder and excitement rippled through the crowd.

The Dance of the Healer was steeped in ritual, and was an ancient sequence of movements performed only by the healer. Mark didn't understand why Milak was insisting Mara perform it, unless it was for the children who had never seen it and might never see it, but he could accept that Mara had the right. She was Milak's granddaughter, and no one else in the village could claim a closer relationship with the healer. He found himself leaning forward, straining to see what Mara would do, whether she'd cut and run, as he expected, or whether she'd stick it out and possibly, likely, embarrass herself out of respect for the old woman.

Milak's single drumbeat signaled the start.

Mark realized he was squeezing his nephew too hard at the same time he saw Mara make the first tentative step. Not even questioning his need, he gave baby Josh to Ann and stood up. He wasn't about to miss this. He moved back against the wall and watched.

Her initial movements were tentative and filled with indecision. She wasn't dressed to give a performance. The only Native garment she wore was the headdress. Her leather flats, designer jeans and orange silk blouse screamed her modern *kass'aq* connections. Mark winced with sympathy as she again faltered. The villagers mumbled. She was blowing it big-time. She was making a fool of herself. Suddenly, almost as if she'd heard his pained thought, she straightened and swung around to face him, her expression pleading.

Pleading? Her eyes, dark as the winter, deep as the Bering Sea, were full of entreaty. He didn't know what to do, how to respond. Did she want him to disrupt the celebration? He could do that, but at what cost? And what if he was wrong, and she wasn't asking for his help? Was he willing to involve himself in a big fiasco on the basis of what he *thought* he saw in her eyes?

And what made him think she would look to him as her savior? He frowned slightly, looking questioningly at her suddenly deadened eyes. A second later, she glanced away.

Mara didn't know what instant of insanity had led her to hope Mark would come to her rescue. After all, she wasn't a silly kid anymore. She was an adult, and the grandmother she loved with all her heart, the woman who had raised and nurtured her, the woman who had not questioned her sudden need to get an education and who had not complained over her granddaughter's long absence, had just asked for a dance. Mara couldn't refuse.

You can do this for Grandmother, she told herself, praying she wouldn't shame the healer. Family was so important to her people. And Mara didn't want to let her grandmother down. *All you have to do is concentrate on Milak and block out everything else.*

Mark sensed the change in her immediately. It was almost as if she'd stepped beyond the boundaries of her insecurity and into the freedom of confidence. Her arms lifted sinuously to the pounding rhythm of Milak's drumbeat, a rhythm that was suddenly steadier, stronger, more confident.

She had become the healer, and the dance was hers to perform.

Milak's whisper-ragged voice chanted the ancient words as more drums joined the song. Mara moved about the room, her eyes unseeing as she executed the strangely compelling movements that few understood. At times, Mark caught a glimpse of something he recognized, maybe the picking of a special herb, the drying and preparation of potions, but he couldn't be sure. But the villagers were enthralled, young and old alike. They pointed to Mara's swirling body when Milak sang of the confusions and cures of the mind, and they watched in rapt attention when she lay on the ground, her swaying body mimicking the moment of birth and then the moment of death.

Mark watched as intently as anyone in the audience, riveted by Mara's athletic movements. It was a dance of rejuvenation, a dance about the cycle of life, and though he tried not to be personally affected, he was anyway. He didn't notice anyone else, his gaze became so intent and focused on Mara. There was nothing in the shabby, crumbling building but the many *naniq* flames and the one woman with the midnight-black hair and swaying body. He leaned forward even more, trying to see her eyes. It was impossible. She didn't look directly at any single person, and he sensed she was off in a world she shared with none but her grandmother.

Gradually the rhythm of the drums changed from an eerie slow traveling into the ancient past to the faster, more urgent rhythms of modern times. Mara's movements echoed the change, becoming lighter, faster, more strenuous in both execution and discipline. Her face began to gleam, and the flickering flames beat with the pounding of the drums.

The rhythm increased as Milak's aged hands pounded a new, different, challenging rhythm that had the other drummers dropping out to listen. Mark watched as Mara's body followed the throbbing drumbeat, and she stepped up her pace. He was amazed at her endurance, aware of a grudging respect for the discipline and nerve and sheer guts she had shown by not walking out in the first place.

Suddenly Mara whirled and crouched. Her hair blazed, and the headdress sang with tiny tinkling sounds, drawing a low murmur of awe and wonder from the villagers. He sensed she was hunting, but he didn't know what, sensed that the low, stealthy half crawl was meant to imitate a wolf, perhaps, or a polar bear on the hunt. With each intricate step, Mara circled the performance area, her eyes focused yet unseeing, her body as tight as the drumbeat beneath her grandmother's hand.

Mara didn't stop until she'd circled the space. Then she jumped up, with a movement so quick that her orange silk blouse seemed to blur. Her hair fanned out as she turned her back on him, giving him a clear view of her sleek yet elementally feminine silhouette. Again she turned, this time to face her grandmother, her hands once again stretched out, but in front, not above her head, her eyes abruptly reflecting the light, their wild, angry challenge and passionate pleading tearing deep into Mark's innermost memories.

He remembered that look.

Lonely, aching rhythms poured out of the drum beneath Milak's hands. Mara's body echoed that loneliness. Mark watched as grandmother and granddaughter seemed to move as one, Mara's body and Milak's hands quickening with the same intensity as the snapping flames in the heated *qasgiq*. The rhythm swept through Mara, exploding into a passionate display of movement that Mark could no longer follow. Beads flying, body gleaming with sweat, her eyes wide with an astonishment he didn't understand, Mark watched as Mara burned hotter than a thousand *naniq* flames.

Milak's hands, so old, yet burning with equal intensity and heat, beat the drum with an almost violent rhythm. Then, suddenly, she stopped, and the room was plunged into silence. Mara was crouched, her head hanging down, her breasts rising and falling with the harshness of the final climax.

Everyone was silent, but a current of reverent, inaudible excitement rippled like wind-whipped tundra grasses around the room.

Mark felt it—and burned.

Palms flattened against the warm wood planks, he attempted to control the drum's primitive resonance as it pounded in his ears and throbbed through his body. His arousal was intense and, after more than four years of abstinence, painful. He suddenly felt confined, felt a need to get out and breathe a chestful of fresh air. But the echoing drumsong wouldn't release him, and his body was too aroused to make movement a possibility.

Slowly, as if emerging from a hypnosis of some kind, the villagers began to clap until the echoes pounded in Mark's ears as loudly as his pounding pulse.

"Quite a performance, wouldn't you say, little brother?"

He'd been so focused, he hadn't even heard Jacob's approach. Deliberately he stepped back, out of the lamplight. "Interesting," he commented, trying to smooth the tremor in his voice.

He failed, for Jacob chuckled knowingly. "I'd say you were interested, all right. She certainly has grown up."

"And? What's the point?" Mark asked, getting irritated. "Everybody grows up."

Now Jacob laughed outright, and slapped him on the back. "Yeah, sure, everybody grows up, but some look a lot better than others when they're done."

Mark forced a chuckle he didn't feel. What he felt was a savage arousal. And a need for some air. He groaned when Siksik joined them.

"Wasn't she great?"

Mark stepped into the light, caught Jacob's sly glance and scowled. "Yeah, great." He changed the subject. "I think I'm going to head out for fish camp a little early."

"Can't take the heat, huh?"

"Stuff it, Jacob," Mark growled, his arousal still urgent within him. He was aware of his sister's confusion, but he was powerless to lessen it.

"When are you leaving?" she asked, her expression anxious.

Mark schooled his features and playfully cuffed her cheek. "Miss me already? Mom and Dad will be along in a week or so. I'll just get everything ready for when you guys arrive. Save you a lot of work."

Siksik's smile didn't quite reach her eyes. "You're not going tonight, are you?"

"No, but tomorrow, probably. I figure sometime in late afternoon, I'll load up and motor over. There'll be lots of runs. I'll probably be busy setting up for a day or two at least."

Siksik nodded and abruptly excused herself, leaving Mark alone with Jacob. Mark's glance roved the room restlessly, unconsciously searching for a wave of liquid energy and fluid strength. Mara.

"She won't be here long," said Jacob. "If you intend to fix things—"

"I don't intend to fix anything but nets," Mark cut in, his glance pausing on Milak. In her face he saw pride, excitement and deep exhaustion. When that all-seeing gaze became aware of his, he wasn't quick enough to step back into the shadows or to school his own still deeply aroused feelings. Damn.

"What about Crosswinds?"

Mark gave his brother an irritated sidelong look. "Drop it, Jacob."

"Okay, then, what about them?"

Mark gazed at the group of young men gathered around Mara. "If she wants them, let her have them."

"And if she doesn't? Say she wants a certain Tuntu? Old habits die hard."

"That one died four years ago." Muttering a curse, Mark pushed open the door and stalked off.

Congratulations poured toward her from every side. Mara smiled, accepting pats and hugs from her friends and her neighbors, unaware of their curious, almost awed glances as she passed through the crowd, intent on reaching her grandmother. Something had happened during the performance, something strange, something she didn't understand. She hoped her grandmother did.

"Mara."

She turned and recognized Siksik.

"I didn't know you could dance like that," the teenager commented, her gentle eyes wide with a friendly kind of envy.

Mara cracked a smile. "Don't tell anyone, okay?" she whispered as she returned the girl's quick hug. "But I didn't know it myself until a few minutes ago."

Siksik giggled and pulled back. "Mark's over by the door, talking to Jacob," she whispered. "I think you'd better ask him soon. He just told me he's planning on leaving for fish camp late tomorrow."

"Tomorrow?" Any euphoria she'd felt faded. Time had run out. "Would you tell Grandmother that I'll be back in a few minutes?"

Siksik nodded. "Good luck."

Mara weaved through the crowd, scanning for a gold studded caribou on the back of a familiar broad-shouldered build.

"Mara?"

Startled, Mara swung her head around, and the beads on the headdress tinkled. Her glance met Jacob's.

"If you're looking for Mark, he took off."

"Took off?" she cried out, alarmed. "Already? But Siksik just told me he wasn't leaving for fish camp until late tomorrow."

Jacob paused and then he said slowly, "All I meant was that he stepped out for some air. He's not comfortable in crowds."

Immediately Mara blushed, embarrassed. The last thing she wanted was Jacob thinking she was running after his brother again.

"Want some advice?"

Her blush deepened. "You want me to stay away from him?"

"No, I want you to go after him."

Mara blinked, surprised. "You do?"

"Yes, I do. I can't get through to him anymore, but maybe you can. You know him as well as I do. Better, probably, considering all the time you two used to spend together."

Mara paled. "That was years ago. I've changed, and—"

"So has he. I know," Jacob cut in. "But he's twisted up inside, Mara. Unpredictable."

Mara couldn't stop her instinctive shudder. She already knew about Mark's unpredictability.

"It's his business, isn't it? Siksik told me about Crosswinds Siberia."

"That's part of it, I'm sure. But he's tearing himself apart. He doesn't care about anything outside of family matters. Hell, he hasn't flown in years."

Mara flinched. She didn't want to hear this. Not when she'd had to learn to live with her own phobias. Four years she'd stayed away from home. For four years she hadn't so much as been out on a date. No, she didn't want to hear about Mark's problems. She had plenty of her own, and they were all his fault.

"Look, I don't know what happened between you two—and I know something did happen, so don't bother denying it—but can't you give him another chance? He didn't mean to hurt you."

*Oh, yes, he did,* Mara thought, unaware that her eyes revealed her pain. "Forget it, Jacob. I know you mean well, but if Mark needs help, if he's truly hurting, I'm the very last person he'd call."

"Then you've changed your mind? You're not going after him?"

Mara didn't want to. God, how she wished she could join her grandmother and enjoy the celebration. But she couldn't. She didn't have a choice.

"I'm going," she murmured. "Just don't expect a miracle."

"I won't," Jacob answered, his expression concerned. "Be careful, okay? We've been friends a long time. As far as I'm concerned, you're family."

For a long moment, Mara looked into his sincere black eyes. There was a knot in her throat. "I'll be careful," she promised softly.

"See that you are. And if he gets out of hand, tell him he'll have me to answer to."

Mara almost laughed. Almost.

"Mark can be tough. And when he gets really upset . . ."

"He's unpredictable," Mara finished for him. "I know. And I'll take care, believe me." She turned to leave.

"Oh, and Mara?"

She paused, but didn't turn.

"Thanks. From all of us."

The door squeaked as she stepped outside. A breeze rippled through her blouse, chilling her perspiration-wet body. She briefly considered returning to her grandmother's house for a jacket, but then she spotted Mark heading toward the open tundra just beyond the village limits.

His powerful body was directed, the length of his stride eating up and stretching the distance between them. She didn't understand why he was pushing himself, but she sensed his determination. Since his back was to her, she couldn't see his face, but she could imagine it—impatient, focused, unyieldingly single-minded. Definitely a man who wouldn't welcome an interruption.

Mara watched him stalk past the village's electricity station, and his father's house, with its four-wheeler sitting abandoned in the front yard. Without looking around, he left the village, struck out through the windswept grasses of the tundra, taking a direct path toward a small knoll about a quarter mile away.

Mara never remembered moving. As she set out, her eyes were trained on the man who was rapidly becoming a speck as he ate up the ground, walking seemingly without effort, faster and harder.

Her pace lagged far behind. Her flats weren't up to the uneven and sometimes marshy terrain and kept falling off her feet, and the headdress kept slipping and getting in her way. Several times she fell; mud splashed on her clothes, ruining her blouse.

Before long she was winded and laboring for breath, wondering why she'd set out on this insanity. She could have waited for him to return to the village. She could have been dry and warm and calm and prepared. But she kept walking. It was simply now or never. She had to get to Mark.

At last the knoll, with its flattened crest, was within her reach. Adrenaline poured into her system, allowing her to cross the remaining distance to the foot of the grassy incline, where she began climbing. Looking up, she could see Mark's stiff back, his body a warning sign to stay clear and away.

Unpredictable, Jacob had said.

When she finally reached the top, her legs collapsed beneath her. Bent over, she hung her head in exhaustion. Her lungs grabbed for air. Her body, so recently exerted in the dance, trembled. But Mara was afraid it might be more than that. Afraid because she didn't have her pills.

Mark was seated, his arms wrapped loosely around his up-drawn legs. His forehead was resting on his knees, his eyes were trained down on the ground, his concentration was absolute. His feet were braced shoulder-width apart. His hands were curled into fists.

He seemed so alone.

Mara struck the errant thought from her mind. She didn't want to feel sorry for him. He didn't deserve so much as an ounce of sympathy from her. But as she watched, she couldn't help remembering the grief she'd brazenly interrupted four years ago. Was he remembering, too? Was that what was holding his back so stiffly erect? Or was it his troubles over Crosswinds Siberia? Only one way to find out.

"Mark."

His head shot up. She looked . . . a mess. Her hair mussed, her face red. The orange silk blouse was mud-splattered and clung damply to her breasts. Milak's headdress was tilted off to one side.

He'd never seen a woman look so beautiful.

"What the hell are you doing here?" The demand shot out, edged with anger and frustration.

Her body stiffened. He watched her eyes, big and black and scared. Her face, flushed from her walk, went very pale.

"You don't own the tundra, Mark. I can walk anywhere I want."

"Then go walk somewhere else. Back to the *qasgiq,* preferably. I'm sure every man in there's missing you."

"Don't look now, Mark, but the days when you command and I obey are over. We need to talk."

Deliberately he turned his back on her. "Go away, Mara. Whatever it is, I'm not interested."

"You will be."

"No, I won't." What a crock. He was already interested. He was *too* interested.

Mara's insides tightened. Nothing had changed. After four years, he was still rejecting her. Only this time she knew she didn't have the luxury of running away.

"Siksik told me about Crosswinds Siberia." She heard him turn around. Brushing at the dirt on her blouse, her gaze avoided his. "She also told me you need an interpreter."

There was a cold, brittle silence. "What business is it of yours if I do?"

Still avoiding direct contact, she brushed more dirt from her blouse. "Don't be dense, Mark. Translating Russian is my business. I've been doing it for several years now."

"I don't need charity."

Her head snapped up. The cold certainty in her eyes stunned him. "I'm not offering any."

*Especially to you.* Her unspoken words floated on the brisk breeze. "Then why are you here? After I dropped you off at Milak's yesterday, I figured you'd be smart enough to stay the hell out of my way, Mara. I'm sure Siksik warned you."

She nodded. "Jacob, too. They both did."

"Well, then?"

She squeezed shut her eyes, willing the threatening tears to recede. This was turning out to be so much more difficult than she'd imagined. When she felt calmer, she opened them again, catching a wary bleakness burning in his eyes. "Why do you do that?"

"Do what?"

"Push people away. They only want to help. Jacob says you even do it with your family." Instantly Mara knew she'd made a mistake, mentioning his brother.

Mark's eyes blazed. "So I hate handouts. As far as I'm concerned, that's good. I don't want to owe anybody anything. And you can tell Jacob that I said so." His voice was a low snarl. "Crosswinds Siberia is *my* business. And I'll run it exactly the way I want."

"Into the ground, you mean."

"Stay out of my business, Mara." Mark hissed the furious words. "Didn't what happened four years ago teach you anything?"

For a long, long moment, there was no sound but that of Mara's gasp as she fought against an overwhelming urge to run. Only her grandmother's image, held in her mind's eye, kept her seated. "I thought—" She swallowed convulsively. "I thought Crosswinds Siberia was important to you."

Abruptly Mark rose and stalked to the far edge of the knoll. He didn't look at her, couldn't look at her. Not and remain sane. He began to swear softly, heatedly, hating himself and his vulnerability to the woman sitting so silently behind him.

"Why won't you answer a simple question?"

"Because it's not simple," he snapped, jamming clenched fists into narrow pockets. "It's not simple at all. Just because Crosswinds makes a little money for the village and buys a few computers for our kids, you seem to think I should bend over backward to save it. Well, I don't. In a year or two, when I get up some cash, I'll start up again."

"In a year or two?"

"If I feel like it."

"If you—" Outraged, Mara scrambled to her feet. Crossing to his side, she whirled him around. Mark took a hasty step back. "What do you mean, *if you feel like it?* How can you be so callous? Our people are depending on you. If Crosswinds fails, they'll suffer. For God's sake! Don't you even feel the least bit responsible? Twilight is already dying! You said it yourself just yesterday. Don't you care?"

At that moment, the only thing he cared about was controlling an intense urge to take her by her slender throat and strangle her. "If you've finished your little temper tantrum—?"

She gaped at him and took an unconscious step forward. Mark took another step back. "I suppose you know that everyone's whispering about it, wondering what you're going to do, what they're going to do if you can't save Crosswinds."

"That's not my concern," he ground out, his eyes flashing a dark warning.

Mara ignored it. "Oh, that's right, you're not *interested,* are you?" she snapped sarcastically. "Well, that's just too damn bad, Mark Toovak. You're responsible. So you'd better start caring, real quick." She forced the words past dry lips, unwillingly disturbed by his sudden pallor. Then she shrugged off the uneasiness. She knew better than most that the truth could hurt. As far as she was concerned, it was well past time he heard some of it.

"You know what your problem is? You're out of touch. Nothing fazes you, nothing gets past that ice-cold exterior. They're scared, Mark. They might not say so, but they are. They don't have much, and you're threatening to make it even less."

She paused, hoping for some response, some indication that she was getting through to him. Nothing. She felt despair spread through her stomach, and clamped down on the feeling. "*Why* don't you care? Is your ego so fragile that you can't admit to a mistake? Are you really planning on making them suffer because you didn't have the sense to secure adequate backup?"

"You want to know about suffering?"

Too late, she recalled Jacob's warning. Mark was too fast. A shocked breath, and his mouth fused on hers. His raging emotions overpowered her. His mouth, his arms, his hands gripping her neck and the curve of her waist, all denied her escape.

He was so angry. Mara trembled and instinctively tried to wiggle out of his grasp, gripping his arms, shuddering at the powerful contraction of his biceps as he tensed against her awkward, puny efforts. His jacket felt worn and smooth, but the muscles beneath were hard and determined.

He could feel her heart thudding, could feel the involuntary and sporadic spasms of her muscles as she pushed back and away from his body. He knew what he was doing was wrong, had known it four years ago, but just as he had been then, he felt overwhelmed by emotion and inadequate to contain it. There was a need in him, a tidal wave of pent-up longing, and now that he held her in his arms, that need wasn't about to let him—or her—go.

Her lips were so soft.... Just another moment, he promised himself. Just one more minute. He could smell her hair, flower-

scented from dried petals, her skin, irresistibly flavored from the
exertion of the dance and the familiar ancient fragrance of the
tundra and the Bering Sea. Each individual aroma assaulted his
body, attacking his heart, storming his thoughts, raiding and con-
quering every cell, every molecule.

He forgot what had pushed him to this point, forgot everything
but the presence of her in his arms. His heart, already revved, settled into a deep, loud pounding. His blood ran hot. The feel of her
lips, so soft even in their unresponsiveness, cooled his anger and
fueled his desire.

Would he never stop? She couldn't breathe, couldn't move,
couldn't even distance her mind from the sensations seizing control of her body. She moaned and her body tightened further as she
felt the anger recede from him and the hot and determined taste of
him seep into her soul. He was wrapped all around her, his shud-
ders no less urgent than her own. Pain centered in her fingertips,
and numbly, absently, she recognized that she was gripping his
arms so tightly that her fingernails hurt.

That she was in his arms was more than she could fathom. The
taste of him, the awareness of his strength, the deep pounding of
his heart . . . Together, they overwhelmed her resistance, exploding all barriers to reveal her own need. Helpless in the face of it, she
parted her lips.

Suddenly, heat exploded through her body. And along with the
heat came the dizziness. Eyes that had been held tightly shut
snapped open, horrified awareness in their depths. She renewed her
struggles even as the familiar reactions took over and the fevered
face so close to hers blurred and dimmed. Desperation made her
fight, for she didn't want to surrender, not to him, certainly not to
the unknown disease inside her.

Vaguely she sensed his sudden stillness, but it was already too
late. She couldn't escape—not now, maybe not ever. Then she
screamed. One silent, pain-filled cry that issued up from the depths
of her soul and poured like a river of flowing ice out of her body.

Mark reared and caught her just as she sagged in his arms.

Then nothing moved, nothing stirred, not even the wind.

## Chapter Six

"What the hell?"

Alarmed, Mark gazed down at the limp woman in his arms, his heart thudding with fear. Quickly he lowered her to the ground, the long tundra grasses surrounding them and creating a natural enclosure, out of reach of the wind. Her eyelids were shut, her breathing was shallow. A knife turned in his stomach as his gaze cataloged her symptoms.

Carefully he removed the headdress, then laid it aside with a gentle respect that would have caused speculation among those who believed in his lack of reverence for traditional trappings. He checked her pulse, felt her forehead, unsnapped her jeans and freed the ruined blouse from the waistband. All this he did automatically, recalling the procedures, not questioning the ease with which he performed the necessary checks. He slapped her chin gently, hating himself for having to do it.

"Mara? Hey! Wake up!"

She responded so immediately he started with surprise. Her eyes were wide with shock and confusion.

He helped her sit up, then moved away to observe her.

"You all right?"

Her hands were shaking, so she hid them in her lap. Abruptly tears scalded up from deep inside her. *Oh, God, don't let me cry. Not now, not here, please.* She turned blindly away, trapped by the raw feelings building inside her—furious, desperate longings to blame Mark for what had just happened. But she couldn't. The illness wasn't his fault. Nor was it his fault that she'd pushed him too hard. Weak tears tracked down her cheeks.

"Mara?"

"Please, don't," Mara said quickly. "I don't want to talk about it, please. Let's just move on." Swiping at the tears, she stole a look at him. Under other circumstances, his stunned disbelief would have been funny. But these weren't other circumstances. Bracing her leg muscles, she stood and walked unsteadily to the edge of the knoll. "I think we were talking about Crosswinds."

"I don't give a damn what we were talking about." Mark watched, impatient, as she shivered and swayed in the wind. "Damn it! Sit down before you fall down!"

It took every ounce of willpower in her to face him again. But she knew she had to, if only to wrest back some of her lost self-respect. "Sit down, get up, get out... I'm really tired of being ordered around by you. I told you a half hour ago, Mark—those days are over."

Mark muttered a searing obscenity and crossed to her side. When Mara made a low sound and backed away from him involuntarily, he paled, but nevertheless caught and steadied her. He could feel her trembling when his hands closed around her wrists.

"What the hell is this?" His voice grated roughly, like his hands. He wanted her to get mad—needed it to appease his growing guilt. "I just kissed you senseless, and now you're telling me to forget the apology and move on, like this was some damned business meeting?"

"That's what it was supposed to be," Mara said, grabbing on to his interpretation as if it were a lifeline. "And that's how I'd like to continue."

She stared at him across a ringing silence. There was something in his eyes that held her gaze even against her will. For just an instant she had the ridiculous impression that he was hurting, hurting every bit as much as she was. Then she dismissed it.

"You can stop a lot of unnecessary suffering, Mark. And you can save Crosswinds, all at the same time." Her eyes swung pointedly down to his hands. "I have a plan."

Mark had to admire her guts. She thought she had it all figured out. But her pulse still pounded erratically beneath his thumbs, and her arms still trembled. She wasn't as controlled as she wanted him to believe.

"What plan?" Mark asked, releasing her slowly.

"I'll do it, Mark. For the village, not for you. And—" she stressed the word as she rubbed her wrists "—so you won't think it's charity, there's a price."

"A price."

"Yes. You help me and I'll…interpret for your clients." Not for anything could she say, I'll help you.

Mark looked at the tense and shaken woman, and was even more suspicious. She would consider helping him after what he'd just done? "Why? You know I can't pay."

"I know. And I don't need your money. What I need is your expertise."

"My *what?*"

Mara blanched when she realized what he thought.

Immediately Mark's hand shot out again and steadied her at the waist. The silk of her blouse was a thin barrier; her slender body was cool and quivered with emotion. Anger? Fear? The latter thought clenched his gut.

"I'm talking about your knowledge of Russia. I need you to take me to Siberia." Stepping back and away, she told him about the letter from Milak's sister.

"So let me get this straight," he said after she finished. "I get you to Sireniki, and in turn you provide me with translation services?"

"Exactly."

"What's the catch?"

"There is no catch."

"There's always a catch, Mara. I'd need your services from July through October. That's four months of your time. At most, you'd need me for a few days of mine. So, I repeat. What's the catch?"

"Fine, you want a catch, I'll give you one." The bleak look she gave him squelched his self-satisfied smirk. "Don't touch me again. You do, and our contract's off. I don't care if you've got the president for a client, I'll leave you flat. Got it?"

Mark looked at the ashen, determined woman and felt the remorse he'd lived with for so many years churn queasily in his stomach. Her contempt and fear were there for him to see. Her feelings tore at his self-respect.

"I got it."

"Good. It's a fair deal, Mark. Crosswinds survives, our people aren't deprived, and Grandmother's life isn't put at risk."

As long as he didn't kiss her. For an instant, she saw his face above hers again, his eyes dark with anger as he covered her mouth with his own. The force of it had sent her reeling. Mara strongly suspected she'd have fainted anyway, illness or no, because during those last urgent seconds before the dizziness overpowered her, something had happened. Something she didn't want to acknowledge, because it frightened her deeply. But just as she was through running from Mark, she was equally through running from herself. She knew that over the fear and the anger, a weak but very real response had swelled.

"Mara? Are you all right?"

She faced him stoically. "Yes. I'm fine. Now that we have a deal, I'm fine."

"I didn't say we have a deal."

Mark wondered if he was finally going crazy. *She asks you not to touch her and you agree. She asks you to take her to Siberia and you consider it. What the hell are you thinking?*

He looked at Mara again. Her eyes were wide, fixed, and the skin around them looked blue. "Translation aside," he asked stiffly, "you don't even know this woman, do you?"

"What's that got to do with anything?"

"She could be a fraud."

"A fraud? What advantage would there be for someone to impersonate my grandaunt?"

"Since you haven't been to Siberia, you'll just have to take my word for it. A rich American relative—"

"Grandmother's not rich."

"She is by their standards," he shot back. "If this woman's dying, she might make all kinds of demands. Demands someone like you would feel compelled to grant."

"Someone like me? What's that supposed to mean?"

Mark started to speak, stopped, then sighed heavily. "It means I think you're tenderhearted."

Mara brutally squashed the tiny spark of hope his words created. "You mean you think I'm a sap."

"I didn't say that."

"But it's what you meant, isn't it?"

"Don't put words into my mouth," Mark grated.

As if pulled there, Mara's gaze lowered to his mouth and lingered, no fear in her expression, just an innocent curiosity. Mark scowled and abruptly turned away. "You're too suspicious," she said, watching his back. The gold studded caribou mocked her racing heart.

"And you're too naive."

"So you've said before."

Mark whirled. "Wake up, Mara! This woman might not even be able to *see* you, much less communicate with you. Have you thought of that? And what if this woman's already dead? You want to chance going all the way to Siberia just to pick up some old recipes? Always supposing, of course, that they actually exist."

"They do exist. And they're not recipes, they're sacred teachings."

"Fine, whatever, but what if she's dead?"

"She's not. Grandmother would know if she were."

"Grandmother would—" Mark began, then abruptly stopped. "Never mind. I don't want to hear it. Whatever it is, it probably makes no more sense than this damn-fool stupid plan of yours."

"I didn't ask for your opinion. Just get me to Sireniki." Frustrated anger made her throw up her hands. "Don't you understand? If I don't go, Grandmother will. She's determined, Mark. She's already told me not to interfere."

"Then don't."

"I've got to! She's ninety-two! She's using a cane, for heaven's sake. The trip could conceivably kill her. Do you want that on your conscience? Do you even *have* one?"

"No, I don't." *Liar.* Lately it seemed all he had was a conscience. "I don't want to be responsible for anyone but myself."

"That's loud and clear," Mara shot back. "I got the message. Once you get me to Sireniki, you're free to leave." And she sincerely hoped he would.

Mark drew a short, impatient breath. Her face was so open. Everything she was feeling, the anger, the hurt, the bitterness, showed in her expression. "And just how," he asked quietly, "do you expect to get back?"

"That's not your concern. I speak Russian, I'll make it. The return trip's not time-critical. If it takes me a few more days to make the proper connections, it won't matter."

He laughed, but the sound was grim. "You don't know what you're talking about. *Glasnost* may now be the new law of the land over there, but not everyone's heard it or believes it, understand?

Russia's not America. Not by a long shot. And the Russian Far East is like nothing you've ever imagined."

Her chin tilted. "That's not important. What's important is my grandmother's health. What's important is my grandaunt and her last wishes. What's important is Twilight. Now, do we have a deal?"

Did they? He'd all but assaulted her, and she was offering to save his business. Try as he might to stick to his creed of noninvolvement, he couldn't quite succeed. Even if she hadn't offered, he still owed her one. No, he owed her two. Four years was a long time to wait to pay back a debt, but he figured it was time. Even if she never knew, he would.

"Do we have a deal?" Mara repeated.

"On one condition." His eyes captured hers. "Just so you understand, once we leave here, it's my show. This isn't some pansy anthropological field trip. Out there, it's survival that counts. I lead, you follow. Step out of line and I'll bring you back, whether or not you want to go. Got it?"

Mara tensed, not bothering to hide her indignation. "Got it."

In the old *qasgiq,* Twilight's healer smiled for the first time that night.

It was ten o'clock the next morning. The Twin Otter that would fly them to Bethel for their commercial flight to Nome, was due to arrive in twenty minutes. She'd decided against calling and informing her doctor of her plans. Private discussions were impossible, since anyone who happened to be at John Muktoyuk's store at the time of her call would unabashedly listen in. She had, however, called Wally, and he'd agreed to inform her professor and a few of her regular business clients of her extended absence. After ringing off, she'd felt strange, unusually detached from Wally and the academic environment that had been her world for four years now. He'd sounded so far off, as if she'd been away for weeks, not just days. So much had happened.

She was completing her packing when Milak entered her bedroom and seated herself on a corner of the single bed. In Milak's left hand lay the beaded headdress; in the other, a leather wristband to which several downy feathers were tied. Mara stilled, recognizing the wristband. It was called a *talliraq.* Milak had fashioned it for her when Mara was just a little girl. For protection, Milak had simply stated, and Mara had contentedly worn it every day of her life, until the night her dreams had been shattered. She didn't remember much after leaving Mark's house, but she did remember ripping it off. Where had her grandmother found it?

"Here." Milak held out the headdress. "My sister will see it and know you as family."

Mara winced and made no move to reach out. "Grandmother, please, try to understand . . ."

Milak interrupted her. "Take it."

With a sigh, Mara did, wrapping the headdress securely in two T-shirts, which she placed in her carryon next to her purse, her pills, her tape recorder and her notepads.

"And the *talliraq*."

"No, I think you better keep it," Mara said quickly, eyeing the talisman warily. It held so many memories, good and bad. The feathers were from the sandhill crane—Mara's own *inua*. "It's not something I'll need on this trip, and . . . well . . . now that you've found it, it would be a shame to chance losing it again, wouldn't it?"

Milak's look was dry and uncompromising. "Take it."

The seconds ticked by, and Mara got the distinct impression her grandmother knew what was going on in her head. Inevitably, she conceded, comforting herself with the excuse that refusing would only further distress the healer. As she tied the wristband on her arm, she experienced a sharp jolt of something that could only be described as homecoming. The *talliraq* was hers and she'd missed wearing it, as some people missed a wedding ring. Mara felt her spirit lift. She smiled. Milak's eyes smiled back. When the healer stood to leave, Mara stayed her with a gentle hand on the healer's shoulder.

"It's better this way," she said softly. Though she couldn't read Milak's eyes, she could feel her grandmother's very real tension. "I'll make sure Mark takes plenty of videotape, okay? And as far as the sacred teachings go, you know I'll be careful, don't you? They're as priceless as your headdress—"

"No," Milak said, abruptly ending her silence. "The headdress is but a symbol of power. The sacred teachings *are* power. They are who we are. Our past, our present and our future. They cannot— *must not* be lost."

Their eyes met. Mara felt herself captured and drawn into her grandmother's thoughts. A fleeting impression of inner conflict and urgency—and then the strange connection was broken, and Milak was turning away.

Mara blinked. What had just happened? For an instant, she'd felt her grandmother's thoughts. Just like during the dance...

"*Maacungaq?*" Mara called out, her voice subdued, confused.

Milak paused and sighed heavily. "You have much to learn."

Although she didn't understand it, Mara felt that she was supposed to. She shook her head. "I'll be careful."

The old healer paused, as if she were about to say something, then shook her head and left the room. Mara let her go, telling herself as she finished packing that she had no choice, and that, hopefully, her grandmother would some day understand that and forgive her granddaughter for loving her too much to let her risk her life.

As she exited the bedroom, she saw her grandmother opening the door to Mark.

"Just checking to see if you've come to your senses," he said, eyeing both the old suitcase in Mara's hand and the old *talliraq* around her wrist. "Guess not." He ignored her glare and glanced down at his watch. "The plane should be here in five minutes. I'll be at the airstrip. Glad to see you without that cane, Milak." He withdrew, and strong footsteps echoed down the old steps, then faded away.

Mara glared after him. "Just checking to see if you've come to your senses," she mimicked, to Milak's open amusement.

Milak crossed to the kitchen. Mara waited a full four minutes, pacing the room, her thoughts both excited and scared.

"Take this tea," Milak said, her voice breaking Mara's stride. "And drink it often."

Mara sniffed at the small plastic bag full of finely crushed leaves. "What is it? I don't recognize this scent."

"An ancient mixture of the women of our family drank during... times of great trial. Now, go."

Was Milak actually pushing her out the door? It did seem as if she were subtly stronger this morning, less despairing and more positive. And, as Mark had pointed out, she *was* walking without the cane. Encouraged by the observations, Mara actually smiled as she hefted her suitcase, placed the tea in her knapsack and kissed her grandmother's cheek. As she turned to leave, she remembered one other thing.

"The letter Grandaunt wrote. Where is it? I'd like to take it with me."

Milak was already shaking her head. "The headdress is all you will need."

"I realize that," Mara said, oblivious to her grandmother's sudden stillness. "But I thought that she could translate it for me. Ever since you told me Sireniski was a dying language, I've been thinking about studying and recording it as a master's thesis. The letter could be one of my most important sources."

All the while she was talking, she was also watching Milak walk to her reindeer-skin suit. Something about her movements gave Mara the impression Milak didn't want her to have the letter. Then Mara realized why: It was the last tangible link her grandmother had with her sister. As Milak pulled the familiar yellowed envelope from the pocket and extracted the letter, Mara almost stopped her. But the opportunity was too good to miss. Even if she did, someday, return to Sireniki, her grandaunt wouldn't be there. As she accepted the letter, Mara sighed.

"Thanks," Mara said. "I'll take care of this, too."

## Chapter Seven

Two days after leaving Twilight, the nine-seat, twin engine Bering Air Navajo Chieftain banked left through the clouds on initial descent toward the Chukotka District city of Provideniya. Mara leaned in close to the oval window, excitedly awaiting her first glimpse of the Asian coastline.

She saw the familiar gray-blue Bering Sea and spotted surf breaking against a sandy beach. Sharp-pointed mountains of gray-colored rock rose from the shore. The sun was a haze-covered ball that didn't look much like it wanted to shine. Mara glanced in another direction and saw concrete-block apartments painted in faded pastels of orange and blue, stair-stepping up the lower flank of the mountain range and dominated by a tall smokestack that belched heavy black fumes into the air.

"And I thought Acapulco was bad! Look at all that smoke! See it, Mara? Over there by the mountains! Ed, come and look. That must be the plant you were reading about."

Mara heard Ed Brandon unbuckle his seat belt. A moment later he was leaning over his wife, Ethel's, shoulders. She'd met the retired couple when she and Mark checked in for the flight. They'd been married for an obviously satisfying thirty-five years, and this was their anniversary present to one another.

"Quite right, dear," Ed commented. "According to my book, that's a coal-fired plant. How the land surrounding Provideniya could have been designated an international park with that plant continually spewing its industrial pollutants into the sky is beyond me."

Just then, Mara heard the distinct click of Mark's seat belt being unbuckled.

"We're almost there. I need to check your declaration form."

Aware of the Brandons' proximity, Mara twisted around, her irritated "Why?" sticking in her throat when she found her eyes scant inches from his crotch. For a second, wild color suffused her cheeks. Then she paled, her gaze dropping hurriedly to her knapsack.

"You know what's on it," she said as she extracted the declaration card and pretended to examine it closely, not reading a thing. "Grandmother's headdress."

"Then you forgot the *talliraq* and the tape recorder." Mark's eyes followed the blush, very narrow, very intent . . . very resigned. "Listen up," he ordered, murmuring something harsh under his breath before hunkering down. "Nothing American is ever outdated by Russian standards. Even old, banged-up tape recorders have value. And while that scrap of leather and feathers may only be sentimental to you, it could be a priceless Siberian Native artifact to the custom officials."

At that, Mara looked up, steeling herself not to cringe away from the set features mere inches from her own. "My *talliraq* is not a priceless artifact."

"I know it, but will they? Can you prove it's yours?" Mara's silence was her answer. "Then if you don't want to be accused of stealing, take the advice you're paying for and *write the damn things down.*"

"Better do as your young man says, dearie." Ethel's head suddenly appeared above Mara's seatback.

Young man? Mara paled, aware of Mark's sharply indrawn breath.

"Ed and I encountered that problem last summer in Egypt, when I forgot to declare the gold cartouche necklace my son gave me years earlier as a Christmas present. You wouldn't believe the ruckus that little oversight caused. If Ed hadn't just happened to have an old photo of me wearing it in his wallet, we wouldn't have had any way to prove it wasn't new."

"Indeed, yes," Ed added. "Russia's not America. You can't just pick up the phone and call your lawyer when something goes wrong."

And that, apparently, was that. Mara watched as Mark stood and returned to his seat. She recorded the two entries, wondering if she would ever do anything right in his eyes, wondering why she was even trying to.

After the plane landed, they disembarked and were herded into an old, decaying building that was, Mara guessed, the terminal. There weren't many locals, and those looked tired and defeated, clutching their meager belongings as if they were afraid to let go. There were a lot of uniformed gray-capped border guards and customs officials. After checking and double-checking their papers, recording who they were visiting with and why and for how long, they passed the party on. When Mark led her out of the oppressive place, Mara sighed in relief.

"Now what?" she asked, stopping just outside to reset her watch to nine o'clock Saturday morning. She guessed the temperature to be around seventy degrees. Just fifty-five minutes earlier it had been noon on Friday in Nome, Alaska, their jumping-off point. Now it was twenty hours later, instead of just one, and she was feeling slightly off kilter.

"We wait for the bus." Mark promptly dropped Mara's suitcase, his camcorder and his duffel bag. Then he plopped down on the ground and stretched out, using his bag as a pillow.

Mara's glance slid uncomfortably away from his long-limbed form. Gazing first left down the gray, rutted and potholed road, then right, she quickly realized there was nothing to see. No airport signs directing travelers in town, no billboards advertising food or lodging, no information of any kind whatsoever.

Somehow, Mara thought as her glance returned to Mark's reclining form, she'd expected Provideniya to be more developed. During dinner in Nome last night, Mark had surprised her by relaxing his tight-lipped restraint. Five thousand people lived in Provideniya, he'd told her. The town served as the administrative center for five outlying villages, one of which was Sireniki. There were a few amenities—a heated saltwater swimming pool and an acupuncture clinic—but there was no taxi service.

"How long until the bus arrives?"

"They don't print schedules, Mara. It'll get here when it gets here."

"I don't suppose we could walk."

"Sure, go ahead. It's only five miles or so. We'll pick you up when we catch up with you."

Mara frowned and settled herself a small distance away. Mark was such an enigma. Handsome and almost considerate one moment, then cold and politely distant the next. From the moment she insisted on paying their dinner bill last night, she'd known their amiable meal was over. He'd been so angry. And then, suddenly... nothing. When she paid for their airline tickets this morning, he'd acted very cool, treating her as if she were a business associate and nothing more.

But then, that was exactly what she was, right?

"Such a depressing atmosphere," Mara heard Ethel comment as Ed set their luggage down next to hers. "Did you see them pull us aside? I almost had a stroke when they started searching our bags."

"You're a doctor, dear, don't exaggerate," Ed commented dryly as he helped Ethel sit on the concrete curb before settling beside her himself.

The gentlemanly courtesy made Mara smile. They seemed to be the best of friends, she thought wistfully, her gaze once again drawn unconsciously to Mark's prone form.

"Any idea when the bus arrives?" Ed asked, once seated.

"I understand they don't print schedules," Mara answered when she realized Mark had no intention of doing so. He wasn't really sleeping, was he? "Excited about your trip?"

"Oh, my, yes!" Ethel rushed to answer. "Ed and I have been planning this vacation ever since Egypt was such a disappointment for us."

"Such a disaster, you mean," Ed mumbled, extracting a thick tourist guide and a yellow marker from his carryon. Mara thought he looked very scholarly when he donned his glasses. "The ambient temperature was an intolerable one hundred and twenty degrees in the shade. And the desertlike floor of the Valley of the Kings..." He shook his head, and Mara had to swallow a smile at his affronted expression. "Well, suffice it to say we found the taking of a simple breath exceedingly difficult indeed."

"Indeed," Ethel repeated, her blue eyes teasing her husband and twinkling at Mara's swallowed amusement. "Before Ed retired three years ago, he was a professor of world history. I don't think he's quite figured out yet that he's not lecturing anymore."

Mara smiled softly. "I just graduated a few weeks ago."

"You did? Well, congratulations! Your parents must be very proud. I know we were when our son, Troy, graduated."

"Yes, indeed," Ed added, saving Mara from having to comment on her parentless state. "We were proud *and* relieved. For a while there, we weren't sure he would."

"Now, Ed, don't start," Ethel admonished him. "What was your subject?"

"Alaskan Native anthropology, with a minor in Russian."

"I don't suppose," Ed asked, looking up from his book, "that you'd be interested in translating some documents for a colleague of mine, would you? He would, of course, compensate you for your efforts."

"As a matter of fact, that's how I earn money for school. Since Gorbachev's *glasnost,* translating is big business. You wouldn't believe the number of Alaskans seeking to do business in the Russian Far East."

"Sounds like you've got quite a head on your shoulders, young lady." Ed sighed. "Too bad our son doesn't have more of your initiative."

*"Ed."* Ethel stared hard at her husband, then turned to Mara. "What are you going to do with your degree?"

"I'm planning to go for my master's. I'm especially interested in studying the cultural ties between Siberian and Alaskan Yup'ik Eskimos."

"You're Yup'ik, then." Ed's question was more a statement. Mara nodded.

"What cultural ties?" Ethel asked.

"Well, it's all very exciting." Mara laughed, enjoying their interest. "Back before the turn of the century and up until 1948, Alaskan and Siberian Yup'ik traded goods and services across the Bering Strait. I don't know if you know, but during winter, the Bering Strait can actually be crossed by dog sled."

"No, I had no idea," Ethel commented.

"Makes sense," Ed replied. "Seeing it's only a fifty-five-minute flight from Nome."

"What happened in 1948?"

"The Cold War. One day Stalin closed the entire region for national-security purposes and forbade the Yup'ik to cross the Bering Stait. Hundreds were stranded in Alaska, cut off from their families, unable to return home."

"What an incredible story," Ethel murmured. "And how awful for those poor people."

Mara nodded. "Stalin's decree created two distinct cultures where there was once only one. I want to study how they've diverged during the forty-odd years they've been separated, especially now that I know my grandmother was one of them."

"She was?" Ethel asked.

"Yes. I just found out a few days ago, when this letter arrived." Unzipping her knapsack, Mara laid aside the T-shirt-wrapped headdress, tape recorder and plastic bag of tea before extracting the single white sheet of stationery. "It's from her sister, my grandaunt."

"My goodness!" Ethel exclaimed. "I can't imagine how your grandmother must have felt when she received it."

"May I see that letter?"

"Sure." Mara handed it to Ed, who studied it with obvious interest.

"Under the circumstances," Ethel said, breaking the pensive silence that had fallen over the trio, "I would have thought your grandmother would be here with you."

For a brief moment, fresh guilt assailed Mara. Then she sighed, reminding herself that she hadn't had any choice. "Physically she wasn't up to it. Grandmother's the healer in my village. People depend on her a lot, and not just for medical advice. She heads our council of elders for example—she's a symbol, really, of our past and our present, and according to Mark, her will is basically what's holding the village together. Unfortunately, I'm not sure what's holding *her* together anymore. She's ninety-two. And she did insist on coming, but I, well, I just couldn't risk it."

Ethel reached over and patted Mara's hand sympathetically. "It's hard to see our loved ones age, isn't it? But it's all part of the wonderful cycle of life. They care for us, then we care for them."

Mara nodded, her expression sad. She loved her grandmother so very much. The healer was the only stability Mara had ever had in her life. Her mother had died in childbirth, her father in a hunting accident. Even Mark had turned away from her. It pained her to think that she might not even have an opportunity to get to know the grandaunt she'd just discovered she had.

Ed looked up from the letter. "This doesn't look like any Russian I've ever seen."

"That's because it isn't," Mara replied. "My grandmother and her sister speak Sireniski, a language very different from my own Yup'ik. One of the things I'd like to do while I'm here is record as

much of the language being spoken as I can. I'd like for it to survive, even if only on tape and in my thesis."

"Absolutely," Ed commented supportively.

"And to think Ed and I had assumed this was a little getaway for
you and your young man," Ethel divulged with a self-conscious
laugh.

Mara's smile faltered. A little getaway? Her young man? She
glanced over at Mark, but he was still pretending to sleep. Or was
he?

"Mark's here because I need to get to Sireniki as fast as possible and he knows the area."

"Why? Has he found relatives here, as well?" Ethel asked.

"No, but he operates a hunting and fishing business here during the summer."

"So he knows the way to..." Ethel paused. "How did you pro-
nounce it?"

"Sireniki."

"Yes, to Sireniki. Why do you have to get there so fast?"

"Grandmother says her sister's dying."

"Oh, dear," Ethel murmured sympathetically. "How old is
she?"

"According to my grandmother's memory, she's one hundred
and two."

"Incredible. Think about what she must have experienced during all that time."

"If she were an American, she'd have lived through roughly half
of our history," Ed remarked absently, his attention still on the
letter.

"She's not suffering, is she? I do hope not. Small villages rarely
have adequate medical provisions."

"Grandaunt's a healer, too," Mara volunteered, though the
thought about the elder woman's circumstances had crossed her
own mind, as well. "And if she's anything like my grandmother,
she'll know what to prepare to relieve any discomfort she might be
experiencing."

Mark absently listened to the conversation as he lay resting, his
concentration drawn to the soft tonalities of Mara's voice, rather
than the content of her words. He realized he'd been doing that a
lot lately: listening to her voice, looking at her face, watching her
body.

The latter thought set loose the memory of her dance Wednesday night. *Naniq* flames flickering, faces held in rapt attention—

especially his, much to Jacob's amusement. Warm, welcoming smells of food and seal oil and drum sounds that filtered into every corner of the *qasgiq,* creating a sense of place and community and history that had soaked through even his progress-oriented mindset, soaked through high-tech court shoes and sealskin mukluks, white *kuspuks* and a certain silk blouse, turning everything redorange and hazy with an ancient and reverent excitement.

Mark knew that Mara had caused that excitement, even as she was unconsciously doing now for Ethel, who sat enthralled by Mara's recounting of herbal remedies. How long she'd danced, he couldn't remember, but her swaying, sensual movements were etched in his mind, like those of a long-ago night when despair had weakened resolve and resistance had seemed impossible. She'd painted pictures without words, calling to a soul he'd thought he'd lost, calling to every watching person. For days afterward, the villagers had talked of her dance. He had remained silent, as always, trying within himself to understand what it was about Mara that had mesmerized the villagers and all but brought him to his knees.

He stirred, uncomfortable. Mara had successfully called forth a response from the villagers that they usually reserved for Milak. He didn't pretend to understand it, he just knew what he'd seen and what he'd felt. He didn't pretend to understand how a young woman whose ties with her village were loose and whose future included a fast-growing business and a master's degree could have accomplished such a feat. But she had. Somehow, even if it was only for a moment out of time, Mara Anvik had unknowingly and unconsciously captured his people's collective imagination. He'd felt it in the air, in the tense and excited expressions on every spectator's face.

He'd envied her. For a moment, maybe two. Then he'd discarded the emotion as useless.

Mara had had no idea what she'd achieved. But he did, and that, at least, he could build on. Somehow, her dancing had succeeded where years of his own logic-driven appeals to his fellow villagers had failed. He'd had no choice but to reevaluate his tactics, and in so doing had painfully acknowledged that reason alone, while clear and straightforward, would not sway his people to relinquish the past and grasp the future. He'd reluctantly concluded that he needed to better understand this bond, this intangible cord, that seemed to flow through him, whether he wanted it to or not, to connect him with his people.

But how? How was he supposed to understand something so removed from the realm of cool reason? Arousal he understood. And loss and pain and fear and hurt and despair. But this was different. This was outside his experience.

Years of distancing had given him a certain edge, an edge he needed, an edge he knew everyone, including Mara, felt. He'd clung to that distance since her reappearance in his life, instinct telling him that without it he'd be vulnerable. He didn't want to need. Before Mara's arrival, he hadn't minded the dawn of each new day, even though he hadn't exactly looked forward to it. Life was smooth, untroubled, physically exhausting at times, but contentedly uncomplicated.

Not anymore. Now his life seemed one big unknown. He woke up thinking of Mara, went to sleep thinking of Mara, even daydreamed of Mara. When she'd offered him this deal and he'd accepted, he'd done so as a form of silent compensation for the pain of his rejection, but he was becoming downright uncomfortable with the rising cost of that compensation.

Mark stirred. He wasn't used to such self-evaluation. Four years ago he'd set himself on a steady course, and not once had he thought to question the validity of his choices.

But he was questioning them now. He was questioning a lot of things.

"In my opinion," Ed was commenting when Mark tuned in again, "I'd say you should complete the master's degree, but then continue on and apply your results toward a doctorate."

Abruptly Mark sat up. "You're kidding."

"A doctorate?" Mara asked at the same time, shooting Mark a warning glance.

"Indeed, yes," Ed commented, not missing a beat at Mark's sudden wakefulness. "From my own experience as an adviser to many prospective doctoral candidates, I believe your project's conclusions could reach beyond the obvious benefits to our historical knowledge and make it possible for your people to enjoy a more prosperous future."

"No offense, Professor," Mark cut in, the bitter edge of cynicism in his voice, "but there's only one way for our people to enjoy a more prosperous future, and it doesn't have a damn thing to do with studying cultural ties or wasting resources preserving a language that's as good as dead."

"Mark," Mara interjected angrily.

He ignored her. "Our people need to move into the future, and we need to do it now. Technology's the key, and Mara knows it. Milak, too, I'd bet. Studying the past won't cut it. Recording a dying language for posterity won't help. Neither will meditating and all that herbal holistic health stuff our people have been practicing for ages and Ethel's so gung ho about. If Mara wants to do something significant for our people, then she should concentrate on creating new ties. Forget the old ones. It's as simple as that."

Ed had pulled off his glasses during Mark's impassioned speech and was absently cleaning the lenses as he listened. Mara could see he wasn't offended by Mark's comments, but rather was enjoying what to him was a debate.

Mara knew right off that Mark wasn't debating. Eyes steely bright, he believed one hundred percent in what he'd just said. There were no sides to this issue. According to him, technology was their people's only chance at a cohesive future, and old ties—like their former friendship—were worse than useless.

Mixed feelings surged through her. On the one hand, she despaired because she couldn't blame him for his intractable philosophy. If Native villages had easily accessible and modern health care, the crash would not have happened. And with modern tracking equipment, Jacob and his sister-in-law would have been located before Lia's death and before Jacob had all but frozen to death.

Yet, on the other hand, Mara felt a compelling impulse to help him understand what he was missing. Technology *was* an answer, but it wasn't the *only* answer. And if she could just make him see that, then she would feel she'd accomplished something, at least.

But she didn't know how, didn't even know why it was so important that she try.

"I've made a career of understanding the results of progress in one form or another," Ed began. "And while the drive for technology has, for most countries, fueled their current success—take Japan, for example—it hasn't come without grave sacrifices. Believe me when I say that only through understanding the past, good and bad, getting it into a proper context and then seeing the big picture, does a society ever progress. And then it can't be done alone. Cause and effect, you know. No one lives in a vacuum. Everything must balance."

Mark was saved from needing to comment by a distant rumbling proclaiming the arrival of the bus. He stood to watch the familiar beat-up old red clunker roll to a stop in front of the terminal.

After forty-five minutes of the Brandons' oohs and ahs over Mara and her bright, promising future, Mark was feeling a definite need to move, to do something physical, to get away from all that nauseating optimism. But he couldn't. As usual, space in the bus was standing room only.

Mark found himself wedged between Mara and Ethel. He let out a long-suffering sigh and just managed to swallow several very colorful curses as the bus lurched away from the curb, propelling Mara against him.

She felt soft, even though she was trying damn hard to be stiff as a board. Strands of her hair brushed across his cheek. The flowery aroma brought a swift, primitive reaction from Mark's body that made him swear under his breath with every pothole. He shifted, hoping to put some small distance between him and the woman centered in his thoughts, but it didn't work. Mara's downturned face was the color of the bus when they arrived.

The passengers disembarked, finally creating space to move, which Mark quickly did, a dull flush suffusing his own cheeks. He picked up his duffel and camcorder, hoping his arousal would subside to a tolerable level. He didn't expect it to fade away completely. Not anymore. Not since last Tuesday, when he'd opened the door on his memories.

"Where are you two staying?" Ed was handing Mara a slip of paper with their Los Angeles address when Mark disembarked, the duffel bag strategically positioned in front of him.

"I don't know. Where are you and Ed—"

Mark quickly cut her off. "We're staying with friends of mine." There wasn't a chance in hell that he was going to spend the rest of the damn day, and possibly the night, plagued by this too-happy, too-interested pair.

"We're at the hotel down the street," said Ethel. "See it?"

Mark didn't even look. "Yeah, well, have a good vacation." He nudged a startled Mara in the opposite direction. "We need to get going. Mara's grandaunt, you understand . . ."

"Oh, of course." Ethel gave Mara a quick hug. Ed shook Mark's hand. "Take care of yourselves," Ethel called as they took off down the street. "Bye!"

For a good five minutes, Mark walked like a man possessed, his subconscious guiding him down the foreign yet familiar streets toward the north end of town. Playing tour guide didn't occur to him. Slowing down didn't occur to him, either, until he heard Mara's soft puffs of exertion. He flicked his gaze sideways, taking in the determined chin, the steely defiance that telegraphed that she'd rather collapse than admit she couldn't keep up.

He slowed down. She was so beautiful. And had tasted so sweet. *Damn.* Hadn't he paid his dues? Didn't he have enough to deal with? His job was to get Mara to Sireniki, not to get Mara into bed. Once again his glance swept over her. She'd felt his arousal, he was certain of it. But he very much doubted she would comment. And he knew for damn sure *he* wasn't going to.

Mara was busy concentrating on her surroundings. Anything was better than concentrating on Mark. There was no doubt in her mind that he had been aroused. She remembered that feeling. It was burned in her mind, along with everything else that had ever occurred between them. What she didn't understand—and knew she would never ask about—was why he'd been aroused at all. In the part of her heart that was safe and secure, hidden away from the concerns of her everyday life, she knew what she was hoping the answer would be—and it literally terrified her. Shaking her head, she determinedly focused on the city before her.

The main street was busy. Military transport vehicles were everywhere, as was the evidence of the old Soviet bureaucracy in the peeling buildings of the Ministry of Culture and the Ministry of Trade. There were women carrying drawstring shopping bags with bread and fruit. Red-cheeked children played tag. The predominant color in the city seemed to be gray.

People stared at them, some whispering comments to friends, others actually stopping to say hello and to welcome them to their city. Surprised at first, Mara happily responded, interpreting for Mark when necessary and listening to their stories and answering their questions about her life in Alaska.

"Mind telling me where we're going?" Mara asked after they started on their way again.

"The Vizdehod garage. It's at the edge of town. If we're lucky and Riabov's here, we might get him to run us out to Sireniki."

"Today? Right now?"

"Don't get too excited," Mark cautioned her. "If he's not there, we'll likely be stuck waiting for him to get back. And before you ask, that could be a while. It all depends on where he is and what he's doing."

"We haven't got a while," Mara said anxiously. "A day might be okay. At least then I could call the village and have someone relay the news that I'm coming. But any longer is out of the question. If Mr. Vizdehod can't take us, you'll just have to find some-one else."

He might have smiled if she hadn't ended her comment with an order. "His name isn't Vizdehod, it's Riabov. Oleg Mikhailovich Riabov, and he runs the Vizdehod garage as the chauffeur for Provideniya's high-ranking government personnel."

"And you think he'll take us to my grandaunt?"

"If there's room, yes. A Vizdehod can carry up to eight people."

Mara blinked. "It's a vehicle?"

"More like a cross between a minivan and a tank." Spotting the familiar building, Mark increased his pace. If everything worked out, he could conceivably be through with his end of the deal in a matter of hours.

Mara entered a few steps behind Mark and watched him being greeted by a thin, approximately fifty-year-old man with an easy smile. Riabov told them he was set to return a group of local government officials to their village of New Chaplino the following morning. If they wished, they could ride along. Then he invited them to spend the night.

Mark smiled. At least something was going in his favor.

## Chapter Eight

Mara nibbled on the pastry known as piroshki, forcing herself to relax. She told herself that everything that could be done had been done. Mark had certainly upheld his end of their deal: He'd helped her avoid what might have become a very uncomfortable customs situation, guided her into town, arranged for their transportation to Sireniki and even helped her secure a telephone to get a message to her grandaunt. Honestly, Mara thought as she smiled at Riabov's wife, Natasha, she had nothing to complain about. They even had a free place to sleep.

Situated across from a monolithic concrete building known as the House of Culture, the Riabov apartment reflected the couple's passion for the wilderness beyond Provideniya's borders. Reindeer antlers served as a coatrack. Dried salt fish hung from a string in front of their kitchen window. A bowl of whale muktuk—cut into tiny slivers for them to nibble on—sat on the rectangular dinette next to another bowl filled with mushrooms Natasha had gathered from the mountains behind town.

"You like the piroshki?" Natasha asked as she handed Mara the bowl containing the Russian summer salad she'd made.

"If you could somehow market these in Fairbanks, McDonald's would probably go out of business," she replied in English, accepting the bowl and ladling out the smallest portion she could without offending the square-bodied woman with the kind but weary eyes. Natasha and Riabov had been so gracious. But she really wasn't hungry, and every time she looked around the small apartment, she knew why: The Riabovs' apartment was a one-bedroom, with a convertible sleeper couch in the living room for their daughter when she came to visit from Magadan.

The fact that there were four people didn't seem to bother anyone but her.

Natasha had insisted everyone speak English, not only for Mark's sake, but also because she and Riabov needed practice. She'd indicated earlier that with the new openness, tourism in Provideniya was a fledgling but growing industry. She and Riabov had agreed that if they were ever to take advantage of it, they would need to speak English much better than they presently did.

Riabov chuckled. "Is that your home, Fairbanks?"

"That's where I attend the university," Mara answered, taking a bite of the beet-and-potato salad. Her glance avoided Mark's. Neither of them had mentioned the incident on the bus. Yet she had only to look at him, or he at her, to remember. "My home is Twilight."

"Ah, yes, I understand." Riabov nodded vigorously, giving his wife's hand a tight squeeze which she returned. "In Provideniya, there is no fighting. We have food. We have work. We have peace. So, we stay. But our home is Moscow."

"Eat," Natasha ordered smilingly, handing Mara more whale muktuk. "You are bird. You must eat."

Mara ate and prayed she wouldn't throw up. Her nervousness was distressing—all the more so because she had to work so hard not to show it.

"How long are you being here?" Natasha asked as she passed mushrooms to Mark.

"At most a couple of days," Mark began.

"That depends on my grandaunt," Mara said at the same time.

Natasha shrugged, as if their uncertainty were normal, though Mara witnessed the quick curious glance she exchanged with her husband. "Mark, you come again for work?"

"Starting in late July and running every third week through October."

"Much work," Riabov commented, stuffing a mushroom into his mouth. "Much money, too, eh?"

"Ten thousand a head," he answered. "This first group wants to hunt *medavedtee.*"

"Brown bear, good meat," Natasha commented as she handed Mara the bowl of mushrooms.

"Ten thousand dollars?" Distracted, Mara accepted the bowl. "For a *week?*"

"Per person," Mark added, enjoying the astonishment on her face. At least now Mara would know she wasn't the only successful entrepreneur. "Arrangements aren't cheap. There are permits, flights, helicopters, food and local guides. And that doesn't take into account the instability of the Russian ruble. The way things have been going lately, ten thousand might not be enough."

At this Natasha joined in. "One month before, we see old friend. His name is Alexander Zorachova. Twenty years he work to save one hundred thousand rubles. He wish to build home for family in Ukraine and buy car. Two days back, I see him. He tell me he pay ninety-five thousand rubles to send family to Ukraine. Twenty years' work, gone. No house, no car, no dream. He tell me same house in Ukraine cost one million rubles, and car, five hundred thousand. He is forty. He must begin again."

"So you see why we stay here and we practice English," Riabov continued, breaking the momentary silence that had fallen. "If we have rich American friend like Mark, we can survive, because we earn dollars, not rubles."

*Rich American friend?* The sardonic look Mark threw her indicated he knew just what she was thinking.

After that, dinner broke up. Mara helped Natasha with the dishes while Mark showed Riabov his camcorder. Too soon, however, it was past eleven, and the Riabovs' bedtime. That the couple had assumed that *they* were a couple was obvious. Mara caught Mark's narrowed glance, and the slight but noticeable shake of his head. She got the message that she wasn't to say anything that might cause the couple embarrassment.

"Good night," Natasha said, entering her bedroom.

"Good night," Mara replied.

The door closed. Immediately, tension filled the small living room. Forcing herself to move, Mara headed across the room to where Natasha had stashed her suitcase behind the sleeper couch. If only she were more sophisticated, Mara wished sadly. Then she would no doubt be able to shrug this situation off. Only she wasn't sophisticated. Mara knew that if she could somehow get away with it, she'd sleep in the bathtub fully clothed. Just thinking about her tentative response during their kiss on the knoll and then earlier today, her heart's pounding when she'd felt his rigid arousal... She let out a deep, slow breath, then squatted next to her suitcase and snapped open the two locks. After all these years, could it be possible? Did she still want Mark?

From his seat at the dinette, Mark surveyed Mara. He watched her pull out a white T-shirt and a small toiletry case, which she nervously unzipped, stuffing what looked like a pair of panties inside. Her movements were secretive and intrinsically feminine, shy gestures made by a woman uneasy with the everyday intimacies of sexual relationships. Or, he decided grimly, a woman uncomfortable with a particular man.

"Didn't you even stop to think," he burst out, startling Mara into looking up, "what you were letting yourself in for when you offered me this deal?"

Mara felt her cheeks grow hot. "Of course I did," she murmured defensively. "But you were there when Grandmother came out of the house. You saw the way she was leaning on that cane. She looked ready to fall down at any moment." Her voice clouded with emotion. "I didn't have a choice."

He snorted. "I know Ed and Ethel swallowed that line, but don't expect me to. Face it, Mara. You chose to interfere in your grandmother's life. It's no one's fault but your own if you can't live with the consequences." His eyes showed the bitterness of personal experience. "There's always a choice."

Mara caught her lower lip in her teeth and stared at him. "You're not being fair," she murmured, dropping a blurred gaze to her belongings, unaware of the pained expression that pinched Mark's already strained features as she held the nightshirt up against her as she'd once held his sheets.

If he said anything more, Mara knew, she would find somewhere else to sleep tonight. She didn't know where she'd go, but she knew she would go. Dropping the lid, she snapped shut the locks, stood, and started silently toward the bathroom.

Mark's gaze narrowed. "Funny, isn't it," he offered with deliberate carelessness, "how your grandmother's so weak, can hardly walk upright, yet she was able to pound that drum for your entire dance the other night without missing a single beat? How long was it? Ten minutes? Fifteen?"

Mara turned and eyed him warily. "I don't know." She'd been so wrapped up in the dance, in the beat, in the astonishing connection with her grandmother's thoughts, that she hadn't taken note of the time. "What are you trying to say? That Grandmother's not as ill as she's making out?"

Exactly. Hearing Mara put it into words, Mark abruptly realized that was exactly what he'd concluded. Milak had waited until this past week to reveal her knowledge of that night four years ago. Why? What was she hoping to gain?

Mark thought about the fine trembling of the old healer's hands, the desperate tension she'd emitted during the two times he'd been in her house since last week. Milak was afraid of something, something she couldn't even tell Mara about.

An oddly primitive warning sounded in his brain. What in the hell could be that bad?

"What you're thinking doesn't make any sense," Mara ventured defensively as she watched thoughts chase their way across Mark's momentarily open features. "The sister she hasn't seen in forty-plus years is dying, remember? This would have been their only chance to meet. If I were ninety-two and had an overly anxious granddaughter, I would have been acting fit and healthy. I would have been trying to make my granddaughter believe I'm capable of making the trip. Grandmother was completely worn out when I came home after you..." She trailed off abruptly. She'd been about to say "after you kissed me." Shifting gears, she picked her way carefully through the admission.

"After you agreed to my proposal. I even had to help her into bed, something she's never asked me to do for her before."

He stood and crossed to the window, looking out at the few late-night lights. "Circumstances can cause people to do a lot of strange things, Mara." He chose his words carefully. "Actions can be deceiving."

Mara searched his stark profile, noting his tense body, his taut expression, his hard, glittering eyes. She sensed his cautious words held a deeper meaning, sensed that he was barely holding some strong emotion in check.

Her throat tightened in response. "Grandmother would never lie to me. She's a healer. She believes that truth heals and that lies hurt."

Mark almost smiled, but the effort would have cost him his hard-won control. He turned, and his gaze swept over her. Everything she felt, the bewilderment, the distress, and something else, something he'd never thought to see again, showed on her face. He drew in a sharp breath. "Then I guess the only thing you need to worry about is separating the truths from the lies."

Mara nodded slowly. What about her illness? Was willful omission considered a lie? Wouldn't such a truth hurt her grandmother?

Mark watched her face, wondering about the pain etched briefly on her soft features. "Not quite so black-and-white, is it?"

"No, I guess it's not. Since coming back home, I'm fast getting to the point where I don't know what to believe anymore."

"Join the club, Mara," Mark murmured, and turned to face the window again. "Join the club."

Mara was turning away when, without thinking how it would sound, she found herself asking, "What do you believe in?"

"What makes you think I have beliefs?"

The loneliness inherent in his statement stunned her. "Everyone believes in something. Even nothing is something."

He studied her quietly for a moment, then decided it wouldn't hurt him to answer. "I believe in myself. Anything else is asking for trouble."

"But what about your *inua?*"

"That's the same thing, Mara. My *inua is* me. It's who I am." He turned away. "Now, if you're done with your questions, I'd suggest you go and take that bath. And don't take all night. It's late. We've got an early start tomorrow morning."

"All right," Mara whispered, then turned toward the bathroom. She wondered if he'd recognized the contradiction in his words just then. Mark had said he didn't have any beliefs. How, then, could he believe in a spirit guide? She'd flicked on the bathroom light and was closing the door when she heard him speak.

"Oh, and Mara?"

She paused, but didn't turn around.

"Don't get any weird ideas about sleeping in the damn bathroom."

When she was gone, Mark found that he was shaking. He heard the sound of running water, muted by the closed doors, and tried to stop his body's surging physical reaction to the mental images of her slick silhouette, wet from the bathwater. Burning up, he unbuttoned his shirt, cursing under his breath as he jerked it loose from his jeans. Then he crossed the room and converted the couch into the sleeper, using the small exertion as a release for his tension. Only it didn't work. Four years of voluntary abstinence could only be eased in one way—and that way was completely out of the question.

He had just shut off the lights when he heard the bathroom light switch then the creak of the door opening. He told himself not to look, but he did anyway. In the dim light of the moon shining in through the living-room window, he could see she was wearing the white nightshirt. Her hair was damp and straight, and the sight of her bare legs and thighs made his stomach clench as the memories crowded in on him. Years earlier he had held the girl, and had touched the soft, rounded contours of breasts and hips not yet fully matured. But she was all woman now, and the physical reality, the obvious womanliness that emanated from feminine curves and shadows, overpowered him.

For a moment, he simply stared as she moved to the kitchenette and poured herself a cup of tea. Then he left the window and headed for the dinette, unaware of her silent gasp.

"Y-you want some of Grandmother's tea?"

For his own sanity, he never let his glance waver lower than her downturned face, with its pale skin and tight expression. "Why not?"

Mara's hands trembled as she poured a second cup. She turned, and her gaze riveted on Mark's chest. His flannel shirt was completely unbuttoned, exposing smooth, muscled chest to her view. He looked frighteningly masculine. Like her worst nightmares, her most secret dreams. How could he be so cruel? To taunt her so heartlessly one minute and tempt her so blatantly the next? Unable to stop, her eyes scanned his chest, comparing new impressions against old and finding no flaws, only the same bronzed perfection. For several unwittingly revealing seconds she did this. Then, finally, she remembered the cup in her hand.

Mark couldn't believe it. After all these years. After all that he'd done . . . and said . . . and all he *hadn't* said . . . Was it possible?

"Here. Grandmother says it's a great stress reducer."

Mark watched as she guided the cup to her mouth. He slowly did the same. "Doesn't taste like any miracle drug to me."

Mara bristled and looked up, shocked to realize his gaze was fixed intently on her lips. Against her will, her heart started a heavy pounding. "Did anybody ever tell you that you could really use an attitude adjustment?"

"Yes."

"Really?" Mara felt heat flush her cheeks at his continued scrutiny. "Who was that brave? Or should I say that stupid?"

"Depends on who you're talking about—Jacob or you," he replied dryly.

Her face really flamed then, as the liquid burned hotly down her throat. At the very least, it gave her something to think about besides Mark's naked chest and strange behavior.

"Thanks," Mark said, passing back the cup. "Now, let's go to bed."

She choked. "Wh-what?"

"Let's go to bed."

"But I thought you said..."

In the sudden, ringing silence in the room, Mark's entire body stiffened. Time seemed to hang suspended as he gazed down at Mara, noting the subtle tremors racking her slender body. Very softly, very deliberately, he reached out one long finger and traced the ribbed and rounded collar of her nightshirt. Nothing in the world could have stopped him. He didn't touch her skin. He'd given his word and he meant it. Yet he needed to know—was willing to torture himself to find out—if the desire he'd seen earlier and again just now was real.

Mara's immediate urge was to run. A million questions crowded her mind, competing for space with the primitive, feminine terror that he was playing with her. That he should tease her like this was offensive. He didn't want her, never had. Why was he doing this? More important, why wasn't she backing away?

"Mark..."

She bit her lip, unnerved by his quiet, watchful gaze, her fingers unconsciously worrying the *talliraq*. When his gaze dropped, then darted back up to hers, something in it made her cringe and flush all at once. She'd never before felt this elemental tension that filled the air between them with all of the awesome power of an arctic blizzard.

"Mark..." she repeated softly. His eyes flashed wildly, but she didn't understand the bleak expression that was the aftermath.

"Damn it, Mara. How could you?"

"How could I...what?" she mouthed, when she realized her throat was once again completely dry.

Mark watched her for another second, then stepped back, intentionally disrupting the darkened intimacy that had built between them.

"Never mind. Just go to bed."

"But I don't understand. What just happened? Why did you—?"

"Do you have to analyze everything? I'm a man. When a semi-naked woman parades herself—"

Mara gasped. "I did not!"

"Sure looks like that from my angle."

His eyes dropped to her chest. And lingered. Heat surged into her breasts, warming them like spring sun after a cold winter. They felt full and heavy and somehow renewed. Her nipples ached.

The reaction both awed and terrified Mara, for it explained so many of her darkest fears. She wasn't frigid. Her body could respond, despite her psychological resistance. Only Wally could never be the catalyst. Mark was, had always been, maybe would always be.

Mara didn't want to find out, couldn't risk finding out. She would control herself, had to. And so did he, for she sensed, astoundingly, that Mark was equally vulnerable.

Mark yanked his eyes toward the bed, and without giving her a chance to comment he picked her up and carried her there. Then he swept aside the blankets, plopped her down and covered her up. "Stay put. We have a long day ahead of us tomorrow, and I don't feel like fighting about who takes the floor."

Mara nodded, too dismayed to do anything but stare at him, too uncomfortably aware of the residual warmth of his arms and hands on her bare thighs. His deliberately inciting comment about her supposed parading of herself barely merited a moment's consideration. She understood now. He wanted to keep her away. If he only knew. Though she couldn't deny her desire for him, she didn't have to act on it. As he'd said, "there's always a choice." And her choice was to do nothing. They were still poles apart, their futures headed in opposing directions. And even if that weren't the case, there was still her illness to consider.

When she focused on him again, he was ensconced in the sleeping bag he must have known was stored in the closet, his clothes strewn in an angry heap beside his shoes. She flushed, noticing the discarded white briefs. A pervasive warmth was spreading through her body, drawing the tension from her limbs. For an instant she panicked. Then she remembered: Grandmother's tea.

"Mark."

"Go to sleep, Mara."

"Do you have any idea how long it takes to get to Sireniki?"

Great, Mark thought. Didn't she even have enough sense to know when to shut up? "No. Besides, it's Riabov's Vizdehod. He knows the area. Why didn't you ask him earlier?"

"I should have, but it didn't occur to me till just now." She turned to lie flat on her stomach, head nestled into the pillow. She felt even warmer, even more relaxed. And talkative.

"Mark?"

"*What?*"

"Do you think we'll get there in time?"

"Maybe."

"What if we don't?"

"Don't think about it."

"I can't help it. You were right. I feel guilty. Grandmother was so hurt."

He listened to her soft sniffling and quelled an urge to hold her tight. "Hurt isn't dead," Mark said bluntly. "She'll survive."

"Like you?" Her breath caught. She hadn't meant to ask that.

Mark spoke after a silent moment had passed. "Everybody dies, Mara. Some sooner than others. No big deal. Now get some sleep."

Mara tried to sleep. For a half hour, she tried, but Mark's fatalistic words kept her awake. Finally, in desperation, she deliberately focused, instead, on her grandmother.

Was the healer meditating? Given the time difference, Mara guessed it would be early morning at home. As Mara pictured her grandmother's serene black eyes, her long, flowing white hair, her gentle, capable hands and wiry little body, she slowly began to relax. The disturbing revelations of the day and evening faded, along with the unfamiliar apartment and her consciousness of Mark. Her mind's frenzied pace slowed, and for a while she drifted, seemingly high in the sky, as her *inua*, Qucillgaq, the Sandhill Crane, flew back across the Bering Sea to Nelson Island and her own village of Twilight. She saw the familiar house, felt the warmth of the already sunny June day and saw her grandmother seated on her favorite fur rug, meditating, as she had guessed. A photo of herself lay in her grandmother's hands, and her grandmother's face bore an expression of such desperate fear that Mara's heart beat heavily with startled anguish and concern.

Instinctively she reached out to her grandmother, and felt the healer's pain flow into her. At first Mara didn't know how to handle it, for it was as if a thousand voices were crowding in on her, a thousand frustrated cries of fear and helplessness. She was unable to retreat, unable to protect her mind, unable even to absorb the message behind the wall of heightened emotion. There was desperation. There was fear. There was yearning. And then, as if her grandmother had gathered her strength, Mara was deliberately pushed away, forced out of the link.

Mara blinked and lay still, listening to Mark's slow, rhythmic breaths, listening to her own erratic counterpoint. What had happened? She didn't question the images she'd seen or the validity of her communication with her grandmother. Both had been shocking and more than a little bit frightening, but that didn't make them any less real. *What was going on?*

Mara had always considered her grandmother's abilities as a healer special, and she had always believed it was those special abilities that allowed her to communicate with her granddaughter, not the other way around.

Obviously Mara had thought wrong. If she could do it—and she just had—so could anyone, probably. Even Mark. Just the thought of Mark being able to read her innermost thoughts made Mara extremely uneasy. Uncomfortable, she shifted beneath the covers.

What had her grandmother been thinking about that could have produced such fear, such yearning? And why wasn't she supposed to know about it? Her grandmother was hiding something. The question of what that something was kept her up a long time.

## Chapter Nine

Mark woke up irritable as hell. Fighting a one-sided desire had been hard enough. Now that he knew Mara wanted him, too, it would be damn near impossible not to touch her. As he stuffed yesterday's clothes into his duffel bag, he knew he should cut her loose. It certainly would be simple enough. All he had to do was cup those luscious breasts, and their deal would be off. Hell, he didn't even have to go that far.

With a frustrated grunt, he zipped shut his duffel bag and carried it to the door, where the rest of their belongings lay gathered. So what was he waiting for? Why was he hesitating, standing silently by as Mara hugged Natasha goodbye? Needing to do something, he pulled his denim jacket from the peg by the door and shrugged it on. He should have finished it last night. She'd wanted him. It would have been so easy.

It could still be easy. Just one kiss ...

The thought was tempting—so tempting, in fact, that he actually shuddered. But that was all he did, and Natasha, who had crossed the room to hug him, mothered him with a gentle command to button up. Mark nodded absently, catching Mara's gaze as she turned back briefly to wave.

Seconds ticked by. She wanted him, all right, Mark observed, watching as she blushed and bit her lower lip. But just as her eyes were telegraphing to him to keep his distance, he was reluctantly deciding against it.

He needed information. Unfortunately for them both, Mara was his only source. Some bond had drawn his people together during the Dance of the Healer, and Mara had been the catalyst. Whatever it was, he'd already decided that he needed to understand it better if he was ever to convince his people of the need to embrace *kass'aq* technology. He figured a summer of frustration was a small price to pay for a people's future.

So, he wouldn't take the easy out. He would instead use today, and every remaining day of the summer, as a research project. And Mara would be his subject. His mouth twisted wryly. How ironic, he thought as he watched Mara don her jacket. If she only knew.

After thanking Natasha for her hospitality, Mara walked between Riabov and Mark through the almost empty morning streets to the Vizdehod garage. She spotted a half-dozen men milling about, and after a short round of introductions, Riabov stashed their luggage and opened the rear of an olive-green vehicle. It had wide treads that revolved around a dozen wheels and did, indeed, look like a cross between a minivan and a tank, Mara acknowledged as she cautiously descended after the others into a dark compartment lined with two wooden benches. Riabov climbed into the cockpit at the front and donned a pair of noise mufflers. As the seven big men settled down, four on one side, three on the other, Mara looked askance at the small bench space that remained. Even if she scooted to the very edge, she wouldn't escape another cramped ride crushed close against Mark.

Wedging her knapsack on the floor between her legs, Mara sat, bracing herself as best she could without anything to hold on to. Then she peered forward over Mark's shoulder out the cockpit's windshield. No sooner had she settled down than Riabov started the engine.

The treads churned loudly as the Vizdehod lumbered through smog from the power plant and forward along Provideniya's main road, past the faded orange and blue apartment buildings she'd viewed from the plane, past a fuel yard fenced off by barbed wire and littered with rusting barrels, and then to the southern edge of town.

Mara tried hard not to stare at Mark's harsh yet handsome profile, tried harder not to lean forward against the broad and curved expanse of his back. But it was the heat radiating from his jean-clad thigh jammed next to hers that created the biggest threat to her concentration. The feelings between them last night had been thick enough to taste, and even the moonlight hadn't hidden the fire in his eyes.

She still could not quite believe it. That fire had been for her.

As the Vizdehod's treads rumbled, she could feel the flex of muscles beneath the denim as he steadied himself, in a subtle series of almost imperceptible movements that Mara felt herself mirror with every bump and sway and every pothole in the rutted street. One particularly deep hole threw her against his back, and she was forced to grab on to him to keep from falling off the bench.

Mara froze. So did Mark. They sat like that for a long time, it seemed, sensing each other, saying nothing. The coldness of the raised gold studded caribou emblem made her nipples harden to tight pebbles of desire.

Mark braced himself and peered out the windshield, trying not to feel the heat of Mara's jean-clad thighs, trying not to visualize their sensuous curves as he'd seen and briefly touched them last night, when he'd carried her to the bed. But the effort was beyond him. He wanted to touch her again, wanted to feel that supple skin against his, wanted to feel her warmth crushed against him.

Sweat beaded on his forehead. He had no idea how long he'd be crushed close to her like this; it was too long already, and he was furious with himself. Why the hell hadn't he entered the Vizdehod first and chosen the other bench? She'd been nervous enough last night, and he had known it. This wasn't helping either of them.

He forced himself to concentrate on the scenery. It was gray and misty out, but that was normal for this time of the morning. In a few hours the sky would clear and the temperature would go up. "That's all I need," he muttered as Riabov turned the Vizdehod sharply off the road and down onto a tundra track. They crossed a treeless river valley and a steep pass clogged with the crushed and rocky debris of winter avalanches. A long, bumpy, frustratingly arousing hour later, they finally rumbled into the village of New Chaplino.

Mara was the first person out. As she walked around to the front of the vehicle, she told herself it was the opportunity to view an aspect of Russian life few Westerners had ever seen that had nearly catapulted her out of her seat. But her heart knew the real reason, and she suspected the reason for her hasty escape wasn't lost on Mark, either. But he let her go, thank goodness, and she watched him walk off somewhere with Riabov, affording her a few minutes of uninterrupted time.

She leaned weakly against the Vizdehod. Desire... hurt. Feelings...hurt. Memories...hurt. And this was just the third day of their trip! How was she going to handle an entire summer in Mark's company, if every second was filled with such emotional turmoil?

There were so many things about him she didn't understand.

Why had he agreed to accompany her to Sireniki, when he could have saved himself the hassle and prearranged for her to meet with Riabov? It didn't make sense. A lot of things about Mark didn't make sense. For so long, she'd thought he despised her. And now...

*What?* Mara admonished herself angrily. *Just because he wants you, that doesn't mean he likes it—or you, for that matter. Do you like him? Or do you just want him?*

*Do you even know what you want?* she asked herself derisively.

"Riabov's about ready to start up again." Mark's voice came from behind her, startling her.

Mara whirled. The events of the night before stood between them, the memory coming alive as his glance fell involuntarily to her breasts. He'd never forget the sight of her hard, beaded nipples, or the gut punch he'd felt when he realized the telling reaction was for him.

"Then we'd better get inside," Mara murmured, and walked quickly past him and down through the rear entrance of the Vizdehod. Picking her knapsack up from the floor, she extracted a pad and pen. She would record her impressions of the trip while waiting for Riabov, she decided.

Mark climbed in and sat down on the now-empty bench, facing Mara. He studied her deliberately downturned face, aware of a vague irritation at the thought that she could so easily dismiss him. "Just how long is this visit going to take?"

"Like I told Natasha, it really depends on my grandaunt." Mara kept writing, pleased with her calm delivery. She didn't look up. "But you can leave anytime you want," she continued, then paused, ostensibly to complete a sentence on her notepad. "If you don't mind leaving your camcorder, you can brief me on how to operate it and go home with Riabov."

Mark raised an eyebrow. "For someone who was so insistent I come along, you sure are anxious to get rid of me," he said, watching her closely.

"I'm just trying to be accommodating," Mara murmured, forcing herself to keep writing. But her eyes weren't focused. "I know you didn't want to come in the first place—"

"You got that right."

Mara paused to control the spurt of aggravation his comment caused, then continued. "But now that you've fulfilled your end of our deal, there's no more reason for you to stick around, is there?"

The very reasonableness of Mara's question further irritated Mark. "Then I take it your sudden need for independence has nothing to do with what happened last night?"

Mara refused to be drawn into asking what he meant. She knew what he meant. She'd been there; she'd felt it.

"No answer?"

Mark murmured an oath before he reached out and snatched the pad from Mara's lap. A quick look at the jumble of nonsense words confirmed his suspicions. He tossed the pad on the bench beside him. "Denying what happened won't change it, you know. It won't go away."

Mara remained stubbornly silent, but her eyes flashed at him angrily.

"What are you worried about? Mr. Donut won't find out unless you tell him."

"Mr. who—?" Mara asked, at first confused. Then, realizing what he meant, her cheeks went pink. "Wally and I are just friends. There's nothing to find out."

"Friends, huh?" Mark ignored her denial. "For just a *friend*, he's awfully familiar with your bedroom."

Mara's flush deepened. They'd had this conversation before. Four years ago, just as he'd thrown her out of his bedroom. Every miserable, frightening word of it was etched on her brain.

*And they damn well weren't going to have it again.*

A hot ache rose in her throat. Even coldly mocking, Mark managed to look devastatingly attractive. All of a sudden, she was furious at her vulnerability to him.

"Why shouldn't Wally be familiar with my bedroom?" she asked, her voice filled with false sweetness. "After all, that's where we spend most of our time."

The thought of that overgrown pup licking Mara all over did something violent to his gut. "Then last night was just a case of raging hormones? You actually wanted *him*, but since he wasn't available, you decided I'd do?"

"You could never take Wally's place," she replied stiffly. "He's a wonderful man, kind and giving and sensitive. He's been a great friend."

"But a lousy lover," Mark shot back gruffly, disturbed more than he wanted to admit by the protective sincerity in her voice. So Mr. Donut was a great friend. What did that make the man who had deliberately pushed away the only good thing in his life? What *did* that make him?

"That's none of your business," Mara continued, uneasy with Mark's sudden silence. "My friendship with Wally has no bearing on our professional relationship."

"It does when you look at me like I'm a particularly edible piece of meat and you're hungry," Mark replied frankly, observing another angry tide of color suffuse Mara's already red cheeks. Her emotional reaction satisfied something inside him. At least she wasn't ignoring him anymore.

"According to our deal, we're spending the summer together, remember? So unless you intend flying back to Wally for a quickie in between tours, I'll tell you now— I'm nobody's substitute stud. And my clients are off-limits, too, so stay away from them."

Mara's face was the color of the beets in Natasha's salad when Mark finished. "I can't very well stay away from them and do my job, now can I?"

"You know what I mean. All you have to do is look at a man like you looked at me last night and he gets hard."

"What?" Mara sputtered, outraged.

"You know it's true," he said. She was about ready to explode, he reasoned. "Out where we'll be, there's no phone to call in police protection, no law other than the survival of the fittest. And I damn well don't want to have to fight a client and compromise my business reputation because you couldn't keep your tongue in your mouth or your nipples covered up."

For a moment, Mara's jaw worked but no words came out. "You . . . arrogant Tuntu!" she finally managed, so angry she wanted to throw things. Her heart was pounding like a fast-moving drum, and bright flashes of color were exploding in front of her eyes.

"Just telling it like it was."

"No, you're not!" Mara seethed, throwing the denial at him like a stone. "I seem to remember *you* looking at *me*. I didn't ask you to. I didn't even want to be near you! You were the one who carried *me* to bed. I didn't ask you to. I would gladly have walked!"

"But you liked it."

"I was disoriented."

"Aroused, you mean. So aroused you were shaking with it," Mark said tightly, his gaze focused on her trembling hands. "A lot like you are now."

Immediately Mara clasped her hands, but they continued to tremble. Her inhalations were fast and furious. "I was not shaking." Each word was distinct and separate. "I was so relaxed I was swaying. Obviously I'll have to be more careful next time I drink Grandmother's tea."

Mark was so surprised that he threw back his head and laughed.

It was the last straw. Enraged, Mara flew off the bench, not sure what she had in mind, knowing only that she had to stop that laugh and wipe that smile off Mark's face.

But she never made it.

Heat exploded through her body, and she swayed, making a wild grab for the side of the Vizdehod to support herself.

Abruptly Mark's laughter ended. "What the hell?" He jumped up and caught her just as she moaned and crumpled. Heart pounding, adrenaline on high, he sat her on the bench, supporting her slack body with his own. "Bend over," he ordered, and pushed her head down between her legs. She moaned, and would have fallen sideways without his support.

He checked her pulse. It was so high he couldn't count it. What in the hell was going on? One minute she was snapping at him, and the next she was moaning and all but unconscious. He shivered, trying to throw off a heavy dose of guilt. That was twice now that she'd reacted so violently.

"You need some air. Help me take off your jacket."

Mara responded by moving her head slightly. Any more and the nausea would become unbearable again. "No," she said weakly. "In my knapsack. Please . . . my pills."

Mark stilled. Pills? As he reached across the aisle with his left hand and continued supporting her with his right on the bent-over curve of her back, his thoughts careened wildly. What were the pills for? he thought as he snagged the knapsack and hauled it next to him. He had to release Mara to unzip it. Dumping the contents, he spied a pill container and popped it open.

"How many?" he asked.

Still bent over, Mara held up one finger.

"Open up." Mara looked up, and he placed a pill on her tongue. He stared down at her tearing eyes. "There's nothing to wash it down with."

Mara shook her head and swallowed. More tears coursed down her cheeks. It didn't matter. Head hanging, she let Mark pull off her jacket, let him release her shirt from her jeans. Not that she could have resisted. When he gently but firmly twisted her sideways then eased her lengthwise down on the bench, she sighed in relief and closed her eyes, knowing there wasn't much she could do now but wait.

Slowly, the dizziness eased. Her head cleared. When she opened her eyes, he was staring at the label on the container of pills. Her heart stopped. He must have felt her glance, for he set down the container and handed her a tissue, hovering over her as she wiped her face and blew her nose. His silence wasn't gentle.

"You want to tell me what's going on?" Mark tried keeping his voice level, but it was impossible. The reality that there was something wrong with Mara shook him. Shook him deeply. He watched as Mara turned her face toward the wall. "Come on, Mara. We're in the middle of nowhere. The nearest hospital is not exactly down the street. I need to know what's going on."

"It's nothing, Mark," Mara finally answered. "Nothing at all. At least nothing for you to worry about."

"Does Milak know?" Her head swiveled back, and her fear-filled gaze was answer enough. "If Milak doesn't know," he said quietly, his anxiety level jumping up another notch, "it's not nothing."

Mara lowered her thick black lashes, too distraught herself to see the dread behind his rigid determination. "Is that a threat?"

Her voice was so soft, Mark had to lean in very close to hear. His glance focused on her lips, and a heaviness centered in his chest. Then he looked up and caught her watching him. "If necessary, Mara."

A tear trickled down her cheek.

Mark straightened and jammed clenched fists deep into his back pockets. If he didn't, he knew, he would reach out to brush it away.

"It's only a hormone problem," Mara reluctantly divulged. "Grandmother's got her own health to worry about right now. That's why I haven't told her."

A hormone problem? He picked up the container of pills. "You take these every day?"

"Only when I need to."

"Which is when, exactly?"

Mara shrugged.

"When you get up in the morning? When you go to bed at night? When you get angry? When you get upset? When?" Mark asked, already upset. When Mara flinched, he sighed heavily and backed away, sitting himself down on what had been Mara's bench, feet spread wide, elbows supported on his thighs, hands clasped around the container. He sat that way for several minutes, waiting.

"I can't really predict it," Mara eventually forced out.

"Why not?"

"It just happens."

Abruptly he stood up. He told himself that he didn't want to know, didn't need to know, that if Mara was sick, it wasn't his problem, wasn't even his business. Resolved, he headed for the stairs.

"Wh-where are you going?"

"To find Riabov. This trip is over. Done. Finished. We're going home."

"No!" Mara struggled to sit up, fighting the remnants of her dizziness. "You made a deal with me, Mark Toovak," she said weakly. "And I'm holding you to it. We're going to Sireniki. Grandaunt's waiting. There won't be another chance. It's now or never, Mark."

"Damn it, Mara!" Mark spun around and pinned her with a level gaze. "Your priorities are all screwed up. Don't you realize you're sick?"

Mara just looked at him, ignoring her own fears and, for the first time, seeing his. Then everything fell into place. She sighed, wishing she could explain, knowing she couldn't. The less he knew, the less responsible he'd feel. He might rant and rave, but his quick action and concern for her just now proclaimed he did care. She wished she could help him, but realized dispairingly that silence was probably the best help of all.

"We have a deal, Mark" was all she finally said.

"No. Forget it. All deals are off." Mark began to pace. He could see the past repeating itself, and he didn't want any part of it.

"Then I'll go alone," Mara said, watching him closely.

Mark quit pacing and met her determined gaze. "Is that a threat?"

"No threat, Mark. Just a statement of fact."

"You can't go if Riabov won't take you."

Mara shrugged. The pill was working; her body was settling down; her thoughts were clearing up. "I'll find a way, Mark. If not today, then tomorrow. If not with Riabov, then with someone else. But I want you to know, whatever happens, the choice was mine."

Mark swore. He figured it was either that or strangle Mara for being so incredibly naive. She thought the choice was hers, did she? Well, maybe it was, but by choosing to continue on, she'd effectively chained him. What was he supposed to do—leave her in Sireniki? What if something happened? Russian medical technology was not up to American standards. Even if she made it to a hospital, he had no guarantee they'd know what to do for her. And how, if he did leave and something happened, was he supposed to explain to Milak that he'd deserted her only living relative?

A wave of anger swept through him. He didn't want to stay, but he couldn't leave. Damn it to hell! How had she done it? How had she made him responsible?

And what was wrong with her? He racked his memory, trying to recall anything he'd ever learned about hormones during his years as a medevac pilot. He had a feeling dizziness and nausea were common side effects, but of what? Abruptly a possibility occurred to him.

Could Mara be pregnant? His gaze traveled the length of her body. She was stooped over, so he couldn't see her abdomen clearly. But he remembered last night, and his stunned amazement at her womanliness. *Was* she pregnant? Was that why she couldn't predict when she'd need those pills, because her nausea just happened? Women in their first few months were prone to fainting, weren't they?

What a mess! Mara was pregnant, and she didn't want anyone to know.

But he did know and, not for the first time, he wished that night so long ago had never happened.

Milak opened tired eyes, her late-afternoon meditation at an end. She gazed down at the worn and yellowed envelope lying so peacefully in her weathered hands. Tungunqut had once more taken her across the Bering Sea. Tuntu, the caribou, she had seen, his eyes bright with fear, his movements angry, caged. Qucillgaq's confusion had torn at her heart; Qucillgaq's pain had burned her soul.

Abruptly Milak ripped the envelope into little shreds, the sound of tearing paper harsh in the silent cabin. No more lies, she promised Qucillgaq. No more pain. Zoya, her sister, would know, as she herself already knew: The time for truth had come. This morning's visit had proved Qucillgaq's power. She was strong for one so young. Hopefully, she would be strong enough.

Sighing deeply, Milak stood and moved to the kitchen, where she watched the trickle of little yellow squares rain slowly down into the trash can. Her granddaughter was a wonderful girl, and one day soon she would become a wonderful woman. Crane mated for life, and so, too, would Mara. Milak's expression lightened, and her heart swelled with pride. Feelings ran deep in her granddaughter. That was important. She would need those feelings soon. Not all life's choices were clear; at best, feelings were the only true guide.

The last piece fluttered and landed. Then Milak turned away, moving slowly, aware that age had weakened her. The will that had guided her through the years was fading, even as Twilight was fading. She crossed to the mantel and picked up the photo of Mara.

There was much she had to learn. Her granddaughter would need courage and strength and love to meet the trials of life. The courage would need to be her own, and Tungunqut could lend her the strength, but the love? The power of love could brighten the shadows, but the question was, would Tuntu see? Would he run or would he stay?

For the first time in a long while, Milak had no answer.

# Chapter Ten

The arrival of the Vizdehod did not go unnoticed. As they entered Sireniki, Mara saw young children stop their playing to run toward them, their parents not far behind. Nervous suddenly, she stood and peered out. What if they were too late?

"There's only one way to find out." Mark spoke from his position behind Mara.

The remaining minutes of their drive to Sireniki had been silent. Mark had had a lot of thinking to do, and he figured Mara hadn't particularly been in the mood to talk, either. But now that they were here, they needed to set some ground rules.

"It's not exactly how Grandmother described it," Mara murmured aloud as Riabov cut the engine. Immediately the floor stopped vibrating and a heavy silence shielded them from the high-pitched shouts of children's voices as they surrounded the vehicle and awaited their exit.

"I imagine forty years makes a difference."

"I guess so," Mara replied, looking around. Sireniki wasn't as small as her grandmother had told her it was. Nor was it as primitive. From what she could see through the windshield, the off-white buildings were primarily one- and two-story and of concrete construction. The streets weren't paved, but the dark brown dirt was hard-packed and clear of debris. Electricity poles dotted the landscape, which meant there was a power plant somewhere. And off in the distance, up on a large, wide knoll, stood a series of open-sided wood-framed and roofed cages. She had to bend down to get a better look.

"That's the state fox farm."

"How do you know?"

"Fox farming is big business here. So is reindeer herding. A few years back, I thought about starting up a farm, but nixed it when the antifur craze hit the lower forty-eight."

Would Mark never cease surprising her? "And the reindeer herd? What happened to that idea?"

"It's still viable. Since I'm here, I may as well get with some of the Chukchi brigades and find out more about it."

Mara turned to face him. From her studies, she knew that the Chukchi were a once-nomadic tribe of reindeer herders that, along with the Yup'ik, had been forcibly relocated from their ancestral lands during the Cold War. "Then you're staying a while?"

He would stay until Mara finished. But she didn't need to know that. "Any objections?"

"No, it's your choice." But Mara couldn't help feeling relieved. Sireniki was a long way away from Twilight, and with her illness as unpredictable as it was, Mark's presence made her feel safer, less isolated. And in a tiny corner of her heart, it also made her very happy. She was turning back to peer outside when Mark forestalled her.

"We need to set some ground rules."

"I'm not leaving until I'm ready, Mark."

"Fine, just don't go off by yourself, all right? Or anywhere, for that matter, without your pills. I'm not about to haul you home in a casket."

Mara winced. "You certainly have a way with words."

Mark just looked at her. "Agreed?"

"Agreed. Anything else?"

"Don't take forever getting what you need here."

*I don't want the responsibility,* Mara silently completed his thought. Would he ever face his fears? she wondered. "Things would go faster if you would record my sessions with Grandaunt," she suggested, eyeing him hopefully.

Mark's face hardened as he bent to retrieve her knapsack. "Sure. Whatever it takes."

Just then, Riabov opened the rear door. They emerged to the welcome smiles of a crowd of curious Yup'ik, Chukchi and Russians. One young Yup'ik male seemed to stand forward, his expression an odd combination of reserve and excitement.

"I am Vadim Ivanova," the slim, dark-haired man said in Yup'ik. "Your telephone message was relayed to me. Zoya is my grandmother. And you are?"

"Your second cousin," Mara said, then introduced Mark and Riabov. Her declaration spread through the small crowd, causing murmurs and hushed exclamations from many, especially the senior adults.

"You say we are related? How is that? To my knowledge, Grandmother Zoya has no American family."

"It's a long story," Mara said, and smiled engagingly. "I didn't know myself until last week when Milak—that's my grandmother—gave me this." From her knapsack, she carefully withdrew, then unwrapped, the headdress and handed it to Vadim. "My grandmother has kept this in a place of honor for over forty years. Your grandmother made it."

"She did? But how—?"

"Let me see."

Everyone turned to watch as an old man worked his way slowly through the rows of adults and children until he was standing in front of Mara. The man stared at the headdress for a long time, and when Vadim placed it in his gnarled, arthritic hands, he nodded repeatedly. "This is Zoya's headdress. I watched her sew on the beads. I caught the ermine myself."

At that, the crowd murmured, many craning their necks to catch a glimpse. Mara couldn't help smiling at their excitement. Especially her cousin's.

"If Mara's passed inspection," Mark interjected, "can we get on with it? I'm sure your grandmother is anxious to meet her grandniece."

Vadim looked instantly uncomfortable. "I'm afraid I didn't tell Grandmother Zoya about your telephone call."

"Why not? Is there a problem?"

"Mark." Mara's tone said, "I'll handle it. That's okay," she gently reassured her cousin, who was eyeing Mark apprehensively. "In her condition, that was probably a good idea. But now that we're here, I'd like to visit with her."

Vadim nodded and accepted the headdress from the old man. He addressed Mark. "Are we related?"

Mark felt a pang of guilt. He shouldn't have jumped down the guy's throat. "No, we're not," he replied, speaking evenly. "Mara hired me as her guide."

"You are a good guide," Vadim replied, and smiled.

Mark couldn't help it. The kid was so happy. He smiled back. "This way."

"Just a minute, Vadim." Quickly Mara turned to Riabov. "I don't know how long we'll be," she began, but he cut her off.

"You call. I be here in something flat."

"That's nothing flat," Mara remarked with a parting smile as she bent to pick up her belongings.

"Leave the suitcase, Mara," Mark ordered quietly.

Mara paused, looked up curiously, then did as he requested, reasoning that she'd make much better time without it.

Mark watched her run off and quelled an urge to tell her to slow down. The children accompanied her. The adults remained gathered around the Vizdehod.

"I'm staying," Mark informed Riabov in English. "I need to talk to the Chukchi about reindeer herding."

"You mean you need to watch out for Mara," Riabov said, and chuckled. A few minutes later, he was gone.

Mara was engrossed in her surroundings when Vadim and the children accompanying them halted in front of an old one-story building. He shooed them away while she took in the plywood door, with its cracked and peeling white paint, the single narrow windowpane, and the incongruous bright white flowers blooming happily in an old tin container of some kind. The house was really no different from any of those she'd passed on her way here. Yet, somehow, it seemed to stand out. Maybe it was the flowers.

"Wait here," Vadim ordered. "I need to prepare Grandmother."

Mara's hand closed around Vadim's arm when he would have gone inside. Startled, he turned toward her questioningly. "Vadim, quit worrying, okay? Let's just go on in. I know she's ill, and I promise, if it looks like she's getting too excited, I'll cut the visit short. All I really want to do right now is introduce myself. After I explain why I'm here, instead of her sister like she's expecting, I'll leave her to rest."

"You say my grandmother Zoya is expecting you?"

Mara saw Vadim start, and felt confused. "Not me, her sister. My grandmother, Milak. Don't you remember mailing this for your grandmother?" Digging into her knapsack, she pulled out the letter.

"What's that?"

"The letter your grandmother Zoya wrote to my grandmother, Milak, a couple of weeks ago. It's because of this letter that I'm here. I didn't even know you existed until last Tuesday." Mara gave him the single sheet of stationery and watched as he scanned the unusual script. "It says that my grandmother Milak is supposed to come for a final visit and receive our family's sacred teachings. But she was too weak, so I've come in her place."

"And you say you received this two weeks ago?"

"My *grandmother* received it a couple of weeks ago." Mara wondered why Vadim was concentrating on such an unimportant fact. "I didn't find out about it until last week, though."

Mara looked at Vadim as he carefully handled the letter. The bright morning sunlight made his frown stand out in stark relief.

"Cousin Mara," he said, looking up, his frown even deeper. "This is not my grandmother Zoya's handwriting."

Mara looked into Vadim's eyes and felt cold. "But what do you mean it's not your grandmother's handwriting? How can it *not* be? My grandmother wouldn't make that kind of mistake. Look again. Maybe you're just not used to seeing your grandmother's handwriting in Sireniski."

"Yup'ik or Sireniski, it doesn't matter, cousin Mara. It's not her handwriting."

"You're positive?"

"I handle all of Grandmother Zoya's business and I know she couldn't have written this letter."

"Why?"

"Because two months ago Grandmother Zoya had a stroke."

Mara gasped. "A stroke? How—" she swallowed past the dryness in her throat "—how bad was it?"

The silence stretched between them. Finally, Vadim admitted on a sad sigh, "My grandmother Zoya is blind."

Mara was momentarily speechless with shock.

"That's why I know she couldn't have written this letter."

"I see." Mara's thoughts whirled. "Could someone else...could someone else have written it for her? Perhaps one of the older villagers. Someone who might still remember the language..."

"It's possible, but not likely," Vadim admitted. "We've lost so much knowledge of our old ways, but I'll find out." He looked down at the letter. "You say this mentions the sacred teachings?"

"Yes," Mara answered, unable to follow his train of thought. "What about them? My grandmother Milak told me that your grandmother Zoya would give them to me so that they wouldn't be lost."

Vadim's eyes widened, and then, as if he had suddenly made up his mind, he pulled opened the door and took Mara's arm. "Let's go inside. Letter or no letter, the headdress is clearly Grandmother's, and you are family. We'll figure out what's going on later."

Mara followed Vadim through the front door, into a room so much like her grandmother's that she stopped and stared, truly astonished. The furniture was different, but the abundance of fur rugs and grass baskets and drying and dried herbs was the same. The atmosphere spoke reverently of things past. When Vadim gestured for her to precede him through another door into her grandaunt's bedroom, Mara didn't hesitate, for she felt—illogically, perhaps—as if she already knew her grandaunt.

Zoya sat upright on an ancient bed. Her features immediately identified her to Mara as Milak's sister. She was a tiny woman, probably less than five feet tall when standing. Her long white hair was parted down the middle of her head and braided, just like Mara's grandmother's. A brightly patterned red-fringed shawl covered her small shoulders. Underneath, she was wearing an all-white *kuspuk*.

The symbolism sobered Mara's excitement. Red fringes symbolized life; an all-white *kuspuk* symbolized her grandaunt's fading strength. Yet the energy that reached out to encompass Mara wasn't weak. It burned brightly, despite the sightless eyes that seemed somehow to see directly through to her soul. Mara smiled and relaxed, accepting the unusual scrutiny, using the time to look back.

Her grandaunt's chin, nose and cheeks, unlike her grandmother's, were tattooed. Mara gazed at the two thin blue lines, about a half inch apart, that ran from the crown of the healer's forehead straight down to the tip of her nose. She wondered at their significance. A dozen more blue lines fanned out from her full bottom lip to the edge of her chin, and each cheek was etched with a fine series of curled lines. Questions upon questions were already queuing up in Mara's mind behind the paradox of the letter. There was such a lot she had to do, to learn. Mara only hoped there would be time.

Mara remained silent and unmoving. Zoya sat alertly, seemingly eternally poised, senses reaching outward, beyond her handicap, to surround Mara with welcome. Even without the knowledge that this woman was a healer, Mara knew, she would have assumed her to be someone of great importance, so awesome was the feeling of immense age and wisdom that emanated from the serene features examining her so thoroughly. Mara felt distinctly intimidated by the wealth of experience and knowledge this woman must have accrued in her one hundred and two years of life. She worriedly wondered if they would have anything besides her grandmother in common.

The silence lengthened. Mara's gaze was drawn to the healer's hands, which were resting peacefully on top of the bedspread. The hands weren't gnarled or misshapen from age. Instead, they looked much like her grandmother's, wrinkled but nimble. Mara had a feeling that this woman continued to concoct her own herbal medicines, despite Vadim's insistence that he did practically everything. Mara also had the feeling that being blind had not stopped this woman from seeing into the hearts of people. Her love flowed out and encompassed Mara, much like the sun's warmth during June—continuously, without end. The feeling was wondrous, the sense of acceptance and welcome, incredible. And it was for her, Mara sensed, not for her grandmother. How she knew this, she couldn't have said. She just knew it.

*"Maacungaq."* Vadim finally spoke into the silence. "Grandmother, you have a visitor. She is—"

"I know who she is, Vadim," the healer said, interrupting him. *"Tallurna,* thank you. Now, leave us."

"But—"

"Leave us, Grandson."

Throwing Mara a worried look, Vadim left. Purely on instinct, Mara waited quietly for the healer to acknowledge her presence. When, after a few minutes, a small hand softly patted the bed, bidding her to come closer, Mara smiled and moved forward, taking the proffered seat.

*"Camai,* hello, Grandaunt," she said, as calmly as she could. Her grandaunt reached out, the weathered fingers exploring the soft feathers of the *talliraq* Mara wore around her wrist before grasping her hand with surprising strength. With her free hand, she

lightly touched Mara's cheek, and then the short strands of her hair.

"You wear the symbols of the past and those of the present. My sister has done well. Tungunqut is wise."

At the mention of her grandmother's spirit guide, Mara felt compelled to explain, "Grandmother wanted to be here, but I feared for her health. I hope you can understand, Grandaunt—"

"I understand," the healer said, interrupting her. "In a dream I saw Tungunqut. He visited me from across the Bering Sea."

"In a dream?" The same one her grandmother had told her about? It seemed so long ago that she'd first learned of it. That dream had brought her Mark. That dream had brought her home from Fairbanks. And now, apparently, that dream had brought her here.

"Tungunqut has sent Qucillgaq, the Sandhill Crane, for the sacred teachings. You will fly high above the shadows and see deep into the light. That is good, for I have little time. There is much for you to learn."

Mara could not disguise the shiver that briefly shook her body. To speak so matter-of-factly about death seemed beyond Mara. And how had her grandaunt known her *inua's* name? Why hadn't she seemed even a little surprised that her visitor wasn't her long-lost sister? Then Mara remembered Vadim's remark that the healer hadn't written the letter summoning Milak, and she was back at square one. If she hadn't, who had? Little was making sense, except for the indisputable fact that she was here. Mara could only hope that the next few days would clear everything up.

"You sound tired."

Mara pressed the stop button on her tape recorder. This was the fifth time her grandaunt had paused in midthought. "Let's stop early today, all right? You should sleep. The potlatch tonight will be very long and tiring."

"Soon I will sleep forever. I do not need it now. But rest I will. Send me Vadim. I wish to speak with my grandson."

Mark watched them head for the bedroom. It was Wednesday. Three days in Sireniki hadn't cleared up anything for Mark. In fact, he felt more confused than ever. As he disengaged the camcorder from the tripod, Mark absently listened to Mara's light laughter as she shared some funny aspect of her college life with her grandaunt.

The woman might be blind, Mark thought as he stored the camcorder in its case, but she saw a hell of a lot more than most people. After three afternoons spent listening and watching and occasionally asking a question, he found himself feeling grudging respect for her knowledge of people and admiration for the endurance it had taken for this woman to lead her people through all the hardships they'd endured during her more than fifty years as their spiritual leader. It made him reevaluate Milak, made him reevaluate a lot of things.

Even Vadim's overly protective attitude. To his surprise, Mark had been welcomed into Vadim's own room in a dormitorylike building set up for the young single men in the village. After a stumbling beginning, they'd realized a mutual zeal for the advantages of progress. Mark had shown the young man how to operate his camcorder and had answered his questions about life in America. In turn, Vadim had answered his about the economy in Sireniki. Monday morning he'd guided Mark through the state-owned fox farm. Tuesday morning he'd introduced him to a Chukchi man who had briefed him on the hardships and rewards of reindeer herding. This morning he'd acted as translator during Mark's discussions with the Russians who managed everything.

Mark had come away from the three meetings totally energized. Reindeer herding just might work at home. He hadn't liked the fact that there was no such thing as free enterprise, but that wasn't a problem in Twilight. Here, everything—the reindeer, the boats, the foxes, the guns, the houses, the people themselves, it seemed—was the property of the Russian government. At home, what one bought, one owned, and what one produced, one could sell.

The only problem was, there wasn't any money to buy anything, and all the meat and fish the villagers hunted and caught went to feed near-starving families through long winters. There wasn't anything left over to "sell." Alaskan Yup'ik were rich in their cultural heritage, but poor in everything else. For the Siberian Yup'ik the opposite held true: everyone had a job and a market within the Russian republics for their produce, but, curiously, they'd lost their connection with their past. Recognizing that had dampened Mark's enthusiasm. Unless he could figure out a way to meld progress with tradition, he realized, his people would never go for the future. But how?

"Are you all right?"

Mark looked up. He'd been so preoccupied, he hadn't even heard Mara reenter the room. "The night of the potlatch, when you performed the Dance of the Healer, what were you thinking?''

The unexpectedly introspective question stopped Mara's progress across the room. Mark had been doing that a lot lately: asking unusual questions. Especially during her sessions with her grandaunt. She looked at him speculatively. Maybe the atmosphere was getting to him. She smiled, pleased by the possibility.

"I wasn't thinking anything," she answered honestly. "I was too terrified."

"You didn't look it."

She immediately wanted to ask, "How *did* I look?" but she didn't. Those long moments had been difficult enough. She didn't need to know for certain what a fool she'd made of herself in his eyes. "Well, I was." She crossed to the reindeer-hide rug she'd been sitting on and scooped up her notepad and tape recorder. "All that pressure. All those expectations, especially Grandmother's. I swear, I don't know what possessed her that night. It could have been a disaster."

"But it wasn't," Mark prompted. "How come?"

"Who knows? For some reason, everything clicked. Steps I'd learned too long ago to really remember came back as clear as if I'd just learned them yesterday. And when the drum began to pound..." Mara's voice faded. Her head tilted sideways, and her gaze became fixed.

Mark stilled, sensing that he was close to getting some answers.

"It was as if every beat spoke to me. Suddenly, all the movements were there, all the gestures, the feelings, the words, everything. I felt like I was connected to everyone, especially Grandmother. With her, I could almost read her mind." She straightened, laughing self-consciously. "Weird, huh?"

"No weirder than a letter nobody wrote," he answered, snapping the lid on the camcorder case. Mind reading? If that was the answer, he didn't have a chance in hell of succeeding with his goal. He didn't even know his own mind most times. Especially lately.

He watched Mara as she stashed her research materials. She walked gracefully—seemingly without any conscious understanding of how sensual and fluid her movements were—toward an old wooden table, where she piled everything neatly. He sat on his walrus-skin rug, staring at her, and wondered what was happening to him. This whole situation was too weird. His relationship with Mara was too strange. His presence here in Zoya's home was too oddly comfortable. Mara was changing him.

Mark was shocked to realize how traditional his feelings about Mara's impending motherhood were. He knew she was intelligent. Fools didn't operate successful businesses. But despite that, despite her facility for languages, she'd gotten herself pregnant. And the baby's father and she were just *friends*.

He winced. Mara should have a husband. The baby should have a father. And he was very definitely going insane. "Did Zoya settle down?"

"Yes, but I think the pace is getting to her. She seems more tired every day. I'm not sure she should go to this potlatch tonight."

Mark wasn't even sure he wanted to go. But the celebration was in honor of their visit. With a grunt, he stood and strode to the door. "Maybe you can get her home early."

"I never could convince Grandmother to do what's best for herself. I'm not having any more luck with her sister." She reached for her coat and pulled it on, then followed Mark outside, intent on fetching Vadim from the beach, where, she'd learned, he spent most of his days working.

Mark had really surprised her the past three days. She and her grandaunt spent long hours talking about the language and about her past. Mark still grumbled about it, but the grumbling had lessened with each successive day. A closeness was developing between the two of them, a bond of shared experiences and knowledge.

Several times, when he'd had to change videotapes, she had turned to find his gaze on her, fixed in an odd expression. There had been no sexual awareness in his eyes, but he'd seemed deeply preoccupied.

And so was she. She was becoming more disturbed by his silent presence with the camera than ever, more sensually aware of his long, tapered fingers, his sharp, efficient gestures. Once, early on, when he'd been engrossed in seeking the best spot to position himself to film her grandaunt, Mara had caught herself concentrating intently on his splayed-out form, memories stripping away the jeans to leave him bare.

"Mara?"

Mark stopped walking and drew a harsh breath, nearly bowled over by the need in her eyes. Then, abruptly, he remembered—it wasn't for him. He started walking again. "How much longer until you're done?"

"I honestly don't know," Mara got out, feeling her face flush. "It seems like all she wants to talk about is my future. She's very interested in my project, you've seen that for yourself. But she hasn't mentioned a thing about the sacred teachings."

"Why not just ask?"

"Because I have a feeling she's not ready."

Mara and her feelings were becoming so commonplace for Mark that her statement didn't even faze him. "You think she doesn't trust you?"

"No, I just think that she's waiting for something. Sounds weird, doesn't it?"

"No weirder than a letter nobody wrote." He repeated his earlier statement, eyeing Mara speculatively. "You haven't asked her about it?"

"This morning."

When Mara didn't volunteer anything, he prompted her. "And what did she say?"

"She didn't say anything," Mara said, remembering. "She just held it in her hands for a while, murmured something about 'our ways must survive,' then patted my hand and gave it back. When I asked if anyone else spoke Sireniski, she said that Milak did."

"But no one here?"

"Apparently not. Vadim checked."

"Our ways must survive," Mark murmured. "Any idea what she meant?"

"Could be she was expressing her happiness that I'm so interested in studying and recording her language."

Mark made a noncommittal sound. "You have your pills with you?"

Mara reached in to her pocket and extracted the vial.

"Taken any lately?"

"No." That was a lie. Just this morning she'd had another episode. She'd been dressing when it happened. Luckily, her purse had been nearby, and she'd quickly taken a pill. The dizziness hadn't lasted long, but when she'd looked up, it had been to see her grandaunt's sightless gaze upon her. The healer had stood perfectly still for a long minute, then she'd calmly asked for some tea. It had surprised Mara to find out that the tea was the same as that given to her by her grandmother. She'd sipped a cup along with her grandaunt, and had begun feeling better almost immediately.

Telling him about this morning's incident was out of the question. It would only upset him and reintroduce friction into their relationship. Mara found she liked things the way they were. Being at odds with Mark was just too draining.

They reached the beach. Mara spotted Vadim and called him over. Surprisingly, several men looked up and called out Mark's name. "What's going on?" Mara asked, noting Mark's sudden discomfort.

"I promised I'd show them how to construct a walrus-skin *umiak*."

Mara couldn't have been more shocked. Apparently her expression showed it.

"I'm not a fanatic, Mara," Mark ground out, faintly irritated. "Just because I happen to believe in technology and its rewards, that doesn't mean I can't appreciate or value a well-constructed *umiak*."

"Is Grandmother all right?"

Vadim's question burst through Mara's startled absorption. For an instant, she remained focused on Mark, until his sardonic expression penetrated her astonishment. She blinked and glanced sideways at her cousin. "Your grandmother's just fine. But she's asking for you."

They both watched him run off. "I guess I'll see you tonight," Mara murmured.

"Yeah, right. Tonight."

## Chapter Eleven

Mara felt a thrill ripple through the crowd as she and Zoya entered the schoolhouse that evening. Everyone was talking and pointing to the center of the room, the young people's fast-paced Russian melding with the slower cadences of the Yup'ik spoken by the elder adults. Looking around, she was astonished at the intricate details in the beaded and fur-trimmed *kuspuks* and mukluks worn by the older villagers. Most everyone was seated, either on the hardwood floor or in chairs scooted back out of the way of the excitement going on at the floor's center. The gymnasium-size room was fully lit. Mara had no trouble zeroing in on the cause.

Bare to the waist, muscled chest heaving from his exertions, Mark was smiling and daring Vadim and a group of eager teens to try their hand at a traditional Alaskan Yup'ik game of skill, the two-foot high kick.

Transfixed, Mara paused to watch Mark demonstrate. As a child, she'd participated in Twilight's version of the World Eskimo and Indian Olympics, but she'd never won any of the athletic events. Striking a softball-size fur ball suspended way over your head was hard enough when you could use your hand to reach out and your legs to propel you upward. But when your body had to jackknife at the waist so that your feet—both of them—struck the ball, the sport took on an entirely different dimension.

Mark had not only won Twilight's two-foot event several years running, but had competed at the national competition in Fairbanks, for which all Indian and Eskimo tribes sent representatives, and he had won that, too. Twice, that she could remember. He was a superb athlete.

"What is happening?" Zoya asked.

Distracted, Mara gazed down at her grandaunt. "Mark has challenged Vadim to beat him at the two-foot high kick," she quickly explained, lightly squeezing the small hand lying serenely within hers.

"And has my grandson accepted?"

"Just now," Mara answered as the spectators cheered.

"Then we will both learn something important tonight."

"And what could that be?" Mara asked as she led Zoya carefully through densely packed bodies to a spot set aside for the five-person council of elders. "I'm sure you already know how to lose."

A smile lifted the corner of Zoya's mouth at Mara's gentle teasing. "That is what Vadim will learn."

"Then I have a funny feeling Vadim's going to learn a lot."

Zoya chuckled. "You are wise, Grandniece. Rarely does Tuntu issue a challenge he cannot win."

As Mara moved aside a large ceremonial drum to make room for her grandaunt to sit, she couldn't help but agree. Mark was a master at avoiding involvement. Zoya would no doubt blame it on his *inua*'s wandering spirit. The caribou was a migrating animal, and its instinct to move was as deeply ingrained as its instinct to survive.

Her eyes zeroed in on Mark. He was standing next to Vadim, his stance supremely confident, his muscled arm flung casually around the young man's shoulders as he coached him on how to proceed. Suddenly he looked up and met Mara's gaze. She watched his eyes flash as he took in her borrowed finery.

She was dressed in reindeer-skin mukluks and an elaborately embroidered *kuspuk*. This time around, she knew she fit in. The fact that the clothes were her own grandmother's, lovingly preserved by her sister, made Mara feel especially comfortable. She willed herself to remain still beneath his gaze, not to squirm, not to breathe in too rapidly, not to give away how this past week around him had reawakened the passion inside her.

She failed. Mark . . . Her eyes widened, and her lips parted. She felt such a wave of longing that she pressed a hand to her stomach. Immediately the mesmerized expression on his face clouded, and he turned back to Vadim.

"*Iluperaq,* Grandniece. Be calm," Zoya demanded softly, then turned her blind gaze back to her council companions.

Mara despaired of ever being calm so long as she was near Mark. Perhaps at summer's end, when her obligation to him had been fulfilled and she was free to return to Fairbanks and her master's studies. Perhaps then she would find calm. Distance would make it easier. It had once before.

She focused on that end, and on the food she was served but didn't taste, knowing that the almost constant daylight of summer would make the months pass slowly.

But it would be worth it, she told herself as she watched Vadim's third attempt and third failure to strike the ball. Mark playfully jabbed him in the side, and Vadim's sour-faced expression changed to a sheepish smile. They were shaking hands when the abrupt pounding of a drum caught everyone's attention. The room quieted.

Mark nabbed his T-shirt from the back of a chair and yanked it on, settling himself on the floor next to Vadim. Along with everyone else's, his gaze focused on Zoya.

She had to be burning up in that full-length white birdskin parka, he decided, as he used the towel Vadim had produced to wipe the sweat off his face and arms. Yet she looked cool enough. Her long white braids were unbound, and her hair was spread out across her tiny shoulders like a living cape. On her feet she wore deerskin mukluks like Mara's, intricately adorned with sky-blue beads and ermine tails. And on her head she wore the headdress Milak had kept and Mara had returned. Her voice, when it came, was soft, yet carried easily across the room to where he sat.

"I have a sister. I know some of you remember Milak. She is very beautiful, very wise. She loves the Bering Sea. Tungunqut is her *inua.*" Mark watched as the remaining elders on the council and several elderly people in the crowd nodded. "One day the Sea took her away. A new home she found, with a new people, a free people. She became wife. She became mother. She became healer. This I know, for Tungunqut comes often to my dreams."

Zoya glanced at Mara, her blind eyes reflecting the past. "Tonight, we celebrate my sister's homecoming. Milak has sent us her daughter's daughter, my grandniece, the anthropologist. Mara

Anvik is her name, and she knows much of the ways of the *kass'aq*. This I know, for she studies our language so that others may know us."

Zoya smiled. The crowd smiled with her. Mark glanced to the side. Mara was watching Zoya, her eyes bright with unshed tears.

"You who are young, listen to my words. In Mara, I see our future. She cares about our traditions, our healing ways, our beliefs. Learn from her example. Study the new ways, but remember and respect the old."

Watching Zoya, Mark had the disconcerting feeling that she was somehow talking specifically to him. When she suddenly looked his way, not through him, as he would have expected because of her blindness, but straight *at* him, he tensed. The last time he'd been looked at like that, he'd wound up in Fairbanks.

"My sister's grandchild did not journey alone. She chose Mark Toovak to guide her. She chose well, for he is Tuntu, the wanderer. Already he has guided us through the shadows of the past to the bright light of forgotten knowledge. A lost skill has been restored, a forgotten game has once again been played. Because of him, our children will have a richer present and a fuller future."

Beside him, Vadim was nodding energetically. Mark, however, was not. His eyes were on Zoya while she talked, and a wild, confused denial rose which he deftly swallowed as tendrils of unease fanned out inside his stomach.

"We are a people torn from our roots. Our young eat *kass'aq* food, wear *kass'aq* clothing, and speak the *kass'aq* language before our own. Though we are employed, though we no longer worry about starvation, though we have shelter, much was lost when we accepted *kass'aq* rule. The young do not understand my words, for they see only the future and do not yet value the past. Mark Toovak knows what we have lost. And he understands its value. In Mark Toovak, we have a link. He will be our guide to the past."

Mark sat perfectly still, as if moving would release a rage he knew he wouldn't be able to control.

"Tonight we renew old bonds and forge new friendships," Zoya continued. "My sister has returned home. Mark has made this possible. And my grandniece..." Zoya slowly turned her head. Her blind eyes were bright, and her expression was oddly beseeching as Mara met her gaze. "My grandniece will make it last."

*Iluperaq?* The plea touched her mind.

Mara hesitated, uncertain she had even heard the unspoken cry. But she squeezed her grandaunt's hand reassuringly anyway, silently acknowledging that she would do what she could to document the language and everyday lives of the Siberian Yup'ik.

Mara caught Mark's tortured glance at the door. The need to escape was stamped all over his face and body. Then his gaze met hers briefly, but it was long enough for her to see beyond his anger, to the very real fear he was trying to deny. *I'm no damned guide to the past!*

Mara turned away quickly, willing her rapidly beating heart to slow down. Conversations erupted among the villagers. Children cheered, drumsong sounded, and the people sitting close around Mark were patting him on the back even as those around Mara were patting her.

Again an elder pounded a drum, and conversations stopped. Again Zoya turned to her, the beseeching expression gone. The woman facing her now was cloaked in her position as Sireniki's healer. "Grandniece, you and Mark are honored guests. Which of you will perform the first dance?"

*I should have realized,* Mara's stunned mind repeated over and over. *I should have realized this would happen.* But she hadn't, and now loud, uncomfortable seconds ticked by as the villagers waited and murmured curiously while she swallowed panic and grappled for a way out. She didn't want to dance tonight. Her gaze swung desperately to Mark, but she didn't hold out any hope. Mark would never dance. And she was right. No help there. Her stomach clenched at the abject denial on his face. He was furious.

"Grandniece?"

Mara closed her eyes, feeling utterly miserable. She had no choice. Like the last time, she would have to dance. She could never disrespect her grandaunt or dishonor the people who had welcomed them so openly by refusing their gesture. Honor was important. Their friendship meant a lot to her. And the sad fact that this would likely be her grandaunt's last celebration also weighed heavily on Mara's mind.

"I will dance," Mara murmured, setting aside her plate of uneaten food. She was about to stand when Mark's voice cut the silence.

"No. I will."

With one furious tug, Mark stripped off his shirt and tossed it and then his shoes and socks aside. Then he stepped to the center of the cleared area he'd just occupied with Vadim. Fury and resentment burned through him. He didn't look at Zoya. He didn't look at Mara. No way in hell would he get through this if he did. Her panic had gone through him like a knife, cutting out his options, making him want to hit something at the way he was being so expertly manipulated. And he *was* being manipulated.

He didn't blame Mara. No, her shock had been real. She'd expected no help from him.

But, help or no help, he couldn't let her dance. He would not risk another fainting spell.

Zoya. He blamed Zoya. And Milak. Both of them enjoyed pushing his buttons. *He is our guide to the past.* Damned if Zoya wasn't forcing him to prove it beyond anyone's doubt. Except his own, of course, right?

No answer came, only the memory of Mara standing where he stood now, her eyes wide and frightened, and Milak watching serenely like a master orchestrator.

Watching the way Zoya watched. Into the soul of a man.

The drumsong started. He didn't announce what dance he was doing, because he didn't know himself. He couldn't remember the last time he'd danced. Sweat beaded his forehead as the drumsong faltered, waiting for him to start. To hell with it, he decided, and moved. The drumsong started up again, the cadence measured and regular.

He had watched Mara dance until he ached with hunger. Would she watch him that way? Did he want her watching him that way?

*Yes.* He could deny it to everyone else, but not to himself. He had wanted Mara long before the glaring light of discovery had revealed her face. He had wanted her long after he had frightened her away. A single kiss on a knoll and he'd known he wanted her still.

Will she see my pain, my anger, my heartache? Will she see the need I reject but can't deny? Will she even look at me?

There was no answer but the lonely song of the drums and the murmured whispers of the crowd as he fought to master the fierce anger and burning resentment jamming his thoughts and freezing his body.

Damn. He'd buckled under Zoya's manipulation. Did he have to humiliate himself, too?

Mark moved his arms across his body, but the movement held no meaning for him. It was just something he'd seen other dancers do.

He'd been so certain he could do it. So certain. But he couldn't. It was too much. Again his steps faltered, but the drumsong continued, pulsing, pounding, slow and steady and even.

The rhythm! God! If he could just shut it out!

Desperate, Mark closed his eyes, forcing himself to breathe at his own swifter pace, to hear the faster beating of his heart. He listened. Really listened. And then . . . and then . . . he heard it. Faint at first, a mere whisper of vibration, beating, irregular, sometimes strong, sometimes weak, illusive and confused, but his. His own drumsong.

Focusing hard, he tried to follow it, aware that he faltered, aware that he felt a half step out of sync, too slow at times, too fast at others.

Soon sweat gleamed on his chest and face as his movements revealed a story his father had told him, the story of a great warrior and an even greater walrus. A crouch, a turn, a mimicked throw of a spear, and he spun an ancient tale of skill and daring, bravery and courage. But the face of the hunter was dark and confused, and all who watched felt the raging cry when another spear and then another missed the walrus, the rhythms off, the strikes, the moves, the steps, either too short or too long.

The drumsong slowed. Or was it that Mark moved faster? Mara watched from her position beside her grandaunt, her heart pounding with dread, her hands slick with sweat. She had seen what the others had missed, could not know, for they saw only the fierceness of a warrior on the hunt. But she saw more, knew more, and that knowledge was causing her acute pain.

She'd been stunned by his intervention. Even now she couldn't quite believe he was actually out there. It hurt her to sit and watch him tear himself apart in front of everyone's eyes. As it had before, again the drumsong spoke to her, helping her see beyond the surface rage, to Mark's pain and confusion. Yet the rhythm was somehow off, too slow for the savage hurt of the man dancing before them, too gentle for the grief he could not express.

Without conscious thought, Mara reached for the drum at her grandaunt's feet and began a fast, arrhythmic pounding that sent a murmur through the crowd, a low wave that soon had all the other drummers bowing out, unable to follow a song without name, a rhythm without direction.

But Mara knew the direction.

From the first beat, the first contact of her palm against the waxy-smooth head of the ceremonial drum, Mara knew where she was headed. The beat was wild and strong and free and matched the movements of the man pawing at the earth like Tuntu caged, like a warrior thwarted. Mara's drumsong didn't cajole, didn't flaunt, didn't hide or soothe. Her pounding hands answered his rage and described her own, a rage that equaled Mark's primitive explosion of movement. Mara was no longer the college graduate with a head for business. She was again the scared girl who'd risked everything for the friend she held most dear. The anguish poured from her fingers, and every harsh, sharp beat proclaimed that pain, and her disillusionment. Torn, wounded, hurting, as all innocents hurt when plundered, Mara demanded attention, the lone sounds loud in the all-silent room, where the only movement was the dancer's stalking of an unsuspecting prey.

Mara didn't look at Mark. She hadn't started this intending to beat out her fury, but now that she had, she found she needed to finish it. Mark would dance for the same reason, she guessed, because he needed to finish it.

Mark heard the anguish in the drumsong, and his quick movements reflected a rage and a regret and an accepting, unflinching responsibility for the pulsing tears of a young girl who had once called him friend and now called him nothing at all. Emotions so long held in check clamored to be freed, seeking an outlet, needing release, forgiveness from the child now grown, the woman who wouldn't even look at him.

He continued dancing, letting her set the pace, following where she led, allowing her to control the outcome of this encounter. Distantly Mark wondered what the villagers were making of this display, what Zoya was thinking. He knew that he could stop anytime, and knew, somehow, that Mara wasn't ready. So he kept dancing, ignoring the stares, ignoring Zoya, as his own rage flared up once more.

Chest heaving, his legs trembling with the unexpected exertion, Mark danced, his own anger no less than hers, no more tempered than hers.

Then, suddenly, Mara stopped. Mark sensed it somehow through the drumsong and stopped, too. They stared at one another as the silence rang loud and stretched. Gone was their audience. Gone was the room itself. As Mark's eyes burned into hers, the distance between them halved, then halved again and again, until it seemed as if he were close enough to see the raw hurt glittering torturously in eyes that reflected his feelings. Then Mara was looking away, down at Zoya, murmuring something before she got up and quickly, quietly, left.

Slowly, slowly, the room returned and the sounds reappeared. He made to follow her. But, as if cued, the crowd surged up and around him, their expressions shocked, awed, reverent. They barred his exit.

It was past nine o'clock when he finally stepped outside. Immediately he cast about, finally spotting Mara sitting on a bench facing the ocean. Releasing a pent-up breath, he took a moment to watch a hazy sun send muted yellow streaks over a glistening sea. A cool breeze wrapped itself around him, and he could hear waves crashing in to shore. It was time to leave Sireniki, he decided as he set out toward the beach.

Pregnancy or no, Mara would just have to take care of herself. Too many of his emotions had erupted just now, along with feelings he hadn't even known he had. And then there were the questions and the doubts and the insecurities.

When had his easygoing life become so complicated? He didn't want to start questioning his life-style. For a long time now he'd managed to survive just fine without a single doubt that what he was doing, how he was conducting his life, was right for him. After that dance, he felt like questioning everything.

The *crunch-squish* sound of his tennis shoes compressing wet sand and rock announced his presence, yet Mara didn't so much as bat an eyelash. He glanced down at her still form. Her back was bowed, and her arms were wrapped tightly around her chest. Head up, she was staring at the ocean and rocking, her face tortured, her eyes dry now, but no less bleak. Slipping off his jacket, he dropped it around her shoulders.

"I brought your bag. You forgot it. I thought..." Mark didn't, couldn't, divulge the fear he'd experienced when he watched how quickly she'd left and was unable to follow. "I thought you might need it."

Mark waited a moment, expecting her to reach out and take it, to at least thank him for the jacket, but she didn't.

"You want me to leave?" he asked tersely when the silence had gone on long enough.

*No!* Mara's heart screamed out as her raw gaze met his. *I want you to hold me. I want you to wrap yourself around me so tight that I can't breathe. I want you to show me the passion that once was mine. Can't you see that? Didn't you feel it in my drumsong?*

"Oh, God," Mara whimpered as she shot up from the beach. Her slim body trembled. Get away! Get away! her body urged. Go, before it's too late, and you humiliate yourself all over again!

"Mara—"

"Don't!" she cried out, as his hands closed over her denim-covered shoulders. She squeezed her eyes tightly shut. "Oh, God, *don't* touch me!"

The near hysteria in Mara's voice shocked Mark. "What the hell's the matter with you?" he demanded defensively to cover the deep stab of pain he felt at her slicing rejection.

Mara shook her head, saying nothing.

"Look at me, Mara. Or don't I even deserve that for taking your place back there?" His hands tightened on her shoulders.

Opening her eyes, she chose to look through him, wishing that, like the arctic night, she could disappear. But the sun was out, and nothing could hide her from his searching gaze.

"You didn't have to go out there," she said finally, in a defeated voice.

"I thought you didn't want anyone to know you were pr—sick," he argued roughly. "What was I supposed to do? Sit and watch you work yourself up into another faint?"

"I told you three days ago that you're not responsible for me."

"And I should have told you then what crap that is."

Mara shuddered. She wanted to wrap her arms around herself, but that would only bring Mark into closer contact with her body. His warmth was already seeping into cold bones, making her weak, and now was the time to be strong. "I would have danced, Mark. I was going to. The very last thing I expected was help from you."

Mark's breath came in sharply. He probed Mara's face, hoping to see even the smallest hint she was lying. But her dark, wounded eyes showed only the bald truth of harsh experience.

He was responsible for that look. He was responsible for the experience. Four years ago he'd stripped her of not only her clothes, but her defenses, and when she'd trembled and pleaded with him, he'd cruelly thrown her out.

In the midst of his own anguish, he hadn't thought about the consequences of his actions, but now that he had, now that he could see the damage he'd caused, he felt hopelessly inadequate to fix it. Though he wanted to—it surprised him how much he wanted to—he didn't know how. It didn't take a genius to figure out that he could be the last man on earth and she'd likely die perfectly happy alone.

"I know you wouldn't expect any help from me," Mark murmured, shaken by the irony that the very same warmth and goodness and budding sensuality he'd rejected back then, he'd kill to have directed at him right now. The truth of it poured over him like a ray of sunlight, scaring him with its intensity.

"Do you?" Her eyes searched his, and the anguish she saw made the warm air rush from her lungs. "Every time I look at you . . . I remember."

"Mara—"

She lifted her hand, shutting off what she felt certain would be another rejection as she shoved away the passionate images. "How does it feel to be a guide to the past? To have three hundred people needing you, and an entire generation of young adults looking to you for direction?"

Mark's eyes slid from hers. She could tell he didn't appreciate the change of subject, or the reminder. "They like you, you know." She spoke softly, looking up at him though he refused to look down at her. "You saw their faces. The kids already admire you."

"I'm no damn hero."

"But they don't know that, do they?"

Mark jerked as if shot. Mara stood still, absorbing the telling reaction, caught between the urge to retreat and the desire to stay. She felt his hands tighten around her shoulders and wondered inwardly why she was punishing herself, why she was pushing him, what she was hoping to accomplish.

There was no answer save that of need. Tonight she'd discovered a Mark she'd never known. Had he also discovered himself?

"It wouldn't even occur to them that you'd want to leave," she continued. "After all, Sireniki is their whole world. Naturally they're eager to share it. They believe you're honored by Grandaunt's announcement. But they're wrong, aren't they? You can't wait to leave. I bet you followed me out here just to tell me that. I bet that, come tomorrow morning, you're history."

"Damn it, Mara!"

"Am I right?"

"Yes...no... I don't know anymore, all right? I don't know!" Mark caught the stunned surprise on Mara's face just as he threw up his hands and spun away, his long stride taking him away from her.

The need to distance himself was so great he actually felt as if he were going to drown right there on the beach. He knew what she was trying to do: make him admit what Zoya already knew and

what he was afraid Mara had guessed—that all these years he'd
been fooling himself. That deep down he was just as traditional as
everyone else. Maybe even more so.

*Was* he a guide to the past? *Had* he been deluding himself? Did
he even know himself anymore? Right then, his desire for Mara
seemed the only reality, the one steadfast aspect of his life.

And he'd ruined even that.

Ruthlessly he reminded himself that he was a survivor. Life had
cut him up before, and he'd mended. The fact that he was feeling
overwhelmed and confused was no reason to get all bent out of
shape. Life was unpredictable. Brothers could get lost on ice floes;
pilots could make fatal mistakes; people could die. There were no
guarantees. He'd learned to go with the flow. At least he'd thought
he'd learned. This summer was certainly turning into a refresher
course.

"Running away never helps," Mara offered quietly. She'd followed him, unable to help herself, compelled by the pain she'd
caused him to feel.

"But it's damned good exercise."

In silence Mara stood looking at Mark's hunched back, looking beyond him and out at the Bering Sea. She listened to the lapping of the waves and watched an occasional gull off in the far
distance, wondering how to proceed. Mark had traveled far enough
that the main part of the village was behind them. Here the beach
was lonely and silent and private. As she stood there, a gust of wind
sprayed a salty mist over her skin. It felt good, refreshing, cleans-
ing. It cleared the senses and calmed the emotions.

"Answer me one question," Mark suddenly said. He kept his
gaze fixed on the ocean. "Why did you pick up that drum?"

The whispered question sent shivers of emotion down her spine.
Oh, Mark, she thought, wishing she could burn all the barriers
between them and just hold him tight, as he had once held her.

"Why did you do it?" he repeated.

"Maybe I don't like being manipulated any more than you do."

Mark turned around so fast he almost lost his balance. "What's
that supposed to mean?"

"I didn't expect you to dance, but when you did…when it didn't
seem as if you could do it…" Mara's shrug was jerky, harsh. "I
suppose I got angry. I knew what you were going through out
there, and it made me mad that I hadn't realized beforehand that
it might happen. And the drummers were making it worse. I don't

know. I just did, that's all. I was angry and I did it. You were angry and you danced. Things seemed to mesh.''

They'd meshed, all right. Mara's drumsong had called to him as the others' had not. A pounding, rhythmic melding of minds, easy to understand, easy to anticipate. That was why he'd followed her. Her rage and her pain had been as clear to him as his own.

"Then you did it for me," he concluded softly.

Mara's breath caught at the altered tone of his voice. Gone was the anger, and in its place . . . She gasped. Her eyes grew huge and dark, as dark as the Sea, churning not with fear but with awareness, acknowledgment and, finally, concession.

As though the last had been his signal, Mark planted his hands on her shoulders and pulled her in to him. "I don't know what's going on inside me anymore," he admitted softly.

Mara lay against his chest, her heart beating so loudly that she felt certain he'd hear. His breath tickled her hair, and his warm body was hard against her own. She didn't move, afraid to break the mood, wanting to prolong this moment out of time. Involuntarily, she burrowed deeper into his chest.

"Mara . . ."

She shuddered and pulled back. Her gaze met his, seeing his need, knowing he saw her own. The pain of it was so sweet, so precious that a tear slowly trickled from the corner of her eye and clung tenuously to her lashes before coursing quickly down her cheek. What did he want from her? What was he asking?

What was she willing to give?

"Mara . . . oh, God, Mara, please."

She sighed, a soft windsong of sound followed by a small nod. Whatever it was he needed, Mara knew she couldn't walk away and push him deeper into the cold and lonely cocoon he'd built so successfully around himself. Mark was slowly emerging. He was asking questions and reevaluating everything in his life, it seemed. And maybe, just maybe, he was reevaluating them, too.

Mark placed his hands on either side of her face, then slid his fingers through her hair as he pulled her lips to his.

The rhythmic slide of the waves crashing into the shore and the whisper of the cool evening breeze were the only sounds around them. Mark's nostrils flared as his lips brushed hers, gently exploring, trying not to overwhelm her with any sense of the crushing need he was controlling.

The ermine-soft touch of her lips threatened to drown him. That she would kiss him, that she felt any desire at all for him, left him breathless. For a long while, it seemed, her soft lips lay still. Then, slowly, tentatively, he felt the increased pressure and knew she was kissing him back.

At that, his need escalated, just barely checked.

He covered her mouth boldly, without hesitation, without awkwardness. Ruthlessly he shut out the past, selfishly deciding to take this one moment and savor it as if the sudden halt of a four-year abstinence were meant to be savored, had to be savored. Her mouth was as exciting as it had once been, as he'd imagined it would be again, the sweet taste of her shattering barriers as it exploded through him. His thumbs caressed her cheeks even as he used his superior height and weight to bend her backward beneath the primitive power of his embrace. His tongue claimed her mouth, coaxing and eventually dueling with hers, until he heard her tiny cry and felt the bittersweet press of her breasts as they strained against his chest.

Mara couldn't breathe, and decided it didn't matter. If she died with the touch of his lips on hers, it would be a good death. Her heart pounded with excitement and wonder. Her blood rushed. She let her head fall back under the force of his kiss, trying to keep up with the spiraling desire flowing over her, knowing she hadn't a chance.

But she didn't care. It was enough that Mark was here, that he was holding her and kissing her and that years of pent-up doubts over her sexual nonresponsiveness were being so explosively exorcised.

Mara felt his heat and his power seep through her ceremonial garment. Her breasts flushed, her nipples tightening. Sensation coursed through her body, shaking her, surprising her with its power. She arched against Mark's body, hearing his groan, feeling her body heat with a long-forgotten fire. She thrilled to the touch of his lips, and when he removed his callused hands from her face and possessively spanned her waist, she felt incredibly feminine. Held so gently, a part of her soul, long hidden away, began a slow healing.

Mark drew back for air, then refastened his mouth over hers, arching her to him with a need that would have been painful had Mara not been equally needy. He knew that he should slow down, that he should relish every moment, but when she stood on tiptoe, trustingly leaning her firm, rounded breasts and long, lean legs against his aroused body, he shuddered and thrust his tongue deeply into her moist mouth, picking her up, swallowing her surprised cry to lay her on the sand in a single fluid motion. He wanted her here. He wanted her now. With the wind swirling around them and the ocean at their feet.

His body covered hers, and the feel of her stretched out beneath him dragged a primitive groan of need from him.

"Mara," he said raggedly. "I want you."

Her answer was a small whimper as her body froze. At first he was too aroused with need to comprehend the change, and he continued kissing her with an even wilder abandon, his hands freed to test the supple resiliency of her thighs and her rib cage just beneath her breasts. But then he realized she wasn't returning his kisses or caressing him with her hands. Her body lay still, and as stiff as a board.

"Mara?"

Mark hoisted himself up on his hands so that he could see her face. Her eyes were wide open and her mouth was pursed in a grim line, as if she were tolerating torture instead of participating in pleasure. Her expression was easy to read.

"You're afraid, aren't you?"

Mara shuddered a sigh and looked away.

Mark took that as an answer. "I wouldn't hurt you," he said. Guilt for his past actions bombarded him. He'd already hurt her.

Both of them acknowledged that unspoken truth. "Don't say it was a mistake. I know when a woman wants me."

Mara closed her eyes tight, but even so, a fat tear escaped and trickled down her cheek. Of course he would know. She was personally knowledgeable about his passionate nature. She was the only sexual innocent in this situation.

Innocent and frightened. Like last time, only worse. Much worse.

Mara inhaled deeply, raggedly. "I can't . . . I can't explain."

But Mark could. He swore bitterly, because he suddenly realized *he* could explain it. Her pills. Mara was pregnant, and she couldn't make love to him because she loved Wally, her so-called *friend*.

Mara searched Mark's face. He had strong, masculine features that pleased her. There was a taut grimness to his lips, but the eyes that watched her stonily were the same eyes that had watched her for years during their childhood.

The hazy sun bathed Mark's upper body in warm yellow light. His chest was broad, and his biceps were strained and visible, bulging from beneath the cuffs of his T-shirt. She almost wished those strong arms would enfold her again, as they'd just finished doing. Almost.

"I'd better go," Mara murmured. Mark moved off her and she stood, brushing self-consciously at the sand on her clothes and in her hair. She didn't know what to say, how to act. The fear she'd felt had been reflexive, debilitating, and unsurprising, considering how much she'd wanted Mark. When he'd picked her up and covered her with his body, she'd balked. It was just too much too soon.

And then again, maybe it was more.

All she knew was that she wasn't ready for making love. She didn't trust him enough. Some, but not enough to blithely forgive the past, or even to simply forget it. Years ago she'd naively trusted him too much, and his words and his actions that night had shattered much more than her pride—they had crippled her confidence in herself as a woman.

She was no longer a naive teenager. She was an adult, and adults, even sexually innocent ones like herself, deserved an explanation, or, at the very least, an apology. And she shouldn't have to ask for it, either.

"I'd better get back," Mara repeated. "Grandaunt Zoya is probably wondering what happened to me."

Mark's rigid expression clouded as the evening's events returned full-force. "Does Wally know you're . . . sick?"

Mara didn't understand what could have prompted that question, but she answered it anyway. "No, he would worry about me," she said, unaware how damning her words were to the man listening. She turned away, only to turn back again. "Are you leaving tomorrow?"

Right then, Mark knew of no words that could erase the wariness gathered behind her passion-clouded eyes. Did she want him to go or to stay? Did she even care?

Holding her had closed a deep wound within him; kissing her had seemingly opened it up again. What to do?

*Running away doesn't help,* Mara had said to him earlier. He sighed, threading his hands through his windblown hair.

"No, Mara, not tomorrow."

## Chapter Twelve

*Iluperaq? Grandniece?* Her grandaunt was speaking to her.

*Where are you?* she asked. *Are you all right?*

*It is time.... Come... it is time....*

Mara's eyes opened. The room was dark, but not so dark that she couldn't identify her grandaunt's possessions.

Everything was in its place.

Her thoughts whirled, caught up in the eerie sensation that she'd experienced this before. Then she remembered. Two weeks ago yesterday. Her grandmother's message to come home. *Time runs out,* her grandmother had warned. And now her grandaunt was telling her, *It is time.*

Time for what?

Not stopping to question her instincts, Mara flung aside the sheets and ran into her grandaunt's bedroom.

It was empty.

Mara froze, shocked by the sight of the neatly arranged bed. Where was her grandaunt? She spun completely around, eyes narrowed and looking for clues, struggling to figure out how the old healer had managed to pass right by her without making a sound.

*Come...*

Mara was sorely tempted to fling wide the door and race outside. But once there, where would she head? In what direction?

For an instant, Mara wished she could ask Mark for help. But he would no more chase after a dream than he would allow her to once she'd told him of her intent. Tears filled her eyes, and she sat down on the bed, trying to think. What if she couldn't find her? How long could a sightless, sick old woman survive before she stumbled and fell, or worse?

*Iluperaq...come...The Gathering Place...*

Like a bird taking flight, Mara shot up off the bed, her heart pounding with relief and fear. The Gathering Place. Her grandaunt had told her about the small, hidden cove during one of their sessions. There she performed her healing rites.

Mara quickly threw on some warm clothes and spared only one extra moment to grab the blankets off hers and her grandaunt's beds. Then she raced for the door, opened it and crashed headlong into Vadim.

His arms reached out to steady her. "Vadim! Oh, thank God! You've got to help me. Your grandmother. She's gone to the Gathering Place, and I—"

"I know." He looked at her oddly, then seemed to sigh. "Follow me."

Together they ran into the dark.

Mark turned over in bed, opened his eyes and knew instantly that something was not right. He sat up and reached for his watch, pressing a small knob on the side to illuminate the dial. Three-thirty in the morning. And Vadim was missing.

Just then, a rustling outside the dormitory room door indicated that the nightwalker had returned. He watched him creep across the room to his bed.

"Hot date?" Mark's voice shattered the silence.

Vadim jumped and banged hard into the edge of his bed. Mark listened to the creative string of oaths issuing from his friend's mouth, and chuckled.

"Don't let Zoya hear you talking like that."

Almost on cue, Vadim banged his toe. Mark chuckled. "A late night out, Vadim?" Mark's voice spoke into the silence. "Where were you? You can tell me, I promise to keep it to myself."

The silence stretched, and Mark's amusement quickly turned to unease. Deciding it was time to shed some light on whatever Vadim was up to, he swept aside the sheet and started across the room to the light switch by the door. He never made it.

"This is family business. Don't interfere," Vadim warned, blocking his way out. His voice was rough, and as menacing as he could make it, considering whom he was ordering.

Mark reached around and flicked the switch. Bright light filled the small room. In silence he took in Vadim's muddy clothes and boots, his dirty hands and mud-smeared face. "Want to tell me what kind of family business makes you this dirty at three-thirty in the morning?"

"No."

"Want to tell me where you were?"

"No."

Mark's suspicions flared. "I'll ask you one more question, Vadim, and you'd better think before you answer."

Vadim's eyes widened, but he held his ground. "This family business you mentioned— Does it involve Mara?"

Vadim's abrupt tension was all the answer Mark needed. Muttering an oath, he stalked back to his bed and dragged on his jeans. Then he reached for his T-shirt.

"I can't let you interfere, Mark. It's forbidden."

Mark sat down and pulled on his socks. He wasn't particularly concerned about forbidden. But he was concerned about Mara.

"They'll be back before sunrise," Vadim offered. "You'll see."

*Damn right they'll—* Mark stopped himself. He fixed Vadim with a "don't mess with me" stare. "Who...is...they?" Each word was distinct.

"Grandmother and Mara, of course. Who else?"

Mark let out the breath he hadn't known he was holding and reached for his court shoes. He wasn't certain exactly who he'd thought Mara was with. Knowing it was Zoya didn't particularly ease his anxiety, though. "You wanna tell me where the hell they are?"

"They're at the Gathering Place. But it's forbidden. You can't go out there."

Mark ignored Vadim's warning. He finished lacing his shoes and stood. When Zoya had described the place, it had sounded damned strange. "Are they safe?" What he really wanted to know was, did Mara have her pills? But he couldn't ask that.

"They're safe. Nothing goes there."

No *thing.* He grabbed his jacket. "If it's family business, what are you doing here? Why aren't you there with them?"

"Men aren't allowed," he confided.

Mark's anxiety increased. The two women were living together. Why did they need to *go* anywhere to talk?

Damn! He'd told Mara not to take any unnecessary risks.

"Stay away, Mark." Vadim's voice cut the silence. "They'll be back in a few hours. You want answers, you wait until then. If Zoya wants you to know, she'll tell you."

For a moment, it was difficult to tell which of them was more surprised by Vadim's unspoken ultimatum. A faint shadow of humor crossed Mark's face.

"And just how would you stop me?"

"I don't know. But don't try it. Zoya asked for privacy, and that's what she'll get."

There was a moment of tense silence. Mark paused, weighing what he'd learned against his instincts. "If they're not back by sunrise, all bets are off."

Vadim visibly relaxed, and a smile managed to tilt up the corners of his mouth. But Mark noted that his eyes were just as clouded as they'd been all along.

"If they're not back by sunrise," Vadim murmured, "I'll lead the way."

Looking around the small, claustrophobic cave, with its striated rock showing the markings of geological time and the power of the Bering Sea, Mara shuddered from more than the cold. Zoya's little fire didn't exactly cheer up the dismal-looking place.

"Grandaunt, what's going on?"

"Do you know why I summoned you?"

The old healer sat cross-legged on a reindeer-hide rug, wrapped snugly in the blankets Mara had brought and insisted she use. Her long white hair was unbound. She wore the traditional white bird-skin *kuspuk* of a spiritual healer, and on her head sat a headdress of white beads and white ermine tails. At her side lay a small pouch crafted from the bladder lining of a small animal. Their ancestors had used such pouches to carry and transport liquids. Sort of an ancient Ziploc bag. Mara's mouth curved upward in a small smile.

"I'm here to receive the sacred teachings, I think," she replied, fairly certain she was right. She'd hit on that as she followed Vadim across the tundra to this place where the Sea had cut a deep, long inlet, gouging out narrow fissures. Behind one of these fissures, lay this cave.

"You speak truth. Calm yourself, Grandniece. Fear has no place here."

Mara decided to reserve judgment. She fidgeted, uncomfortable in the dark, damp surroundings. The air was heavy with sea mist and salty odors. The lonely echoes of waves added to the sense of timelessness. Save for the blankets she'd brought—which Zoya now used—and the fire and the pouch, they were alone. Even Vadim was gone, his departure having been as silent as his arrival. But Mara had held his gaze and absorbed his worry seconds before he left her at the mouth of the cave with instructions that Zoya awaited inside.

Eerie, Mara decided. This entire situation was strange. The sooner they got home, the better off they'd both be.

"Come. Sit close to the fire," Zoya commanded.

Mara did as Zoya requested and felt marginally better.

"You have learned much of me and my people," the old healer suddenly said. "Before you receive the sacred teachings, I would know more of you."

Mara closed her eyes as hurt burned in her stomach. "You don't trust me," she murmured softly. "You wish your sister were here."

Zoya was silent for so long that Mara finally looked up. The sightless eyes were peering directly at her. "The sacred teachings are very powerful, Grandniece. Only the chosen can receive them. This is not a matter of trust."

"But I took Grandmother's place."

"I would know more of you," Zoya repeated.

Mara's heart beat faster. "You already know I'm an anthropologist," she began, haltingly. "I plan on using your language and customs as the basis for my advanced degree, possibly even my doctorate. I also plan on expanding my translation business."

Zoya nodded. "That is how others see you. What I wish to know is how clearly you see yourself. What of being wife? What of becoming mother?"

Mara's heart jerked painfully. Was motherhood a requirement? If so, then she'd just failed the exam. Motherhood wasn't even an option in her present state of anxiety over matters strictly sexual. And the part about the wife, well, she couldn't imagine herself in that role with anyone other than Mark.

The ease with which that truth slipped through her slowly numbing defenses stunned Mara, and for a moment she was caught up in the unrealistic fantasy of a dark-haired girl-child with Mark's zest for progress and her reverence for the past. Then she shook her head. "I don't know, Grandaunt," she admitted honestly, her voice wavering slightly. "I love children, but they're not in my immediate future."

"Then Tuntu has not made you his woman," Zoya stated matter-of-factly.

Mara's reaction was not matter-of-fact. "Made me his *what!*"

"His woman. You feel much for this one. I sense this. Though my eyes cannot see, I am far from blind."

The gentle admonishment dropped heavily into the misty atmosphere. Mara blushed, thinking about all those long silences this past week, silences during which they had stared at one another, their actions and their words stilted and awkward because of what they had exposed during and after his dance. Mara knew Mark wanted her. Mark knew she wanted him. She knew Mark was afraid of change. He knew she was afraid of intimacy.

They knew a hell of a lot about each other. And yet, they knew very little about things that counted between a man and a woman. Things like marriage and children. Things like shared goals and a common outlook for the years ahead.

"Mark believes our people's future lies in accepting the progress of the *kass'aq* way."

"This I know," Zoya said, her expression sad. "Tuntu is confused. He battles his nature. But he will lose, as my grandson lost, and therefore he will learn."

"How do you know? How can you be so certain?"

"I am healer. Pain is not only of the body. For him, it is of the soul. Tuntu has closed his eyes to many things, not only to my people. He does not wish to see truth. He is afraid. But truth requires no light. It shines bright in darkness."

Mara shivered and watched Zoya warily. She had the feeling there was very little the healer didn't see, very little she didn't know about her, as well. And though this made her feel oddly exposed and vulnerable, she wasn't afraid. Zoya was family. Mara could sense only comfort and serenity and love flowing out from the watching woman.

"As Mark is our guide to the past, you are our key to the future. The time of beginning is now. You heard my call. You are here."

For a long while, they sat in silent communion, watching the fire. Then Zoya stirred.

"My sister— What has she told you of the sacred teachings?"

"Nothing, really," Mara answered. "I didn't even know they existed until I read your letter."

"Ah, yes. The letter. The letter you say I wrote."

Not a question, a statement. "Well, Grandmother must have confused the handwriting, because you couldn't have written it, could you? Someone else must have, and you've just forgotten."

Mara noted Zoya's raised white eyebrow and blushed at her tactless comment.

Suddenly Zoya laid back the blankets and sat forward, her sightless eyes fixed firmly on Mara. "What I tell you now, cannot be repeated. You cannot write it down, you cannot record it, you cannot speak of it with anyone."

Even Mark? Mara automatically thought, but what came out was "Even Grandmother?"

"Your grandmother knows. It is because of her knowledge that you are here." Zoya's voice was formal, stiff, heavy with warning.

Mara's calm shattered, and her heart skipped a beat.

"When I was a young girl of your age, I became very sick. My hands would sweat. My heart would race. I would get dizzy. I would faint."

Mara gasped, but if Zoya heard it, she gave no indication.

"My brothers thought I would die. My husband hoped I was with child."

Mara looked across at Zoya's pained expression and was reminded of her grandmother's haunted eyes as she'd left with Mark. She felt guilt twist deeply inside her.

"And Grandmother? What did she think?"

"Milak knew I was not with child."

"She knew. And it turned out you weren't?"

"I was not."

"Then what happened? You're not sick with it anymore, are you?"

"I am healer" was Zoya's simple reply. Then she continued. "My mother was also healer. She prepared a special tea, which I drank. Later, Milak also drank of this tea."

"*Grandmother,* too?" she whispered, stunned. "But she never said anything."

"We do not speak of it. As I said, what you now learn, cannot be repeated."

"But she gave me that same tea just before I left. I didn't even know she suspected I was sick. But she must have, mustn't she?"

Mara focused on Zoya's silent countenance. The healer's blind eyes met hers, unreadable, steady. But the old hands trembled visibly. Somehow, that telltale sign managed to frighten Mara.

"Grandmother's not sick now."

"She is healer," Zoya replied.

Mara's thoughts whirled. Both Zoya and Milak had suffered as she was suffering. Both of them had been given a special tea to drink. It stood to reason that if their mother, Mara's great-grandmother, had prepared the brew, then she must have needed it, too. And if they had all been cured, then ... Mara stopped her spiraling hopes. *One step at a time.*

"Your mother," Mara asked, just to make sure. "She also drank the tea?"

"And her sister. And her mother's daughter before that."

Mara gasped. "And Vadim? What about him?"

"Only the women, and then only a select few. That is why I would know more of you." Zoya leaned forward. Her intensity reached out to Mara, making her catch her breath. "You say Milak gave you the tea. How long have you been ill?"

Mara's heart thudded painfully fast. "Six, seven months. A year, maybe, I don't remember exactly. It's just lately, now, that it's getting worse, that I'm always on edge."

Mark's ultimatum came abruptly to mind. *Just don't go off by yourself. Or anywhere, for that matter, without your pills. I'm not about to bring you home in a casket.*

As if Zoya had sensed the direction of Mara's thoughts, she asked, "And what of Tuntu? Does he know?"

Mara shuddered, recalling Mark's fury. "Yes. I fainted before we arrived. He...he was going to force me to go home unless I gave him some idea of what was happening. I told him I didn't know, but I did tell him."

"He protects you."

"Yes, I guess so. But he doesn't like it."

"I sensed this in his dance, heard it in your drumsong."

The formal way she said it made goose bumps rise on Mara's arms. She swallowed, sensing that something momentous was about to happen. The waves stopped lapping, as if they, too, were holding their breath. "How?"

"The sacred teachings." Zoya smoothed a wrinkled, trembling hand across the pouch at her side. "You must drink this."

Mara jolted and eyed it warily. "Why? What's in there?"

"Your future."

"My—" Mara gulped "—my future?"

"Yes."

Mara shook her head. "I don't understand. Tell me exactly what's in there."

"An herbal potion passed down through the ages from healer to healer, from mother to daughters."

"What will it do to me? Is it a cure?"

Had an old pouch ever looked so wonderful and so frightening at the same time?

"Perhaps."

"What does that mean? You're not sure what's going to happen once I take this?"

"The cure must come from within you. From your belief. From your faith. This potion provides a path, but you must walk this path."

Mara's voice shook. Suddenly the salvation Zoya offered didn't look quite so alluring. "How?"

"You must choose."

It wasn't the words so much as the expression on Zoya's face that had the breath backing up in Mara's lungs. It was unwavering, fierce and desperate. Instinctively she cringed, not wanting to ask the next questions but knowing she had no choice.

"Choose what?"

"To become healer."

Mara scrambled to her feet, backing away so quickly she almost fell. "You're kidding aren't you? Grandaunt, *please,* tell me you're kidding."

The flickering flames stilled as the silence between them stretched. The waves were silent. Nothing moved. No sound filled the void in the cave.

"But what about my career, the one I was just telling you all about? The one you've been so interested in since the first day we met?"

"You must choose."

"No! No, I won't. I can't. It's not fair." Mara backed away another foot, slamming into the ragged edge of the cave wall. She had to fight for each breath, fight it past a million questions, a million fears. "How can you do this? How could Grandmother? You know I love you both. How can you manipulate me this way?"

"Healer to our people, or teacher, anthropologist. Not both."

Mara watched as Zoya reached for the pouch with hands that trembled badly. "It is time. You heard my call, you have the sickness. You know this as truth." Their eyes met, held. "For you the decision is difficult, this I understand. This my sister understood. But it does not change the fact that you must choose. It does not alter the truth." Zoya reached out, extending the pouch.

Mara recoiled. "You expect me to choose tonight? *Right now?*" Mara nearly screamed it, then closed her hands over her mouth, because she was afraid she wouldn't stop, once started.

"No. Not tonight. But soon."

Mara stared at her dazedly. Wave after wave of fear and doubt and confusion bombarded her until she looked desperately at the fissure beyond which freedom lay. Her grandaunt and her grandmother had planned this. Mark had been right. The two women she loved most in the world, the two women she had thought would never deliberately hurt anyone, were hurting her. They were tearing her apart. And in a flash, one of those crazy insights that come out of nowhere, Mara knew.

"The letter," she asked jerkily. "Who wrote it?"

"Milak."

Mara cried out and squeezed shut her eyes. She hadn't even known that her grandmother *could* write. Had they planned this that many years ago?

"Why?" she whispered. "Why not just ask me? Why go through all of this?"

Zoya didn't pretend ignorance of her question. "You are the last female, and we are old. Too old to await a girl-child you have said may never be." Her head hung low, then raised again. Her expression was pained, but not guilty. "Our ways must survive."

"Our ways must survive," Mara repeated, her voice trembling, tortured. "No matter what."

Zoya didn't answer, for the question required no answer.

Mara gazed at the pouch. "You say I don't have to choose tonight."

Zoya nodded. "But you must choose before I die."

A cry escaped Mara's tightly compressed lips. "What happens if I don't? Will I—" She forced herself to say it. "Will *I* die?"

Zoya paused, almost as if she were consulting with someone. "No. You will just be sick."

"What about if I *do* take it? Can that stuff kill me?"

This time, Zoya didn't hesitate. "You must be committed to a life of healing. That is the test. Before you can heal others, you must heal yourself."

Mara turned her back on the healer, needing visual, if not mental, privacy. What to do? What to believe? Zoya's words were so farfetched. Yet they did make a weird kind of ethical sense. If she couldn't minister to herself and succeed, then she most certainly shouldn't be out there doing for others, risking their lives, their futures.

"How do I do it?" Mara's voice cracked as she whirled on Zoya.

"That is what you will learn," she said quietly. "That is what the sacred teachings will tell you."

Mara opened her mouth to ask how, but Zoya raised her hand, wordlessly asking for patience. Mara didn't have any, but she shut up anyway. "Our knowledge is ancient. It has been gathered through generations of healers. That is why it is so powerful. That is why only a few are chosen."

"And I'm one of the lucky ones?" she snapped, her voice high and thin and strained close to breaking.

"Yes. From my mother to me, from me to Milak, and from us to you, knowledge will flow through a rite of passage."

God! Would this nightmare never end? "Explain."

"Two times you will take this potion." Zoya's hand patted the pouch. "And two times you will sleep. When you wake, you will know who we are. You will understand our knowledge. And you will know who you are. Teacher or healer, not both."

Just then, Mara was understanding very little. With a supreme effort, she tried to focus. "Then I'll be cured?"

"No. There is a third potion. Different from the other. More powerful. If you choose teacher, you may not take the final potion."

"Because if I did, it would kill me?"

"Because there must be no doubt in your mind that you wish to be healer," Zoya replied. "You must clearly see your future's path. Then you must walk toward the light of knowledge."

Mara paled and made a small sound of denial. "Can't you just give me the third potion and let me take it to my doctor? He can analyze the active ingredients and remove any toxins. That way, I could be cured without the risk."

Zoya shook her head. "The potion itself is not the cure. *You* are the cure, your belief in our healing ways, in your ability to heal others and your desire to do so. That is what will cure you. The potion is powerless without your commitment to make it work."

"And why do I have to decide now? Why couldn't I take it home, think about it and decide later?"

"The final potion loses its power, and the herbs are rare. They do not bloom every year. They do not grow in Alaska."

With those last words, any hope Mara had harbored of a way out died. She felt trapped, completely unequipped to make such a momentous decision. She loved her work as an interpreter and, since meeting Ed and Ethel, had actually begun contemplating the possibility of a doctorate with great enthusiasm and excitement. Could she give up those plans? Did she want to?

Did she have any choice?

More than just her good health was at stake here. According to Zoya, in her womb lay the seeds of future healers, daughters who would one day be forced to make the same difficult decision.

Unless she made it for them.

Could she delude herself with the notion that to walk away was to protect them? Could she live guilt-free, knowing that with her rejection hundreds of years of medical knowledge was sacrificed? That she had severed a family chain that had grown stronger with each passing generation?

She'd felt guilty just taking her grandmother's place! How would she handle this? To walk away now, to reject the potion, was to lose something so ancient, so valuable, so utterly incredible, that only the direst reason could suffice. And Mara knew what that reason was.

Fear for her own life.

Nothing would be gained by her death. Therefore, Mara knew she had to be absolutely one hundred percent certain that she would be a good healer. *If* she chose to do it. And that was the biggest *if* she'd ever encountered.

She had no proof of her capabilities beyond Zoya's certainty. And for Mara, in this very special instant, even Zoya's certainty wasn't enough.

There were other questions beyond that of capability. Could she settle in Twilight? Could she live what amounted to just a few doors down the street from Mark? Could she live out her life, wanting him as she did, knowing that he wanted her, too, but not enough to overcome his own fears?

Could she live with the possibility that he might one day want someone else?

Reminding her of their kisses, this latest question hurt Mara the most. The only man she had ever wanted was Mark. She had grown up wanting him as a friend, and now that she was grown, she wanted him as a lover. But he didn't want her that way, at least not enough. What was the point of saving herself for her future daughters if there were never to be any?

What to do? God, what to do?

"Grandniece." Zoya's voice interrupted Mara's thoughts. "You think too much. This is not a decision for the mind. It is for the heart." She patted the pouch. "Come. Take the potion. Learn about us, about yourself. Then you will know what to do."

Emotionally exhausted, Mara hesitated for a long, agonizing moment. Then she nodded, reached for the pouch and drank.

## Chapter Thirteen

Mark stared through the mist across at Zoya's house, unhappily aware that he was wet and cold, but not caring enough to get up from his shadowed position reclining against a horizontal barrel. Vadim had just left, presumably to get some sleep. Mark was relieved. He needed some time alone to think.

He'd watched the two women as they returned from their mission, noting their silence, noting how Zoya seemed to be leading Mara down the street. He hadn't liked that. Mara hadn't been carrying her purse, either.

As if in response to his thoughts, Zoya's door opened and Mara stepped out. His eyes narrowed on her slender figure, and he watched as she took a deep breath, then raised clasped arms high above her head and stretched. The sinuous movement thrust her breasts forward against the fabric of her T-shirt. Abruptly, Mark's chill turned into a slow, frustrated burn.

"I thought—" Mark pushed himself upright, projecting his voice across the deserted street "—we agreed that you wouldn't go anywhere without your pills."

Mara gasped and dropped her arms. She watched Mark approach, noting how his mist-soaked jeans molded him snugly, sensuously. His hands were stuffed in his back pockets, and his face was all affronted attitude. She shoved suddenly shaking hands into the deep pockets of her jacket. "What are you doing here?"

"Waiting for you. Have been for over an hour." He looked down at her, noting the fatigue she couldn't hide, and the nervousness. And something else. Something new had been added. Something that was making her avoid his glance. "Are you all right?"

The drizzly morning air shrouded them in a soft cloak of quiet. "Are you all right?" he repeated, watching the question jerk through her body. Her eyes looked dazed, her expression unnaturally tight. He felt a chill creep over him. "Vadim told me you two were at the Gathering Place."

Mara remained silent. "Fine, never mind," he murmured, and turned away.

"Wait." Mara expelled the breath she'd been holding while he spoke, barely hearing his words, caught in an emotional turmoil that had nothing and everything to do with him. She wanted refuge. She needed to be held. But the only place, the only comfort, wasn't hers to seek, maybe never would be. "I'm all right," she lied.

When he turned back and met her gaze, he stood still. His eyes reflected her own disbelief, showing a bitter resignation, a hint of anger, a lot of hunger.

Her stomach knotted tightly, and she looked down at the ground. But she could still feel his fire-hot gaze. Or was it the aftereffects of the potion?

The sleep had come quickly. Mara had barely stretched out on one of the reindeer-hide rugs with her head resting on Zoya's lap when she dozed off. For her, time had moved slowly. Later Zoya told her less than an hour had passed.

But in that hour, her life had been forever changed. And I can't ever tell him, she thought.

"What?" Mark asked, watching her hands clench.

"What?"

"I thought you were going to tell me something," he said, aware his tone was hopeful, aware he probably didn't have anything to hope for.

"No, I . . ." She glanced up at him, met his eyes for a long moment, then glanced away.

"Mara," he said, and when she didn't look up, he sighed.

Mara looked up then, and it was as if she'd made some decision. "Mark, I want to ask you a question. You don't have to answer if you don't want to. Just say so, and I'll drop it."

Mark looked down at the woman he so desperately wanted and wondered what question could have made her beautiful black eyes so deeply disturbed.

Taking a deep, fortifying breath, she blurted out, "Before you crashed, when you were working as a medevac pilot, how did that make you feel?"

"What the hell kind of question is that?"

"A private one. Like I said, you don't have to answer."

"Damn right I don't."

Mara shuddered. "I'm sorry. I should have realized. It's just that I needed . . . Please, just forget it. Forget I asked."

Needed what? Mark didn't know. But he would, he promised himself. He'd never been asked that particularly familiar question in quite that way. Normally he got "Why did you give it up?", or "When was the last time you flew?" But Mara had asked how he'd *felt*.

"Free, that's how I felt. Free."

Mara stared, unblinking, waiting for him to continue, hoping he would continue.

"I . . . went where I was needed. Out over the Bering, inland to the mountains, across the tundra. But it was more than that. To me, it wasn't really work. I felt if they'd let me fly all day, I would."

Mara had suspected as much, but had needed to hear the words. "And what does it feel like to give it up?"

Mark's expression grew blank. "You go on." He shrugged. "Nothing else to do."

"That's it? Too bad? The best thing in your life's over, and that's all it cost you?"

Mark studied her, wondering what she was after.

"Mark, please. I need to understand."

"Like losing my best friend," he found himself saying. "I suppose it felt like . . . dying. But I gave it up anyway," he quickly added. "I had to. It was the second hardest thing I've ever done."

"The second?"

It was time. Time to get rid of the baggage, and to explain. As far as forgiveness was concerned, Mark didn't hold out much hope.

"The hardest thing I've ever done—" he forced his gaze to remain locked with hers "—I did . . . that night . . . to you."

There, it was out. He wasn't surprised by the way she instantly recoiled. Instinctively he reached out and captured her wrist, crushing the delicate feathers on her *talliraq*.

"You asked, damn it," he said, pinning her to his side. "Now hear me out. It's not exactly easy for me, either, you know."

"Then don't do it. Don't say anything." She whispered the plea, trying to wrest her arm free of his grip. It was like pushing against a concrete wall. "Just let it go. Please, Mark. Not now. Maybe tomorrow, okay? Right now I've got enough to handle."

"Then tell me what it is, and we'll share it," Mark heard himself say. "There is something, isn't there?"

Mara gazed at him, stricken.

"It's been four years, Mara. If you can't share it, we both know why. Don't you think we *should* talk?"

"Yes." She tried to stay calm, but she knew her voice was shaking. "But not now, *not tonight.*"

"You mean this morning." Mark watched her back away toward the house until an arm's length stood between them.

"Leave it be, Mark," Mara whispered.

"I can't. Maybe it's not the right time, but I need to explain, and you need to listen. At least stop denying that."

For a long, endless moment, there was no sound but that of Mara's ragged breathing as she fought to control an irrational spate of self-anger. She should never have come outside. Why hadn't she just gone to bed, as Zoya had urged?

Because she obviously wasn't thinking straight, was still reeling from shock. The potion had been powerful, just as Zoya had said. From the instant she'd fallen asleep, the images had come. Visions of her *inua* and Mark's, hers flying over the tundra, his running headlong across it, together yet not together. Their rhythm nonsynchronous and loudly disharmonic. To Mara, the disturbing message had been only too clear: Whatever decision she made, Mark would play a key role.

But not tonight—or rather, not today. Too much had happened. She needed time. She needed space.

"Mara, I didn't mean it—" began Mark.

"Don't." Mara interrupted him quickly, cutting across his words, staring past him and up at the sky. "I understand. Really, I do. You wanted to be alone. I interrupted your privacy." Her eyes focused on Mark. She knew what he must read in hers, the confusion, the overload, her rejection of him at this time, at this moment.

Mark flinched.

"I'm sorry. I should have knocked. But I didn't, and what happened ... happened."

"You think what I did to you was your fault, don't you?"

"Please, Mark, let me go. Grandaunt's waiting."

"Grandaunt's asleep. You two have been up all damn night," he replied roughly, shaking his head. "I can't believe this, Mara. I can't believe you actually think it was your fault!"

A cold knot formed in his stomach. He looked at Mara's pale face and felt a profound regret over his actions, a regret that went beyond shame. Because of her innocence, she'd blamed herself. Because of her feelings for him, she'd surrendered her home and her family, the only security, the only life, she'd ever known. He didn't want to believe it. But he had no choice.

"You wanted to comfort me, remember?" he said softly.

"Yes, but I did it all wrong, didn't I? You're not turned on by naive little girls with teenage crushes."

For a moment, Mark thought he would be sick. Those were the exact words he'd hurled at her that night. Every one of them had been a lie. A lie she'd believed.

"Mara—" Mark's voice was raw with shame, but she had turned aside, uncaring of how the motion twisted her arm at an uncomfortable angle, her eyes unfocused, seeing the past as he'd created it through his own fear. He didn't know which was worse, watching her cringe away or feeling himself do it. All he knew was that he couldn't let her continue suffering.

*"I'm not turned on by naive little girls with teenage crushes."*

Mark swore, and when he felt Mara flinch he realized she was at the edge of her control. "Mara—" His voice broke. "For God's sake—it wasn't your fault. It was mine, do you hear?" He captured her chin and turned her around to look at him. "I *did* need you that night. And I *was* turned on."

"Don't. Don't lie. I saw you. You made me look." This time her voice broke, and she gasped on a sob. "You made me...."

Mark closed his eyes, praying for guidance as he'd never done before. *She offered me heaven, and in return, I gave her hell.*

The knowledge of how terribly he'd scarred her was there in the pale face gazing fixedly at something just beyond his shoulder. She looked bruised, emotionally wrung out.

*Damn it, man! Say something!*

"Losing people you love is damned hard," he began stiltedly, his heart torn by the sight of her tears. "And I'd, well, I'd just had a gutful of it, okay? I didn't want—couldn't stomach—the possibility that it could happen again with you." Mark reached up and stroked her cheek, dropping his hands altogether when she flinched back. "So I pushed you away."

"Because you thought I'd hang around." Mara forced the words through a ragged breath.

"Because I was scared what would happen if you did hang around, yes," Mark admitted, his voice raw and tight as he tried to make Mara understand. "You were eighteen, don't forget. You were young and beautiful and incredibly sexy." She flinched again. "You were! When you touched me, I went a little insane, but I wasn't so far gone that I didn't realize what loving you would do. You had your entire life ahead of you. I didn't even want mine all that much that night. Don't you see? I just couldn't watch you waste yourself on me. You deserved better. You deserved more."

As Mara watched him, she was humiliatingly aware that had he given her the slightest encouragement, she would have stuck around, waiting to marry him, bear his children and live out her life with him in Twilight.

Only the last part was still an option, would become fact, if she survived the third test. If she took the potion at all. But the part about the marriage and the children... She couldn't imagine Mark accepting her in the role of healer. Even if he was admitting that he could accept her in his bed.

"So it was a noble impulse. You sacrificed us so that I could get an education?"

"Yes."

"But I didn't care about that then."

"But you care about it now, don't you?" Mark's voice fairly shook with the intensity of the emotions washing over him. He released her, even though he didn't want to. "You're so excited about your work and your studies that you're going to go for a doctorate."

Numbly Mara turned away, but with hands that trembled, Mark captured her waist and turned her around. "For what I said, I'm sorry." He shuddered, but forced himself to endure her glazed eyes and stunned expression, to get to the worst part of it. "For what I did, the way I acted, I can only say I was out of my mind. I shouldn't have treated you like I did. I shouldn't have taken my pain out on you." Unconsciously, he stroked her, wanting the connection, seeking to ease her turmoil any way he could.

"Stop it," Mara insisted, her hormones humming crazily to life with the knowledge that the arms she sought, the refuge she needed, were so close within reach. His touch was rhythmic and mesmerizing, tugging at her senses, urging her forward when every fiber of her mind shouted for her to stand firm and stay put. "This isn't the time or the place," she said, her voice shaking with suppressed need. She wondered if Mark could hear it. She hoped not.

"I know." Mark spoke softly. "But we could make now the right time, couldn't we? Then all we'd need is a bed."

The tempting offer floated in the mist between them.

Mark stood and waited. He hadn't stopped to analyze the possible dangers such an offer could present, he'd just said it. But now that he had, he couldn't retract it, didn't want to. He decided to stop worrying about Wally. Mara obviously wasn't. Her wide eyes were focused solely on him, to the point that he could see a shiver flutter through her body as she thought about what it would be like. He thought about it, too, and forced his arms not to reach out to enfold her. The choice would be hers.

The unexpected thought rocked him backward. Not since last week, when Zoya had forced him to dance, had he felt such a fierce wave of need and protectiveness. Mara deserved so much more than he could offer. He wasn't ready for a commitment. Maybe he would never be ready. He didn't know. But he *did* know that he wanted her, and that his desire was honest, without strings or hidden agendas.

She could use some healing. Would she let him try?

Losing his silent battle, he pulled her close, positioning her soft, inviting lips just inches from his own. And then he waited for the signal that would tell him what she wanted.

Caught between her physical needs, which were urging her forward, and her psychological needs, which were screaming for caution, Mara wavered. She closed her eyes to feel the warmth of his breath on her cheek, to feel the security in the strength of the hands wrapped firmly about her waist. He wanted her. She could feel it in the trembling stillness that held him as captive as she was. And, opening her eyes, she could see it in the blazing closeness of black eyes searching hers for the smallest response.

Her heart was pounding. She was amazed at his control, aware that he was trying to tell her something by it, something about himself, how he'd changed.

"Mark," asked Mara, her voice a whisper of sweet, aching desire, "what exactly does this mean? Are you saying you're interested in a future for us now?"

The question was an answer in itself. He should have known it was too good to be true. She didn't want him enough. Dropping his hands, he stepped back, his arousal so full and tight that it took him several moments to control the bittersweet pain enough to speak, enough to think. "What were you and Zoya doing at the Gathering Place?"

Mark's abrupt change of attitude and subject startled Mara and
brought everything that had happened to her that morning rushing back. Her breasts ached, and her lips felt abandoned. It could
have been so easy. It would have been so wrong. She attempted
humor. "We were doing a lot of that hocus-pocus stuff you don't
believe in."

"Try me."

Startled, Mara blinked. "You serious?"

"Do I look like I'm laughing?"

"No, but I didn't think... I had no idea— When did you change
your mind?"

"I haven't exactly said I have, Mara." He sighed, aware she'd
attempted to redirect his thoughts. "You're not going to tell me,
are you?" he asked quietly.

"I'm sorry, Mark," Mara began, reminded of Zoya's edict of
secrecy. "But if it were just about you and me..."

"This *is* about you and me," he insisted, watching her desire to
share thwarted by some higher objective.

Mara shook her head. "I can't. I'm sorry."

"Family business, huh?"

Mara's eyes widened, and she nodded. "You... you didn't answer my question."

"The only future I'm interested in is Crosswinds."

Mara thought a lot about her conversation with Mark during the
ensuing week. Every evening, while her grandaunt slept, she would
pass the time reviewing her notes, cataloging the growing bank of
tapes, trying to organize what she'd learned about the old language. She found the work more engrossing than ever, but the decision was never far from her mind. She knew the clock was
ticking, knew Zoya's strength was waning with every passing day,
but she couldn't decide. She still had no proof.

And then there was Mark. The oddest thing was happening between them. Whenever they were together, which was mostly during Zoya's sessions, Mara would start a sentence, only to have
Mark finish it. Or he would start and she would finish. Little by
little, day by day, Mara felt the strange mental connection between them strengthening. She started handing him things before
he even asked for them, anticipating his needs almost as if she were
reading his thoughts.

Mark felt it, too. She could see how it put him on edge, and it
wasn't hard for her to understand why. When he looked at her, she
could read his yearning to fly again, his fear that he never would,

his pain at the very private admission. And she could also read a deep driving hunger for herself that dominated the confusion he felt over his discovery that the past and its traditions were as much a part of who he was as his drive to take advantage of technology.

One afternoon he'd even told her to get out of his head. She'd laughed it off, not willing to acknowledge verbally what they both knew was happening to them, for the prospect frightened her deeply. She carried too many secrets—the decision to become healer, the truth about her illness, her need to reexperience his passion. These were intensely private, and she was finding she didn't want him in her head either.

Early yesterday morning, she'd drunk the potion for the second time. Her sleep had been deep and immediate, the images of Tuntu and the crane blurred by a darkness whose shadow seemed to be pushing them apart, rather than together. And there had been something else. A feeling. A vague, elusive song, almost a calling, that had seemingly floated in and through and around her. Mara had awakened with it ringing softly, barely audible, in her ears. The message had stunned her.

She'd turned to her grandaunt. "Why didn't you tell me?"

"I did," Zoya had said. "From my mother to me, from me to Milak, and from us to you," she'd intoned, repeating the exact words spoken during their first visit.

"From us to you..." Mara had murmured dazedly. She should have realized. With Zoya's passing, Sireniki would be left without a healer. With Milak's weakening, Twilight would soon suffer a similar fate. That left only one solution.

She would have to be healer for both.


Mark entered Zoya's home as he did every morning lately: tense, frustrated, mentally on edge. But as he stepped inside, he didn't hear the usual shy greeting or sense what he'd come to think of as Mara's unique mental signature whispering in his mind. Her essence was absent; the shield barring her thoughts to him was gone. It took him a moment to figure out why. Mara wasn't here. Her special scent wasn't floating in the air, her thoughts weren't swimming around in his head.

For an instant, he felt curiously empty. The feeling surprised and worried him, telling in its strength, for it warned that he was becoming too used to sharing himself with Mara, even if that sharing was only mental.

Zoya sat where she usually sat, in the only cushioned chair in the room. But she was unusually still, her blind gaze focused *on* him, not *through* him. Mark immediately felt his mental barriers strengthening. He figured if Mara could read him, Zoya could likely blow a hole in his brain.

He smiled at the ridiculous thought, but noticed he didn't lower his defenses. "Where's Mara?"

"The Gathering Place."

Mark frowned. Mara was spending altogether too much time there lately. He didn't like it. Didn't like the fact that she was alone there. Anything could happen.

"This disturbs you."

He met her eyes, guarded. "Did I say it did?"

Zoya chuckled. The lingering resentment Mark still harbored against her flourished as embarrassment heated his cheeks. A moment earlier he'd been grateful for a reprieve from Mara's mental presence. Now he wished she was back. Frustrated, he crossed to where his camcorder lay and began assembling the tripod.

"You are a stubborn Tuntu," Zoya said. "Why do you fight? I had thought that by now, you would see."

"I see plenty."

"Tell me. Tell me what you see."

"I see that you're not above using others for your own purposes."

"You speak of the dance. It was necessary, Mark. You are our guide to the past. Your eyes were closed. Now they are open."

"And that makes it okay?"

If Zoya noted his lack of protest regarding his new role, she didn't comment on it. "Our ways must survive."

"You know what?" Mark ground out as he set the assembled tripod upright. "I'm sick to death of hearing that. You say it, Mara says it, Milak said it. What about my ways?"

"Your ways *are* our ways," came the cryptic reply. "You teach Vadim a new sport, you instruct our men to build strong *umiaks*, you show our women how to prepare and preserve the walrus hides. In you we rediscover ourselves. Your ways are our ways."

Her clear, simple logic unsettled him.

"What else do you see?"

"I see Mara's pregnant. I see that you have her running back and forth to the Gathering Place. I see that she spends hours there sometimes. Why? She shouldn't be alone. It's not safe."

"You protect her."

"Yes." He didn't understand her lack of reaction over the pregnancy, but abruptly decided he might as well lay it on the line. "No one else seems to be."

Again Zoya chuckled. "You are angry."

"Yes."

"Good."

"Huh?"

"You hold too much within. Rage, I feel. Fear, I feel. Guilt and love combined. You must face your feelings, Tuntu, release them from your heart. Only then will you once more be free to fly."

Mark's mind cringed at the prophetic-sounding words, trying vainly to hide, to formulate a reaction. He felt anger at her invasion and abruptly decided there was only one appropriate reaction.

"I'm leaving," he said with finality. Zoya nodded, as if she'd expected his decision. Her reaction only angered him more. Was she manipulating him again?

*To hell with it.* Whether she was or she wasn't, he was out of here. He faced her, hands clenched and shoved into his pockets. "And I'm taking Mara with me."

"It is time. I have said and done all that I can."

Mark couldn't escape the feeling that her words held a double meaning. He packed the tripod away and strode purposefully to the door, where he paused. Would he ever see her again? Deeply rooted emotions flowed through him at the inevitable reply. He might still resent the old woman's interference, but in the close to three weeks he'd spent in her company, he'd come to admire and respect her deep love and commitment to her people. He turned when he felt Zoya's soft call.

"I will say this one thing, and you must know it for truth."

Mark tensed, gazing back at this woman who, despite her advanced age, reminded him of Mara. He was pierced by the feeling that she sensed his deep feelings for her and returned them, loving him despite his resentment of her.

"What?" he asked quietly.

"My grandniece carries no man's child."

## Chapter Fourteen

Flipping back the nylon flap, Mara emerged from the tent. They were camped along the Kachalan River, somewhere in a remote section of the Chukotka District. Three days had passed since their abrupt departure from Sireniki. She was still fuming from the way it had happened. She'd returned from the Gathering Place, no more certain of her decision than before, to find her notes and recordings and tapes stacked by the door alongside her suitcase, which Zoya informed her Vadim had graciously packed.

To say she'd been shocked was an understatement. But Zoya had been oddly insistent she accompany Mark, saying that if she hadn't yet found answers, then she wouldn't, not in Sireniki. Then she'd handed her a pouch so small Mara had known instantly what it was. Mara had cried as she stashed it carefully in her knapsack. Zoya had smiled and wished her the Yup'ik equivalent of Godspeed. They had hugged, kissed, sensed each other's fears and hopes, then silently parted. Riabov had picked them up, and they'd returned to Provideniya.

Mara inhaled a ragged breath. So far, their hasty departure hadn't accomplished anything tangible. Except for a heightened sensitivity to people's emotions—which could just as easily be attributed to the strain she was under—the potions hadn't miraculously "made her into a healer." She was still plain old Mara Anvik. She still didn't know what to do. Frustrated, she looked up through the forest of tall birch and larch trees at the blue sky of the bright, sunlit morning. The helicopter that was to return them to Provideniya should be arriving soon. Mark had had her order the pilot to return in two days.

Thank God the two days were up. Since leaving Sireniki, Mark had taken to staring at her when he thought she was engrossed with the inventory they were conducting of his camp provisions. She could sense whenever his gaze lingered too long on her hair or her legs or... her breasts. It was almost as if he'd forgotten the end result of their conversation that early morning in front of Zoya's home.

Well, she hadn't. Mark's future was Crosswinds. And hers? She didn't know. But she did know it wouldn't include making love with Mark, no matter how Mark's nonverbal signals tempted her.

And they did tempt her. Inwardly she smiled. She'd bet her degree that he had been counting on two days of passion. Instead, he'd ended up with two days of work, work and more work. And, just as clearly, she knew that he hadn't quite realized how difficult being together every moment would be.

Mara's sole diversion was the work. For two days she'd labored, Mark opening every box and bag, checking every piece of equipment while she recorded it against the accompanying inventory. There was an incredible amount of stuff: fishing poles, life vests, tents, dry goods, rubber wading boots, kitchen utensils, sleeping bags, sleeping pads, tarps, lanterns, batteries and more. So much more, it amazed her. And the perishable items wouldn't arrive for another week. While she'd worked, her mind had been occupied.

Thank God, she wouldn't have to spend another night in that tent, Mara thought as she crossed the campsite toward the two-burner stove she'd set up following Mark's instructions. Testing the small coffeepot, Mara sighed in relief. Hot. She poured herself a cup of coffee.

Lying still in that sleeping bag next to Mark was one of the hardest things she'd ever done. His heartfelt apology had rung in her ears, playing over and over in her mind, building her desire and weakening her resistance. He'd likely known, for he had lain as still as she. But then she'd remembered his glib one-liner about Crosswinds and his future, and she'd felt a renewed burst of willpower. The emotional roller coaster was getting to her. She lifted the cup gingerly to her mouth, took another sip and looked wistfully up at the sky.

"He's not coming."

The abrupt sound of Mark's voice startled Mara. Hot coffee went down the wrong way. She whirled and coughed, spotting him at the far edge of the campsite, where the cleared area met virgin forest. "What do you mean, 'he's not coming'? How—how do you know that?"

"The radio." Mark scowled as he crossed to her side and poured himself a cup. Did she have to make it quite so obvious that she couldn't wait to leave? "He checked in while you were asleep. Even I can understand 'Engine, she broke'."

"The engine's broken? How can that be?"

"Do I look like a helicopter mechanic?" He looked at Mara, noting her white-knuckled grip on the cup. "Look, all I know is that it's broken. That means we're stuck here until the damn engine's fixed and he comes to pick us up."

They were stuck. Stranded. The helicopter wasn't coming. The implications staggered Mara, and she stared at Mark, dumbfounded. "How long?"

"He couldn't be sure."

"A day? Two? A week?"

Mark could see she was really getting worked up. "Does it matter?" They both knew it did. "We won't starve, and he knows it. There's enough fish in that river to feed us from here until doomsday." Which, as far as Mara was concerned, had just arrived.

"Wasn't there another helicopter available? I can't believe there's only one."

"This is the hunting season. You had enough trouble arranging for this guy to fly us out here on such short notice."

He was right. After leaving Sireniki with Riabov, they had spent the bulk of the day finalizing the approvals, permits, fees and arrangements for his summer tours. The last arrangement she'd negotiated had brought them out here. Setting down her cup, Mara started toward the radio, which was sitting next to the fishing gear. "Maybe I should try talking to him."

"Go ahead, try. Just don't get your hopes up. My guess is that the guy doesn't want to give up the dollars he'd earn picking us up. So even if there was another helicopter available, he wouldn't tell, because he'd lose the job to another pilot."

Again Mara knew Mark was right. "You should have offered him more money."

"Why? We're a captive audience. I could offer him a hundred bucks and it wouldn't make any difference. If he's waiting for a part, he's waiting for a part." Mark watched her kneel beside the radio. The denim stretched tightly over the rounded curve of her buttocks.

"So we're stuck?"

"Until he can fix it, yes." Tossing back the rest of his coffee, Mark slammed the cup down on the closed lid of a box holding dried foodstuffs. Then he stalked over to a pile of provisions and grabbed an ax.

"Where are you going?"

Mark stopped himself from saying, "Away from you," and said instead, "To cut wood. We're going to need it. If you haven't noticed, we're in Siberia. Even in the summer it gets cold at night."

So saying, he struck out into the forest, oblivious to the occasional thorny branch that brushed across his face and clothes. When he located a fallen tree, he stripped off his shirt and started hacking away at branches.

Leaving Sireniki had been surprisingly hard. The people had been warm, open, and almost pathetically eager to listen and learn about anything he had in mind to teach them. He'd liked that, liked being their guide to the past. He hadn't realized how much he'd come to care for them until he decided to leave.

He wished the villagers of Twilight were as eager to embrace the future as the people of Sireniki were to embrace their past. Watching Mara and the easy way she interacted with people of all ages, and listening to Zoya's stories of her past struggles and triumphs, he'd tried to formulate a theory, something tangible that he could use: Do this or say that and everyone in Twilight will see the future as you do. But he didn't believe in magic. And while Zoya's discomforting habit of reading his innermost thoughts certainly was eerie, he didn't think it was anything more than the wisdom of age. She saw into people just as Mara saw into him.

He thought about Zoya's words regarding his soul and wondered why she'd thought he wasn't free. He took on no responsibilities he didn't want, had no dependents, worked when he wanted, and as hard or as little as he wanted. Wasn't that freedom? Hell, he didn't even have to worry about Mara being pregnant anymore.

Mara again. Did his every thought have to begin and end with her? Ever since Zoya had dropped her parting bombshell, he'd thought about little else in any concrete way. He'd followed her all over Provideniya, sat next to her in that cramped helicopter, opened boxes and assembled tents, but all he'd really been thinking of was how she'd look stripped of her clothes and tucked warm and wanting inside his sleeping bag, how she'd feel wet and wild and curved around his—

"Agh!" He couldn't prevent himself from crying out as the ax caught the edge of a branch and ricocheted into his leg. The force of his momentum sent him sprawling; he fell backward and landed on his backside. The pain was immediate. He reached over with both hands to pull the embedded ax out of his leg. Tears came to his eyes as he did it. Instinctively he wrapped his hands around the wound. Damn, that hurt! He saw blood pouring everywhere, and felt another wave of such excruciating pain wash over him that for a split second everything went dark.

Back at camp, Mara was just signing off from an unproductive talk with the pilot when she heard Mark scream.

Instantly she was on her feet, heart pounding, senses on full alert. She didn't stop to think, she just reacted, running into the woods, grabbing Mark's multipurpose knife on the way out of camp. As a means of defense, it was pitiful, but it was better than nothing. If Mark was in danger, she'd need something besides her wits to defend him, to defend them both.

The import of her actions was lost in the frightened rush of adrenaline that propelled her headlong through the forest. She actually ran up on him from behind, spotting the fallen tree first. She saw the ax. Then she saw his dark head and bared back. He was hunched over, as if in pain. "Mark!" She ran around front. When she saw the blood that covered his hands and legs, she gasped and fell to her knees beside him. "Oh, my God! You're bleeding!"

In a flash she dropped the knife and was reaching out to see.

Mark reared back, his eyes tortured. "Don't!" he ground out. "If you want to be useful, get me some bandages."

Later Mara would wonder at the raging anger and icy calm that settled like a shroud over her. "And if *you* want to be useful," she said, her voice low and absolutely unyielding, "kindly lie back and shut up. We don't need you going into shock."

Mark stared at the rock-hard intent blazing in her eyes. Curiously, it reassured him as nothing else could have, and after another half second he groaned and lay back against the tree.

Immediately Mara reached out, her concentration complete as she gently separated his clamped fingers from around the wound. Before she could stop herself, her breath dragged in sharply.

Hearing it, Mark started to lever himself up on his elbows. "What?"

"Lie down," Mara ordered again, swallowing the panic that was threatening to overwhelm her. The left leg of his jeans beneath the knee was soaked bright red with blood, and his sock was drinking it up like a sponge. She picked up the knife and slipped it from its scabbard. Lifting the blood-soaked denim, she slid the knife about an inch under the rim and sliced open the thick hem before ripping neatly up the entire leg. The rough sound of tearing fabric rushed across their ears. Gently, carefully, she flipped back the severed panels. "I hope you like red," she murmured.

"Why?"

"Because your hundred-dollar court shoes are never going to be the same again."

Oddly, he appreciated her attempt at humor, but the pounding from his leg wouldn't let him smile. He looked at Mara. Her face was white from shock and fear. Suddenly her features swam and his head began to buzz. He felt as if he were going to throw up.

Mara, who had grabbed his shirt to soak up the blood, heard him groan. "Damn it, Mark, stay with me, okay? I need you awake, Mark. *Stay awake.*" Without considering her own exposure, Mara swept her T-shirt over her head. The morning air was cool and quickly sapped the warmth from her upper body. But that didn't matter. Only Mark mattered. Only Mark.

"I'm going to bind the wound, all right? Then you're going to help me get you back to camp." She knelt down over him, fearful of his disorientation. "Do you hear me? Don't conk out on me now. I need you."

*I need you. I need you.* The words swam dizzily in his brain. Opening his eyes, he blinked, once, twice, certain that the half-nude woman kneeling over him with the wide, frightened eyes couldn't be Mara. It couldn't be her because she'd said she needed him.

Using the knife, Mara quickly cut her T-shirt into strips, which she bound tightly around his leg. It would have to do. Again she knelt over Mark. Gently she patted his cheek. He blinked and moaned. "Mark, let's go. Help me get you up."

His soft curse reassured her as nothing else could have. He would make it. Crouching, she levered her shoulders under his arm and heaved upward.

"I can do it myself," Mark murmured, his instinctive dislike of being dependent forcing him to utter the all-but-useless words. And from the hard expression on Mara's face, she knew it. But all she said was "You can carry the knife." She replaced the scabbard and handed it to him.

Mark took the angry-looking blade, looking pained and astonished. "You brought a knife?"

"This is bear country, isn't it?" she shot back, daring him to make anything of it.

Mark gazed pointedly at the plush breasts barely hidden by the white lace cups of her bra. So feminine, and yet so fierce. "Yeah, you never know what's going to reach out and bite you."

Her lips twitched with the need to smile, but her eyes didn't make it. "Okay, up we go," she said, avoiding his gaze and concentrating on their footing. They couldn't afford to trip.

By the time they got back to camp it was past noon and the sky, which had been perfectly blue and clear for three days, had started clouding up.

"Easy does it," Mara said as she gratefully lowered his considerable weight onto his sleeping bag. "How do you feel?"

"Like I've run a marathon."

"Well, you're not finished yet. I need to clean the wound, find out how much damage there is, stop the bleeding."

"I can do it my—" Catching Mara's expression, he shut up.

"Lie down. I'll call you when I need you."

There they were again, those three words. *I need you.*

It didn't occur to her how calmly she was dealing with Mark's injury. She just set about gathering the necessary materials, as she'd done for her grandmother countless times. Only this time there wasn't much available to choose from. In fact, there wasn't anything but more T-shirts from their luggage and a single small bottle of peroxide.

"You definitely need to upgrade your first aid kit," she murmured as she positioned herself to one side of his injured leg and removed the soaked strips of cloth. She set them aside, knowing she'd likely need them again once they'd been washed in the river and dried by the sun.

"Can I do anything?"

"You've done enough, thank you," she replied, swallowing a gasp at the sight of his injured leg. "God, you're lucky."

Hearing that, Mark roused. He tilted his head up and looked down at his leg. "You call that luck?" Along his shinbone back toward his calf, a deep, ragged, triangular-looking cut had been gouged out of flesh and muscle.

"You didn't break the bone. I'd call that darn lucky," she replied as she set about sponging up the blood with another stripped shirt. The amount of dirt and debris inside the wound worried her. Getting it clean wouldn't be easy. Maybe Mark would pass out. That just might be best for them both. "Lie down, damn it."

"You really need to work on that bedside manner," Mark said as he focused his gaze on the pointed canvas roof and tried to ignore the pain. "Milak would be right disappointed. In fact, Zoya would— Ow!"

"You've got to stay still," Mara ordered as she doused the corner of yet another shirt with the peroxide. His remark had hurt, but she pushed it and her growing fear aside. She'd need strength to get her through the next few minutes. She didn't want to hurt him, but she was very much afraid that she would have no choice.

"This is going to sting a little."

He chuckled, but the sound was very definitely forced. "That's like saying a blizzard is a little sprinkle."

Mara felt the pain he was denying, then leaned forward to press the pad on the wound. As the antiseptic penetrated, Mark stiffened; a grinding oath tore from between his clenched lips. Then, suddenly, his body went limp, and Mara knew he'd passed out.

For a long while, Mark stared up at the canvas roof and listened to a hypnotic pounding that he finally recognized was rain. He felt as though his lower body were being crushed by something big and heavy, and he found it difficult to concentrate. Then he remembered why. His leg. He'd damn near cut it off.

He turned his head, instinctively looking for something, someone. Mara. She stood with her back to him, and he could tell she was soaked clean through. Her hair was a slick black mat, and her T-shirt was plastered to her back like a second skin. Her cotton panties left little doubt as to her womanliness.

For the life of him, Mark knew he should say something, at least make a sound, but he couldn't.

Off came the T-shirt. Off came the bra. His body jerked, and he sucked in air, the hasty movement making his leg throb painfully, but not anywhere near as painfully as another part of his body. He watched her bend down and reach for one of the towels lying on her sleeping bag. The movement put her in profile and caused her breasts to sway forward with an agonizingly enticing jiggle. Her nipples were a dusty rose, he noted, and puckered from the cold.

Unaware of his gaze, she swiftly, efficiently, wrapped the towel sarong-style around her head. The distinctly feminine movement lifted her arms above her head, and he broke out in more of a sweat than he already had watching the tantalizing sway of those beautiful, luscious, full breasts. When she slid into a fresh pair of jeans and then proceeded to dry her upper body, Mark clenched his fists. Inadvertently he moved, and he moaned out loud this time. Damn, but his leg hurt!

"You're awake." Mara hugged the towel to her breasts in embarrassment, her startled expression quickly turning to relief as she stared at him from across the small space. Hastily she turned her back and tugged on a sweatshirt. Then she crossed to his side. Being careful not to jar him, she sat down on a sleeping bag that she'd rolled out next to him.

"How do you feel?" Mara asked gently, resisting the urge to take his hand. The gesture would have been more for her comfort than his.

"I'm about to explode," he said honestly. Maybe too honestly, for faint color tinged her cheeks.

Mara stood and walked over near the tent flap, where she picked up a cup and a small cylindrical container. "Here, take these. They'll help."

*Not as far as he was concerned.* But he accepted the three aspirin she placed in his palm and popped them in his mouth.

"Water?"

The thought of sitting up was too much. He swallowed, then grimaced as the pills stuck in his dry throat. "No thanks."

Mara's glance hardened. Making her decision, she slid one arm under the makeshift pillow and lifted Mark's head, placing the cup she held against his lips and tipping it forward. He either had to drink or be doused with it.

Mark drank. The cool water poured down his parched throat. When he'd emptied the entire cup, Mara laid him back down.

"More?"

Their eyes met and held. Mara's expression was sympathetic, even understanding. It made Mark nervous, and his leg started throbbing even more. She saw him too clearly. Like Milak. Like Zoya. Into his soul.

"I've tried the radio several times, but I guess this storm has wiped out transmission," she informed him quietly.

"Which means we're stuck," he translated gruffly.

"I'm afraid so."

Mara felt an instinctive need to comfort him. But she'd done that once, and she'd learned her lesson. Still, his pain was so obvious and his wound so severe that she prayed he'd fall asleep quickly. Checking the wound was easier when he wasn't conscious.

They sat there together for a long while, listening to the rain tap its song all around the tent. Inside, it was quiet. Eventually the rhythm lulled Mark to sleep. His breathing leveled and steadied. Only then did Mara move.

But Mark heard. "Mara?" he called out.

"I'm right here." Mara placed her hand on his forehead and smoothed back the perspiration-soaked waves of his hair. He was hot. Her heart started thudding, but her voice gentled. "You're okay, Mark. I'm right here," she repeated, over and over, until he quieted again. Just before he fell asleep, he mumbled something. Mara had to lean close to his lips to hear.

"Your breasts . . . they're beautiful."


"Wake up, Mark."

The little girl's voice cried out in his dream. He was standing to one side, oblivious to the blowing snowstorm, the ambulances, the strained faces, oblivious to everything but the little girl's anguish as she climbed on her mother's lifeless body and clung.

"Wake up, please." Mara didn't want to shake him, but she had to do something to get his attention. "I can't hold you down, and you're going to hurt yourself if you don't wake up!"

Mark groaned, then blinked. It wasn't the little girl crying out for her mother, but Mara, her eyes frightened as she yelled orders at him. What was she saying?

"Stop moving," Mara cried out, her chest heaving with her exertions.

Abruptly Mark stopped. The air in the tent was cold on his skin, and he realized with a start that he didn't have a shirt on. On her knees, straddling his chest, Mara was bending over him. One hand was clamped on each shoulder, holding him down.

"You can let go now."

"Not until you tell me who you are."

"*Mara.*" Apparently, that he was lucid enough to recognize her and say her name sufficed, for Mark immediately felt Mara move off him. For an instant, the tips of her breasts passed right over his mouth. He felt himself shiver. "How bad is it?"

Mara hesitated. How much to tell him? She wished her grandmother were here. She could use the healer's advice, for she was very afraid that she was running out of medical supplies and options.

"Give it to me straight." The weakness in his voice was answer enough. His teeth started clicking together. "Chills?"

Mara nodded.

"Fever?"

Mara nodded again.

"How long?"

"Two days." She watched his eyes widen with disbelief as he absorbed the information. How much to tell him? she asked herself again.

"What? Tell me."

"I'm running out of aspirin," she blurted out. In truth, she already had. A small lie—more a compromise, really. It would afford him some time, some mental relief. Because he still didn't know everything.

"What about the radio?"

"Useless." She gazed up. "It's still raining."

Mark shuddered. Two days had passed. He couldn't believe it. Two days, and no helicopter. The radio was useless, and soon he wouldn't even have any aspirin.

Scooting down his body, Mara unzipped the sleeping bag completely around so that she could uncover his injury without having to expose the rest of him. As she had so often during the past two nightmarish days, she unwrapped the makeshift bandage and stared down at the open wound. Then she looked up.

"It's infected, Mark. I used up the supply of peroxide yesterday."

Mark's stomach clenched. *He didn't even remember yesterday.* Raising himself up, ignoring the splinters of pain the small movement caused, he looked at his leg. Only his need not to show his fear kept him from rearing back at the sight of the raised, purplish flesh and the pockets of pus. Beads of sweat lined his brow, and some slid down his face. He flopped back down and closed his eyes, his breathing rapid and shallow.

Suddenly a cool cloth smoothed across his brow. He sighed. "God, that feels good."

"I'm glad," Mara murmured, happy to do something positive. Mark's face was so pale. Too pale. The infection was stealing the strength from him, and he'd need his strength for what was to come. "Do you want to lance out the pus, or shall I do it?"

Mark's entire body bucked at Mara's question. He couldn't help it. He stared into the depth of her eyes, seeing her pain for him, seeing her fear, as well. It came to him that she wasn't simply offering him lip service, even though she had to know he couldn't do it himself. She was, in effect, offering a measure of control, of independence. He could decide how they would proceed.

"We don't exactly have a lot of choices, do we?"

"Can you think of something else?"

"No."

Mara sighed, thinking about the concoction that had popped into her mind last night while she concentrated on watching him sleep. She hesitated to call it a vision, because she'd been awake. Four plants she'd never seen had appeared in her mind's eye, leaving her with the feeling that, applied as a poultice, they were supposed to draw off Mark's infection.

Should she tell him? Would Mark believe her? Did she believe it herself? And without the plants, what difference did it make? To Mark, none.

"There's no other way," she repeated softly.

"Then you do it," Mark said gruffly. Seeing the anguish flare up in her eyes, Mark was reminded of how much pain he'd already caused Mara. He wished this hadn't happened. Mara felt too deeply, cared too much. And though she wouldn't think of it this way, her desire for him made her particularly vulnerable. He winced as a wave of pain shot up his leg. Mara was afraid. He had to do something to help her.

"I trust you," he murmured.

Mara's eyes widened at first, but then her glance slowly softened into an unconscious caress. "Thank you."

Something warm and wonderful passed between them. Mark focused on Mara's perspiration-wet face, on the dark hollows under her eyes that showed so vividly that she hadn't slept. He was amazed at the feelings she generated in him. This woman was as nonviolent as they came, yet she hadn't hesitated to grab a knife and rush into the forest to find him, and defend him if necessary. He moved his hand out from under the sleeping bag, extending it, palm up.

Mara linked her hand in his, and for a few silent moments neither said a word. Then she released his hand and moved near the door of the tent. She wasn't proud of herself for what she was about to do, but Mark needed something to bolster him during the next few minutes. Rummaging in her suitcase, she withdrew a small container of vitamin C pills. Pouring two of the little round white pills into her hand, she returned with a cup of water. "Here, take these while I set up."

"What are they?"

"Pain pills," Mara answered. "My doctor prescribed them. They'll cut the edge. Drink up."

Mark drank and wondered briefly why she'd had the pills, then decided now was not the time to ask. He returned the cup, then watched her switch on one of his new battery-operated lamps and position it close to his leg for maximum exposure. Then he watched her select a fresh T-shirt. And, lastly, he watched her sterilize the knife blade in the flame from the camp stove. She must have carried the stove into the tent sometime in the past two days, he decided as he watched her return to kneel by his leg.

"Ready?"

Mark noted that she was sweating almost as much as he. But her hands were steady. Remarkably, she was in control. That control calmed him. He was certain that if their positions were reversed, he'd be shaking like a damned leaf for fear of hurting her. If she could do this for him—and he knew how much it was costing her, for he could see it in her eyes—then the least he could do was co-operate. For someone so young, she was handling this remarkably well. He was proud of her, he realized. Proud and—what? At the moment, he felt . . . connected. Connected to her in a way that went beyond the physical. He felt a reserve of energy flow through his body, lending him a strength he needed so that he could help her help him.

"Ready."

The seconds ticked by. When nothing happened, Mark raised his head. "What's the matter?"

Mara looked up, her eyes pleading. "I need you to talk to me while I do this."

*Talk?* Mark had the feeling he was going to have enough trouble keeping from passing out. "Okay. Fine. What about?"

"Anything. The nightmare you were having. Tell me about that." She looked down, knife poised.

Mark faltered. To talk about the nightmare... Then he groaned. If that was what she needed, then he would try. "It's always the same," he started. "I hear the little girl crying."

"What little girl?" Mara lifted the knife and punctured one of the blisters. Mark cried out, unconsciously yanking his leg from her hand. "No, Mark! Don't move! God! Please, don't move."

They stared at one another. Mara breathing heavily, Mark panting. It took a supreme effort of will for him to lie down and once again extend his foot.

"Go on," Mara coaxed him on a shuddered sigh. Her hand gently captured his foot. Tension vibrated down his body, through his leg and into her arms.

Mark sighed at the feel of her gentle touch and tried to gather coherent thoughts. He knew the pain would be bad, as bad as that in the nightmare. He decided to use the nightmare, to let it rip through him in words as the pain lanced through him physically.

"What little girl?" Mara repeated the question, waiting for him to begin.

"The little girl whose mother I killed." At the first touch of the knife, he tensed, and just managed not to pull away. The pain was bad. Real bad. Fighting for concentration like he'd never fought before, Mark continued. "There was a storm that night. I don't . . . know what it is about babies . . . but they sure as hell like to arrive during storms."

"I missed you while I was in Fairbanks," Mara heard herself confess.

Mark paused, blissfully distracted for a second, maybe two. Then the pain returned and he forced out, "I missed you, too." Suddenly, his rage at himself overflowed. "I should have been more careful, taken more time landing in Bethel. But the storm was bad and the woman was real sick . . . dying . . . Kathy said so."

"Kathy?"

"The nurse. And Mandy, the copilot. Both dead. My fault."

"But, Mark . . ." Mara paused in her ministrations. She couldn't let him go on thinking that. "You're one of the best pilots in the sky. You have to be, otherwise they wouldn't have let you fly rescue."

"Well, they made a mistake."

"No, they didn't. You're the one making the mistake. You can't take responsibility for a storm."

The minutes ticked by so slowly. She couldn't rush through the work. She had to make sure she was getting everything. For a while Mara didn't even hear Mark's mumbled sentences as she sliced, then drained, sliced, then drained. Her back hurt, and her legs were numb from kneeling and bending down over Mark's leg. She felt chilled, tuning in as a way of tuning out the reality beneath her fingers, and only vaguely aware that, as she'd planned, talking about the nightmare was keeping his mind occupied, at least to a certain degree, at least enough that she could do what was necessary.

"We didn't even know if we could save her baby," Mark continued. "I took a chance. . . . The fog was so thick that night . . . the wind so strong . . . so strong."

"Listen to me." Mara looked up and murmured, "I know you. You always check out your plane. You always make sure it's ready. But if it wasn't ready for that storm, then nothing you did, or anyone else would have done, could have helped."

For a fraction of a second, Mara thought she saw his eyes waver, his pain-filled expression ease.

She resumed lancing, speaking in gentle tones. "Please, don't be so hard on yourself. Despite how you may feel, I bet no one even blames you. My God, Mark, you could have died in that crash, too!"

Mark's expression hardened instantly. "I'm not being too hard on myself."

"You are. Every time you look up into the sky when you hear a plane and then look quickly down again, you are. Stop punishing yourself."

When Mark didn't respond, Mara looked up to see him staring at her, and the expression on his face said he was nearing the end of his control. But it also showed a hint of something else that took Mara's breath away. "We're almost done, Mark," she told him, her voice faint from the strain and the tears she was blinking wildly to control. "Just one more. Hold on, okay? Hold on."

Mark stared at Mara's bent head. Her forehead was sweating, but her hands remained steady. He couldn't believe she'd defended him just now. He'd killed three people—four, with the baby—and she was reminding him how lucky he was to be alive!

Abruptly his head began to spin, and he thanked God that those pills of Mara's were finally kicking in. He struggled to stay awake, knowing Mara needed him, needing that need. But the pain and the trauma were greater than his will. Finally, he could fight no longer.

Mara finished. Quickly she set aside the knife and cleansed the wound with rainwater. She wished she had something stronger. Then she bound it tight and scrambled up to where Mark lay unconscious.

"It's over." She barely mouthed the unnecessary words. Gently, she covered him, making sure not to jostle his leg. His bronze skin was a chalky, pasty white. She didn't know if what they'd done was good enough. Only time would tell.

## Chapter Fifteen

The waiting was the worst part, Mara soon discovered. He kept fading in and out of consciousness. Sitting and listening to the rain in the damp, shadowy tent, watching his restless sleep, watching his shallow breaths, watching him tremble one minute, then sweat the next. Dread filled her heart. And anguish at his pain. And fear, because she was helpless. And, finally, terror, because she knew she was not.

"Wa—"

Mara started at the raspy sound and quickly crawled to his side. "Mark?" she whispered hopefully.

"Wa-water," he repeated, in a pleading croak that wrenched Mara's heart.

She reached for her cup of now-tepid tea, moving him so that his head was cradled against her breasts. "It's lukewarm tea," she informed him, then quickly held the cup to his mouth, tilting it so that the liquid trickled down his throat.

He sighed, and his eyes flickered open and seemed to focus on her.

"Mark?"

"More . . ." was his reply.

He didn't recognize her. She gave him more tea. When his eyes closed, she lowered him down again. "Sleep now," she instructed. "Don't try to talk. Just rest. Just rest."

"Getting worse. Feel it."

"No," Mara told him, even as tremors racked his body. She pulled the covers up to his chin. "You'll be fine. You just need to rest."

"Stay with me."

"Always," Mara replied, over and over, until they both dropped off to sleep.

"No!"

Mara woke, panicked by the scream. Mark! She reached for him. "It's all right," she murmured, stroking his tangled hair from his face. She'd long since given up lying separated from him in her own sleeping bag and had zipped the two together. "It's all right."

"Can't see. So much snow! My fault!"

"Shh. It's not your fault. Shh. Not your fault, Mark. Go to sleep."

Her soft words and slow, rhythmic strokes across his forehead calmed him. He woke, his eyes dazed, unseeing. With a choked sound, he turned toward her, instinctively seeking her comfort.

Mara gathered him into her arms, careful to move herself and not him. "Mark?" she asked softly when her arms were tight around him.

"Baby?" he muttered.

Mara felt her heart contract. He was shifting restlessly, his head moving from side to side against her breast. He kept muttering.

"You don't understand. I didn't mean it, I didn't mean—" His voice cracked and fell silent, then rose again. "My fault, baby, my fault!"

"No, no, no," Mara murmured, her eyes tearing. "Shh. It's over, Mark. It wasn't your fault. Shh."

Mark half woke and lay still, listening to the rain. He felt a softness next to him and turned his head just slightly. Mara. He sighed, listening to her even breathing, too weak to do more than touch her hand. Nevertheless, the small contact comforted him somehow.

Dimly he realized the infection was worse. Yet Mara's presence kept him calm. He thought about that as he drifted off again.

Thought about how she'd run into the woods to protect him, how she was caring for his needs, soothing his nightmares. God, he was glad she was here. He didn't want to be alone.

*Where was she?*

As she came in from outside, Mara's gaze automatically zeroed in on Mark. His eyes were open, but that was no guarantee he was lucid. She watched his eyes travel over her soaked clothes, then up to her face.

"Mara?" he asked in a husky voice.

Mara's eyes widened. She dropped the wet plants she'd just gathered on a towel and rushed over to where he lay.

"Oh, Mark, thank God!" She unzipped the bottom end of their large sleeping bag. "How long have you been awake? How do you feel?"

"I don't know how long, and bad," he said truthfully as she examined the leg. Though the swelling had eased somewhat, new pockets of pus had formed. If anything, the infection was worse. He didn't have to look to know. He could feel it. He could see it on Mara's face. "Any luck with the radio?" he asked weakly, though he already knew the answer. Shivering, he closed his eyes. The dizziness was starting again. He was so tired. So very tired.

She was losing him. Mara gazed fixedly at the drying plants, then down at her trembling hands. *Tell him,* her heart urged. *Trust him. Give him a chance, give him a choice.*

"There's something I need to tell you," she blurted out into the heavy silence. He didn't respond. She tried again, leaning forward this time to place her hand around his. It was a completely natural gesture, and, feeling it, Mark opened his eyes.

"There's something I need to tell you," she repeated. "Something that might—" she swallowed "—might help you."

It wasn't the gravity of her words that captured Mark's attention and helped him focus, it was her expression. Both fear and hope warred there. "What is it? I thought we ran out of everything."

"We did," she replied. "At least, we ran out of...conventional medicines."

He sighed. He'd done this to her. Made her afraid even to talk about what might just save his life, what was likely Milak's and Zoya's legacy to her.

"Did Zoya give you the sacred teachings?"

"In a way, yes." Three potions her grandaunt had given her. Three potions, and a choice. *When you wake, you will know who we are. You will understand our knowledge.* Mara hadn't comprehended just how that was to happen. Now she did. At least she thought she did. If she needed knowledge, it would simply arise from her subconscious, like a long-lost memory. Question was, did she believe in that imagery? And if so, had she interpreted it correctly? Was it fair to use Mark as a guinea pig? Was it fair to him not to?

"Mara..." Mark searched her eyes for a moment, then shivered. "It's all right. Whatever it is, you can tell me."

Mara stared at their linked hands, feeling the depth of her indecision weighing heavily on her shoulders. Then, slowly, she lifted her gaze to meet his. Her soul ached to see him so ill, but she knew she wouldn't be able to live with the guilt if she convinced him of her plan and the poultice made him worse, not better.

"Tell me."

*Trust him. Give him a choice.* "There's a mud pack," she forced out. "I've got an idea how to prepare it ... I think I know what to do.... If I make it right, it may draw off your infection. But I don't know for sure."

Their gazes held as he absorbed the impact of her announcement. She was offering him hope. So why wasn't she more excited?

"What's the problem?"

"I'm just not sure. You don't believe in this stuff, and I don't really know what I'm doing. I don't want to hurt you. I don't want to make it worse."

Mark caught her distraught gaze and held it, reading past her words to the need beyond. Mara wanted his support. Needed to know he shared the risk willingly.

"Do it."

Mara's eyes widened. "Didn't you hear what I said?"

"I heard it. Now do it."

"But, Mark! I've never done it before."

"Doesn't matter."

"Without Grandmother or Grandaunt..." Her voice faded, then picked up again. "What if I gathered the wrong plants? Or put them together in the wrong proportions? I don't even know their names."

"Who cares? That's not important. What is important is that you get on with it. I know you'll do it right," he concluded firmly, wishing he could hold her close and convince her through the strength of his arms.

Mara stared at him, eyes huge with tears. "I'm afraid," she admitted. "I'm afraid it'll hurt you. I'm afraid it'll make things worse."

The only way things could be worse would be for him to be dead. But he didn't say that. Mara needed his unconditional support, not his hard realism. "It won't," Mark said, never taking his eyes off hers. "You've never hurt a living thing, and you're not about to break that record now."

He'd never meant anything so deeply in his life.

Mark watched the tears overflow as she struggled within herself.

"How can you be so certain, when I'm not?"

"Would you use it yourself?"

"Yes, of course—"

"Then that's all I need to know," Mark said. "All you needed to say."

She looked at him with guarded eyes, trying to believe him, wanting to, needing to, for both of them. "You truly believe it'll work?"

Mark understood what she was asking. "All I can say is that I see things differently now than I did four weeks ago."

"But is that good enough?"

"I believe in you," Mark answered. "That's good enough for me."


With Mark's words in her heart and her ancestors' knowledge in her head, Mara prepared and applied the poultice. Then they sat back to wait. An afternoon passed, and another night. Though Mark's restless movements had ceased, she hesitated to call that an improvement. She slept, but never for long. She ate, but never much. And she watched over Mark, occasionally plying him with tea she'd made from the leaves of a yarrow plant, a natural fever reducer she'd recognized when she went in search of the ingredients for Mark's poultice.

The next morning, she briefly left the tent to relieve herself. She gazed up at the sky, surprised that it wasn't raining, surprised that she hadn't even heard it stop. As she returned from her short trip into the woods, she felt a sudden and inexplicable urge to hurry to Mark's side.

She ran across the clearing and flipped back the tent flap. And there he was, levered up on his elbows, a huge, ear-splitting grin on his pale, no-longer-fevered face.

"Got anything to eat?"

Mark's improvement was rapid. Twenty-four hours later he was up, walking slowly around with the aid of a tall stick. His infection and fever were gone, and his outlook one hundred percent improved. The old Mark was once again reaching out to ensnare her emotions.

"What are you doing?"

Mara looked up briefly from the inventory list she was updating. "Just recording everything we used during our five days. Have to restock when we get back."

"How long before the helicopter comes?"

Mara stopped zipping up the duffel-bag cover for the tent and glanced at her watch, then across to where Mark stood. "Two hours," she said, catching her breath at the predatory gleam in his eyes. "He said he couldn't get here before noon."

Two hours. Mark looked up at the sunlit morning, feeling the warmth seep into his bones. God, it felt good to be alive! He smiled, unaware of how his entire face radiated his deep contentment. A lot could be accomplished in two hours. When he again looked at Mara, he'd made his decision.

"Then let's take a break," he said huskily, holding out his hand.

Mara could no more have kept from going to him than she could have turned back the hands of time. It was a joy to see him standing there so tall and healthy. What he wanted was there in his eyes, had been locked in her imagination for more years than she cared to admit to. With his belief in her as a healer, she'd found the proof she'd sought, the proof Zoya had told her to go out and find. His health was the icing on the cake.

She would take the third potion, she decided as she linked her hand with his. And she would become healer for both Sireniki and Twilight. But first, before she gave her life over to the service of others, and before the helicopter arrived, she would allow herself this one selfish moment with him all to herself.

"Where are we going?" she asked, though she really didn't care. All she wanted was to hold him close and to experience the wonder of the passion blazing brightly in his eyes. The trepidation was there, off in a small corner of her heart, but the love and the need were much stronger. She grabbed the two sleeping bags Mark had just finished rolling up.

"To the river. There's a place I know."

"Yes. I found it a few days back."

Mark walked slowly, picking his way carefully because of his leg. He was reluctant to speak, unwilling to interrupt their silent communication with unnecessary words. Her ready agreement had thrilled and relieved him, for though he knew how much he wanted to make love with her, there had been no real certainty in him about Mara's feelings. Both times he'd tried—after the dance, and outside Zoya's home—she'd declined, if not with her body, then with her words. But this time, the music of her need was as loud as the birdsong around them, and as clear as the swiftly flowing river he led her to.

Mara was grateful that Mark didn't want to talk. Had he uttered even a single question about the reason for her consent, her mood would have changed. She knew that he saw no future for them. Knew it, had accepted it, and, more important, was even relieved, for she now saw no future for them, either. With her decision to become a healer came a responsibility greater than any she'd ever borne. And while she was eager to shoulder that weight, she knew Mark wasn't ready to share it with her. He'd claimed he'd changed. But how much? Enough to help her guide Twilight into the future? Enough to help her lead the people of Sireniki in rediscovering their past? The responsibility would be tremendous. No, there would be no future for them, but hers was now set in motion. She owed it to Mark, she owed it to her grandmother and grandaunt, she owed it to her people.

But this one moment in time she owed to no one but herself.

As they exited the woods, Mara paused behind Mark and gazed in silent tribute at the sun-warmed clearing he'd brought her to. They were surrounded by nature's wonders, trees whose leaves were a glorious array of greens and golden browns, and mosses that were so dark they seemed almost black. Mara inhaled the crisp, clear scent given off by the trees and trembled again in anticipation. Only Mark could do this to her. Her *inua*, the crane, mated for life. That Mark had not chosen her did not alter that truth. She needed him now, as a woman needs the man of her dreams, if not of her future. And now that the moment was here...well...she was impatient.

Mark led her to the center of the small clearing and watched as Mara spread out the sleeping bags. Then he dropped the stick and gingerly lowered himself down beside her, reaching out and brushing a stray strand of midnight-black hair away from her face. "If you don't want this, Mara—" he spoke gently, feeling her shudder, seeing the stiffness of her spine "—it doesn't have to happen. We can just lie back and watch the sky for a while."

The significance of his statement was lost as she shot him a dismayed look that immediately eased his fears. Then she smiled and lightly squeezed his hand before withdrawing.

"I want this, Mark," she whispered. "I'm just ... nervous."

"Me, too." He smiled a little at her obvious astonishment. Then his gaze focused on her lips as he deliberately lowered his own guard. "Four years is a long time to wait."

His softly whispered confession floated in the warm, sweet air between them. Mara started to speak, to ask him if he could possibly have meant what she thought he'd meant, but the answer shone in dark eyes that, for once, were clear of shadows. In a voice filled with wonder, Mara admitted. "I've waited forever."

Mark glanced at her flushed cheeks and wary eyes, saw the spine she kept so stiffly straight and the trembling hands that stroked his arm with such hesitant desire. The woman in her was ready to experience the passion he was offering but the girl, the teenager he'd so cruelly rejected, continued to live in a nightmare of fear and insecurity.

He would destroy that nightmare, he promised himself. Destroy it and replace it with a golden memory of warmth and caring and a passion equally shared. Silently he caressed Mara's hair again, watching with pleasure as she turned her head gently into the palm of his hand. He would fulfill that sensual promise, he told himself. He would give her a man's honest passion in exchange for her trust. He would give her all that he had to give.

Beneath the sun's yellow-white brightness, tiny flowers emitted their scents into the air around them. A gentle breeze eased through the trees, which rustled in reply, as if their need to be stroked with a sure and knowing hand was no less than her own. Nature's scents intermixed with Mark's, bringing Mara a sensory awareness almost beyond description.

Mark's finger swept down Mara's shoulder and along the back of her hand. She shivered and opened her eyes, following the sensual path that was repeated over and over and over. He had such sensitive hands, she realized. Strong and big and capable, the skin smoothly bronzed, the fingers long and tapered. A pilot's hands. A guide's hands. A lover's hands.

Her lover. She stiffened.

Mark sensed the change. "It's all right," he said gently. "We'll take all day, if necessary."

"We've only got two hours," she murmured, unconsciously flexing the fingers captured beneath his, telling him without words that she missed his gentle strokes.

"We've got all day," he answered without hesitation. "He can wait. Or he can come back. Whatever. We're not rushing this."

Upon hearing his words, Mara relaxed and her eyes closed. When the stroking didn't continue, she opened them again.

"I could use some stroking, too, you know," he teased her gently with a crooked smile that didn't quite hide the vulnerability behind his words. "Want to give it a try?"

Incredibly, Mara found herself laughing. That they could play as they learned about one another hadn't occurred to her. "Where shall I start?"

The look Mark sent her was all too clear, and way too much. She blushed a fiery red, and he laughed, reaching out to gently pull her close.

"How about a kiss? Think you can manage that?" Again he sensed her hesitation before she turned to face him and put her hands on his shoulders. Then she leaned forward and placed her lips softly against his.

A low moan broke free as Mark tasted her sweet willingness to yield to him. "You taste like sunshine."

"Don't be silly," she whispered.

"Come closer. I can't get enough of you." As she settled herself deeper in his arms, Mark kissed her as if there were nothing in the world that could be more important.

*Two hours or two days,* he silently pledged. *Whatever it takes. Before we leave, I promise that your fears will disappear and only pleasure will remain when you think of me. You deserve to be happy, you deserve so much from me. Tell me what you need and I'll make it happen, show me and I'll follow your lead. Whatever you want, whatever it takes, for now, in this private place, forever, in my heart.*

He tried to tell her all that with his kiss—and when he raised his head far enough to see her lashes flutter open and her eyes gaze at him dazedly as she whispered his name, he knew she'd understood. He kissed her again, quickly, then again, his tongue dipping into her mouth, dueling with hers before withdrawing to guide her down onto the sleeping bag. Then he pulled off his T-shirt.

Mara watched the bronze chest she had bathed nightly come into view, and knew he was reading her helpless fascination. Health and vitality radiated from him in waves of heat and desire. He was broad-shouldered and starkly defined, the muscles of his chest firm, resilient, the muscles of his stomach rippled and tightly clenched with the evidence of his need and his reaction to her helpless exploratory caress. Looking at him now, so strong and virile, made it difficult to recall how much he'd needed her just a few short days ago. The man facing her now needed her, too, but in a potent, primitive way, a way that made her breath catch as she lowered her eyes to the straining evidence of his arousal.

It made her nervous, it made her excited. She felt caught between her growing needs and her meager knowledge. And when Mark tugged on the edge of her own T-shirt, she couldn't help her reflexive clutching at the hem. She wasn't ready for that yet.

"I'm sorry, Mara." His words reassured even as his hand traced the tender outline of her lips. "This is your show. We'll move on when you're ready."

"Mark . . ." Mara said softly, wanting to explain, not knowing how.

"Do you know," he asked, lying down on his side and tracing a lazy, winding path of sensual delight across her stomach with his free hand, "why I almost cut my leg off?"

The seemingly incongruous subject piqued Mara's curiosity. "Why?"

"Because—" and his finger traced lazily higher, until he was grazing the underside of her lace-edged bra, then moved away again "—I was thinking about the way you would feel, warm and wet and willingly wrapped around me." He shifted closer to her, his finger never ceasing its aimless, winding glide of discovery.

Mara's body jerked, and she made an audible sound that was half shock, half disbelief.

"It's true," he continued, teasing her, teaching her how beautiful she was, how wondrous he thought her. Slowly, taking his time, he traced the path of a horizontal figure eight around the gentle mounds of her breasts, the valley between earning double duty as the crossing point. With each completed journey, the next would start, shorter this time, and higher up, nearer the tips of her breasts, his goal. And each time, Mara's breath would rush out until he knew she was not only waiting for him to reach the top, but taking every step with him. With a thick sound of understanding, he traced one hardened bud, then the other.

For a moment, Mara stiffened, not knowing what to expect. The feeling of Mark's fingers pulling, tugging, drawing from her a rush of warmth and heat and desire, was awesome. Her breasts tingled and ached in a way they'd ached only once before. They swelled, and she listened to his moan of satisfaction, knowing he'd felt the change and was rejoicing in it along with her. Heat flushed her body as he continued the teasing caresses, the tugging on nipples that were tight with need and hungry for less confining contact. Pleasure fluttered deep in her womb, along with an intense burst of heat. Mara began pulling at the restrictive fabric of her shirt, telling Mark without words that she wanted more, and that her earlier uneasiness had been replaced by need. Her back arched as she offered him access, and Mark was quick to accept, pulling her shirt off in one smooth motion.

Cool air rushed over her hot skin, and Mara took a deep, clean breath that filled her breasts and thrust them tightly against the lace edging of her bra.

"Do that again," Mark murmured as he fit his mouth to hers in a kiss that spelled out his needs and made Mara aware of the delicious feeling of his bare skin against hers. But the lacy bra was in the way. She realized she didn't want it there, that she wanted nothing separating her from him, not even her modesty.

"Please, Mark, stop. I need to—" she started to say, but Mark bent down and licked at the lace edging, just flicking her nipple with his tongue. Her breath came out in a ragged exhalation, and she stilled.

Could she really want to stop? A low murmur of pain ground out against the softness of her breast. Again he licked. Again she moaned.

"Mark, please, I need to take this off."

It took a moment for the words to sink in, but when they did, he couldn't contain his fierce surge of triumph. He drew back, his eyes burning with sensual messages that made Mara's body tighten with obvious need. He smiled. He couldn't help it. He moved off her and pulled her up to sit in front of him, aware how his eyes must show his anticipation, because she blushed, suddenly shy.

"Be my guest," he murmured, licking his lips.

Mara was torn between a laugh and a moan, feeling a nervous sort of pride in his obvious delight. Never in her wildest dreams had she ever imagined herself in such a role, an equal participant, seeking to please and wanting to be pleased. But with Mark the improbable seemed likely, so much so that when her left hand crossed her chest to slide the silky strap off her right shoulder, she did so with just the tiniest flare of wantonness. She kept her eyes firmly fixed on Mark's face, watching him watch her as she repeated the movement with her right hand. His breath caught in anticipation; his face was tight, almost pained, and his eyes flared out of control. Delicious tremors quaked through her body at this unguarded evidence of her desirability. Her lacy bra slid slowly down the engorged fullness of her breasts, exposing them in little bursts of her nervous, rapid-fire breaths.

Just looking at her was enough to arouse Mark. But when the scrap of lace snagged on the tightened buds of her nipples, he couldn't stop himself—he leaned forward and licked free first one nipple and then the other.

Another low sound of primitive triumph came from Mark as he once again bore her willing body down onto the sleeping bag, tracing the dusky areola of one breast, learning its texture, exploring its resiliency, drawing it deeply into his mouth. Then he repeated the gestures with her other breast, taking his time, not wanting to rush, even though his body was nearly exploding. "Touch me," he whispered, his voice husky.

Mara needed no second invitation. With a throaty cry of need, she raised her arms and buried them in his hair, holding him to her breast as if she were afraid he would leave her. When he moved down her body, trailing kisses along the slender curve of her waist, she shuddered and closed her eyes at the hot tremors building in her womb. Her hunger for him was as potent as the poultice had been, affecting her life and changing it forever.

Had Mark known what she was thinking, he would have agreed. He felt as though he'd waited a lifetime for this moment with Mara. The feverish touch of her hands guiding him to her pleasure nearly undid him. He did the next best thing— He undid her.

"Lift up," he ordered, and felt Mara's automatic reply in the lifting of her hips off the sleeping bag. Even as Mark unsnapped her jeans and slid them quickly down her body, he was busy flicking each nipple, having missed their sensual texture already.

Mara opened eyes that blazed with desire. She looked down at her almost nude body as if she couldn't quite believe that things had progressed so far so fast. When her silky underwear followed before she could even protest, she stiffened, half expecting Mark to touch her there, knowing that she wasn't ready for that.

Their eyes, like their memories, met and meshed. "Forgive me," he pleaded hoarsely, looking away from the tempting perfection of Mara's breasts and the womanly curls at the apex of her legs.

Mark closed his eyes, his breathing painful and labored. He knew that he couldn't look at Mara and see the return of the uncertainty that he'd just worked so hard to dispel. He cursed his own barely restrained need, praying for control, wishing he'd continued to let her set the pace. But his hunger was that of a thirsty man faced with a wellspring of water. Restraint was impossible, and unnecessary, for as thirsty as he was, Mara was equally eager to let him quench that thirst.

At first, Mara thought that Mark was deliberately turning away from her, that, somehow, despite the shame clouding his eyes and the remorse he'd forced past stiffened lips, she'd disappointed him. But though his back was now facing her, she could see how heavily he was breathing, how tightly his shoulders were knotted. This wasn't rejection, this was a man close to the edge of his control, a man willing to put her needs before his own so that what had happened once before would not happen again.

Understanding melted the last of Mara's reservations, and she reached out, the sensitive pads of her fingers contacting his spine, feeling him flinch. So much heat, so much need! And all of it for her.

"Oh, Mark..." Mara moved to fit herself against him, her aroused breasts heavy as they settled flush against his back. Her arms slid around his waist, her palms pressing tightly against his rippled stomach. He moaned as she did it, whispering her name, and she shuddered in response, wanting him to know how much his restraint had meant to her, how much his remorse had freed her from the past.

Mara's hand slid down to release the snap fastening Mark's jeans. Feeling her way, aware of Mark's abrupt stillness, she tugged at the zipper.

It wouldn't budge, and they both knew why.

When Mark eased up so that he was kneeling, with her still clinging to his back, Mara understood he was giving her access. Heart pounding, she returned her hands to his zipper. The rasping, grating sound rang in Mara's ears, a loud and undeniable signal that she was taking the last steps toward womanhood.

Freeing him was difficult, because the denim had been stretched tight against his arousal. And by the time Mara accomplished the feat, both of them were breathing heavily. Mark was about ready to go off, but he held on so that Mara could learn him with her hands, feel how much he needed her and understand it as only a woman holding a man so intimately could know. Her gentle exhalation of awe fortified him as she peeled down his shorts, running hot hands down his even hotter thighs. When she grasped him, he couldn't help it— He cried out.

"No," he ground out when she would have withdrawn. "Not yet. I need this. I need you."

The words were a bare whisper of agony, but Mara heard them and rejoiced. She wasn't ready to let him go. She'd discovered she liked the velvety-smooth texture that ran hot and hard within the sheltered cove of her hand. With her body pressed against his back, she couldn't see what she was doing, didn't want to, not yet. Without sight, there were no memories, and she felt free to touch and caress and form new memories of pleasure and anticipation. Gently she explored him, touching him. It could have gone on forever, had Mark not stilled her hand.

"If you don't stop now, I'll explode," he murmured, removing her hand. He edged forward on his knees, separating their bodies, sitting down to remove the jeans and shorts pooled around his feet. Then he reached out for Mara, aware that she hadn't moved from her spot, aware of her flushed gaze as it caressed his naked body with an uninhibited desire that rocked his soul.

She lay down, pressed close against him, and he felt the shudder that quaked through her body as her taut nipples grazed his chest and his arousal lay hot between them. Slowly, gently, Mark edged back so that his hand could glide from her breasts to her waist, and to the heat emanating from between her thighs. He paused there to explore, nudging a finger into the dew-wet softness, breathing a sigh of relief when Mara's legs shifted, allowing him access.

The feel of Mark's hand cupping her made Mara tense. Mark knew it. Mara knew that he knew it, but she couldn't help it.

"It's all right," Mark murmured, brushing his lips across hers. "I won't hurt you. I just want to touch you like this, like you touched me. You're so warm and wet, and I want you so much."

Mara focused on the words as she felt the first gliding penetration of his finger. She cried out his name, overwhelmed by the bittersweet pain building where he touched. Over and over he stroked, until she was dizzy with feeling, her hips lifting and following his hand in a silent demand for more. The sleek, wet touch robbed her of will, and the deep suckling of her breasts made her melt in his hand.

She was so tight! But she was ready for him, Mark knew as he watched her writhe beneath his hands. He shifted, positioning himself over her, seeing awareness dampen Mara's wild readiness. He paused at the realization that she wasn't as ready as he'd imagined.

When Mara sensed Mark's hesitation, she strained up to kiss first one masculine nipple and then the other. Sometime during their play she had learned he found it as exciting as she. "I need you, Mark," she said, lying back and urging him to come with her.

The words triggered an avalanche of emotions, freeing the lingering restraint and burdensome shadow of memory. He took her slowly, wanting to savor the feelings, needing to control himself even in this last instant, for her sake. When he nudged up against a barrier, he paused, dawning shock darkening his eyes. He started to pull out.

"Why?" His voice was hoarse. "Why didn't you tell me?"

"But I did!" The likelihood that he would leave her made her frantic. The hands grasping his shoulders tugged at him, but Mark refused to budge. "I told you, Mark! I said I'd waited forever. How much clearer could I get?"

Mark groaned at the need she wasn't bothering to hide from him. All these years. All these years she'd suffered from the cruelty of his words. Suffered so much that she hadn't even been able to... Mark couldn't even say it. Self-disgust churned inside him. What had he done?

"Mark, listen to me," Mara urged tightly. She was losing him, she could see it, for he wasn't bothering to hide his emotions from her. She couldn't let it happen, couldn't let Mark destroy something so powerful. "We need this," she whispered, refusing to let go of him. "I need this, you need this. Don't stop. You'll see, it'll be okay. What happened happened. How I reacted was my choice. What I'm doing right now is my choice, too. Don't leave me now. Not when it could heal us both."

Her hurried, frantic words settled over him like a balm. She was right. They did need this. Maybe for different reasons, but they did need it. But as he braced himself, then pushed through the barrier, he couldn't help the tear that streaked down his face at her swallowed gasp. He'd promised himself that he wouldn't ever hurt her again. Maybe he just wasn't any good at promises.

They lay still, each feeling the other, Mark giving Mara time to adjust to his presence, Mara giving Mark time to sense her warmth around him.

If she died tomorrow, Mara knew, she would never forget this moment: the shock on his face; the tear in his eye; the moan when he felt himself sheathed within her, the sense of peace and belonging and rightness. She'd never forget any of it, because it would have to last her a lifetime of tomorrows.

Mark didn't know how long he'd lain still, but the pressure inside him was demanding more. Slowly he moved within her, watching her face carefully, seeing only welcome and encouragement and a dawning sense of her feminine power. That last humbled him, for even in this first-ever instant of discovery, Mara was giving, healing, seeking to bring him fulfillment and release.

As their comfort with each other grew, their rhythm increased until they were acting and reacting, like the dancer and the drummer, Mark thrusting out the movements while Mara, her hands positioned on his hips, produced the rhythm. They created a beautiful song together, a song that rose in a climax of shimmering, pulsing beats that exploded for Mara in a blaze of such brilliant light that she felt completely surrounded. She sighed and closed her eyes.

It wasn't until a full minute later, when Mark rose off her, that he realized Mara was unconscious.

*Chapter Sixteen*

When Mara blinked and opened her eyes, she was smiling. She stretched sensuously, aware that she felt a little drained and a whole lot giddy. Loving Mark had been everything she'd imagined it would be—and more. As his handsome features appeared above her, her breath caught. In a gesture as natural as sunlight, she reached up to caress his face.

Mark captured the wrist and firmly, deliberately, returned it to Mara's side. Then he let go. "We should get back," he said tightly as his gaze traced coldly over her naked breasts. "He'll be here in a few minutes, and there are still some things I need to wrap up."

Immediately Mara's euphoria shattered. She sat up, suddenly conscious that she was in the sleeping bag, not on it, and that while Mark was fully clothed, she remained naked. How had he dressed without her knowing it? Reflexively, her hands covered her breasts while she looked around for her clothes. The silence between them was awkward and stilted.

"What's the matter?" she asked, spotting her T-shirt and jeans peeking out from under the far corner of the sleeping bag. Mara cringed, realizing that she'd have to reach for them. Apparently Mark realized the same thing, for he took pity on her and nabbed them, along with her panties. She wasn't about to ask for the bra, because it wasn't even in sight. She dressed quickly, conscious that he hadn't answered her question. When she was clothed, she tried again. "What's the matter?"

Mark said nothing, just looked at her as if he couldn't contemplate her even asking such a ridiculous question. "You ready?"

"No. I want to know what's going on."

"Yeah, well, join the club." So saying, he stood, slinging the sleeping bag he'd been sitting on over his arm. Grabbing his makeshift cane, he walked off.

"Wait!" Mara gathered up the other sleeping bag, found her bra underneath and scrambled after him. "Slow down, Mark! You shouldn't be walking this fast. Not yet, anyway. It's bad for your leg."

He slowed down and stopped. They stared at each other for several tense seconds.

"What's the matter?" she asked softly.

Hurt shadowed Mara's eyes, but confusion reigned uppermost. Was it possible? Could she really not know? Only one way to find out. "You've been down for the count for the last twenty minutes."

Mara hadn't given any concrete thought to what she'd expected Mark to say, but she knew one thing— That wasn't it. She shrugged, a sensual smile playing around the corners of her mouth as she attempted to diffuse his unusual tension. "Can I help it if you exhausted me?"

Mark stared at her, nonplussed. Then he turned and took off. He was furious with himself. How could he have forgotten she was sick? How *could* he?

"That was supposed to be a compliment."

"I'm sorry, but it doesn't particularly turn me on to think that I satisfied you into unconsciousness."

"Unconscious? What are you talking about? I was sleeping—"

Mark whirled, and Mara bumped into him. He steadied her automatically, the brief contact with her softness further fueling his anger. He set her aside, his eyes narrowed to slits as they looked at her. "You were unconscious, Mara. Out cold. Comatose. However you want to say it. I know the difference. At least give me that much credit."

Her jaw went slack with disbelief. "But—but how?"

"You're the one taking the mystery pills," he shot back, watching Mara's expression turn from confusion to understanding to alarm. He had to stop himself from reaching out to comfort her.

He'd done all the comforting he was going to do. "All I do know is that we climaxed and you zoned out."

He shuddered. He couldn't help it. The past twenty minutes were the worst he'd ever survived. The crash had been a nightmare, with all of the screams of pain, but Mara's cold, unresponsive silence had surpassed even that. When had his own mind stepped out to lunch? She was sick, damn it! And all she knew was that it was some sort of a hormone deficiency. What the hell did that mean? Could she die?

At that, Mark stopped his mind's tortured analysis. He didn't want to know. Whatever was wrong with Mara, it was none of his business. He wished now that Zoya hadn't told him Mara wasn't pregnant. This never would have happened had she not.

Mara looked at Mark and felt betrayed. Not by him, but by herself, her body. The beauty of their time together had been marred by the harsh reality of her illness. It was too late to try to rekindle the bond they'd shared. She loved Mark too much to be that selfish. She just wished she'd had a little more time. Just a little.

"How long did you say I was out?" she asked, watching him.

"Twenty minutes."

"Oh, Mark . . ."

"Save it for the next guy," he said, the crude words torn from him. He strode the remaining few yards into camp and immediately started gathering gear to stuff into boxes.

Mara stared at him, the words easily penetrating her mind. He was afraid. *Mark was afraid!* And his fear for her was showing itself in a burst of angry, crude words. The realization only made her love him more. "I'm not worried about other men," she revealed softly, honestly. "After what we just shared, I can't imagine wanting anyone but you."

His back stiffened and he paused, as if she'd struck him. Then, a few seconds later, he started packing again. "You'll get over it."

"I don't want to get over it," Mara said reasonably.

"Fine. Just don't start thinking about any repeat performance."

"I don't want one."

That stopped him. He glanced at her, and there was something in his eyes that broke her heart. "You don't?"

"No," she breathed softly. It took every ounce of willpower she had not to go to him. But he wouldn't welcome her comfort, and he didn't want her commitment. "Once was enough." It would have to be. She'd known that going in. Tears gathered in her eyes.

Mark saw them and started forward. "I hurt you, didn't I? Damn it, Mara—"

"No, Mark!" She backed away from him, when all she wanted was to rush into his arms. "Stay where you are."

Mark froze where he stood, drawing in a harsh, agonized breath. "Then for God's sakes, don't look at me like that!"

"Then don't come any closer," Mara warned, grappling with her swinging emotions. "You didn't hurt me, Mark," she confessed, aware she couldn't let him think that. It would be too cruel, and it was so obvious to her now how much he cared. Yet it wasn't enough. Not enough for a lifetime. Not enough to forget his fears, and nowhere near enough to accept her future. "We just have different goals in life. Crosswinds is your future. You told me so, remember? And I have my own interests...." She let her voice trail off. "Look, what happened between us was wonderful, but it was also inevitable in a weird sort of way, wasn't it? But now that it happened, we can put it into its proper perspective and get on with our respective lives."

Mark's expression went blank, as if the piercing pain inside him had made him numb. He felt curiously calm. Mara was telling him exactly what he wanted to hear, that he was free, independent, that she wasn't going to try binding him to her with any trumped-up emotionalism or even the more common ploy of the possibility of a baby. He shuddered and forced himself to resume packing. She was telling him exactly what he needed to hear, exactly what he'd planned to be saying to her right now.

Damn her. Damn him. Their lovemaking had been more than just wonderful. It had been the most intense sexual experience of his life. Feeling himself sheathed within her, he had never felt so close to another soul. And when they'd reached the pinnacle, he'd felt such an explosion of bright light and warmth, he'd felt... awakened somehow.

*He loved her.* Nothing else could possibly make him feel this bad or this good. But there was no way in hell that he was going to spend his life watching her, waiting for her to faint, afraid to lose himself within her for fear that he'd once again drive her over the edge.

No. Forget it. He couldn't do it. He'd allowed himself to be pushed a lot in the past four weeks, but not over this. He loved Mara, but he could never live with her. Even if she weren't sick, there would always be the specter of it in the future. Good health wasn't a right— There were no guarantees. And after witnessing the years of despair Jacob had struggled through after losing his first wife, Lia, Mark knew he wouldn't consciously choose to put himself in such a vulnerable position. Thank God she hadn't asked.

Off in the distance, the distinct sound of rotor blades reached his ears. He glanced at Mara. "You ready to move on?"

"I'm ready."

They flew from Provideniya back to Nome, and from there to Bethel. Mark stayed to have a doctor look at his leg. Mara arranged for a flight home. If he wanted her to interpret for his tours, she'd be there, but if he didn't, Mara had decided, now was good a time as any to get on with her life. Neither spoke much during their last hours together. They'd said it all, apparently, done what they'd needed to, and done one thing that they shouldn't have. But when the time came to go their separate ways, there were no kisses, no lingering touches, no tearful farewells.

Her grandmother was not among the people waiting when she deplaned Sunday morning in Twilight.

"So, how did it go?" asked Siksik excitedly.

"Did you get the sacred teachings?" asked Sharon.

"What about souvenirs?" asked Patrick.

"Son," warned Ann. She turned to Mara. "Where's Mark?"

Accepting Ann's hug of greeting and then Sharon's, Patrick's and Siksik's, Mara was thankfully occupied for the few moments it took her to think up a reply that wouldn't alarm them.

"Mark decided to stay over in Bethel," she informed them. In actuality, when he'd stopped by the hospital to show them his leg, they'd immediately admitted him for observation. He hadn't been at all happy. "He injured his leg and wanted to have a doctor check it out."

"His leg?" Siksik gasped.

"What's wrong with Uncle Mark?" asked Patrick.

"Mark doesn't like hospitals," Ann observed shrewdly.

Jacob, who'd just arrived, greeted her with a warm hug. But when he pulled back, his eyes were narrowed with concern. Mara felt the weight of it. "He's all right," she said, trying to soothe everyone, listening to Ann's quick summary for Jacob's benefit. She kept her voice falsely upbeat. "Why don't I tell you all about our trip at dinner later? Grandmother still goes over to your house on Sundays?''

Jacob nodded.

"Good. How is Grandmother?" This she addressed to Siksik.

"She's fine!" Siksik's smile was wide. "I don't really understand what was wrong with her just before you left, but she's better than ever, actually."

*I'll bet,* Mara smiled inwardly, aware that she carried no residual resentment in her heart for either of her manipulative relatives. Their legacy would soon be hers, and she now understood its vital importance. And while their tactics hadn't been the best, their desperation justified their actions. At least to her.

"So, what was her sister like? Really spooky, probably, huh?"

"Later, Patrick," Ann admonished.

The crowd dispersed. Everyone, that is, except Jacob, who had gone to retrieve her suitcase and recordings from the cargo bay of the Twin Otter. Together they walked to her grandmother's home.

"Mark called a few minutes ago."

Mara forced herself not to react. She kept walking, her eyes focused on her surroundings, mentally comparing the poverty around her to the relative prosperity in Sireniki. There was so much to do, to think about, to plan. Absurdly, she wished Mark was going to be involved. She could have used his support, his advice. Her heart ached at the impossibility.

"Did you hear what I said?" Jacob asked.

Mara looked up at him and sighed. "Yes, Jacob. I heard. And?"

"He told me what happened."

"Everything?" Her response was too quick. Mara blushed.

"No, not everything," he replied, looking at her pointedly. "But enough for me to know you've had an interesting few weeks."

Interesting? Try mind-boggling. Try life-altering. "Yes, I guess you could say that," Mara replied. She spotted her grandmother's home with a mixture of relief and trepidation. Ascending the two sagging steps, she paused, looking down into Jacob's worried eyes, eyes so like his brother's, yet without their ever-present bitterness.

"Want some advice?"

"I already know he's unpredictable," Mara pointed out, unaware of how the pain in her eyes told of her experiences.

"Sometimes I wish I'd never sent you after him," Jacob admitted. "But Mark's my brother. I love him and don't want to see him hurting forever over something that's not his fault. I'd hoped that you could teach him to live life, not just to exist. Maybe I was asking too much. Neither of you seems particularly happy."

There was another long silence as Mara debated what to say to ease his conscience. "I am happy, Jacob. It's just that there are different kinds of happiness. And as far as Mark goes, I tried. Believe me, I tried every way I could, but I can't force him to change, because that's not really change. He's got to want to. He's got to do it for his own reasons, for himself. Not for you and not for me."

"I'm sorry I involved you. I shouldn't have, and now I can see nothing's any better. I just hope you understand that I was doing it for the both of you."

"I understand. And for my sake, it *was* worth it." Despite everything that had happened, she wouldn't ever wish away her love for Mark. What he'd given her was irreplaceable. Her love for him filled her with wonder and contentment. She was a better, more understanding person because of it. She would be a more compassionate healer because of it.

"You love him," Jacob said, reading her expression.

"Yes." So much so that she'd set him free.

"Does he know?"

Mara thought about how much she might have revealed when she picked up that drum to ease his confusion, how much he might have understood when she was prepared to defend him with a knife, how obvious she'd been in her care of him, and, finally, how open in her trust in him to teach her of love.

"Yes, he knows," she murmured. "And he cares."

"Then what's the problem?"

"He cares too much."

Mark lay in bed Monday afternoon, looking out the small hospital window, wishing he were at home, in the secluded privacy of his cabin. He couldn't stop thinking about Mara. What was she doing now? Talking with her grandmother? Packing to return to Fairbanks? They hadn't discussed his tours, which were scheduled to begin in another two weeks. He didn't know if she was still planning on interpreting for him or not.

Did he want her to? He sighed. If she didn't, he'd have to shut down for a year, maybe two, to recoup his losses. If she did, he'd probably go quietly insane. Everything about his campsite would forever have Mara's presence stamped all over it. Would nothing ever be the same?

No. His love for Mara had changed all that, had changed him. He wasn't the same man who'd pounded on her door, four-plus weeks ago, full of bitterness and fear. The nightmare was gone, and while he still acknowledged responsibility, he was willing now to accept that he'd done everything humanly possible the night of the crash.

The bitterness was gone, too. Watching Mara's struggle to steer clear of her own justifiable bitterness over his treatment of her, he'd recognized he didn't have a right to claim his own. Her courage had healed him, had shown him he was more than an empty shell. And her gift of trust and of love had reawakened the man inside him.

In a flash of insight, he saw his life as he'd structured it these past four years. Everything about it was temporary: His work was seasonal, his commitments—those he accepted—were always short-term, and his friendships superficial. He'd been living on the sidelines of life as a watcher. Mara had forced him to play the game, to get involved.

And he had. So involved, he'd fallen in love.

There was no way out of it or around it. Denying that he needed her was futile. He did. But in telling her so, he had to accept her illness, and, though it shamed him to admit it, he just wasn't certain that he could stand by, day after day, year after year—hopefully—and watch her suffer. He was strong, but not that strong. Jacob had looked like a walking corpse until the winter Ann arrived to teach at their high school. Only Ann wasn't sick. Mara was.

In the end, it all boiled down to two questions: *What was the meaning of life?* and *What did life mean without Mara?*

Simple, right? He groaned and buried his head in his pillow.

## Chapter Seventeen

Mara stood outside the *qasgiq,* unable to stem her trembling. The time had come. After leaving Jacob the other day, she'd greeted her grandmother, telling her of the decision she'd made. The ceremony going on now inside the *qasgiq* was the result.

"It'll be over soon," Siksik murmured, her gentle eyes compassionate in their understanding of Mara's nervousness. "Everyone thinks you'll make a great healer. And there's not really much for you to do, is there?"

No, Mara thought, allowing herself a wry smile as she fingered the ever-present *talliraq* on her wrist. All I have to do is save my own life. That ought to be easy, right?

But she didn't say any of that, because she couldn't. Tonight's ceremony had two distinctly separate parts: the public ceremony, similar to an installation, where she would take the healer's oath; and then afterward, the private ceremony, where she would take the third potion. Both were necessary trials, neither one more important than the other, Milak had explained to her. For without the people's faith, there could be no true healing, and without belief in herself, it would be wrong for her to *be* healer.

Mara sighed and changed the subject. "How are your studies going? Still planning on taking the GED?"

Siksik nodded, though her eyes were worried. "I've tried to make time, but it's hard when there's so much to do. Dad and Jacob brought in a good salmon harvest this year, so there's lots of fish for Mom and me to process. And then there's the berries we need to pick and the grasses that need drying.... You know this year I'm sixteen." She gazed at Mara, a sudden sparkle in her eyes. "Did you know my mom married my dad when she was sixteen?"

Mara started. "No, I never thought about it, but I guess it makes sense. She's, what—in her mid-forties?" She glanced sideways at Siksik. "Your mother's not getting ready to marry you off, is she?"

Siksik smiled, though Mara noted that a wistful expression flashed across her face. "If she is, she's going to be disappointed. I'm not marrying anybody but Billy."

The young teen's innocent enthusiasm was painful to Mara. It reminded her of what was going on inside her, what had brought her to this place in time. "Well, there's no rush. You have your whole life ahead of you. Plenty of time for marriage. And, as far as the test goes, it'll be there when you're ready for it."

"Yeah, but will Billy?" Siksik murmured under her breath.

Mara heard. "Have you heard anything from him?"

"He called and talked to his dad while you and Mark were in Sireniki. He's doing great at basketball camp. Apparently his coach thinks he's got real potential."

Mara read in Siksik's false brightness a deep disappointment. "Phone calls are expensive," she said consolingly. "Maybe there wasn't time for him to talk to you."

"Yeah, I guess so."

Just then the door opened and Jacob appeared. Mara felt his bright smile lift her spirits, though it did nothing to curb her suddenly pounding heart.

"It's time," he said. "Ready?"

For a brief instant, Mara wished Mark were here. It was odd how much more focused she felt when Mark was with her. But it wasn't meant to be, and she'd better get used to that. She'd known he wouldn't be there for her in the future. He'd made it perfectly clear when he left her so abruptly at the airport. Her future, her life, lay beyond that door, among the supportive community of her people. She would be loved, and she would love them in return. Only a woman's passion would be denied her. She raised her chin, aware of Jacob's silent, steadfast support and the increased pounding of her heart, and nodded.

"Ready."

Jacob and Siksik entered first, stepping to the side to hold open the double-sided door so that she could make her entrance alone.

And that was what she would be, Mara knew, as she started confidently forward down the wide path that led straight to the council of elders and her grandmother. Mara felt the villagers' stares taking in her ceremonial sealskin mukluks and white cotton *kuspuk*. Her head was bare. There would be no headdress until and unless she earned the right to wear one.

Mara kept her gaze fixed forward, her ears aware of the muted murmurings of the crowd, her mind fixed on placing one foot in front of the other. Most of them had never witnessed this ritual, and in that they were taking this journey together, starting off their new lives with this common joining. As she walked through the large building lit by a hundred *naniq* lamps, a thousand memories played like a film through her mind. Memories of her childhood, of her graduation, of Zoya and the Gathering Place. Memories of Mark.

There would be changes in the ways of the past, Mara had decided. The potions were valuable, too valuable to keep from a world that could use their healing powers. She would bring forth this knowledge, teaching the *kass'aq* world. And, in exchange, she hoped to bring some prosperity to her people, and some respect from a world that seemed to consider them a forgotten people, living in forgotten times.

Mara reached the path's end.

The air fairly shimmered with hushed tension and excitement. Surrounded by it, at the focus of it, Mara stood tall, controlled and determined, now concentrating all her attention on the lone woman on the council—her grandmother.

Milak sat proudly on her sealskin rug, her wrinkled hands still, her face serene, her eyes telegraphing a shining, prideful, satisfaction that she should have this honor. Mara understood the mix of emotions. Of all the people here, her grandmother was the only one who really understood what Mara was seeking to accomplish this night, what she was willfully consenting to undergo for that privilege. Her life, for the lives of others. The price was fair. The price was just. Helped up by Ben, Milak stood and faced her.

"We are the 'real people,' the Yup'ik," the old healer rasped. "Since Raven created Earth, our people have had the protection of a healer. So that the young may prosper, so that our ways survive, we call on you."

Milak took a ragged breath and stepped forward two more paces.

Mara felt a hush come over the crowded *qasgiq*—some three hundred and fifty people, sitting, standing, jammed against the walls watching, all without movement. It made her feel very small and very scared, suddenly.

"Mara Anvik, child of my daughter, hear me now. Tonight is a time of great joy and of great pain. So it is with all beginnings, with all births. I, Milak Nayakik, whose voice speaks for the healers before me, say this to you. Tonight you must choose."

"Tonight you must choose," voices in the crowd repeated.

Milak nodded and continued: "I am old, my will grows weak. You are young, we will test the strength of your will if you choose the rite. Do you so choose?"

Mara, feeling as if her entire life were being compressed into a blazing pinpoint of time without beginning, middle or end, nodded. This was so much harder than she'd imagined it would be, and she'd imagined the worst, given the stakes. Her throat closed tight, but she held fast to her control and her belief.

"To the people I say this. I have trained this woman, this grandchild, to know the proper ways of the healer. She has the knowledge. This I have seen. She has the will. This she has said. Now we must learn truth, for only in truth is there trust." Milak then turned and motioned to Ben.

Mara watched as Ben handed Milak the tiny pouch Zoya had given her. Her heart started a wild, frenzied slamming against her ribs. She felt herself at a turning point, knowing of the danger inside the pouch, knowing of the salvation it offered, knowing that of all the eyes watching, there was one pair, one familiar pair, that was missing.

Jacob made a crooked path through the jammed room to stand beside her. Mara looked up at him, dimly aware she wasn't shielding her fear, but managing, just, to question his surprising presence by her side. His eyes flared for a brief second, but he said nothing, just stared back at her, then forward at Milak and his father.

Was he supposed to be a guard or a guardian? Mara wondered.

"We now begin," Milak said, and handed Jacob the pouch.

"It begins," the crowd repeated.

Mara watched Jacob handle the pouch containing the potion. With extremely careful attention to detail, he untied the caribou sinew holding it closed, then spread wide the tiny folded orifice.

Using a small wooden bowl that he'd carried in his hands and that Mara just then noticed, he poured out the liquid.

"The potion is ready," Jacob said when he'd emptied the sack of what amounted to no more than a quarter cup of liquid.

Milak motioned to him. Jacob stepped forward and lowered the bowl. Milak sniffed. Mara watched the healer's eyes close as she inhaled the scent. For just a brief second, the healer's hands trembled. Then she opened her eyes, once again in control.

"The potion is as I, and the healers before me, remember it."

Jacob returned to his place beside Mara.

"As in all birth, there is need of both man and woman. You will accept the potion of your rebirth from Jacob. You must drink now," Milak directed.

Mara felt the sense of danger, high and charged, in the atmosphere. She watched Jacob kneel, understood that he was both guard and guardian, but that he wished Mark were in his place, for it was right that he should be here, now, when the woman who loved him needed his support.

A restless murmur passed through the crowd, an uneasy stirring created by the elder watchers, wary of the fact that Mara had no life mate. She glanced at Milak, saw that the healer had also felt the disquiet.

Had she known this would happen? Mara wondered. Was that why Jacob stood next to her now, his presence somehow prearranged without her knowledge? She pressed a hand against her stomach, trying to think quickly, to analyze the effect her single status would have on the villagers' faith. The concept of completeness was fundamental to their beliefs. A healer without a mate was unfinished, lacking in basic knowledge of the complexities of relationships between the sexes.

The disquiet gained momentum, moving around the room like a storm gathering strength. Mara felt it, felt their collective support fading, and knew that she would have to do something, say something, to return the ceremony to its original path. She understood their unease. In this they needed to know that she shared their understanding. Well, she did. Making up her mind, Mara knelt and faced Jacob.

Jacob lifted the bowl toward her lips and while he did it, Milak said, "Here is the essence of truth, the potion that will decide your future. If you are a true healer, it will allow you to see us as we are, as we were, and as we hope to be."

Would Mark ever understand the path she'd chosen? Would he ever forgive the words she was about to speak? Mara accepted the bowl.

The potion smelled fruity, flowery, welcoming. Mara knew that for her, it would be. For her, it had to be.

"You must drink it now," Milak said.

Standing, Mara turned and faced the crowd, striving to control her fear. "I, Mara Anvik, granddaughter to Milak, our healer, choose to drink the essence of truth. I choose this future as I choose my mate, Mark, brother to Jacob. Tonight Jacob stands in his stead, but, as I know, and now you know, Mark is here, in my heart, forever in my soul." Then, before she could think or even say another word, she raised the bowl and drank the contents.

There was no applause, no loud exclamation of sound, no drumsong. Every person gathered there knew that what they had witnessed was only the first of two parts, and that for her, the hard part was just beginning.

As it had earlier, a pathway opened for her to exit the building. But before leaving, Mara turned and stared at her grandmother, whose features were so clear, almost transparent.

*You have done well, Granddaughter. Now go. Sleep.*

Silence settled around Mara as she exited the *qasgiq* with Jacob's solid, protective presence by her side. From her earlier two experiences, Mara knew the sleep would come quickly, so she walked fast, aware that it was her right to find a place of comfort where she could rest undisturbed. Mara concentrated on controlling her panic and maintaining even breaths, even as she felt the potion begin its swift route through her body. In all the village, there was only one place where she knew she would find the privacy she sought and the security she needed—Mark's bed.

She spotted the cabin, dimly aware that Jacob had figured out where she was headed. He ran on ahead, likely preparing her space, and Mara watched him from a greater and greater distance, aware of her steps, yet somehow not.

Entering the room, she headed straight for the bed. Her movements were automatic, her thoughts focused inward. She didn't hear Jacob turn off the light, didn't hear him quietly shut the door behind him. Her actions seemed guided by something other than herself, because, instead of lying down as she desperately needed to, she paused to undress, to remove the garments of man for this journey into herself. Then, wrapped in the cushioned comfort of

Mark's bed and covered by the security of his blankets, she closed her eyes.

Mark was sitting up in his hospital bed, eating a dinner he didn't want and grumbling about the fact that the doctor had kept him another day, when an inexplicable urge to go to Mara came over him. The impulse was strong, the image of her naked body lying in his bed crystal-clear. It made him uneasy, this unusual daydream, and he wondered if he'd feel like this, connected to her somehow, for the rest of his life. He pushed aside the food. Now he really wasn't hungry. He stood and walked over to the window, looking out at the sky, wondering selfishly if she was thinking of him.

Mara felt free.

Her body did not exist.

Despite the life-threatening circumstances that had brought her to this juncture, she felt a moment when all the troubles and concerns of her twenty-two years were pushed away, and all that mattered to her was that she was free.

Every fiber of her being rejoiced in that freedom. She felt changed, different, greater than the sum of her parts, outside the physical realm bounded by the laws of nature. What was happening to her seemed impossible, yet it was happening and she was able to comprehend a reality that was aphysical yet breathtakingly real.

But her time was short, and, even in this floating, formless limbo, she sensed her body's urgency. She had responsibilities, and a task to perform. She had to heal herself, and she had to do it before the faint but noticeable tug of her physical body ceased altogether.

But how?

Tentatively she reached out, opening her mind's eye to observe a flat, grayish, featureless tundra that converged like a cone on a distant horizon that shone with a bright, brilliant light. Mara recognized the tundra, but the light was new. And Mark's *inua*, the caribou, was nowhere to be seen.

The brightness drew her inexorably closer. To reach the light would be to complete the ritual. Mara did not question the knowledge, for here, in this place, it seemed self-evident.

Mara soared swiftly across the tundra. But then something happened. No matter how fast she flew, the distance between her and the horizon grew greater, not shorter. Dark shadows began obscuring the tundra, blurring her path. Instinctively she slowed her flight, unwilling to concede that she would not reach her goal, could not reach it, was, perhaps, not supposed to reach it. Eventually, Mara became tired and frightened.

*I wish Mark were here,* Mara thought again as she sought a place to land. It frightened her that the shadowy darkness had grown so quickly. The tundra was all but obscured now.

Mara continued soaring, confused by her inability to complete the ritual. What had gone wrong? Why were the shadows growing stronger, not weaker? Why was the caribou not even present?

Time seemed suspended as she soared to save her waning strength. Fear strengthened and edged itself through her earlier euphoria.

Mara began to lose confidence. Again she cried: What had gone wrong? Why were the shadows growing stronger, not weaker? *Where was Mark?*

Mara's focus shifted, and as she began searching for Mark, the horizon receded. The next time she looked toward it, it was gone, and she was surrounded by shadows.

And then she knew— She had failed.

Zoya had insisted she be committed. Until this instant, Mara had genuinely thought she was. But here there could be no illusions. Without Mark she felt incomplete, she could give no absolute commitment, that which Zoya and Milak both sought from her as healer.

She had failed. Her public acknowledgment of Mark as her soul mate had soothed only the villagers' concerns. It had done nothing to ease her own loneliness. Without Mark, without his love, the commitment just wasn't there. It wasn't enough.

Disoriented and helpless, Mara soared alone in the midst of the shadows, aware that she had made her choice, that she had taken her chance. Now, as the last of her energy drained away, her last question answered itself: Mark would not appear, because he was no longer a part of her life.

And soon there would be no life to be part of.

Twilight was silent when Milak left her home late that night. The sky overhead was cloudy; the air smelled wild, angry. A storm was coming. She walked quickly, her old muscles stretched to their limit by the grueling pace. She ignored the pain. If she failed, it would become much worse.

"Our ways will survive," she muttered as Mark's home came into view. Jacob sat guard outside. He slept.

"Jacob."

He came immediately awake, his eyes alert, reading Milak's tension. He stood. "What is it?"

"Mara needs help."

Jacob's hand automatically reached for the door. "No, Jacob." Milak spoke quickly. "You have served well. What Mara now needs, you cannot provide."

Again he read her glance. "Mark."

Milak nodded. "Bring him to me. Time is short."

"But he's in Bethel. How—?"

"Bring him to me." She turned and walked away.

Mark was standing by the window. He'd been there all night, staring out at the storm front gathering over the Bering Sea. He felt uptight and restless, as if he were waiting for something. When he heard the soft footfalls of the night nurse on his rounds, he knew he should jump into bed. His release tomorrow depended on his cooperation tonight. The nurse wouldn't look kindly on his silent vigil by the window.

Mark didn't move. He stood still and tense, eyes watching the storm, ears listening to the footsteps. Odd, he thought, as the cadence increased to that of a semirun. His heart started a loud pounding. He had a feeling....

The door opened. The orderly rushed in and stopped, startled, when he realized Mark was not only awake, but standing.

"You have an emergency phone call."

*Mara.* Something had happened to Mara. His uneasiness, his refusal to sleep, the unusual daydream ... It couldn't be anything else.

Mark didn't say a word. He just followed the orderly down the corridor to the nurses' station. "Mark here," he said into the receiver the nurse handed him.

"Mark?"

It was Jacob. "What's going on? Is Mara all right?" Mark didn't stop to think how the directness of his question revealed his feelings.

"No. At least, I don't think so."

"What the hell does that mean?"

"I don't know!" Jacob sounded scared. That fact chilled Mark to the bone. "She's been shut up in your house, sleeping in your bed, since the end of the ceremony. Milak says you have to come home."

*Mara was in his house? Sleeping in his bed?* Mark didn't say anything for several deafening moments. The vision hadn't been a dream at all. His leg started hurting, and he felt a tightness close his throat. This was what he'd wanted to avoid: the pain, the fear, the anguish that came with loving someone. "No." His voice sounded strained.

"What?"

He wanted to hang up, to sever the connection, but he couldn't. "I can't, Jacob. Don't ask me. You, of all people, should understand."

Mark could almost see Jacob's mind working, grappling with his refusal, trying to see beyond it to the underlying message.

"My guilt over Lia's death was wrong, Mark," Jacob said after another silent moment had passed. "Ann helped me to see that. Don't let yours over the crash blind you."

"But what about—"

"Let it go, Mark."

*"I can't."*

"You can. You just have to want to. Isn't Mara worth it?"

"Damn it, Jacob! That's not fair!"

"Neither is life," Jacob said bluntly. "But sometimes you get lucky and you get a second chance. I did. Looks like you did, too. She loves you, you know."

The rumbling confession was like a punch in the gut. Mark thought of her sweet, soothing voice, her healing heart, her penetrating eyes, her hands, gentle with compassion, needy with desire. He'd asked himself what his life meant without Mara. And he'd come up with a simple enough answer.

Nothing. It meant nothing.

But was that realization enough? Did it warrant the leap of faith Jacob described?

"Come home, Mark. She needs you. Milak said time was short."

Mark made up his mind. "I'll be there as fast as I can."

Jacob hung up, leaving Mark holding a dead connection. He turned to the nurse. "I'm leaving." His tone left no room for discussion. Then he gazed across the counter at a digital clock displaying the hour. Three o'clock in the morning. How in the hell was he going to get home?

A phone number he hadn't used in four years popped into his head. Before he could so much as blink, he punched in the numbers. On the third ring, a man's familiar voice sounded in his ear.

"Hello?"

"Lou? It's Mark. Mark Toovak. I need—" Mark swallowed and forced the words past stiff lips. "I need to borrow your plane."

When Mark reached the airport, driven there by a doctor going off duty, his friend Lou Greene was already there. Mark had learned to fly using Lou's Cessna. The man operated a fly-in hunting and fishing business.

"She's fueled up and all ready to go."

Mark wanted to shake the man's hand, but his own was so slick with sweat, he was embarrassed. "Lou, I don't know what to say, how to thank you—"

"Forget it," Lou broke in. "You've done a lot for people around here. It's good to pay you back. Take care. Fly high and fly safe." With a wave, he ran off.

Mark watched him go, stunned by Lou's casual confidence. The Cessna was his family's livelihood. And he had to know that Mark hadn't flown in years.

Shaking his head and wondering, if their situations had been reversed, whether he would have done something so risky, Mark quickly ran through his preflight check. His motions were automatic. He didn't want to think. Thinking was dangerous.

He leaned over and opened the door, his inhalations fast and shallow and rapid. He was in danger of hyperventilating and he knew that there was only one thing that would relieve it: He had to fly the plane. He looked around, minimally comforted by the familiar layout. He'd flown this plane many times. Mark strapped himself in, pulled on his headset and radioed the tower that he wanted to take off. He knew he shouldn't be in the air. After years of down time, recertification was mandatory. But there wasn't time. A commercial flight wasn't available, and a charter was out of the question. He supposed Lou could have flown him to Twilight, but . . . no. He had to do this alone. No one, not even Lou sitting in the cockpit with him as a passenger, could ease it. If he was ever going to do it, now was the time. Jacob had said he needed to come home. Milak had said time was short. It was now or never.

The tower okayed his takeoff.

Mark pumped the throttle and touched the starter. The engine roared to life.

*You can do this. Just think of Mara. She needs you. When you needed her, she came through. You can't let her down.*

The words became a litany as he monitored the illuminated switches and dials, double-checking and triple-checking everything he could think of. The storm front would make for a bumpy ride. His intellect absorbed the data, but his emotions, his memories, recoiled.

He remembered the swirling snow blinding his sight, and then the sudden, unexpected impact. The sound of Kathy's screams, the sound of his own, the smell of burning fuel and then more screams of excruciating pain and then finally the awful roaring absence of sound . . .

With a fierce oath, Mark swiped a trembling hand across his blurred eyes. Then, slowly, almost imperceptibly, he brought up the power.

The plane began to roll forward along the smooth tarmac. *You can do this. Just think of Mara. You can do this,* he repeated to himself. By the time he'd maneuvered the plane into takeoff position, he had himself under grim control.

He knew he could do this. He had the skill. He had the knowledge. *You're one of the best pilots in the sky,* Mara had said. *You have to be, otherwise they wouldn't have let you fly rescue.*

The prophetic words guided him down the tarmac and steadied his hand as he gave throttle and gently, expertly, coaxed the nosewheel into the air.

*Yes!* Exhilaration poured through him, but he didn't lift his attention from the controls. Sweat still ran into his eyes; his hands still trembled as they clasped the controls, but damn it, he was in the air! He'd done it! And with those words, he soared into the night, headed for home—headed for Mara.

## Chapter Eighteen

Forty minutes later, he was landing in Twilight. After securing the aircraft, he pulled off his set gear and tossed it aside. Then he leaned back against the seat and closed his eyes. A deep, ragged sigh issued from his lips. A minute later, Jacob swung open the door.

The two brothers stared at one another. Mark wondered tiredly if he looked as shaken as he felt. Probably, if Jacob's half smile and worried eyes were anything to go by.

"Piece of cake?"

Trust Jacob to make it sound like he'd just taken an evening joyride. His gaze held his brother's a moment longer. Then, with a faint smile that attested to his near exhaustion, he managed what was likely the understatement of the year: "Yeah. No big deal."

"I brought the four-wheeler. Wasn't sure how your leg was doing."

Mark jumped down onto the gravel runway and climbed on behind Jacob. He wasn't concerned about his leg. Jacob started the engine, and they roared toward the village. "How's Mara?" Mark shouted into the wind.

"No change. Milak won't let anybody inside."

"So why am I here?"

"Except you. You can go in."

Mark thought about that as they neared his home. The village was curiously busy for four-thirty in the morning. And people were waving to him like he was a long-lost relative. Another one of those strange feelings feathered up his spine. "What's going on?"

Jacob must have heard the confusion in his voice, for he slowed the four-wheeler to a stop some distance from Mark's home.

"They're happy to see you."

"I can see that. Why?"

"Because Mara told them last night that you two were soul mates."

"She what?" Mark stared at Jacob as if he couldn't possibly have heard right.

"You have to understand the circumstances—" Jacob began, but Mark cut him off.

"You've got to be kidding."

Jacob looked at him, the heavy sadness in his eyes penetrating Mark's runaway emotions. "I thought something wasn't quite right. Her hands were shaking when she took that potion."

"Potion? What potion?"

"The healer's potion. Mara swallowed it last night at the cere- mony in the *qasgiq*. Then she went straight to your house, where she's been ever since. Milak won't let anybody inside, though we've all figured out something's not right. That's why you're here."

"How can I fix something when I don't even know what's go- ing on?" Mark asked tightly. *"What ceremony?"*

"Mara's. Last night she drank Zoya's potion. I gave it to her myself."

"You gave her some crazy potion?" Mark's voice was hoarse, and his gaze was dazed. "For God's sake! Why?"

"Because, Mark," Jacob answered, an edge of impatience en- tering his voice, "you weren't there. Anyway, she gave this little speech about you two being soul mates, and then she drank it. We've been waiting for the results ever since, only something's gone wrong."

*Only something's gone wrong.* The ominous words echoed harshly in Mark's overloaded brain. "Back up. What results?"

"What—" Jacob broke off, his eyes narrowed, assessing. "Are you all right? I know the flight must have been—"

"What results?" Mark repeated.

Jacob hesitated, clearly torn. "We're waiting to find out if she's going to be healer for both Twilight and Sireniki."

For a moment, Mark was nonplussed. He felt betrayed. He didn't have the right, but that didn't stop him from feeling it. "I see."

And he did see. He saw how very far apart they really were. He didn't say anything else for several moments.

"You didn't know, did you? After what she did for your leg, I would have thought…" Jacob stared at him for a split second, then started the four-wheeler again. "I've got to get you home. Don't be surprised by the people sitting outside. Milak will explain. I just thought you should be prepared."

Jacob sped up to the house. Mark jumped off, immediately surrounded by a throng of happy faces that couldn't hide a deep concern. He spotted his father and sister— Siksik was crying! Blocking everyone out, Mark entered.

The one-room space was dark. A single *naniq* lamp flickered solemnly on the nightstand by his bedside, where Milak sat in a straight-backed chair, in silent vigil. She motioned to him.

Mark moved, his eyes glued on Mara's too-still form as she rested like a real-life Sleeping Beauty on his bed. His gaze traveled over her flawless skin, her jet-black hair as it fanned out on his pillow, on the visible swell of her breasts beneath the thin sheet covering. His breath caught. She was hardly even breathing.

"She lives," Milak told him, in answer to the question he couldn't bring himself to ask aloud. "But she needs you. Your indecision about your feelings for her clouds her commitment to become healer. She denies herself relief."

Mark didn't understand any of this. "What—"

"No more talk! You must listen!"

Mark stopped his questions. But his eyes still burned with an underlying anger.

"Time is short," Milak said to him. Her very intensity turned Mark's feelings of anger and replaced them with alarm. "You must join her. You must free her to make a choice. Go. Tell her of your decision. It matters not what that decision is, only that you tell her and free her to fly."

There was no time to think. "What do I need to do?"

Milak gazed at him, into him, apparently finding the belief, the strength, she sought. "Remove your clothes. Lie down beside her."

Mark did as she asked, sliding in next to her, covering them both. Contrary to what he'd imagined, Mara's skin burned, though no sweat shone on her body. Milak handed him a long, narrow, paper-wrapped tube that looked like a cigarette. She lit the end.

"Inhale deeply. Let the smoke fill your lungs."

"But what's going to happen? How do I help Mara—"

"You will know," Milak said, interrupting him. "You will see. Now inhale twice more."

Mark did. Whatever the stuff was, it was potent. Before he'd even inhaled the second time, he was feeling the effects. By the time Milak doused the flame and left the house, he was out.

Mara felt so weak. The shadows had all but obscured her vision, making any sense of purpose, of direction, useless. And where, even if she could, would she go? Her career as an anthropologist seemed so far away. Her translation business, with all its complexities, even farther. She wondered, now that it was too late, whether she should have told Mark of her plans, whether his knowing might have produced a different ending, a joining rather than a parting.

She would never know....

As she spiraled down through the shadows, an image emerged. With a weak flap of her wings, Mara recognized her grandaunt's *inua*, Arlunaq, the polar bear.

How had the old healer found her? Mara wondered as she zeroed in on the moving vision of white. The illusive tundra was now a frozen ocean, but the faint outline of the horizon was still there, and the brightness continued to exist, far away. Zoya's appearance energized Mara, renewing her sagging strength, giving her a replenished sense of hope and focus, a path through the shadows.

For a while, Mara rejoiced in her grandaunt's help, flying low, following, allowing herself to rest from the confusion the shadows had caused. But her grandaunt was weak, too weak to guide her for long, and when Arlunaq disappeared beneath the shadows and did not resurface, Mara watched her go with a calm detachment, then began to close her wings.

Mark wasn't sure how long he'd watched the scene unfold, but when he heard Mara's cry and saw her spiraled dive, every primitive protective instinct he possessed urged him to her aid. He found that he could move, that he could feel, that he could see, just as Milak had promised. He found that he could run, faster than he'd ever run before, and with the strength of his *inua* form he pounded across the frozen ocean turned tundra toward Mara.

He felt a yearning for Mara, a fear for her life that directed him through the thickened shadows. They seemed to part for him, to allow him through, to allow him access.

With his senses so expanded, he looked up and saw her, just as she saw him. For an eternity she hovered, questioning, neither flying toward him nor retreating. Mark did the only thing he could do: He called her to him.

Mara came. Swiftly, unsteadily, she glided down and settled lightly onto his back. At the contact of her *inua* form with his, the horizon flared explosively to life, almost blinding him. Mark absorbed Mara's joy in the manifestation of his love, and he realized that he'd made his choice. He loved her, had probably always loved her in some form or another.

Traveling swiftly, he crossed the tundra with Mara on his back, his own amazed confusion over what was happening pushed aside by the irrefutable fact that it was, somehow, happening. That he didn't understand why this was happening didn't matter. What mattered was that the shadows around them diffused, then cleared away entirely. Mara had her focus back. Admitting the truth to himself had freed her to make other choices. And as he watched her fly off, now close enough to complete the journey on her own, the feelings of the real world once again claimed him.

He opened his eyes. Milak was gone. He looked sideways at the woman he loved. Then, unwilling to stop himself, he gently, reverently, turned onto his side and kissed her lips. Her eyes fluttered and opened.

Mara's emotions were on a roller-coaster high as she quietly searched his face, seeing there the same wonder and joy that continued to burn in her heart. She was still having a hard time comprehending the enormity of what Mark had admitted to, what it signified to her, if not to him. She was happy. So incredibly, awesomely happy.

"I love you," she whispered.

For a moment, Mark was paralyzed. He didn't breathe, he didn't move, he couldn't respond. He just lay there, letting her words flow over him, around him, through him.

"Mara, I—"

"Don't." She snuggled close against him, holding him tightly. "I didn't tell you that to hold you, but because . . . after what just happened, I had to. If you need me, I'll be there. If you want me, I'll want you, too. Forever."

The promise was as important to her as the oath she'd taken to become healer. Her fingers trembled as she lifted them to smooth his troubled brow, to guide his mouth to hers.

Mark kissed her. He'd never truly understood what it was that set Zoya and Milak apart from everyone else. But now that he'd experienced something of their inner journey, he saw that distinctive brightness shining in Mara's eyes. He felt humbled. She'd been changed by what had happened. And, in a smaller measure, so had he. Again he kissed her, rejoicing in her immediate and wholehearted response.

"You're beautiful," he murmured. Deftly he kicked off the sheet to pull her on top of him.

Mara's lips formed his name on an echo of sound. The look in his eyes was everything she had ever hoped to see, and as she held his gaze and felt his hands roaming, kneading, learning her body again, she didn't try to stop the tears that formed and flowed down her cheeks.

She started to say, "I should have told you about my decision back at the campsite—"

"No." Mark rolled over so that he could look down at her. "I wasn't ready to hear it then." He wasn't even sure he could talk about it now.

Lowering his head, he trailed light kisses along the valley between her breasts. Her nipples tightened to luscious buds of desire. Had anything ever felt so good, so right? Immediately he felt himself harden.

"Oh, Mark..." She accepted his mouth, the sweet, painful kisses that penetrated deep, all the way to her soul. He kissed her until she was gasping for breath and calling out his name in short, erratic bursts. Mara felt herself melting, changing, flowing around him as he parted her thighs, then paused, lightly nudging the entrance to her feminine core. When his mouth suckled at the tip of one breast, she cried out. "Mark... Mark, please... I need you."

How could he ever have pushed her away? How could he even be thinking about it now? Four years ago, the innocent promise of a girl almost grown had captured his heart. Tonight, that promise had been fulfilled. Mara was everything he could ever want in a woman. And she was also more. The depth of her commitment to her people—their people—was right for her. He understood that, even as he understood why she hadn't revealed her plans. But what about him? What would be expected of the man at her side? Could he, with his uncertain future, fulfill that role? Could he honestly let someone else even try? As she flowed beneath him, Mark knew he had never truly understood how crazy love could make a man until now.

His smile was bittersweet as he opened his eyes to find her watching him, watching his hardened manhood as it teased her wet heat. He could hurt her, hurt her so easily, with the strength of the passion that flowed through him. Did he dare take her again?

"Seeing you fall through the shadows...struggling like that...it was more frightening than my nightmare over the crash. More frightening than getting here tonight after Jacob's phone call," he admitted, leaning over her body. The action nudged him forward, and he felt her muscles contract as they closed around him, grasping him. His blood pooled hotly, expanding him, threatening his control, as Mara felt the change and moaned. "You looked so small, so still, so lifeless, when Milak let me in." He drew a shaky breath, inhaling her comforting aliveness. He let his eyes close and slid in a little farther. *Just a little more,* he promised himself, *and then I'll leave.* She gave another excited cry. His thighs tensed, rock-hard with restraint. So good. So sweet! "There just aren't any words to describe what I felt when you landed so softly, when you trusted me to see you through. And after everything I've done and everything I didn't do."

"*Mark!* Please." Mara took control and pushed down as she pulled him into her.

"No! Mara! Wait! Ahhh . . ."

She held him tight, not allowing him to slip out, to escape. The fierce thudding of his heart, the feeling of him throbbing within her, relayed its own message of need. "It'll be all right," she breathed, wrapping her legs around him.

Mark let out a throaty, agonized moan. "I don't want to hurt you."

"I know," she breathed softly. "And you won't. I promise, you won't. Please?"

Her husky plea carried him beyond his fear, and once again he gave in to the urge to stroke her with a man's need; to claim her with a man's honest passion; to conquer and caress her with a man's heartfelt love for a woman so much more than his dreams. And when she splintered into a thousand pieces of bright, brilliant light, he greedily absorbed them all, loving her with infinite tenderness and devotion, with a commitment that transcended the uncertainty of his future, though not his fear over her illness.

When she fell into a deep, exhausted sleep, Mark watched her for a few minutes to make sure. Then he rose and dressed, covered her gently and quietly left.

When Mara woke up later, Milak was there. The coldness of the bed told her Mark had gone. She pushed aside the pain, aware she'd expected it, and gazed at her grandmother. Something had happened during the night, something great and something sad. Looking inward, Mara already knew the answer, but she asked it anyway: "Grandaunt's gone, isn't she?"

The bright tears in her grandmother's eyes spoke her answer.

# *Chapter Nineteen*

The Cessna soared over the Kuskokwim Delta with Mark at the controls. He'd officially checked out of Bethel's hospital for the forty-minute flight to Nelson Island over an hour and a half ago. But every time he skirted the familiar coastline, he veered off in another direction, Mara's words echoing loudly in his ears: *"If you need me, I'll be there. If you want me, I'll want you, too. Forever."*

Was she crazy to have made that kind of promise? Had the joy of the moment spilled over into words she would now regret? He hadn't promised her a thing in return: no future, no commitment, no occasional "visits." Hell, he hadn't even said goodbye!

But as he nudged the nosewheel skyward, he knew why. He hadn't said goodbye because he hadn't been able to. I love her, he thought, not for the first time. God knows, I love her. And she probably knows it, too. Even though he hadn't said the words, Mara couldn't help but know.

Mark smiled grimly. Zoya had told him to face his feelings. Well, he'd done that. Only now he was having trouble facing the consequences.

These past weeks had been hell. He hadn't realized just how successful he'd become in keeping friends, even family, at bay, never letting anyone touch him more than superficially.

Except Mara, of course. For several minutes, Mark concentrated on the landscape far below him, watching as Twilight came into range. Automatically his thoughts veered back to his dilemma.

What *was* the worst thing that could happen if he committed himself to Mara? If he let himself love her as she wanted to be loved?

She could die. Today, tomorrow, next year. Whatever the illness was that had Mara in its grip, it could take her from him, instantaneously, irrevocably. Or, worse, lull him into a false sense of security and hope and then—whammo!

He shuddered. "God! If I've ever done anything to deserve a favor, don't let Mara die. She's too young, too alive!"

The anguished prayer exploded into the small cabin. Mark gripped the steering mechanism, aware he had a tough choice to make: to land in Twilight and be there for Mara, or to return to Bethel and stay out of the picture altogether.

Mark snorted. Who was he trying to kid this time? He couldn't stay away from home indefinitely, and he would see Mara when he did go home. And there really wasn't any hope that he could behave as if he were "out of the picture." He *was* involved. Had been since Mara was a little girl, tagging along behind him. And what about this healer thing? If he teamed up with Mara, he would become part of a life filled with more responsibility than he'd ever imagined. Hell, Milak still ministered to the people of Twilight at ninety-two! And Zoya had been over a hundred! As healer to both villages, Mara would be stretched thin. Too thin? It was a lot of responsibility. Who was going to watch out for her? Could he take care of her while she cared for everyone else? Did he want to do that?

There would be times when she'd need more than his caring. She'd need his strength, she'd need his support and belief.

Could he give her that? Could he face the fact that there were things going on around him that he didn't understand, things that weren't concrete and explained by science, but intangible and only sensed through feelings? And could he accept it as a regular part of his life?

It occurred to him that, after last night, acknowledgment and acceptance were moot points. What he had to face was that, by acknowledging this heightened awareness, he had changed. And what he had to face was that there was no going back.

Mark weighed the thought critically as he maneuvered the nosewheel down, dropping altitude. Because of Mara, he was flying again. Because of her, he was dancing and teaching and rediscovering the value of his roots. He'd even accepted himself as Sireniki's guide to the past!

"Who would have thought it, eh, Jacob?" Mark voiced his own quiet astonishment and pride to the empty cockpit, knowing his big brother would have shared the laugh with him had he been there. Mara had already faced the reality of her illness and had, quite unselfishly, decided to accept the trust and responsibility of healership. Mark admired her courage. It would take a man equally strong to stand by her side. A man committed not just to her mission, but to her. For as sure as he was flying today, Mara could be counted on to put everyone else's needs and concerns first. The man at her side would be responsible for taking care of her.

It would be the greatest risk he'd ever taken. It would mean he'd have to consciously choose to live a life very different from the one he'd planned, a life that would be filled with a great deal of love, but an equally great uncertainty.

He honestly didn't know if he could do it. But he did know one thing: For the woman who had given him back the sky, he was going to try.

Mara was packing when the infrequent sound of a small plane's engine drew her attention. Her heart started a furious beating. So few planes landed here. And this wasn't Tuesday, so it couldn't be the Twin Otter with their weekly supplies. Could it be—?

She cut the thought short and stoically resumed packing. Mark would come back when he was ready. She had to believe that, had to trust those instincts. And until then, she'd just have to begin her new life on her own.

For ten, maybe fifteen minutes, silence reigned in the house. But then happy sounds of animated conversation and laughter, familiar voices—Jacob and his family, Siksik and her parents—filled the air and flowed in through the open window to where Mara was packing her suitcases at the dinette. One voice stood out from the rest. Her hands paused in their routine task of folding clothes.

He was here. Mark had come back.

"Sure," he was saying, and in his voice there was a lightness Mara hadn't heard in years. Her hopes lifted, in spite of her reservations. "Now that I'm back in the air, I've got plans. Big plans. We'll talk later, okay?"

Mara heard the purposeful steps approach the house, the confident knock. "Come in," she called past the dryness in her throat.

Mark entered, and his eyes held hers for a long moment. Then, with a distinct frown, he nodded toward the open suitcase.

"How— How's your leg?" Mara forced out, ignoring his silent question for the time being.

Mark managed a disturbed smile. He hadn't expected her to leave so soon. But all he said was "Fine. Good as new. The doctor wants to know about the poultice. I figure he's thinking he might have stumbled onto the next best thing to an ouchless suture."

"Well, he did, and he knows it," Mara answered, thinking about her plans. If only Mark— Again she stopped the enticing thought. She'd just overheard him saying he had plans of his own. Big plans. Plans that likely would take him away from Twilight. She sighed, turning to fold a sweater, setting it on top of the clothes already in the suitcase. "What did you tell him?"

Mark crossed the room to stand by her side. Mara jumped when he reached out to brush aside an errant strand of hair falling into her eyes. Her tension was immediate, and he felt it keenly. "I told him to talk to you," he said quietly. He let his fingers caress her pale cheek. "That's your department now."

Mara knew she couldn't meet his gaze without revealing everything, so she stared at the contents of her suitcase. "Thanks. I'll make sure to call him before I leave."

"But you just got back. Aren't there things you have to do now? Can't Fairbanks wait?"

*No, it can't wait. I've been waiting forever for my life to begin. No more waiting.* But all she said was "I've already called my professor and told him the news."

"Bet he wasn't happy."

"Actually, he was. More than happy." Mara returned to her suitcase with another armload of clothes. "He urged me not to give up on my degree plans. Suggested I work on the thesis as I find the time. I agreed, but warned him my priorities had changed."

Mark thought about the "as I find the time" part, but didn't say anything. She was kidding herself if she really thought she'd have spare time to do a thesis. "And that's okay with you? The fact that it may be a while before you get your master's?"

Mara looked up, then quickly lowered her eyes again to her task. "My doctorate. If I'm going to do this, I might as well go all the way." She bent to pick up a stray sock that had fallen from the pile of clothes on the bed. "Hand me my T-shirt over by the door, will you? And, yes, it's okay. Maybe I won't get to it. Who knows? What I want to do is introduce certain examples of our healing medicines to Western doctors. If I have my Ph.D. at the time, I'll get more attention, the kind of attention we need, and, hopefully, I'll be able to garner more bidding competition from the medical industry."

Sound enough plan, Mark thought. Zoya had been right. Mara *would* be their guide to the future. "So where are you going, if not to Fairbanks?"

Mara replied, her voice carefully devoid of inflection. "I'm going back to Sireniki. With Grandmother here, my priorities have to be with Vadim. He'll need a lot of support. And I feel I should help make the arrangements for Grandaunt's funeral."

The import of her softly spoken words didn't register for a moment. But when they did, the scene he'd witnessed in his mind's eyes just before he called to her, suddenly made sense. He sighed, filled with a deep regret. Zoya had been a great lady. "Ahh, Mara, I'm sorry, honey." Mark pulled her unresistingly into his arms.

"Oh, Mark..." Mara bit back a sob, her arms seemingly of their own volition, wrapping tight around his waist as the emotions of the past few days broke through her restraints.

"Mara, honey, don't cry...." Mark soothed her with his softly spoken words.

But the tenderness and concern in his voice was a catalyst, opening the valve locked against the strength of her emotions. She cried as she hadn't in a long while. For her grandaunt, whom she'd come to love in so short a time; for her grandmother, who had lost a dear sister, and for herself, who had to sacrifice an incredibly precious thing—the love and support of a wonderful man.

How would she make it through life without him?

Maybe she was being a fool not to tell him she'd been cured. If he knew, he'd probably stay. He loved her. Last night he'd declared it in a way that could leave her no doubts. But if she told him, she would be weakening the very strength that she now sought as comfort. Mark needed to make his own decision, for the sake of his own self-respect. And if that meant he left her, then she'd have to be strong enough to let him go.

As Mara continued to cry, Mark lifted her and carried her across the room to Milak's lounge chair. Standing her beside the chair, he tugged off his denim jacket, sat down, and pulled her onto his lap, wrapping his arms tightly around her and holding her as he had when she'd been a little girl with long black pigtails.

As Mark held her, he realized that he'd made the right decision. To stand by her side, to protect her, to advise her when necessary, to share with her his plans, his ideas for the future— Those were the things that mattered to him now. And he could do those things for a week, a year, forever. Just so long as he could do them!

The afternoon sun shone in through the dusty window, refracting the light in a hazy pattern along the walls. A look of tired resignation passed over her features as Mark gazed down at the woman he loved. Gently he tilted her face for his kiss. He would be her man, if she'd have him, he decided.

This he could give her. Though she would become a symbol to their people, she would always be a woman to him. A woman who felt love and pain, who laughed and cried, who needed a place and a man with whom she could express that essential part of herself.

Yes, if she'd let him, he would be that man.

"Mara . . . Mara, it'll be all right," he promised. "Zoya loved you. She did what she felt she had to do."

"I know." She shuddered. "And when I think of what might have happened if she hadn't . . ." She closed her eyes, feeling utterly miserable. "It's just so hard, Mark, so hard to lose someone you—" her voice broke again "—someone you love."

Mara trembled as another feather-soft kiss claimed her lips. She understood Mark's gentleness, but it confused her nonetheless. Why was he here? What was he doing, kissing her, comforting her, when he had to know how painful it would be for her after he left?

Mark caught her intense, questioning glance. With her wrapped tight against him, he said, "Last night we shared something I didn't know it was possible to share. Afterward, when you told me you loved me—" his eyes squeezed closed "—I rationalized that it was just the moment. But it wasn't, was it?"

"No . . ." Mara shrugged to hide her confusion. "I meant what I said."

"'If you need me, I'll be there. If you want me, I'll want you, too. Forever,'" he quoted.

"Yes," Mara repeated, her mind a crazy mixture of fear and hope. "Forever."

"I thought about those words as I was flying, working up the guts to land and come see you. And I realized that as much as you meant them, I meant them, too. You knew that, didn't you?"

"Yes . . . I knew."

"But I was scared. I didn't want to make that final commitment, so I left."

He grinned, his mood suddenly buoyant, and cupped her face with his hands. "Mara, I refuse to be scared anymore. I'm tired of running away. Before last night happened, I admit, I wasn't ready for any of this. But that was last night, and this is now."

"I—I should have told you what I'd planned. . . ." Mara stammered.

"And I'll say it again. It wouldn't have made a difference. What I did last night had nothing to do with Zoya or Milak. If you want to be healer, fine. If you decide to get that doctorate, that's fine, too. I didn't join you because I need a translator, either, although now, I guess, I still need one."

"We'll work it out, Mark." Mara's heart sang with dawning delight.

"I did it because I love you," Mark admitted. "Because I couldn't watch you struggle when I could help. I did it because I couldn't bear the thought of being without you forever. And that's why I'm here, Mara mine, because I don't want to be apart from you anymore. It's ten times worse than being together."

Mara almost laughed through her tears, because it was so obvious that he'd meant that rather backhanded compliment. "Mark, there's something you should know...." she began, but he cut her off.

"Wait. Now that I'm on a roll here, let me finish. Then you can talk all you want, or..." His hands slid up to the undersides of her breasts. He grinned at her blushing amazement. "I've decided to renew my pilot's license."

Jacob had told her about Mark's early-morning flight through the storm to reach her. Her heart ached to think of what he must have gone through for her. Her gaze searched his face, reading there how hard it had been. But there was also an excitement, a spark of energy that she'd never seen before. Her breath caught. She told herself she should be happy for him. She told herself that, only it didn't quite ring true.

"Then you're going back to flying rescue?"

Mark gazed at Mara and shook his head and hugged her briefly. "No. I told you, Mara. We're not going to be apart."

"But then, how... what... ?"

"I'm thinking of expanding the business. Bringing some tourist dollars into Sireniki and employing people here as the business grows."

"What are you talking about?"

"Vadim's old enough to assist with my tours. Hell, if I give him an intensive course in English, and he bones up on his Russian, I'll eventually be able to expand Crosswinds Siberia and employ more people from both villages. We could even tie the villages together on the tour, stopping in Twilight for some tourist-type stuff and then the hunting and fishing over there."

Mara stared, caught completely off guard by the vibrancy in his voice. She hadn't lost him after all! "And what about—"

"Us?" he said, finishing her question. "Can't allow someone else to fly my wife back and forth between the two villages, now can I? Besides, I have a lot to teach those people over there. And we have a lot to learn from them. If I can just make everything work out so that everyone benefits." Mark brought Mara's hands to his chest, clasping them within his own. "I figure we're both going to be pretty busy for a long—"

Mara's fingers trembled as she lifted them to caress his lips. "Mark, it's okay."

Mark stilled, his grip around her body almost painful as his gaze bored into hers. "There's nothing Milak can do?"

"She did her part. That's why she wrote that letter. That's why she sent me to Sireniki."

"Milak wrote the letter? When did you find this out?"

"I figured it out myself. You were right about their manipulating us. But I won't fault them. There was a lot at stake."

He was afraid to hope. "Mara, are you saying what I think you're saying?"

"Yes." Her smile was pure sunshine.

"But how? What happened? When?"

"You were there, Mark. You freed me so that I could do it."

Mark's expression went blank for a moment, trying to recall where he'd heard those words before. And then he remembered. Milak had spoken them: *Tell her of your decision. It matters not what the decision is, only that you tell her and free her to fly.*

Free her to fly... Free her to fly! Mark's lips formed Mara's name as understanding dawned. The light. The healer's light. Somehow it, and the potion, had cured her.

"Mara— Oh, God! Are you sure? Are you absolutely certain?" He started kissing her, soft kisses, trembling kisses, reverent kisses that deepened into a heat that quickly consumed them both.

"I'm sure." Intense joy bubbled in her whispered response.

"I love you. Mara, Mara!" In his exuberance, he stood up with her pressed tight against him and swung them both around. Her laughter sounded in his ears, exploded in his heart. "My God, there's so much we'll do, so many plans to be made." He laughed with the sheer joy of the moment, then settled her down on her feet and gazed into her glowing eyes.

"I love you," he vowed. "I'll be there for you, I promise. From now on, we're together, forever."

Mara thought her heart might burst from so much joy. She gazed up at the face of the man she loved. "From now on, we're together, forever."

And they would be.

\* \* \* \* \*

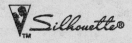

# Take 4 bestselling love stories FREE

## Plus get a FREE surprise gift!

**BABY'S CHOICE**

Those mischievous matchmaking babies are back, as Marie Ferrarella's Baby's Choice series continues in August with MOTHER ON THE WING (SR #1026).

Frank Harrigan could hardly explain his sudden desire to fly to Seattle. Sure, an old friend had written to him out of the blue, but there was something else.... Then he spotted Donna McCollough, or rather, she fell right into his lap. And from that moment on, they were powerless to interfere with what angelic fate had lovingly ordained.

Continue to share in the wonder of life and love, as babies-in-waiting handpick the most perfect parents, only in

*Silhouette*
R O M A N C E™

## by Christine Rimmer

Three rapscallion brothers. Their main talent: making trouble. Their only hope: three uncommon women who knew the way to heal a wounded heart! Meet them in these books:

### Jared Jones

hadn't had it easy with women. Retreating to his mountain cabin, he found willful Eden Parker waiting to show him a good woman's love in MAN OF THE MOUNTAIN (May, SE #886).

### Patrick Jones

was determined to show Regina Black that a wild Jones boy was *not* husband material. But that wouldn't stop her from trying to nab him in SWEETBRIAR SUMMIT (July, SE #896)

### Jack Roper

came to town looking for the wayward and beautiful Olivia Larrabee. He never suspected he'd uncover a long-buried Jones family secret in A HOME FOR THE HUNTER (September, SE #908)....

**Meet these rascal men and the women who'll tame them, only from Silhouette Books and Special Edition!**